THEIR VIRGIN

MISTRESS

THEIR VIRGIN MISTRESS
Masters of Ménage, Book 7
Shayla Black and Lexi Blake

Published by Shayla Black and Lexi Blake
Copyright 2015 Black Oak Books LLC
Edited by Chloe Vale and Shayla Black
ISBN: 978-1-939673-07-7

THEIR VIRGIN MISTRESS

Masters of Ménage, Book 7

Shayla Black and Lexi Blake

Bonus material and excerpts at the conclusion of this book.

CHAPTER ONE

London

Melinda Torrance Glen glanced across the elegantly appointed table, watching her sister pour steaming brew into delicate cups. "You look almost graceful serving tea. Lots of practice these days, I suppose. Remember when you broke the play set Mom bought us, and she had to glue it back together?"

Piper al Mussad, now known as the Queen of Bezakistan, still flashed the same bright smile she had growing up in rural Texas. Though she wore designer clothes and sat in the penthouse of one of London's most exclusive buildings, Tori still saw Piper, first and foremost, as her older sister.

"I cried until she repaired it, as I recall. Mr. Bear simply couldn't be without his afternoon tea." She glanced back at the bodyguard waiting in the background. "Thank you so much, Tanner. I'd like to be alone with my sister now."

The massive bodyguard frowned. "Dane gave me strict instructions not to let you out of my sight."

"I need to talk to my sister about girl things. He'll understand if you wait just outside the door. We're sixteen floors up, and the windows in this building are bulletproof.

Dane made certain of that when we bought the flat. The only way in is through a private elevator, and any intruder would still have to pass multiple guard stations. My husbands wouldn't have left me or our sons here unless they felt certain we'd be safe."

The guard didn't move.

"All right, then. I hope you can be discreet, Tanner." Piper sighed and turned to her. "You know, Mindy, since I last gave birth, I'm struggling with my vaginal walls contracting painfully during sex. It's been difficult, and I wonder if you have any advice."

The door slammed as the guard disappeared.

Tori pressed a hand over her mouth to smother her laugh. Despite her sister's now regal polish, she glowed with happiness. She had three gorgeous husbands and two precious sons. She'd been blessed.

Piper had married the Sheikh of Bezakistan, Talib al Mussad, and his two brothers, Rafiq and Kadir. In Bezakistan, the practice of brothers sharing a wife was both ancient and common—very unlike the West where primogeniture, which meant the first-born son inherited all the wealth and land, had been the norm. But Bezakistani nationals preferred to honor all their sons, keeping the riches within the whole family through the practice of polyandry. The world seemed utterly fascinated by the queen and her three sheikhs.

Tori constantly reminded herself that she didn't live there and having three husbands would be quite frowned upon in London, even more so in the great state of Texas where she fully intended to return in a few months.

"You're so bad," Tori teased her sister. "You probably scarred that poor man for life."

Piper giggled. "One of these days Dane will realize that a female guard would be so less easy for me to handle than these ex-military types. Then I'll be in trouble. For now…" She shrugged. "It's amazing how quickly they run once I start talking about the royal vagina."

"You'd better hope Dane never figures it out," Tori agreed. "If he does, he'll tell Tal, Rafe, and Kade. Then you'll have hell to pay."

Clearly aware of that fact, Piper pressed a finger to her lips. "Shh."

Tori just shook her head. "So, how is Dane doing? I heard Alea had another baby."

Alea al Mussad was Piper's cousin-in-law and had married the head of Bezakistan's royal guard—all three of them—Dane Mitchell, Cooper Evans, and Landon Nix.

"Yes, a girl. She's *beautiful*," Piper groaned. "I want a girl, but it seems my husbands only produce male sperm. I might try one more time, but then my womb is closed for business. Two boys is enough. Three would be more than any woman should have to handle and keep her sanity. Hopefully, we'll be blessed with a princess next, but if not, surely my little sister can give me a niece to spoil, right?"

"Me?" Tori reared back. "I'm not even dating anyone, much less married or looking to become pregnant."

"Hmm." Piper sent her a speculative stare. "I see the way Oliver looks at you. If he hasn't already, he's going to man up and ask you out."

The mere mention of Oliver Thurston-Hughes made Tori's heart flutter. The eldest of the three British brothers she worked for was a golden god of a man in a perfectly pressed three-piece suit. When she'd met him six months earlier, she'd been dazzled by his good looks, but his sharp intelligence and ruthless business acumen had truly lured her in. He did his best to maintain a wide distance and make others believe he was heartless, but over time, Tori had come to know him—the employer, the brother, the friend. She'd seen under his harsh façade. And she'd fallen in love. The only trouble was she could say the same for his two brothers, Callum and Rory. Athletic and model-gorgeous, Callum could be funny and surprisingly sweet. According to rumor, he was magnificent in bed. Brilliant Rory had the most intense focus of any man she'd ever met, and the idea of being the center of his attention made her shiver.

But Tori didn't live in Bezakistan and couldn't have them all. She reminded herself of that every single day.

"He's not going to ask me out." She answered her sister with what she hoped sounded like a matter-of-fact tone. "We work together. So if he did, of course I would turn him down. And you're the only one in the whole world who still calls me Mindy. Can you stop it?"

She'd started using her middle name when she'd realized that going to med school wasn't for her, after failing organic chemistry. Instead, she'd gone into public relations. Torrance Glen sounded far more worldly and professional—exactly what she needed to become a competent image consultant.

Piper's nose wrinkled. "You're my kid sister. You'll always be Mindy to me. Now stop trying to change the subject. You know I care about Oliver. I think you do, too."

"Yes, but as the Brits would say, it's bad form to shag your boss. I'm already considered young in a game usually won by seasoned vets. I don't need any whispers circulating that I slept my way into this lucrative job. I took on this challenge precisely to build myself some professional credibility."

Her decision hadn't had anything to do with being close to the Thurston-Hughes men. Well, not much.

"Oliver needs a woman to love far more than he needs a PR consultant." Piper paused, as if trying to weigh her next words. "I was there that terrible day Yasmin nearly killed him and destroyed his life. Even when I visited him in the hospital afterward, I could tell he was a changed man. If you can look past his gruffness—"

"I have," Tori assured softly. She'd seen Oliver's heart underneath, no matter how desperately he wished to conceal it. "But he's not over her yet."

His late wife, Yasmin, had not only lied to and cheated

on him, but she'd taken betrayal a step further and aborted two of their children during the marriage. At the end, she'd attempted to kill him. As past lovers went, she was kind of the be-all and end-all of badness.

"Then you could help him."

Tori shook her head. "I don't know that he will ever be over her, and I can't get caught up in his damage. I'm sure that sounds cold. I like Oliver a lot, probably more than I should. But a personal relationship would ruin our professional one. He's nice to me now because we merely work together, but the man has built an invisible wall around himself, and I think if I ever tried to breach the sucker he would defend himself. It wouldn't be pretty."

Piper leaned in with a sigh. "Under all the hurt, he's a good man with a big heart."

Yes, but Tori didn't dare want more with Oliver. "Do you know why Claire Thurston-Hughes hired me?"

The brothers' sister had recognized how badly the company needed an image consultant. Since Tori had already done some work for the Bezakistani royals, which had led her to a few high-profile European jobs, Claire had assured Tori that she would be a good fit for the Thurston-Hughes company.

"I know the stock has taken a hit in the last couple of years," Piper replied. "I heard Tal talking to Kade about it."

"Most of the financial problems had everything to do with the slowdown in the world economy and nothing to do with management. The strange thing is, the quarterly reports are actually on an uptick, but no one wants to hear that. They want to hear about Oliver Thurston-Hughes getting into pub fights. They seem to enjoy focusing on him acting more like a hooligan than a CEO. Then there's Rory. He's one of the smartest men I've ever met in my life, not to mention rich and incredibly interesting. Apparently, that combination is kryptonite for females. He goes through a six-pack of supermodels each month, like he's consuming beer, not women. And he's incredibly generous with them all."

"I haven't seen Rory mentioned in the press for a few months." Piper reached for a scone. "So you must be doing an admirable, if not heroic, job of keeping the gossip about him quiet."

If Piper thought that, she clearly hadn't seen the tabloids for the last week. Rory, it seemed, had suddenly embraced his old habits because it looked as if he had a new bedmate. Tori hurt with a physical pang every time she saw photos of him with a "date." Every woman he showered his time and attention on seemed more interested in fame and fortune than in the man himself. "He's been more circumspect since I pointed out how much of his trust fund he's spending on what amounts to high-class hookers."

Piper's eyes widened. "You did *not* say that to him."

Tori shrugged. She shot straight with her clients and saved her tact for the press. Candy coating a situation rarely benefitted the one signing her checks. She was there to make them look better, not feel better. "Actually, I believe I told him he'd spent the GDP of a small country on the last Slutasaurus Rex he called girlfriend and if he didn't quit, he'd be both broke and foolish."

Her sister's mouth hung open. "Seriously?"

"I stand by my judgment. She was about eleven feet tall and weighed ninety pounds soaking wet. And those teeth could seriously kill a man. I have no idea what he saw in her, except breasts done by the best surgeon England has to offer."

"You sound jealous," Piper pointed out.

Tori sipped her tea, hoping the cup hid her grimace. God, she needed to keep her mouth shut. Piper was both astute and happy, so if her sister knew how deep her feelings for her bosses ran, she wouldn't hesitate to play matchmaker. And if Piper learned how far she'd gone to keep herself "safe" from the Thurston-Hughes brothers, she would gasp in horror. Her sister wasn't big on lies, even for the greater good.

"I'm simply pointing out that while Rory is an amazing man, he's got issues, just like his brothers, that I don't want to deal with," Tori murmured.

"Even the soccer player? Excuse me, the football god."

She sometimes forgot that what she'd called soccer all her life was football over here. And Callum Thurston-Hughes had been one of the best—Manchester United's star player until a career-killing injury had taken him out the year before. But Tori gave him credit. Rather than being bitter, Callum treated every new day like a gift to be used to its fullest. It sometimes made him reckless, dangerous. "You must have heard that I'm dealing with a paternity case for him. It's all over the press."

"All right. That headline was hard to miss," Piper conceded. "Hey, at least they're keeping you busy."

Tori scoffed. "I just love the phone ringing at three in the morning with some new Thurston-Hughes surprise that ruins my night of sleep."

"Well, if you won't consider your very hot bosses as potential mates, Dane has hired a couple of new guards who are smart and funny. I think you'll find them attractive. My husbands also have some cousins who would love to meet you. I have to warn you, though. There are five of them and they're very traditional."

Tori felt her jaw drop. Had her sister lost her damn mind? "Five? I don't know where you put three."

"Oh, that's easy," Piper began. "One in—"

"Stop." Sometimes her sister overshared, and Tori didn't need to hear more of this. "I don't want to know. I would like to keep my ears as virginal as the rest of me."

Piper froze. "You're kidding. Still?"

"You were a virgin until you got married. I don't understand the shock."

"After Dad died, I had you to raise, so I didn't date. What's holding you back?"

How did she explain her choices to a sister who had been

swept off her feet and made a queen literally? "I watched a couple of friends get their hearts seriously broken by guys who used them for sex. I don't want to end up like them.

Tori refused to give up that piece of herself to someone who didn't value her. Her friend Brooke had once had a one-night stand. Nine months later, it turned into a battle for child support fought by two parents who couldn't stand each other. But it wasn't simply pregnancy or single motherhood that worried Tori.

"You have to take a chance at some point." Piper sat back, her eyes soft with empathy as she looked her sister over. "You can't hide away all of your life. Mom and Dad had a great marriage."

Of course Piper had to bring up the one subject guaranteed to send her into a tailspin. Unfortunately, not even that kept her from thinking about the Thurston-Hughes brothers—all three of them.

"Yes, until Mom died and Daddy turned into a shell of himself." Tori took a long breath. Her chest tightened, as it always did when she thought about her parents. For most of her life they'd been blissfully happy. Then her mother's long fight with cancer had ended. Afterward, her father had faded away until a car accident had stolen what had been left of his life. "Do you ever wonder?"

Piper sniffled, her eyes glazing over with a sheen of tears. She didn't pretend to misunderstand. "If he let it happen because he wanted to end his suffering? All the time. He knew those roads like the back of his hand."

Had their father driven off that road so he didn't have to live without his beloved anymore? "The thought of a love like that scares me, Piper."

"Sweetie, life is basically meaningless if you don't love like that," Piper argued. "Dad wouldn't have taken back the years he had with Mom, even if he'd known how they would end. He wouldn't have chosen to spend his life with anyone else. We don't know what happened the night he died,

Mindy, but he was a good father. Shouldn't we give him the benefit of the doubt?"

Tori nodded because she didn't want to talk about this anymore. It was easier to deflect this subject with the Thurston-Hughes family. They didn't know her the way Piper did. Tori easily handled them with a fake engagement ring and a couple of phony calls to her "fiancé."

She used that pretend engagement like a blunt instrument. It worked best on Oliver. Callum and Rory still flirted, but the moment Oliver had heard the "news," he'd become chillingly polite. Every now and then, she still caught him looking at her like a hungry lion. Whenever that happened, she flashed her cubic zirconia rock, and *poof*, they were merely work associates again.

"Tell me about Sabir's birthday party," Tori said, completely changing the subject. The elder of her two adorable nephews was having his birthday soon, and Tori intended to forget her romantic issues for a while and play auntie. It was her favorite role.

For a moment, Piper looked like she would press the subject, but she finally stirred her tea again and sipped. "I'm so glad you're coming. I hope you can stay for a while. The boys miss you. I think we're going with a pirate theme."

While her sister chatted away, Tori thought about the men she should never, would never touch.

* * * *

Oliver Thurston-Hughes clenched his fists and tried to quell his urge to punch someone. Then again, a day rarely went by that he didn't feel it. "What do you mean?"

"I need a place to stay temporarily." His younger brother Callum leaned forward, wearing an earnest look on his sunbronzed face. "Just until the crack pot births her spawn and I get the results of the DNA test. Apparently, I can't force her to do one until the nipper makes his actual appearance, so

13

we've got some months to wait."

Oliver bristled. "You're talking about a child, potentially your own."

Yet his brother treated the baby as if he or she meant nothing.

Callum's remark gnawed at Oliver's brain. The rage that constantly seethed inside him rose. He breathed through the violent urge but couldn't deny the fact that he'd enjoy beating his brother right now. Usually he preferred strangers, but the former footballer would be a nice change of pace and provide a good challenge besides.

Drawing in a steadying breath, Oliver stood and looked out the rain-splattered window over St. James's Park from the office that had once been his father's. What would Albert Thurston-Hughes do if he could see his three sons now? Likely shoot the lot of them and start over.

Outside, everything looked peaceful, and he tried to find his calm. A light drizzle fell. Down below, pedestrians hustled about. Women held umbrellas over their prams as they rushed to shelter where their babies would be dry and warm.

Oliver gripped the sill. His children would be too old for prams now—or would have been if that bitch had allowed them to be born.

"Nothing against the baby," Callum assured. "But I couldn't possibly have fathered that insane woman's child."

He turned back to his younger brother, brow raised. "So you're telling me you didn't sleep with her?"

Callum paused, giving Oliver precisely the answer he'd expected.

With a shake of his head, he stared out the window again, refusing to look at his brother. The rage grew, and he needed to find an outlet to release it. He'd been a perpetual volcano set to explode ever since he'd realized Yasmin had betrayed him and he'd learned his whole life was a lie. "You have a flat worth millions. Why can't you stay there?"

"Because she knows where I live and keeps popping 'round," Callum admitted. "She's mental, I tell you."

"Maybe you should have figured that out before you shagged her," a familiar feminine voice offered.

Oliver turned slightly to find Rory and their sister, Claire, entering the room. The entire family was now here. Hurrah for him. Younger than Callum and older than Rory, Claire tended to be the voice of wisdom. Most of the time that was a good thing, but on the days when pent-up violence nipped at his gut, Oliver didn't want to hear reason.

"Then again, he's always liked the crazy ones," Claire went on.

Oliver glanced back out the window. Below, a yellow umbrella caught his eye. He was fooling himself if he thought for an instant that he stared out the window because he couldn't stand to look at Callum. He was staring because he was waiting for *her*.

It seemed that everyone else in London carried a black umbrella. Tori looked like a bright canary amongst all the crows. She disappeared as she walked into the building. Only then did Oliver turn to the others and step into the middle of the room to join them.

She was safe now. He could focus on the meeting at hand.

Oliver had no idea what he would do when she returned to the States and her fiancé. Watching Tori Glen had become his favorite pastime. After his last brawl, he'd come away with a black eye and split lip. He'd told Tori he had gotten pissed at a pub and started a fight. Oliver still wondered if he should admit that he'd beaten the holy hell out of a bloke who'd been stalking her. When she'd gone down the wrong alley, the bastard had whipped out a big knife and followed.

Tori had never noticed that he'd put her would-be attacker in the hospital. Instead, she'd just blithely gone her way. The following day, she'd told him about her misadventure, laughing that she still sometimes got lost in

London.

She was going to be the death of him, and he wasn't so sure he minded.

Only two things kept him from taking her bright light for himself: One was James Fenway of Texas, her loving and endlessly patient fiancé. The second was the fact that he was a black hole, which tended to consume and destroy all light in its path.

"I didn't know she was cray cray before I slept with her. Also, I might have had a wee bit to drink. However, I can assure you that the baby is not mine," Callum said.

"Cray cray? What is that nonsense you're spouting?" Oliver glared at his younger brother.

Callum waved him off. "It's an expression Tori uses. I very much like the way she talks. In fact, I appreciate the way she does everything. We need to discuss her."

"First, explain how this can't be your child," Claire demanded.

"I'd like to hear this as well." Rory took a seat beside Callum. "You know condoms break. Did she tell you she was on the pill? I know you think no one would ever lie to their favorite footballer, but really... Do you even watch telly?"

Callum groaned. "Yes, Mummy and Daddy, I did use a condom, and I know how it feels when one breaks. This one stayed solid. But I know this baby isn't mine because I haven't had sex with the woman in almost a year. If fact, I haven't slept with anyone since the injury."

Oliver felt his jaw drop. "You've been celibate all this time? Impossible. Unless something is wrong. Anything we don't know? Has the medication adversely affected your...sex drive?"

Callum chuckled, his expression open, happy even. Oliver didn't understand how his brother had survived such a backbiting, throat-slitting profession with his ability to smile like that still intact but he appreciated it.

"No. Little Cal is in perfect working order, thank you. I'll admit that at first I was somewhat depressed, but I've come out the other side of that. I haven't shagged anyone because I'm only interested in one woman, and until very recently, she was off limits. But did you note that I couldn't possibly have fathered whatever beast is in Thea's womb? She claims she's two months pregnant. I will admit to seeing her at a party at Reggie's a couple of months back. She started the creepy stalker stuff then. But my willy stayed firmly behind my zip all night."

Oliver sighed with relief and sat behind his desk. That was one worry out of his way. His younger brother might make a hash of his life on a regular basis, but he was honest about it. The tabloids would calm down once the results of the DNA test were in. Directly after, they could ensure the woman stayed away from Callum. "All right, then. You can stay at the Heights. There's a vacant one-bedroom, I believe."

He couldn't miss the way Callum's whole face lit up as though being told he could go from his posh digs in Chelsea to a nondescript building that temporarily housed visiting workers was a godsend. "Brilliant. I'll take my suitcases over there tonight. You have no idea how grateful I am, Oliver. I promise once this is all over, you'll see I'm a changed man."

"Happy to hear you're in proper working order..." Rory stared at Callum with narrowed eyes. "But who are you interested in? It best not be the woman I told you to stay the bloody hell away from."

Wearing a calming expression, Claire stood, stepping between them. "Stop it, both of you. Sit down and work this out like brothers."

"Have you touched her?" Rory ignored his sister, leaping to his feet, fists at his sides.

"Not yet," Cal admitted. "But I intend to very soon."

Rory looked ready to kill. "Don't you dare."

Oliver held up a hand. "I'm a bit confused. Who are you two arguing over?" He frowned at Rory. "I thought you were seeing some actress."

"I was," his youngest brother admitted. "I broke it off. It was never serious."

"I'll touch her if I want to." Callum ignored him to warn Rory, then turned to Oliver. "He's seeing at least three different women. Or rather, he's seen at least three so far this week."

Claire scowled. "I always thought Cal was the walking venereal disease."

"Not at all," Callum assured their sister. "I'm perfectly clean. All the doctors' reports say I'm STI free. Perhaps I should have a button announcing that fact made for my lapel."

"Being disease free for the moment hardly makes you prime relationship material," Oliver shot back.

"At the very least, it should be on every girl's checklist. I know it's on mine." Claire sat once more, obviously hoping she'd seen the last of her brothers' theatrics for now.

Oliver tsked. "Rory, we pay Tori for a reason. Have you heard a word our publicist has said? You're supposed to be discreet."

"I assure you, I am. You won't find any YouTube videos of me drunkenly dropping my trousers at a bar in Brazil to shag a girl on a stool."

"That was nearly two years ago," Callum objected. "I've matured since then."

Rory shot him a skeptical glance.

Oliver wanted to punch them both now. "This isn't about Cal, and you know perfectly well that dating three women in a week isn't discreet." Rory needed to grasp the bloody concept. "Our stock is still unstable. If we're not careful, the stockholders will soon ask for my head. Do you want to watch the company our family spent decades building crumble around us?"

Rory and Callum both backed down.

"You know I don't." Rory sank into his seat. "I'm not indiscriminately dating women, just escorting a few girls around as a favor. One is an old schoolmate's sister who's working on a movie here. He asked if I would take her to a few dinners. For her, the publicity is helpful."

"And for you, it's toxic. For all of us, in fact." Oliver pressed his thumb to his forehead, massaging between his eyes, though he knew it wouldn't stave off the inevitable headache. "I understand that I'm more than a bit to blame. I started this cycle."

All three of his siblings went on the attack then. Or rather in defense of him, all talking loudly over one another. Oliver managed a grim smile. It was good to know they didn't believe him at fault for the Yasmin incident. Unfortunately, they were wrong.

"Stop," he insisted. "I married her even knowing that I didn't love her. I didn't want to deal with her, so I turned a blind eye to her behavior. And in doing so, I landed our family in every known tabloid. Now we're synonymous with bad behavior. It needs to stop. This is precisely the reason we hired a publicist in the first place. We need to listen to her."

And that meant he couldn't pop in at the pub 'round the corner and pick a fight whenever the whim grabbed him by the balls. He couldn't beat on someone deserving until the chap collapsed. Oliver knew he would simply have to find another way to burn off the angry energy bubbling in his blood.

A vision of Tori assaulted him. He could see her laid out on his desk, her legs spread, arms open and welcoming him inside.

He sucked in a breath, glad he sat behind his desk because the last thing he wanted his siblings to see was the fact that he had an erection. He liked to pretend he no longer got those.

"I agree." Callum stood again and smoothed down his shirt. "Tori insisted that I start looking more serious. It's why I've been working so hard these last few months. I think you'll find that tomorrow night's charity ball will be a smashing success. I've managed to lure a ton of press, and most of my old team is coming out to help. We'll easily raise a hundred thousand pounds for the fund. I'll prove that I'm more than a bloke who kicked a football."

For as long as Oliver could remember, playing midfielder had been all Callum ever wanted. He'd practiced constantly as a kid. He'd made it to the top of his profession, and now, at age twenty-eight, that part of his life was over. Tori had advised him to give Callum a high-profile position within the company. Given both his brother's contacts in entertainment and his charm, she'd suggested marketing. Remembering the debacle of his brother's school years, Oliver had immediately shoved him somewhere he couldn't do too much damage—the director in name only of the corporation's charity wing. Thurston-Hughes had a long history of donating to good causes, specifically London's children's charities. It had been his mother's lifelong passion.

If what Callum said about the charity ball was true, maybe he'd found another calling.

"I'm looking forward to it, but we must present a united front when the press asks about the paternity suit." Oliver wished he could forget or ignore this unpleasantry, but they'd been planning this fundraiser for months and everyone looking for a scoop would attend. Hopefully the press—and the stockholders—would take note if the family united behind Callum. "In a bit, let's ask Tori what we should and shouldn't say when asked. Then tonight, you'll move into the corporate housing. It's got decent security. And stay away from this mad woman. In a couple of weeks, we can escape on holiday and head out to the countryside. Until then, let's all keep a low profile." Oliver frowned. "Callum, please tell me you're not bringing someone new to the fundraiser."

Twin flags of red stained his face. "I was planning to."

"Don't. The last thing we need is for you to be seen with another woman when you've supposedly already got one pregnant."

"Fine, but I'm ready to move on with my life. I'm not waiting forever. Tell me when we're meeting with Tori." Callum stood to leave and headed for the door, looking back at Oliver. "None of us blames you. What happened with Yasmin was terrible, but none of it was your fault. I'll do whatever I can to help right this ship."

The door closed behind him, and Rory stood. "I will, too. I'll be in my office if you need me."

Oliver was left alone with his sister. He rather wished she'd left with the lads.

"What are you doing, Ollie?" She moved across the room, settling into the chair by his desk.

He flipped open a binder. "I'm reading through the latest R&D reports."

"That isn't what I meant, and you know it." She crossed her legs at the ankle, every bit the elegant British lady. "You weren't in a pub fight. If you're going to lie, at least get your facts straight. The pub you mentioned was closed that evening due to a small fire in the kitchen."

He stared at his sister—not as a brother, but as a man who didn't like having his secrets pried into. "You checked up on me?"

"I have to. You lie. And before you tell me it's none of my business, consider that you've just been grilling Callum and Rory about their personal lives. Now you weren't in a pub fight that evening. Tell me what really happened."

He didn't want to give Claire anything else to worry about. "Nothing."

"You sent that man to the hospital." She bounced her Prada heel against the plush carpet as she spoke, almost punctuating her every accusation. "I started to put it together a few days ago. I watched you follow Tori after work. I didn't mean to. I happened to be on the street when I noticed her walking toward Westminster Station, then saw you dash after her. I was curious since you'd said not half an hour before that you were heading home. You never go home that way.

Imagine my surprise when you got on the Line 12 bus. She didn't see you, did she? At first, I thought you two had some kind of assignation planned."

Oliver felt the blood drain from his face. "Did you follow me?"

"Yes, in a taxi."

"Tell me you stayed in the cab."

"I would love to, but I'm afraid my curiosity got the better of me."

"You walked around Peckham by yourself?"

"Never mind that." Claire waved him off. "That thug was waiting for Tori, Oliver. It wasn't random, but you knew that. Right? You were following her because you knew she was in danger."

Her words nearly knocked Oliver over. He'd known no such thing.

"What do you mean he was waiting for Tori?" He'd seen the man creep up behind her. "She said she'd intended to visit a friend and got lost. She went down the wrong street and ended up in an alley where a predator awaited some unsuspecting prey."

Claire reared back. "You didn't notice that man followed her from Westminster on to the bus and then off when they reached Peckham?"

He hadn't noticed anything but Tori. He'd been utterly fixated on her until the big man with the knife had crept after her in the alley. "How did he get between us?"

"He seemed to know the area. Somehow, he beat you there." She shook her head. "If you weren't trying to protect Tori, then why were you following her, Oliver?"

He didn't have a reply and tried to answer his sister's question with a shrug.

She pursed her lips in displeasure. "I was shocked by what you did to that man. When did you learn to fight like that?"

"Like what?" *An animal?*

Oliver stood and turned away from her. He'd never wanted any of them to see that side of him. Every day he had to fight harder to control it.

"You nearly killed him. Even when he was down, you kept beating him until the police came."

"Are you the one who called them?" He'd been lost in blood rage, beating the man senseless for even having the notion to hurt Tori. Somewhere deep down he'd known the bloke was done, but he'd kept at it.

Oliver suspected he'd kill someone one of these days. Then he would get what he deserved.

"Yes. I'll admit you truly frightened me for a minute. I needed to think about what I saw. I called the police because I didn't want you to do something we'd all regret. I also noticed you didn't stay around."

He'd fled when he heard the sirens. He'd felt the blood pumping in his veins and he'd run. For a brief moment, he'd felt alive again. "I should frighten you. To answer your questions, I followed Tori because I'm a pervert and can't seem to help myself. I kept hitting him because I was in a blind rage. I get them every now and then, ever since…"

"Yasmin nearly killed you. Ever since you found out what she'd done to you."

"To this whole family."

"Oliver, don't distance. You're fooling yourself if you think this rage is for the rest of us. It's for you. She betrayed you on every level. And stop saying you didn't love her."

At least he could be honest in that. He turned back to Claire, settling his palms on the desk. "I might have thought I was in love, but it was a young man's infatuation with an exotic woman who was very good in bed. It wasn't love."

"That's the bitterness talking."

"No, it's experience. I know what it really feels like to be in love, and what I felt for Yasmin is nothing compared to what I feel now. This is a million times worse."

"You're in love with Tori." His sister's eyes went wide.

"Oh, what a mess."

Oliver felt his jaw tighten. "I won't act on it. She's marrying someone else. You must know that I, of all people, would never come between a man and his woman."

He knew what it felt like to be the cuckold in that scenario. All too often, he looked into the faces of his former friends and wondered which of them had been his wife's lovers.

Claire bit her bottom lip. "I know you won't...but perhaps you should. She can't be terribly mad for the man—or he for her. She hasn't seen him in six months. Six months, Oliver, and neither has visited the other once. Her sister is both the queen of an entire country and mother to two boys—enormous responsibilities—and yet Piper has already visited Tori twice. I've been thinking about this fiancé of hers. We should look into him."

His sister sometimes enjoyed sticking her nose where it didn't belong. "Absolutely not. You'll leave the situation alone. Tori's contract ends in a few months, and she's already said that she intends to return home. And that will be the end of it."

"It won't be. Can't you see that? You've suffered this malaise for the past two years, Oliver. You can't stay this way. How many other fights have you been involved in? Can't you see you have a death wish, and she might be the only one who can save you? Do you think I haven't noticed the way you look at her? I followed you because I was praying I would find out you're sleeping with her, even with all the trouble that would cause between you, Rory, and Callum."

"It's not going to happen. I'm not good for anyone. I never will be again." And he didn't apologize for it. "As for the death wish, well...we all have to wish for something." His brain finally caught on to the rest of her speech. "What did you mean, trouble between me and our brothers? What do they have to do with my ill-timed fascination with Ms.

Glen?"

"You really don't pay attention to anything, do you? Who do you think Callum was talking about bringing to the fundraiser? And why do you think Rory looked ready to take his head off? They both fancy her. Callum believes himself in love with the girl and he intends to make his move. If you tell them that you want her for yourself, I think they'll back off. They love you."

Oliver gripped the side of the desk, seething, his knuckles turning white. "He will *not* touch her. I'll make sure of it."

Rory would have to get in line to take Callum's head off because if their middle brother laid one finger on Tori, Oliver would be more than happy to do the honors.

Without a backward glance at his sister, he strode out of the office, itching for a fight.

CHAPTER TWO

Rory managed to close the door to Oliver's office with a quiet snick. He had to force himself not to slam the thing because he was so bloody angry. What did Callum think he was about? Had the bastard listened to a word he'd said last night? Or had he simply nodded his pretty-boy head and decided to do whatever he wanted, no matter the cost?

"Which direction did my brother go?" Rory asked Oliver's fifty-something assistant.

Silently, he pleaded for the proper reply. The only good answer was to the west wing where Callum's office was located.

"Mr. Thurston-Hughes went toward the east wing. He seemed in good spirits," the woman said. "That's nice to see after all the nasty business of late."

Anger flashed through Rory's system. Good spirits? Callum wouldn't be after a thorough throttling. The prick was headed for Tori's office. Callum might be six foot six inches and almost sixteen stone of pure-muscled imbecile, but Rory could hold his own in a fight.

"He won't be for long," he mumbled under his breath as he jogged down the hall to intercept Callum before he reached Tori. He couldn't let his brother botch everything.

According to Claire, Oliver was following their lovely publicist around. That likely meant their eldest brother finally intended to do something about his obvious infatuation with her. If not, that meant Oliver was stalking her. While Rory wondered if his big brother had turned predator, he also had to believe the warm, giving sibling who had practically raised him still lurked inside, waiting for the right woman to free him.

Damn Yasmin. If she weren't already dead, Rory would cheerfully murder the bitch himself.

And damn Tori for being so fucking lovable that she was going to break at least two Thurston-Hughes's hearts. If he couldn't have her himself, Rory intended to make damn sure she didn't hurt Oliver. He'd been through enough.

He turned the corner and found Callum in front of the lifts, impatiently pressing the button that would take him down a level to Tori's office. Thankfully, he was alone.

"You bastard."

Callum turned, his jawline taut and stubborn. "I'm not talking about this any longer. Oliver won't have her, so I intend to. That's all that needs to be said."

They'd been through this before. What would it take to get through his brother's thick skull? "He can't admit it yet, but I finally think he's close. Damn it, Callum. I want her, too, but I want Ollie to live more. We have to step back and let him have his chance. We owe him that."

"I know we do, but I'm not convinced he'll pick himself up by the balls enough to take her. If that's the case, I don't owe him my happiness. Or hers. If he has his way, she'll be alone forever."

"You forget her fiancé."

Callum flushed slightly. "What sort of man leaves her all alone in a foreign country? As far as I'm concerned, after six months he's given up his rights to her. And Tori doesn't seem to miss him. She might still wear that pitiful nothing of a ring, but I keep her company. I make sure she's not alone at night."

A red mist descended over Rory, shocking him with a fury that made his whole body shake. He'd heard some people talk about losing control when their anger took hold, but he'd never been that man. Callum's words pushed him to the breaking point, and he fought to repress the crimson haze. "Exactly how are you keeping her company at night, brother?"

Callum raised his hands as if in surrender. "Not sexually. I haven't touched her beyond a friendly hug."

One of the things Rory loved about Torrance was her genuine, frequent affection. He'd loved his parents, but their open shows of fondness had been few and far between. Now he craved the way she hugged him when she thought he needed it. At first, he'd been put off by it. Now he wouldn't let a day go by without her embrace. "Explain it to me then."

"I call her. I sometimes convince her to let me buy her dinner so we can talk about the fundraiser, but we spend hours talking about all sorts of things. We click, she and I. I've never met anyone like her and I'm not willing to give her up because Oliver won't pull his head from his sphincter."

"He's gun-shy. Can't you see that? Don't you think I feel the same way about her you do?"

"Then may the best man win." He turned back to the lift doors and reached out to press the button to call the car again.

They weren't done yet. He slapped his brother's hand away and lunged in front of the doors. "No. We're not playing it that way. We had an agreement."

"That was months ago, and Oliver has shown no signs of coming out of his shell. I'm not certain he'll ever be ready." Callum's eyes softened. "Rory, I know you feel terribly guilty that you introduced him to Yasmin. You think she got to him through you, but this mess isn't your fault any more than it's his. Yasmin is to blame and she's dead. I'll be honest, I don't understand this desperate need he seems to have to punish himself for something that wasn't his fault."

"I think he blames himself most for the two children she aborted. He didn't even know she was pregnant."

"How could he have known if she didn't tell him? And

given what we know about her now, how can he be certain the babies were even his? I feel for Ollie. He can mourn his lost children, but he doesn't honor them by dying as well. I feel the loss of my career every day but do you know why I didn't go immediately into coaching or broadcasting?"

"No. I have wondered. I know you've had offers."

"Because that part of my life is over. I don't want to be some pathetic, middle-aged, washed-up former pro. I don't want to be a former anything. I was an athlete. I can't do that anymore so I'm going to take all of my energy and put it into something new, something worthwhile. I've got one life and I won't live it in the past. I won't wallow in misery. And I'm through helping Oliver do it. I love Tori. I've never felt this way about a woman before. I won't let her go because Oliver might someday wake up and want her. If he truly cares for her, then he'd better be ready to fight. She deserves that."

Callum had a point, but he hadn't been the one to introduce his brother to the devil. He didn't know how deeply that gouged. It was one thing to lose his career and carry on. It was quite another to aid the ruin of a beloved brother's life and try to move forward without profound regret.

"I told you what Claire said. He's been following her after work. I think he's trying to make sure she gets home all right. That has to mean something."

"Rory, I have a woman who follows me home from work all the time, and we call her a stalker. Don't make this something it's not. Unless he steps up and declares his feelings, I'm not backing down. I'm going to Tori's office and I'm going to make a few things plain to her."

"What is going on here?" Oliver asked the pair of them as he turned the corner, his eyes narrowing as he took in the sight of them awaiting the lifts. "Where do you think you're going, Cal?"

Callum flushed a nice shade of pink. It was good to know someone could still bring the bugger to heel. "Downstairs. I have business that needs tending."

Shayla Black and Lexi Blake

"He's going to see Tori," Rory explained between clenched teeth. "For personal reasons."

"You're such a suck-up," Callum said, turning on him like they were still ten and seven and Oliver had been the authority figure in their lives at the ripe age of thirteen. "My intent is none of your business. Neither one of yours."

"Everything is my business. What is going on between you and our publicist, Cal?" Oliver's tone dripped with chill. His face could have been carved from arctic ice.

Rory was actually quite pleased not to find himself on the receiving end of that stare.

Callum glared back stubbornly. "Nothing."

"Good," Oliver replied.

"Yet," Callum clarified.

Hell. Rory got between his two older brothers. "I'm handling it, Oliver. He's got it in his head that he can date her. You know what he's like when he's at loose ends. It's not serious. She's a pretty girl, and this is what Cal does."

"It *is* serious and I won't pretend otherwise. I'm not a child with a new toy," Callum replied.

"Then stop behaving like one," Oliver growled back.

Callum didn't seem to understand the threat their eldest brother posed because he stepped into Oliver's personal space. "I'm in love with her and I intend to give her what she needs and deserves. I want to be a better man for her, provide for her, and build a life with her."

"I forbid it," Oliver pronounced, then turned to go.

That annoyed Rory a bit, too. Did Oliver truly think he was some sort of king who could dictate his siblings' lives? It rankled, but he told himself Oliver needed more time to heal. He needed to feel in control until that day came.

"I think what Oliver is saying is that, according to company policy, we really shouldn't date anyone from the office," Rory ad-libbed.

"There's no rule." Callum didn't know when to stop. "I looked. And he can't stop me."

"I bloody well can," Oliver turned back, shouting. "I control the purse strings, Callum."

"Maybe Rory's but not mine. You might think I don't have a brain in my head, but I was careful with my money. I was paid millions and I didn't spend it like it was water. I put it all away and it's waiting there for me and the woman I love. It was always for her. I simply didn't know who she was until now."

"She is engaged," Oliver said, his voice tight. "Promised to another man. She wears *his* ring, yet you would go after her? You would take what doesn't belong to you?"

"Does she truly belong to him? He can't put a ring on her finger, then leave her for months at a time." Callum softened marginally. "It isn't right. And it's not what happened with you and Yasmin. I'm not intending to seduce Tori into cheating. I intend to show her I'm the right man for her."

Oliver flushed a furious red. "You don't think all the times my friends took my wife to bed they weren't trying to show her they were right for her?"

"I think we should calm down." Rory realized he'd have to be the voice of reason.

Oliver utterly ignored him. "You think they gave a damn about her wedding ring when they fucked her behind my back?"

Callum stood his ground like the idiot he was. "They didn't love her, Oliver. They used her. And she used you. This situation is different because I love Tori."

"You told Oliver you wouldn't bring a date to the fundraiser." The argument was stupid, but Rory couldn't think of anything else to say just then. He needed time to talk Callum out of this foolishness.

Instead, Callum rolled the famous blue eyes that had gotten him laid repeatedly since puberty. "I'm not. Tori is not a mere date. If I do this right, she'll be *my* fiancée. That should solve many of our problems. My wild reputation will certainly die down, especially after we've married and I've gotten her pregnant a couple of times."

That did it. The notion of his athletic god of a brother impregnating the woman Rory loved finally unhinged his red rage. A vision of Tori, belly curved with a baby, floated through his head. In Rory's estimation, those children should be his. He'd been willing to give up his happiness for Oliver, who'd been devastated by his late wife. But he refused to relinquish Tori to his selfish, good-for-nothing-but-scoring-a-damn-goal sibling.

Before Rory could think, his fist connected with that pretty-boy face that had always gotten Callum every woman he'd ever wanted. By god, it wouldn't land him Tori.

"What the hell?" Callum cupped his jaw. "Why on earth did you do that?"

Rory didn't bother to answer. He punched his older brother again, forcing him back to the wall.

Then Callum struck back, the force of his blow smashing Rory against the lift doors. Years of physical training had given Callum the edge, but Rory looked up and realized Callum's strength was nothing compared to Oliver's rage.

Oliver lashed out, nailing Callum in the jaw. "You're fired, you little shit. I won't let you use her like that."

Rory straightened away from the lift doors as the display above indicated the car stopped on their floor. Through the big doors, he heard a familiar feminine voice.

"Thurston-Hughes Incorporated is one of the last great British family companies, and I think you'll see that the siblings work together to run the company in a harmonious fashion." Tori spoke with soft confidence.

Hell. They were supposed to meet with a reporter this afternoon. Rory feared their sweet Tori was escorting a representative from one of the big financial news sites through the building as a prelude to the fundraiser and Thurston-Hughes's renewal.

The elevator doors opened then.

"Yes, I can see that," a male voice chuckled. "That will

make a good headline."

Rory looked into Tori's horrified face and prayed she didn't quit on the spot.

* * * *

Callum placed the ice pack over his jaw and wondered where Ollie had learned to throw a punch like that. It had been like a battering ram. He'd nearly seen stars, and that hadn't happened since Spain's defender elbowed him in the final round of the World Cup two years before. He wasn't entirely sure he didn't have a concussion but then he tended to get those like most people got headaches.

"What is wrong with you three?" Tori raged at them back in Oliver's office.

Callum tried to focus on her words, not the way her golden brown hair whipped around her like a lusciously soft windstorm or her blouse tightened over her breasts as she railed. "Sorry."

"You knew the reporters were coming. I know you knew that because you all responded to my e-mail advising you. Is fighting like this some British thing I don't understand? Do you normally greet reporters by brawling with your brother?"

Her pretty cheeks flushed pink. He'd bet she would turn that very same color when he spread her legs and fucked her hard. Damn, but she was pretty when she was mad. He was getting an erection that stiffened and throbbed every time she screamed at him.

Lord, he sounded half mad. Sometimes he wondered if hitting the ball with his head so many times had led to brain damage.

Tori turned her attention to Oliver. "And you... I thought you were better than that."

Oliver's eyes narrowed and he stood, leaning over his desk so he could properly intimidate her. His older brother had perfected that maneuver in the last two years. He stood a good foot taller than petite Tori and loomed over her like some snarling beast. "So sorry to have proven you wrong, but I think you forget exactly who you work for."

If Tori was at all intimidated, she didn't show it. She planted her palms on Oliver's desk and leaned in, mirroring him. "And I think you forget what you hired me to do, what you swore we were all working toward."

The sexual tension between them was so bloody thick he could cut it with a knife.

And sweet, smart Tori was in the perfect position for a spanking. She was leaning over, her pert ass in the air. Callum could almost feel his palm connecting. He would give her one rough swat to get her attention, then pepper more across that lush ass to sensitize her skin and prepare her for the fucking to follow.

A big hand swatted his arm, jerking him from the fantasy.

"What is wrong with you?" Rory leaned in and hissed quietly.

His brother's eyes were focused on his slacks. Damn it. He shifted, trying to hide his unruly cock. "I can't help it."

"Try," Rory bit out.

Tori snapped her head around like a predator sensing prey. His sweet bunny actually had a few layers of sharp teeth. That was the trouble. She was so very kind, but in an instant, she could turn into a raging bitch. God, that got him hot. *She* got him hot.

Callum shifted again and tried to think of past games. 2011. Manchester United vs. Arsenal. Their opponents had lost the coin toss, so he'd taken the kickoff.

"Is he listening to a word I've said?" Tori now stood in front of him, but she'd posed her question to Rory.

"Give him a minute. Cal has taken many a thump to the head. Sometimes he requires a moment to focus and get himself back under control." Rory's words provided the time needed to tamp down his arousal and get his head back in the game.

But he knew how to play this scene to his advantage. "I'm all right. Now what were we saying?"

Tori stared at him for a moment as if trying to decide whether to believe him. "I was saying we're screwed."

Nope. Just hearing her utter that particular word got him hard again.

Callum stood and shifted his suit jacket for better coverage. "We're brothers. You were saying that we're one of the last great family-owned corporations in Britain. We proved it by acting like brothers."

He didn't see the problem. Brothers sometimes fought. Then they made up with a pint and a laugh. Most men functioned that way, and it had nothing to do with stocks or bottom lines.

Tori's head sank forward like it was simply too heavy for her to carry anymore. She sighed and when she looked up again, she wore a sadly earnest expression. "The press won't see it that way. The original story I crafted described a unified family rising again in both spirit and sales. Now it will be about three brothers tearing themselves and their company apart. They'll bring up everything from Oliver's marriage to Rory's playboy status to Callum's loss of career and descent into paternity hell."

"I didn't mean to collide with the opposition and break my leg in such a way that I can no longer play."

She sighed tiredly. "Don't apologize for that and don't be flippant. I'm merely pointing out that the press uses the video of your injury and the fact that they had to clean your blood off the field as a metaphor for the company. You're all damaged and someone needs to clean you up."

"Pitch," he corrected.

"What?"

"We call it a pitch. They cleaned my blood off the pitch after they carried me off with my tibia sticking out." He forced himself not to shudder. He still felt a bit sick when he thought of it.

Tori turned pale. "Sorry. I'm not trying to bring back bad memories, but they will use everything against you." She sighed. "Do you want to tell me what all this squabbling is about?"

She stood so close and she looked tired. Callum wondered how her visit with her sister had gone. Hadn't seeing Piper cheered her up? All he wanted to do was haul Tori close and promise that everything would be all right. But he couldn't—yet. Callum wasn't sure how he and his brothers would solve this mess. Oliver and Rory were excellent at unraveling puzzles. He was the workhorse really. He simply did what needed to be done.

"Nothing for you to worry about," he said softly.

"None of your business," Oliver stated at the same moment.

She whirled on Oliver. "You ruin my press conference before it even begins and it's none of my business?"

Maybe, Callum thought, he was more necessary than he'd imagined. Oliver obviously lacked a soft touch these days. "Of course it's her business. Bolstering us with the press is precisely the reason we hired her."

"Can we all calm down?" Rory held a chair out for Tori. "Claire is having tea with the reporter and she'll smooth things over. She's very good with them, unlike the rest of us."

Naturally, Rory had given her the seat closest to him. *Bastard.*

"At least she didn't fall asleep during media training." Tori huffed as she sat.

Callum knew that particular comment was directed straight at him. "Sorry, love. I sometimes get sleepy about midafternoon."

"He's also easily distracted," Rory said pointedly.

Tori sat with her back ramrod straight. "I think it's time to try something different."

Oliver relaxed into his chair and nodded. "I'm all ears."

"I don't think I'm helping you as much as you need. I have a colleague in New York who might be better suited to your PR needs. I'll leave you his contact information. We spoke yesterday about another matter, so I know he's working on something right now, but he could probably be here by the end of the month."

He tensed. "We don't need to bring in anyone to help you, Tori. You're doing fine."

"That's not what she's suggesting," Oliver explained grimly.

Rory turned to her. "Oh?"

Tori trained her stare on Oliver. "It's been six months, and I haven't made a substantial difference here. Perhaps the company should try someone new. I suggest a man because I think you might listen better to one."

"No." Callum wasn't about to let her go, not before he could see whether he and Tori could have a go at a future together. "Absolutely not. You saw what happened. We're on testosterone overload as it is. We don't need more. We need you."

Oliver held up his hand, a clear signal he'd decided to take over. "So now we're misogynists, is that it?"

She frowned. "No. You're all normally quite polite and kind. You're very much gentlemen around me, which is why I think you need a male. You might talk to him more...openly. He might be able to get to the root of the problem."

Tori was the root of the problem. How the hell could they tell her that?

Well, love, we all want in your knickers and we're battling it out to see who gets to go first. Yes, she would love that.

Who goes first? Callum intended to be first—and last. He would be her only. Hell, he and his brothers couldn't share a room, much less a wife, without fighting. Right?

A little voice in his head had been picking at him for

weeks, ever since he'd talked to his friends in New Orleans who shared a wife. Three lawyers. One beloved beauty. He kept waiting for their relationship to fall apart, but they seemed happier than ever.

Oliver sat back, looking positively arctic. "Do you want to leave?"

"Of course she doesn't," Callum said, trying to be an optimist.

"Don't interrupt, Cal," Oliver snapped. "Tori has been through a great deal with us in the past six months. My situation—and the company's—was already challenging enough. So what did you give her? A paternity suit. Brilliant." He turned to Rory. "And you heaped on a parade of apparent sluts. I wouldn't blame her if she preferred to go home." He quieted for a moment, then his expression softened as he regarded Tori. "Do you miss your fiancé? You're not wearing your engagement ring. Is there any trouble?"

Callum bit back a retort. For once, he knew something they didn't. Finally, he was ahead of his brothers in the knowledge department, and he'd been saving this nugget for his own use. He wasn't about to let Tori leave. But for now, he sat back and waited to see how she responded.

Tori glanced down at her hand and seemed surprised to see it ringless. Then she fumbled for her purse and slipped the meager gem on once more. "I took it off so my sister could look at it. She loves diamonds. I guess I forgot to put it back on."

Yes, because the Queen of Bezakistan couldn't tell a real diamond from that piece of shit fake. Callum held back his snort. He suspected that if he asked Piper, she probably had no idea her sister was "engaged."

For months, it had bothered him that Tori talked about that ring as if James Fenway had spent his last dime on it. He'd assumed that she was either overcompensating because she knew it was synthetic or terribly naïve. If the latter,

Callum had itched to beat the liar to a bloody pulp.

Except now he knew. *She* was the liar. Tori had bought that silly ring for seventy pounds, and according to his private investigator, no man by the name of James Fenway existed in her little Texas hometown.

Yes, he definitely intended to spank her for that, the little minx.

"You're under contract," Rory reminded her with a quiet bite.

"I can release her from that contract," Oliver countered.

"Not without the support of the board." Rory sat up straight, thrusting his chin out stubbornly, the way he used to just before he did something sure to land him in trouble. "I think we need her. Callum will vote with me."

"Damn straight." At least they were in accord on this.

"Claire will vote with me." Oliver shot Rory a tight smile.

"I'm not so sure about that," Callum said. "Claire likes Tori. She might vote to keep her around just so she's got another female, but if not we go to our tie breaker, Uncle Walter."

Uncle Walter loved one thing and one thing only these days. He'd been given stock in the company on the marriage of his only sister to Albert Thurston-Hughes, but he'd never had a head for business. He taught mathematics at university but he only worked so he could afford tickets to his favorite football team.

Manchester United.

"Yes," Callum said with a satisfied sigh. "I think I should ring him up and assure him I can get him an executive box this year."

"You're a smug bastard." Oliver clearly knew he'd been defeated. "Ms. Glen, we'll be enforcing your contract, it seems."

"I thought that contract was for my benefit, that it guaranteed me a year of work." She swiveled her gaze at

Rory, who had written the contract. "You said it protected me from being fired. Isn't that what sacked means?"

"Contracts work both ways. Since you were coming here from America, I had you sign the same contract I would give any non-British national we host for a prolonged period. We have to deal with your work visa and a lot of paperwork. It only makes sense that you would agree to a time frame advantageous to us both."

"I'm trying to do what's best for y'all." As she grew more agitated, her Texas accent became more pronounced. "You can't force me to stay here."

"No," Oliver agreed. "We can't force you to honor your contract but I believe there's a clause that states you must repay us the expenses we incurred during your employment, should you resign early. Between the legal fees to get you into the country, the travel expenses, and your flat, I think we're somewhere close to fifty thousand pounds."

"We'll need that in cash," Rory added, looking smug.

Tori blinked, obviously stunned.

They were making a hash of this. Callum sighed. "No one wants you to go, love. What happened this afternoon was entirely my fault. Oliver and I were arguing over how to handle some of the advertisements for the fundraiser. I might have lost my temper a bit and called him some names. Mentioned he's losing his hair and getting the slightest bit soft in the middle. He was trying to show me he wasn't."

Tori shook a finger at him. "You can't talk to your brother that way. You know he's sensitive about his hair."

Oliver frowned. "I bloody well am not. I've got all my hair."

She sent him an enthusiastic nod. "I know you do." She turned back to Callum. "You need to be more professional. And sensitive."

At least she was back to henpecking him. He could handle that. He couldn't handle her leaving. "Yes. Of course. I'll apologize to the reporter and explain everything."

She stood and crossed the room to him. Callum rose to his feet, looking down at her as she straightened his tie. "Wash up first. There's a speck of blood on your shirt."

God, he loved being close to her.

"Where?" He pretended he didn't see it.

"Here." She pointed to a spot high on his chest, her finger brushing him.

Callum's cock went rock hard again the instant she touched him. "I've got a clean one in my office. I'll change straightaway. I'm sorry, Tori. I can't tell you how much. My behavior was immature and ridiculous. It won't happen again."

She sniffled a little, looking up at him with bright blue eyes. "We all make mistakes. I'm glad I'm not leaving, though I'm kicking myself for not reading the contract more thoroughly. Please be polite to the reporter. He's a huge fan. It might be good if you took him out for a beer. A pint, I mean."

He grinned. "We'll make a Brit out of you yet. Now go on and try to forget this afternoon. We've got a ball to put on tomorrow. You're supposed to meet with Sheila at Harrods at four."

She looked down at her watch. "I forgot. I'll have to run."

"I'll have my driver take you," Oliver offered.

"You have a driver?" she asked. "I thought you walked everywhere."

Stalked was more like it, but he wasn't going to get his brother into more trouble. "We keep one in case of emergencies. Go along. His names is Charles and he'll be waiting for you in the car park."

She gave him a radiant smile and was off.

Rory shook his head, his eyes still on the door. "Did she not read the contract? I didn't think I had to mention anything since she's perfectly well educated. She's able to read. It was right there."

Oliver ignored him, turning to Callum. "I am *not* losing my hair. Don't you dare tell that reporter some daft story about my anguish over my nonexistent hair loss. And I'm certainly not turning to fat. I proved that by the elevators."

Callum had to hide a smile because this was the most animated Oliver had been in years. "You're right. I'll tell the pesky reporter that we were scrapping over a bet we'd made. Everyone understands football fights. Just a tiny bit of hooligan in you, brother. I'll smooth it over."

"And what about Tori?" Oliver asked.

"I'll handle her, too." He'd already handled the problem of her dress for the next evening.

Despite the fact that she was related to one of the wealthiest families in the world, she seemed determined to make her own way. That meant she couldn't afford the kind of designer gown she should have for tomorrow night. Given Tori's pride, she would naturally balk at him paying if he tried to buy a gown for her. Instead, he'd arranged for her to try on some "clearance" dresses at Harrods. The clerk there would take a small portion from Tori and bill Callum for the rest.

"Whatever scheme is running through your head is wrong," Oliver reminded through clenched teeth. "She's engaged."

The truth sat on the tip of his tongue, but Callum couldn't risk telling his brothers. If he did and Oliver crooked a finger in her direction, would she choose his eldest brother? Would she prefer Rory's intelligence? Or would she actually saddle herself with a past-his-prime bloke who'd only ever been really good at kicking a ball into a net?

Callum didn't like his odds.

"I'll handle that, too." He walked out, his good mood gone.

He might be a bastard, but she was the prize. And he intended to win.

CHAPTER THREE

Tori stared down at the grand ballroom and wondered if she was doing the right thing. Not about the fundraiser. The event itself seemed to be a very elegant success. The money was rolling in. As an added bonus, the Thurston-Hughes brothers all looked lip-bitingly hot in their tuxedos.

What she really wondered was whether she should have given in so easily and agreed to stay in London. Seeing the three brothers every day made it far too likely she'd keep fantasizing they were her men. What if, one day, imagining herself surrounded and beloved by them was no longer enough?

She winced. She should probably quit before she did something stupid she couldn't take back, something that would leave her with a shattered professional reputation *and* a broken heart. If she'd been smarter—if she could have managed to want the three of them less—she could have used that dumb fight yesterday as the excuse to hand them over to another publicist. If she'd pushed a little harder, they would have given in. If she'd cried about how much she missed her fiancé, Oliver would have bought her plane ticket himself.

Instead, a wave of relief had overtaken her when she realized they had no intention of letting her leave. She was trapped here by that contract she really should have paid more attention to. Yep, she was a glutton for punishment.

From the balcony above, Tori swept her gaze around the ballroom and saw her sister in Talib's arms on the dance floor. A wistful feeling overtook her as she watched them waltz in perfect time. Her sister's beauty and happiness was an almost palpable thing. Who could have guessed how well her seemingly ill-fated business trip to Bezakistan would turn out?

"Hello, little sister," a deep voice said. "You look lovely tonight."

She smiled at her brother-in-law. Rafiq al Mussad was a gorgeous man with pitch-black hair and eyes a girl could get lost in. She held out her hands in greeting. "And you look dashing as always, brother."

Tori loved having family again. For so long, she and Piper had struggled to make it on their own, and now she had all these amazing men to count as brothers.

Rafe took her hands in his and shook his head. "Do you have a guard? I don't like the idea of you running about London in that dress. Piper saw it on the runway two weeks ago, and I feared if she wore it that she would start a riot."

Tori laughed and gave Rafe's hands a squeeze before turning back to the ball. "I don't think I'll be starting any riots, but the fundraiser seems to be doing well. I can't thank you enough for the generous contribution."

"We do what we can." He settled in beside her. "I've been thinking."

"That is a dangerous thing." Tori was only half-teasing. Rafe thinking usually meant some plan to move her into the palace where he could keep his whole family under the watchful eye of the royal guard. Talib and Kadir would naturally concur.

"The world is a dangerous place. I think you should come back to work for us."

She sighed. "The royal family doesn't need my services. You're not bad boys. You're all family men and model royals."

"Sabir and Michael are complete hooligans."

She laughed. "I'm sure my nephews get terrible press because they don't pick up their toys or poop when you want them to. Call me when they're teens. *Then* you might need my services."

Rafe leaned against the banister, studying her like she was a problem he must solve. "I worry about you. So does Piper. From a security perspective, you're the weak link in our chain. Some radical factions out there would love to strike at Talib and would think nothing of hurting his family. Piper and the children are surrounded by tight security at all times. But you're living here in London with no one to watch over you."

"The building I live in has security." Though lately, she'd had the oddest feeling someone was watching her.

"Rented guards who don't make enough to truly put their lives on the line for you." Rafe rolled his eyes. "We'd prefer you at the palace, but at least allow Dane to assign you a competent security detail while you're in London."

The idea horrified her. The one thing she couldn't stand about palace life was the lack of privacy. She loved her family. She adored spending holidays and vacations in Bezakistan with Piper and Alea and their husbands and kids, but sometimes she felt as if she couldn't breathe there. She wasn't allowed to leave the palace without a guard. Even when she walked around the gardens, someone was watching to make sure nothing dangerous occurred. Tori knew the guards watched her for security purposes, not to spy, but she couldn't live that life.

"No, Rafe. I have to be able to go where I want, when I want. I need to make my own way. I love London and I love my freedom. I can't enjoy either in Bezakistan or with your rent-a-cops breathing down my neck."

Rafe's eyes narrowed. "Is that truly your objection? I'm thinking it is more likely that a man keeps you in London. Or several."

She pretended to misunderstand. "I'm not being kept. Didn't that whole antiquated mistress ritual die out decades ago? I work a challenging PR job for every dime I make."

Rafe waved a conciliatory hand. "I don't mean to insult you, sister. Forgive me for wanting to protect you, but I must say that the Thurston-Hughes brothers are trouble. I dislike the way they watch you. I've looked into them, and I don't think they're worthy of you."

Tori felt herself flush and anger took root. "You can't set private investigators on all the men in my life."

"We don't discriminate. We had them check up on your female friends as well."

Her jaw dropped. "That is completely unacceptable, Rafiq."

"Damn. You weren't supposed to tell her," said another deep voice.

She turned and found Kadir striding up the stairs to join them. He was slightly shorter than his older brother, but filled out his tuxedo coat with a bit more brawn. His eyes held a glint that told her he intended to enjoy the drama his brother had unwittingly created.

"Kade, explain to me why the al Mussad family seems so bent on poking into my life."

"Of course. You see, Tori, this is what we do. And don't call us the al Mussad family. We are *your* family." He sent her a steely gaze. "You have no parents to watch out for you and no man of your own to protect you. But you do have three brothers."

"Yes, but I did not ask for three overprotective, busybody brothers. You really should find better things to do with your time. You have a country to run."

Rafe and Kade exchanged a look before Rafe shrugged. "That is true, but our country is peaceful. Ensuring your well-being is a good hobby."

Kade's stare drifted down to her hand. His eyes narrowed. "Do you have some news you wish to share with us?"

She glanced at the fake ring. They matched the fake diamonds around her neck. The woman at Harrods insisted they went with the dress. Tori had paid fifty pounds for the necklace and matching earrings. She had to admit, they looked good. They were much better fakes than the CZ ring she'd bought off an infomercial. Before she'd put them on, she held them up to the light and watched them sparkle. "You have your secrets. I have mine."

Rafe lifted her hand and examined the ring. "Did they tell you this was real? Which one? I wish to have a talk with him."

She pulled her hand out of his. "What does that mean?"

"It means I'm not stupid, Tori, but I am confused," Rafe said, his eyes sweeping over her.

"I am, too." Kade stood by his brother as they exchanged a few words in their native language.

Tori really wished she'd caught on to the language.

"What's going on?" Piper walked up the stairs, escorted by her husband.

The Sheikh of Bezakistan looked at his brothers with a narrow glare. "I thought we agreed to do this in private."

"Look at her left hand," Kade murmured.

Damn. Her two worlds were colliding. She hadn't even thought about the fact that Piper or her husbands would question the ring. She'd been thinking about how Oliver, Rory, Callum, and Claire were picking her up in their limo. "It's nothing."

Piper gasped and her whole face lit up. "I knew it. Which one of them is it? The soccer player, right? He's a doll."

"Football, please," Talib said with an elegant shake of his head. "Americans are the only ones who call it soccer and, sweetheart, really look at that thing."

Piper frowned. "So what if it's not real. Money isn't everything."

"These men have billions and they propose to my sister-in-law with such a paltry token?" Talib smoothed down his tuxedo coat. "I'll talk to them about expectations."

She couldn't let that happen.

"They didn't buy me anything. I bought it all for cheap, even the ring. I know it's a fake. But I don't think it's that bad. I did good with the dress and shoes. I only paid two hundred pounds for the lot." She lifted the hem of her gown to show off the gorgeous shoes that had been on clearance. "The engagement ring is to keep men from hitting on me. Okay? So back off, you lovable Neanderthals."

Piper raised a brow. "I can't believe you're lying to the Thurston-Hughes brothers about a fiancé. I've seen the way they watch you. They'll discover your ruse and they will not be happy."

"At least one of them already has," Rafe said. "Or they no longer care that she is 'taken.' Whoever bought you that dress is putting his brand on you."

She wasn't sure what he was talking about. "I told you, I bought the dress."

Kade huffed. "Not for two hundred pounds. Are you certain you didn't run up your credit cards? I didn't think your line of credit would extend far enough to purchase all that. Why go into debt? Why refuse to use the accounts we offered you?"

Because they would come with so many strings, including that dedicated guard who would steal her privacy. "I swear I used my own money. I bought everything off the clearance racks at Harrods."

Piper took her hand, and her sister had that look on her face that told Tori she was about to hear something she wouldn't like. "Sweetie, that dress is a Versace."

She'd been shocked at her good fortune. "I know. It was a steal."

"It premiered two weeks ago. It's from the fall line, straight off the runway. I bought another one from that collection for six thousand dollars in New York last week.

That dress is limited edition. And the shoes are brand new Louboutins. That's another grand. I couldn't even begin to tell you how much the diamonds cost."

"At least fifty thousand pounds," Talib said. "With the earrings, perhaps seventy-five. Are they borrowed?"

Tori couldn't breathe. They must be wrong. No way could she have afforded any of that, and she'd never heard of real diamonds being on clearance. Then what had happened? "But I have a receipt for everything."

"I assure you whoever paid the rest of the bill has the proper receipt if he has a brain in his head," Kade said.

Callum had arranged her appointment at the upscale store. Oh, what had he done?

Normally, Tori would think Rory far more capable of such a ruse, but this proved that she'd deeply underestimated the footballer.

Furiously, she scanned the ballroom and spotted Callum talking to Rory. He laughed at something his younger brother said, and she was taken aback again by how gorgeous they were. Though possessing similar statures, sandy hair, and strong jaws, Callum stood a bit taller than Rory. Then again, Callum was taller than almost everyone at the ball, and his brothers were no more than an inch or two behind. Callum was all lean muscle, his body honed from his years as an athlete. Rory obviously spent an enormous amount of time in the gym. The corporate lawyer wore his hair cropped short, as though he feared that if it grew too long, he would lose control.

Callum looked up suddenly. Their gazes met, fused. His smile nearly took her breath away.

"I know what it means when a man wears that look," Rafe said. "We should take our little sister back to Bezakistan."

"I concur. The footballer isn't the only one staring." Tal gestured to his left.

Oliver lingered by the entryway, his gaze steady on her.

His lips curled up in a dangerous smile that made her think he fantasized about damp skin and breathless nights. Tori's heart began to pound.

"I definitely think you should come with us." Kade wrapped a protective arm around her shoulders. "Tonight."

Oliver's stare zeroed in on the touch. His expression turned from seductive to deadly in a heartbeat.

She pulled away from her brother-in-law. "I'm staying here."

"Talib, she's my sister." Piper stepped in. "And it's her life. I chose to marry the three of you without interference. Well, I chose not to kill you after I found out you'd tricked me into becoming your bride."

"That is not true, *habibti*." Tal pulled her close. "There were no tricks. We were madly in love from the very beginning."

Piper scoffed. "That's not exactly true."

"I say otherwise."

"Then you're rewriting history to suit your purposes." She rolled her eyes.

Tal shrugged with a mischievous grin. "I am a sheikh."

"You're also an overbearing jackass at times," Piper teased, then softened. "My sister wants to stay."

"I have a job," Tori added. "Responsibilities."

With a reluctant sigh, Tal caved. "I will relent in this. Brothers, back off. Allow Tori to handle these men until such time that she cannot."

"I can handle them," she insisted.

Grimacing, Piper gripped her hand. "That's the biggest concession he's going to give you. You know that if the Thurston-Hughes brothers hurt you, my husbands won't care that you're an independent woman. They'll only care that you're their sister."

"Precisely," Tal agreed.

"I'll be fine," she insisted. She really hoped she was telling the truth. "Excuse me."

Tori marched down the stairs to find Callum. If what she suspected he'd done was true, she had a few words to say to him. Then…well, she might lose her job today after all.

* * * *

Rory took another glass of champagne from the waiter and looked up at the second floor balcony overlooking the ballroom. "Where did Tori get that dress? It should be illegal." He let out a rough breath. "She looks edible."

Tori leaned lightly on the railing, a fond smile on her face as she looked down, her cleavage displayed to ripe perfection. Rory followed her gaze as she watched her sister dance with the sheikh. Did she fancy a dance herself? How would she react if he asked her?

Surely, she wouldn't object. There could be no betrayal in squiring his potential sister-in-law around the ballroom floor. Certainly, Oliver would approve of him looking after her when his eldest brother couldn't take care of her himself. As long as Rory shoved his own lust for her aside, they'd be fine.

"The dress is Versace. I knew she had a good eye." Callum's gaze drifted up to where she stood. "I picked out four gowns I thought would suit her, but I have to admit, that's the one I would have picked for her myself."

Rory wondered what Oliver would say about Callum selecting her wardrobe. "Did the other three come with a bodice?"

Callum shot him a confused glare. "What do you mean?"

His brother shouldn't be allowed to dress Tori again. Not only would Oliver find it inappropriate, but Callum seemed to have forgotten important bits. "That dress is missing the proper fabric to cover her breasts. Every man in the room is looking at them."

Including him. He'd nearly salivated when she'd walked out and those breasts had caught his eye. The green of the

51

gown provided a gorgeous contrast to the creamy expanse of her skin.

Callum shrugged as he took a sip of champagne. "Let them look. She's beautiful and tonight she feels that way. She knows every man in the room wants her. What she doesn't know is that if one of the buggers makes a pass at her, he'll find his head relocated up his arse."

"Still, you could have given her some more modest choices." Rory knew he sounded like a prude, but he didn't like the idea of all those other men staring at her. She had three already. She didn't need more.

He actually liked how she dressed for the office. She wore bright colors, but her skirts were always professional length and she tended to button up. He constantly wondered how it would feel to strip off those prim cardies, then rip off the pretty blouses and skirts until he eased down her knickers and spread her across his desk like a virgin sacrifice.

He had a suspicion that's exactly what she was—a virgin.

Rory knew Oliver needed her, that she alone could lead him from that dark place in his soul and back into the light. But he worried Oliver would tear her up.

Perhaps he should rethink everything. If he told Callum what he suspected, his middle brother would be gentle with her. He could be a playboy, but when he cared about a woman he tended to take excellent care of her.

Yes, but then Rory would spend the rest of his own life wanting her for himself. At what point should he figure out what Tori needed and do whatever it took to make certain she got it? He'd spent so much time worried about Oliver's happiness that he'd neglected to consider hers.

"She doesn't need modest choices," Callum argued. "She needs to know how beautiful she is. She needs to see that marrying royalty isn't the only way to be a queen. She looks like one tonight." Callum sighed. "Ah, the al Mussad brothers have found her again. I'll be happy when they're gone.

They're practically barbarians. Did you know the youngest one threatened to play football with my cock if I so much as thought about getting Tori into bed?"

Bastards. "Yes, I was accosted by Rafiq. Seems he doesn't think much of the three of us."

Rafe al Mussad had briefly spoken with him at the beginning of the ball. He'd explained that Tori might be an orphan but that didn't mean she was without protection. Rory had tried to convince the man that Oliver was perfect for her, but Rafe had merely scowled and told him to get his brothers on the same page or leave her alone.

Rory doubted the man had meant persuading Callum to align with him in supporting a marriage between Oliver and Tori. He rather thought Rafe meant all three of them should pursue her.

Together.

"I don't think I'll travel to the country this year," Callum said suddenly, jarring Rory from his thoughts.

The family always ventured to their country home for three weeks during the summer. In years past, when Callum hadn't been busy practicing or promoting his team, he'd joined them. The holiday had been a tradition since they were children. "It's your first year free. Why would you not come? We were all looking forward to being together."

"I don't want to leave Tori alone." Callum held a hand out. "Before you berate me, I'm not simply plotting to seduce her. She's a bit too trusting when she's wandering around the city. She's made some friends in very bad parts of town and she walks or takes the bus to see them. I want to make certain she stays safe."

And it gave Callum ample opportunity to press his claim, Rory thought wryly. "Let me see if I understand you. You've managed to move into her building and now you're going to pounce on her the minute Oliver and I leave town. Is that correct?"

Callum threw back his head and laughed. "I don't know

that I would have put it quite so bluntly, but yes, I intend to make my feelings and intentions known."

Rory fully understood why Oliver had thrashed Callum earlier today. He contemplated doing the same right now. "Don't. You think she's too trusting whilst wandering the city? You can't imagine she'd be any less trusting when you're wining and dining her into bed. I don't think she's even had sex with that fiancé of hers. I suspect she's a virgin."

Callum stared at him like he'd grown two heads. "I can assure you she's never had sex with the fiancé, but a virgin? Isn't finding one over the age of twenty a bit like finding a unicorn these days?"

Rory glanced around because this wasn't a conversation for the tabloid reporters almost certainly lurking about. Oh, they wouldn't be allowed inside, but they always had ears and eyes at events like these. The last thing he needed was an article about the Thurston-Hughes brothers speculating on whether or not their publicist was a virgin.

He dropped his voice. "None of it matters because you're going to leave her alone."

"I won't do that and I told you why." Callum glanced up. "Damn, they're all on her now."

He followed his brother's line of sight. Sure enough, the al Mussad brothers, along with the queen, hovered around Tori. "I don't think the sheikh approves of your choice of clothing, either."

Callum went a little pale. "Actually, I think they might be asking her how she afforded the dress."

"Didn't you ask Sheila to find her something she could afford?" They had a personal shopper who could work miracles at times. Of course a man like Callum didn't need a miracle. He could buy whatever he wanted and he definitely wanted Tori. "Tell me you didn't."

"I wish I could. I sincerely do right now. Do you think they know those diamonds are real?"

"They buy jewels for their wife all the time. Of course."

"Shit. I might be in a bit of a pickle then."

"You idiot! You paid for the jewels and the gown and let her think she could afford them."

"And the shoes. Don't forget the shoes. They were ridiculously expensive and I bet she looks like a dream in them." Tori suddenly glared Callum's way. "She's going to murder me."

"I might help her," Rory snarled.

"Do you think the al Mussad brothers will kidnap me and drag me to their desert to kill me slowly? Or will they simply do it here for the sake of swift vengeance?" Callum straightened. "No. I won't let them intimidate me. I'm going to talk to the sheikh and explain that I'm serious about Tori. I'll get his permission to court her."

"And if he won't give it?"

"Then I'll watch my back and pursue her anyway. Her sister already likes me. I sent her boys signed footballs and promised to coach them when they get older. Hell, I'll take on the country's World Cup team if I have to." Callum had always known how to use his resources.

"You'll do nothing of the sort." Maybe it would be best if the al Mussads dragged her out of the country. Otherwise, Rory wondered if the mutual desire he and his brothers had for Tori would tear them apart.

Unless she was the one who brought them all together. It had worked for the al Mussads.

But Oliver would never share, and they didn't live in Bezakistan. Foolish notion. Such a relationship would never be accepted in England.

You've got a billion pounds at your fingertips. If you never made another, you could live happily for several generations. What good is all that bloody money if it doesn't give you freedom?

Sometimes the voice in his head made too much sense.

"We've got a problem." Claire approached them as

quickly as her four-inch heels allowed.

"Yes, we seem to have many of those tonight," Rory drawled. "And you've clearly forgotten the top of your bloody dress, too. I should have wondered why you came down wearing that shawl. You knew very well I would have told you to change."

Her lips curled up in the sweetest smile as she patted his cheek fondly. "You're a dear, Rory. But I'm almost twenty-seven and I don't need my brothers to choose my wardrobe. It's smashing that you would watch out for me, but I think our dear Cal needs our attention just now."

"Why?" Despite Callum's worries, Rory didn't really think the al Mussads would kill him. They would be far more subtle and dangerous. Besides, the queen really did like Callum.

She glanced over her shoulder, toward the entry. "Security fetched Oliver a moment ago. There's a woman at the door without an invitation, insisting on seeing Callum. She claims to be his fiancée."

Callum cursed. "Bloody Thea."

Did the drama never end? "I'll talk to her."

"No," Callum said. "I'll do it."

The press would be all over that.

"No," Rory insisted. "You stay here. Oliver and I will deal with her. Don't you dare show your face. It will do nothing but encourage her."

Callum's lips flattened. "She's my problem."

Claire shook her head, blond curls brushing her bare shoulders. "No, she's *our* problem and we'll deal with her. Trust me, if I ever acquire my own creepy stalker, I'll let you handle him."

After a long moment, Callum yielded. "All right. I'll keep Tori nearby in case we need some damage control."

Claire reached for Rory's hand. "Let's put this to rest. And keep an eye on Oliver. I'm a bit worried how he'll handle this."

Because Oliver was something of a psychopath lately. Rory turned and left his horniest brother in order to deal with the most violent one in a situation guaranteed to rev up Ollie's temper. Brilliant.

Rory sighed. Sometimes, being the reasonable one was bloody difficult.

* * * *

Oliver stormed toward the security guard. He wanted to blame Tori for wearing that next-to-nothing gown and making him feel so damn possessive. If her breasts hadn't been on display, maybe he wouldn't have wanted to murder every man who laid a hand on her, even her brothers-in-law.

He'd watched Kadir touch her as though he had every right. Granted, the contact hadn't been sexual, but... It was plain to see the al Mussads wanted her back at the palace where they could watch over her and very likely choose whom they believed would be a proper husband for her.

Or husbands, as was their custom.

What did Tori's brothers-in-law think of her poor fiancé back in Texas? Did anyone give a whit about him?

As he reached the security station, Oliver felt more than ready to deal with any man who stood in his way. Instead, he found a woman beside the gate, wearing a stunning, form-fitting ecru gown that barely covered her. Gown wasn't the right word actually. Mini-dress might be more suitable. The tiny garment showed off her breasts and brushed high on her thighs. The poor girl couldn't possibly bend over without showing the world her backside.

If she was pregnant with Callum's baby, it certainly didn't show.

"I don't understand the problem." She pouted at the guard. "My fiancé is inside. He simply didn't leave me with the proper paperwork."

"You need an invitation to get in, miss." One of the

guards sent her an expression of grim apology.

She stamped her designer heel. "I don't need an invite. My future husband is Callum Thurston-Hughes. You will allow me in this instant."

Ah, the young and delusional. He looked her over for a moment. Thea Palmer was an "actress." She'd landed small roles in three films and large spreads as a page-three girl before she'd taken the plunge and gone under the knife. Between the lip enhancements and the overly large breasts that looked ready to pop at any moment, she'd probably spent everything she had on surgeons. Besides being "enhanced," she had absolutely no education whatsoever. So naturally, his younger brother had thought she'd make a proper bedmate.

According to the reports Oliver had received on her, she'd most recently landed a small role on a show in America that had been canceled after only three episodes. She'd returned to England and apparently decided that Cal was her meal ticket.

By contrast, Tori was smart. A few weeks back, they'd had a long talk about politics, and she'd known far more about European systems of government than he'd imagined. Discussions with her were a pure pleasure. He found himself engaging intellectually in a way he hadn't since university. He'd debated with her for nearly two hours, their easy camaraderie making the time fly by. He'd been shocked when he'd finally glanced at the clock. He usually felt the weight of time…except when she looked at him with her soft blue eyes and that smile that lit up the world.

The woman in front of him had absolutely none of Tori's easy intelligence. His publicist handled people with a deft hand. This woman used a hatchet.

"I'll have your bloody job, I will." She stared up at the guard.

"What seems to be the problem?" Oliver stepped out from the hallway and into her line of vision for the first time.

Her eyes widened. "Mr. Thurston-Hughes, thank

goodness. Please speak with your guard. There seems to be a mistake."

Out of the corner of his eyes, Oliver saw an intrepid twenty-something woman in a modest black dress designed to help her blend in. As she loitered around the guard station, he recognized her as a reporter from *The Sun*. Damn. She likely intended to snap pictures of the celebrities coming and going, but the minute she realized the drama playing out here, Callum and Thea's "love child" would be front page news. Again.

And Tori would be furious.

He wanted to throw Thea out, but the chit would likely find the reporters stalking about and give them a tearful story about how the man who had fathered her child was dancing the night away while she was left on the streets to fend for herself.

He should have thrashed Callum more thoroughly. His unruly cock had landed them all in trouble.

"Come with me, Ms. Palmer." He unlatched the velvet rope and allowed her to pass through. He couldn't miss the look of triumph on her face as she passed the guard. Oliver shook the uniformed man's hand. "Thank you. You did well. I'll handle her from here."

The guard leaned over. "Be careful, sir. She walked up with a man who looked a bit thuggish to me. He disappeared once she got close. I don't think she wanted me to see him."

Oliver nodded. "Keep an eye out for him. And don't hesitate to work with the al Mussad guards." Of course, they'd brought their own. "They're some of the best in the world."

He turned back and had to hustle to catch up with his prey. She wasn't lollygagging about, waiting to talk to him. She marched straight for the ballroom, likely prepared to hunt down Callum and cause a scene—along with massive problems for the whole family.

Luckily, Rory blocked her path before she could rush in.

"Hello."

Thea eyed him as though weighing whether she could rush past him.

Oliver intended to shut down that line of thinking. "Why don't you join us in the office? We'll have a good chat."

He tried to sound non-threatening, friendly even. Surely he could manage that for a few minutes. If they could pass the evening with only minimal damage, Tori might not even have to know anything had happened at all. She might believe the Thurston-Hughes brothers could make it through one night without being at the center of a tabloid-worthy story.

Thea's eyes narrowed. "He's in there with that whore, isn't he?"

And just like that, Oliver abandoned the non-threatening approach. "You had better not be talking about the woman I think you are."

Her lips curled up in a smirk. "She might be related by marriage to Middle Eastern royalty, but that pathetic American is nothing more than a whore looking to elevate herself."

"That's the pot calling the kettle black," Rory said under his breath, scanning the area. "Oliver, we should move this somewhere private."

When Oliver glanced behind him, he winced. Sure enough, the reporter from *The Sun* was talking to the guard. She wouldn't get anything out of him, but if Thea didn't keep her voice down, that professional gossip in the black dress would hear far too much.

With a scowl, Oliver took hold of Thea's arm and began escorting her toward the security office.

She struggled. "You can't keep me from Callum. He's the father of my unborn child."

Oliver dragged her into the little room and slammed the door, flipping on the glaring light overhead. He dissected the conniving bitch with his stare. Instantly, he knew his brother was telling the truth. Callum might make mistakes, but never one this big. Oliver sensed that Thea and Yasmin were kindred spirits, the sort of women willing to tell any lie to get their way.

"I don't believe you, Ms. Palmer. I grant that my brother fucked you last year before his injury, but not since then. You cannot possibly be carrying his child."

She had the temerity to look shocked by his bluntness. "How dare you!"

Oliver ignored her. "I'll make you a one-time offer. I'll write you a check for a hundred thousand pounds if you agree to recant the story that Callum is the father of your baby. You'll have to sign paperwork to that effect, of course."

"Oliver," Rory barked. "You can't reward her lies."

"I'd rather not, but I won't have this hanging over our heads for the next year." They had enough problems to deal with. "Once she's signed, if she comes after Callum in any way, we'll sue her."

"And if she's truly pregnant?" Rory argued.

"Then she shouldn't be doing cocaine. There's a bit of it still on your nose." A smudge of white powder clung to her nostril, and her eyes had gone a little glassy. The fact that he'd ever believed, even for a moment, that his brother might impregnate such a creature made Oliver sick.

Tori, on the other hand, was a different animal. He could imagine perfectly well Callum trying to get her with child. He would do it to secure a future with her, but Oliver refused to allow that. Callum might think it was all right to pursue her because her fiancé apparently neglected her, but he must see the dishonor in that play. Tori had chosen another man. The people in her life should respect that choice, no matter how badly they wanted her for their own.

Thea rubbed her free hand across her nose. "It's not what you think."

"It's exactly what I think. You're looking for a payoff. I'm offering you one."

Again, she pulled out the mock distress. "I want Cal. I

love Cal."

"I seriously doubt that. I'll do what I need to protect my brother. This is a one-time offer, Ms. Palmer. If you don't agree now, I'll come after you with everything I have and destroy your credibility. And I assure you, I have a great deal of pull."

Tears filled her eyes. "You can't do this to me."

"I can and I will. I'm the head of this family. I protect it. I have no qualms about eradicating any future you have in order to help my brother. I've had a private investigator look into your basic background. I already know some very interesting things about you. If you refuse me now, tomorrow morning I'll have him dig deeper, especially into your sexual habits these past few months. I have no doubt he'll find enough dirt to make a mockery of you and your claims in every paper across the country."

Her mouth pursed and her face turned purple with fury. "I want to talk to Callum."

"You may be used to getting what you want, but I'll make certain you don't get anywhere near him."

"Because he's with that whore, isn't he? I know exactly who she is. I've seen them at dinner together, watched Callum escort her around London as if she's some fucking princess. If I see a single negative piece about me in the papers, I'll make sure everyone knows what a slut Torrance Glen is." Thea pulled away. "I won't allow her to take my man."

The need to wrap his hands around the bitch's throat rode him hard. He barely managed to quell his rage. "Are you refusing my bargain?"

"Bloody right, I am."

"Then we're at an impasse, but you should know your clock is ticking. If you are pregnant, science will easily prove the baby isn't Callum's. Until then, I recommend that you keep your mouth shut. Your life will be much easier."

"You're a fucking wanker."

Oliver smiled tightly. "And my offer is now rescinded. Get out. If I see you again, I'll have you arrested."

"This isn't over. I won't let you or anyone else keep me apart from Callum." She whirled around and jerked open the door, stomping out of the room and toward the guard and the exit.

Oliver waited until she'd walked past the reporter, blithely licking her wounds. For now. He was sure Thea would be back—and become an enormous pain in his arse.

"She's rather frightening." Rory's lip curled up in distaste as he watched her. "She knows about Tori. We need to do something about that."

"That's precisely why you should have allowed me to send her back to the States." Oliver wouldn't mention the utter relief that had flooded his system when he realized he didn't have to let her go. It was perverse, but then that word described him perfectly these days.

Rory sighed. "I don't want her to go."

"God, not you, too."

Besides Callum's obvious desire for her, Claire had done her best to capitalize on his growing feelings for Tori and push them together. Until this moment, he hadn't realized how badly Rory wanted her as well. "Can't you see we're terrible for her? She won't mean to, but if we're not careful, she'll tear this family apart."

"We won't let her. That's not what she wants."

"She wants to go home at the end of this assignment and marry her fiancé. She made her choice months ago, and you and Callum will bring great dishonor to our name by trying to seduce her out of it. I will not marry again. Even if I did, I certainly wouldn't pick a naïve girl like Tori Glen. I have no interest whatsoever in having a relationship with her."

He charged out of the room and nearly ran into another reporter. They were everywhere. With a curse, he stepped back into the ballroom, hoping the fundraiser would end soon.

Claire strode toward him instantly, her face tight with concern. "Oliver, I can't find Callum. He appeared to get into some kind of an argument with Tori and now they've both disappeared."

No. This ball wouldn't be over anytime soon. Oliver sighed. In fact, it looked as if he was in for a long night.

CHAPTER FOUR

Tori descended the ballroom stairs with a charming smile in place, but Callum saw the furious glower underneath. He started up to meet her. Bugger. No doubt, he was in hot water. Over his shoulder, he watched Oliver disappear past a sea of balloons and into the front entryway, Rory following behind.

His brothers intended to deal with his problem, and he felt guilty about that. Well, they would deal with one of his problems. Tonight, he had two, and they both involved women.

"Where are you going?" Claire climbed the stairs behind him.

Callum didn't know what to say. If he had arranged the same shopping experience for the surgically enhanced loon in the lobby as he had for Tori, Thea would have fallen to her knees and happily expressed her gratitude. Not his little publicist. Instead, he'd insulted her independent nature and now she meant to show him the sharp side of her temper. Which was precisely why he wanted her. She wasn't interested in his money or fame. If he won her, it would be because he was worthy of her love.

He turned to his sister. "I need to talk to Tori. We seem to have a misunderstanding."

Tori approached, her smile more brittle with every step.

Even so, she looked breathtaking. Her hair fell in loose waves around her pale shoulders and made him long to shove his fingers in and wrap them around her soft, shimmering tresses.

"We need to talk." She scowled as if he was a child she intended to take to task.

Now might be the time to play his ace with her. "Yes, I think we do."

"What's going on?" Claire glanced between them, confusion on her face.

"Your brother is playing some kind of game with me and I don't like it," Tori said, anchoring a hand on her shapely hip.

"I'm playing a game? You're the one who started it, love. But I plan on winning." His heart was thudding in his chest as it always had before a match. Callum had to admit that being close to her now, preparing to admit his feelings, gave him a rush.

"Cal?" Claire prompted.

"This is nothing for you to worry about," he reassured his sister. "Please help Oliver. I think he could use it."

Tori didn't miss a beat. "Win? So this is a game to you?"

"If I'm being honest, no." He gripped her elbow and turned to the crowd with a plastic smile as he started to escort her down the stairs. He certainly wasn't going up. Her rather frightening family awaited there, and he intended to be on much firmer footing with Tori the next time he faced them.

She hurried beside him. "Where are you taking me?"

They left Claire on the stairs, staring after them. Guilt prickled Callum, but he couldn't pause to soothe his sister now. He'd explain everything to her later, but at the moment he needed a quiet place to hash this out with Tori.

He knew exactly where to go. Several smaller rooms adjoined the ballroom. When he and Claire had come for a final site visit before the charity ball, he'd explored a bit. He'd stumbled across a particularly nice conference room that hadn't been locked. He hoped the same was true tonight.

"Somewhere private. You see, a very intelligent woman once told me that arguments should remain private. Clearly, you're about to yell at me, so I thought we should nip out, away from prying eyes and ears, so you can express yourself freely."

They crossed the ballroom floor. Orchestra music swelled and elegant couples danced, London's wealthiest citizens gossiping all around them. He'd much prefer to take Tori out on the floor and show her off as his, but he hadn't earned that right yet. Instead, he led her into the empty, shadowed hallway on the far side of the ballroom.

"I'm not going to yell," she said in a hushed voice. "I don't ever yell. I'm just going to ask you not to lie to me. How much did this dress cost?"

Yes, he'd been caught, but at least he wasn't without a play. "That dress looks stunning on you and it's worth every penny I paid for it."

She sucked in a sharp breath, clearly trying to keep tight control on her temper. "I asked for help in finding a suitable dress I could afford. You offered me your personal shopper. Fine. Nowhere in that conversation did I agree to let you buy my gown."

He reached the door, thankfully finding it unlocked again, and opened it. Some of the event staff had used a corner for storage, but the room lay empty now, so Cal dragged Tori inside. The noise of the ballroom faded away as the door swung shut behind them. "You couldn't begin to afford anything you're wearing, which is precisely why I bought it."

She whirled on him. Ambient lighting shimmered around the perimeter of the room, a soft, golden glow that illuminated the space. The diamonds around her graceful throat and her shimmering skin caught the light as she paced in front of a good-sized table and several leather chairs. "You bought it so I wouldn't embarrass the company or your family at this occasion?"

He shook his head. "You could never embarrass me. I bought it because I think you deserve to have a dress as beautiful as you." Telling her the truth felt good, freeing.

Eyes wide, she stepped back, her body coming into contact with the conference table. "I believe you meant this as a lovely gesture, but my brothers-in-law pointed out to me that I'm wearing a fortune I didn't pay for. Do you know what they think of me now?"

He didn't particularly care what they thought. "That you look beautiful, too?"

"That I'm your mistress." She crossed her arms over her chest. "Your whore."

Anger flashed through his system and burned hot. Usually, he wasn't a man with a quick temper, but this pushed his buttons.

He whirled and stormed toward the door. "I'll handle it."

She grabbed his arm, halting him before he left. "Stop."

This wasn't something he would be moved on. "No. I won't allow anyone to talk to you that way. Do you understand me? I don't care who they are. Which one was it?"

It didn't matter. He'd take on all three if he had to.

She took a long breath and stared up at him. "Cal, no one used that word except me, so don't get angry with my brothers-in-law. I'm telling you how I felt when they pointed out that any man who spent this much money on a woman meant to put his brand on her."

All right, then. He could agree with that. "It wasn't my intention to make you feel like my mistress. I simply like seeing you in clothes I bought for you."

"Callum, I'm engaged." And she was right back to putting space between them. Clearly, she meant to play this lie out to the bitter end.

He moved in, obliterating that space she used as an invisible wall between them. He inched closer, closer…until she had nowhere to go. "So you've told me. But if you're in love with your fiancé, why do you spend so much time with me?"

He watched her, carefully noting her responses. Her breathing picked up. Her skin flushed lightly. She licked her lips as she gazed up at him. Cal saw no signs of fear, but he would bet her nipples were hard pebbles now. He wouldn't have to expend much effort to touch them. Just a little tug, and that bodice would fall. He could cup a breast, pull its tip into his mouth, and drink her in.

Her gaze slid away. "Because we're friends."

"We are friends. But I want more than that." He cupped her cheek and forced her to meet his stare once more.

"I can't." The words came out breathy and soft, without an ounce of real willpower behind them.

Normally, Tori had no problem defending herself. She could argue for hours, but all her self-possession seemed to have fled. Her blue eyes looked soft as her gaze tangled with his.

"Because you love your fiancé?" He leaned in, his mouth hovering above hers. "Think carefully before you answer. I won't like it if you lie to me."

She gasped. "You know."

"I do."

Panic flitted across Tori's face. She tried to pull away, but Callum didn't give her an inch. "What did you do? Sic a PI on me?"

"Yes."

"Don't do this. Please…" She raised her hands, palms flat on his chest. But she didn't push him away. "You have to let me go."

Callum had suspected she'd react this way. After all, she'd invented a fake fiancé for a reason. He had to uncover what in order to move past her objection or fear. "Why?"

"Because I won't be another link in your chain of conquests."

Was that her worry? He might have taken many of the

opportunities available to him as a professional footballer back in the day, but he'd put all that behind him.

"I don't have a chain of conquests, Tori. For the last six months, all I've had is my bloody hand and an image of you playing in my head twenty-four seven. If you think for an instant I'm not serious about you, think again. Why else would I pay a ton of money for a PI to hop across the pond to locate this mysterious man of yours? In the beginning, I meant to have a long talk with him about how he treats you."

"Treats me?"

"Tori, if you were mine I would never allow you to spend half so much time away from me. I've even come to hate weekends because I don't see you and can't make certain you have everything you need. I couldn't imagine six months without you. I'd go mad." He took a risk and gripped her shoulders. Bloody hell, her skin felt so soft against his fingers. He swallowed a lump of lust and pressed on. "In the beginning, I wanted to confront this man because I thought he was a bastard. Then I find out he doesn't exist at all. Why would you put a fake diamond on your hand when another man might well want to give you a real one?"

She shrugged from his grip and blinked up at him. "I thought it would keep me safe."

"From me?" She was about to find out that nothing could keep her safe from him.

"From all of you," she whispered.

He gripped her hips this time, dragging her closer. "You're interested in all three of us?"

Her lips closed stubbornly.

"Well, I can't speak for my brothers, but I intend to show you why you should choose me."

"Do they know about my engagement, too?"

Finally, his real bargaining chip. He aligned their bodies together, not missing the way her breath hitched the minute he crushed her breasts to his chest. "No. I haven't told them. You don't want them to know how you lied to them, do you?"

"I wasn't really lying," she demurred.

"You were, Tori. Every time you spoke his name or flashed that ring." His cock hardened as he rubbed against her. "There won't be any more lying. I'm taking control of the situation. You're scared, but I want to show you there's nothing to be afraid of."

"For me, there is, Cal. I don't want to talk about it. Besides, you're in the middle of a paternity suit." She stopped. "You said you haven't…"

"Not since the day I met you, sweetheart. Not with her. Not with anyone."

Shock had her gaping, and she searched his face with her wide eyes, clearly seeking the truth. "So it really can't be yours?"

"No. Clearing everything up will take time, but Thea will go away." He breathed her in. Now that he was here with Tori, he wanted to take his time, focus on them, revel in the moment. "I promise there won't be any more like her. I intend to be utterly faithful to you."

"This is insane." She shook her head. "I can't have a relationship with you."

"Why?"

"It's unprofessional."

Some might see it that way, but Callum suspected that wasn't really her objection. "We have no HR policy against employees dating. Danvers, our CFO, is dating one of the sales managers. Would you call them unprofessional?"

"I-I…" Tori opened her mouth, but no other sound came out.

Cal knew he'd trapped her neatly. If she said yes, she insulted a man she often worked with. If she said no, she opened the door to a romance between them.

"What's the real objection? Your feelings for my brothers?"

Even in this lighting, he saw her face flush. "I realize

that's not normal here in London. Maybe I've spent too much time in Bezakistan. And I know it's wrong, but…"

Was it? Really? Again, he pushed the thought aside.

He leaned in, breathing over her plump lips. "I'll make you forget them. I'll show you I'm the right man for you."

"I'm not here for romance. I don't want it."

The hell she didn't. Her pounding heart and hitched breaths said otherwise. "Kiss me, Tori. Kiss me once. And if it isn't as good as I think it's going to be, if you don't want more, I'll walk away."

It was a lie. There was no chance of that. He wanted her far too badly to ever give her up, but she needed the comfort of that small fib.

"You won't tell them I lied?" Her voice all but pleaded.

"Not if you kiss me."

She took a shaky breath. "All right. Just this once."

His whole body leapt with anticipation. This was the start of his life. One kiss. One woman. Forever.

He waited as she rose on her tiptoes, her hands brushing against his face. She studied him as if memorizing the moment. Fingertips moved along his jawline before her thumb skimmed his bottom lip.

"I think you're the most beautiful woman in the world, Tori." He wasn't going to play around or pretend he wasn't in love with her. She should know that during every moment of her life, from this day on, he would be thinking about her, wanting her.

"And I think you're crazy. I'm taking the dress and the jewelry back." She brushed her lips against his.

He scowled as she pulled back. "No, you're not and that wasn't a kiss."

"Hush, I'm not done." Again, her mouth briefly met his. "And yes, I am taking them back. That's not negotiable."

"You think this is a negotiation?"

"Isn't everything?"

"No, love. Some things aren't up for negotiation. Some

things require dominance, and it's time I show you what I mean." He cupped her nape, fingers clamping around her delicate neck, and lowered his mouth to hers. She'd used the word conquest before. He was going to show her what it really meant.

* * * *

Tori's heart raced as his head dipped lower and his lips crashed over hers. She felt a rush of arousal burn through her veins. She didn't need to be more aroused. She hadn't been thinking clearly from the moment she realized she was alone with Callum and that he wouldn't play politely anymore.

He knew she'd been lying about her engagement. She looked like a fool, but he wasn't laughing at her and telling her she'd never needed protection against him. No. He was proving her point by invading her space and making her whole body come to life under his touch.

His mouth covered hers, heat flashing across her skin like a lightning fire.

She'd been kissed before but never like this. Softly at first, but Tori felt his leashed strength. When he kissed, he didn't just move his lips. His whole body engaged, teasing her to slide against him. With big hands, he drew her deeper into his embrace, caressing her back, down to cup the curves of her hips. Seemingly of their own volition, her arms wound around him, her breasts crushed to his hard chest.

Tori lost herself in his scent and taste, in feeling both desired and adored. She shouldn't kiss one of her employers, shouldn't encourage this man. But they were alone; no one would see them. It was only a kiss, and she owed him for his silence. She didn't have to give him more. She certainly didn't have to give him her heart. Why couldn't she just bask in this one moment?

With a sigh, she surrendered to his embrace. The instant she did, everything changed. The predator in him pounced, as though he scented her submission. Too late, Tori realized she and Callum shared far more than a mere kiss and she was in danger.

As he pressed deeper into her mouth and his tongue touched hers, she couldn't seem to care about the reasons giving into him was a terrible idea. She could only feel.

The kiss turned carnal, their mouths mating. Tori had no real experience with this sort of passion, so she followed his lead, toppling into a dizzying whirl of need. It felt like the times she'd spun around and around as a child until euphoria took over.

She shoved aside the thought that now, like then, she'd eventually fall down.

As Callum tightened his hands on her hips, she met the stroke of his tongue and brushed her body against his, so lean and strong. She caressed the strength of his back, sinking her fingers into the solid bulges of muscles under his wool tuxedo coat. Having that material between them felt wrong. She wanted her hands on his skin, to know how hot it ran when he was aroused and how smooth it would be under her touch.

Over and over he kissed her, their breaths loud in the silence. Then he nipped at her lips and pulled back to stare into her eyes. The jolt of their connection zinged through her like an electrical charge. Tori couldn't catch her breath.

"Tell me you feel it, too," he demanded in an impassioned whisper.

"Yes." The word fell from her lips.

Callum didn't wait another second before diving deep into their kiss again. His hands roved over her body, tracing the curve of her waist, cupping the swell of her ass. Restlessly, he smoothed his fingers up the line of her spine, over her shoulders—then began again, each time skimming closer to her breasts.

They ached for his attention. She moaned in need.

"I want you, Tori." The words rumbled across her skin as he left her lips and started kissing her cheek, her ear, down to her neck. "You want me, too."

She let her head fall back. She would stop him in a moment. Just a little bit longer. She could have a few more minutes before reality intruded. In these stolen moments, she would pretend there weren't a million reasons they shouldn't be together and that this closeness could last in the real world. For these few seconds, she could fool herself that Oliver and Rory hovered nearby, aching with need and lust, to put their hands on her, too.

Suddenly, Callum lifted her onto the conference table, settling her on the glossy wooden surface. He shoved her dress up around her hips and stepped between her legs. Then he took her face in his hands and looked at her as if he could barely wait to unleash all his pent-up lust on her. At his sizzling expression, pure heat coursed through her, sparking down between her thighs.

She needed to stop this.

But when he kissed her again, instead of pushing him away, she latched onto him, arms around his waist, and tilted her head back to give him unfettered access.

With a growl, he delved into her mouth again, possessing and devouring, while he slipped a hand inside her bodice and cupped her breast, thumbing her sensitive nipple.

Tori's breath caught, then she groaned.

"You feel so good, love. I've never wanted anyone the way I want you," he murmured against her lips. "Let me make you feel good, too."

"We can't do this," she managed to say.

Tori was well aware her actions didn't match, but she couldn't stop herself from pulling him closer when she should have pushed him away.

"Not here, anyway." He pinched her left nipple and gave it a sharp pull.

The sensation startled her, penetrated her. Her breast swelled against his hand as though asking for another tug. That little bite of pain had her panting.

"Just let me touch you now." He stroked his way from her breast to her thigh, curling her leg over his hip. "Let me show you how good it's going to be between us. It will be my punishment for tricking you into the dress. You'll know all night that I'm aching and hard for you. After your pleasure, we'll return to the ball, and I'll keep your secret from my brothers. We'll do nothing else until you're ready, but let me have this moment with you, Tori."

She nodded before she could think twice. What would it really hurt? With her heart pounding and her body poised, she felt so close to something she wanted so badly. Yes, she'd experienced orgasm…but not one given by another person. She ached to know that sensation, why Piper glowed when her husbands entered the room. No one ever had to know. She could keep her heart intact. And when she returned to Texas at the end of her contract, she would have a special memory of them together.

Callum moved quickly, pushing her skirt up higher. Then he dropped his hand right over *that* spot, barely covered by her lacy undies. "You're so wet."

She hadn't realized that. "Sorry."

He groaned and slipped his fingers under the elastic, directly over her flesh. "Don't be. That's all for me. If I had time, I would get on my knees and lick up all that cream. Would you like that? Would you like my tongue in your pussy?"

She didn't know from experience, but if he did so with the same gusto and finesse with which he kissed, Tori bet having his mouth down there would feel divine. "Yes."

"Good, because eventually we'll get to that. We'll get to all of it."

She couldn't breathe. He dragged a single finger up her thigh, over her labia, before finding her clit and rubbing in soft circles. Tingles and heat rushed her. Sure, she'd touched herself, but experiencing a man's deft fingers made it different. Callum's hand was huge and deliciously callused.

So masculine. She spread her legs, wanting more of him.

"There's something you haven't asked about," he whispered in her ear as his thumb kept up the decadent torture. His fingers played at the entrance to her sex.

Tori could barely maintain her train of thought. "What?" Was that her voice? She sounded so breathy and come-hither, like a vixen capable of tempting a man to insanity. Tori had never imagined she could sound so seductive. She liked it.

"This is my punishment," Callum ground out. "I'm going to please you. Then I'm going to walk around with my cock in knots all night. Eventually, there will be punishment for you too, love, for lying to me, for keeping me away from what belongs to me. Don't you want to know what I'll do to you?"

"God, Callum, that feels so good." Why did he keep talking? She writhed closer, moving against his hand, trying to steal more of the shocking pleasure. "Don't stop."

His free hand tweaked her nipple hard. "No. You don't control this. If you move like that again, you'll get the punishment I'm promising you much sooner."

She stilled. His voice had gone so hard, so rough. She'd never heard him be anything but gentle with her. "What are you doing?"

He circled her clit again, so achingly soft. He took her right to the edge again. "I'm taking control. You're excellent at your job and you should know I will attempt to follow all of your advice when it comes to the boardroom, but I'm the Master in the bedroom—or wherever I happen to be fucking you." He inserted a finger inside her, and he hissed. "You're going to squeeze my cock so tightly. You're so hot and wet and ripe. It will be hell to wait to get inside you."

His words melted her, along with his touch. It took everything she had not to move against him. By forcing her to remain still, he robbed her of all control. He took the power, drew out the sensual torture. Stole her ability to think.

Normally, her mind didn't have an off switch. Now, she could only focus on doing whatever necessary to keep his hands on her.

"Please, Callum."

His finger worked inside her, marking perfect time against the thumb at her clit. Pressure built between her thighs. So much glorious pressure. She was moving toward something she'd never felt. All those little pleasures she'd managed to give herself were nothing compared to the shimmering explosion she sensed right around the bend. So close. With her body poised and on the edge, she knew she was close.

"Oh, all of this pleases Callum," he murmured. "But you're going to give me even more. Once we're settled in and we've negotiated all the terms—yes, we'll negotiate, despite what I said earlier—you'll pay for the lie. You owe me for all the long months you kept us apart. I would have seduced you the day we met had it not been for that silly ring on your finger."

She sat, spread open wide, trying to be so obedient. She clutched his free arm and held on as he eased his thick finger in and out of her. He pressed his hard cock against her thigh. As often as she'd fantasized about being the woman who made him ache, the reality felt surreal. But it was true. Gorgeous Callum Thurston-Hughes had an erection for her. The bad boy of the football world wanted her and he was proving it.

As much as she should, Tori wouldn't refuse him now. If he stepped between her legs and tried to make love to her, she would likely welcome him. Decorum and professionalism didn't stand a chance against the blistering want he created inside her. Therein lay the danger of getting too close to any of them. She'd always known it, felt the sizzle from the moment she'd met them all, but now the roar of arousal drowned out the warning bells gonging in her head.

"Your punishment, love? I will spank that gorgeous

backside of yours," he promised. "Very soon. Until it's pink and perfect and you're begging me to fuck you.

Tori sucked in a breath. She wasn't shying away from his soft threat. Instead, she envisioned how he would spank her. Would he lay her across his lap or tell her to bend over in front of him? Would he slowly draw her skirt up or order her to stand naked in front of him?

The concept of Callum smacking her backside with his hand shouldn't be appealing. She'd always considered herself a strong, independent woman, so taking such a punishment from a man who meant to control her sexually should horrify her. Instead, it just made her flesh slicker and more ready for Callum's cock.

"Let me see you fly, love. Let me see how beautiful you are when you surrender." Callum pressed against her thigh, his erection nudging her insistently. "Come for me."

His thumb pressed down hard and his finger curled inside her channel, finding the exact spot that sent her straight over the edge. The pressure converged. The burst of pleasure dazzled. Euphoria swam through her veins as her body bucked. With his kiss, Callum captured her cry, swallowing down the sound of his name on her lips.

Then bliss took over, and she sagged in his arms, perfectly content with the haze of pleasure she found herself wrapped in.

Suddenly, a stronger beam of light flooded in from the door and she heard a familiar voice speak. "So while I'm dealing with one of your ex-lovers, you're in here with another."

Oliver.

Tori's haze lifted and cold reality set in. She gasped and tried to scramble off the table.

He froze and stared. "Tori?"

She closed her eyes, horror spreading through her. What was she doing? No, what had she done?

In no hurry at all, Callum slipped his hand out of her

panties and threw his arm around her. "Sorry, Ollie. We tried to keep quiet."

She realized what she must have looked like when Oliver opened the door and saw her with her dress askew, her legs spread and wanton. She'd looked every inch like Callum's mistress. Like his whore.

She scurried out of Cal's embrace and wobbled onto her heels. Oh, dear god. The best of London society and many of the worst of its tabloid reporters were not a hundred feet away, separated by a few thin walls, and she'd allowed herself to be groped by a playboy who'd taken hundreds of women to bed because the instant he'd touched her, her brain had melted.

Tears filled her eyes as she pulled the bodice of her stupid dress up higher. When she'd first tried it on, the silky green gown had made her feel elegant and sexy. Now, despite the expensive dress, she felt cheap.

What kind of twit behaved this way and expected to keep her job? Only a stupid one.

"Tori?" Callum was at her side, smoothing her skirt. "Love, let me help you."

She jerked away from him. "No. I have to go. Oliver, I understand that my services are no longer needed. Please let me know what I owe you to buy out the contract and I'll send you a check." She'd figure out how to raise the money later. "I'll leave you the name of that PR person in New York I mentioned yesterday."

But no way could she walk back into the Thurston-Hughes offices with her head held high. Never again. Certainly not, given the pure ice in Oliver's eyes. She shrank back from his seeming fury and contempt.

"We'll discuss that at a later date," Oliver bit out. "If the two of you are through, rejoin the ball. Miss Glen, you should take a moment to make yourself more presentable, unless this fundraiser was merely a pretense to focus the tabloids on you. If that's the case, then feel free to enter the party looking like you've just had intercourse. The press will write a nasty story about you, but don't think a little embarrassment will have any effect on my brother. He's used to getting caught in the act."

Callum stepped in front of her as though he meant to shield her. "If you're angry, take it out on me. Don't you be a prick to her."

She hated standing in their shadows, feeling like a piece of white trash, when only moments before she'd felt so close to Callum. That was the lie of sex for women, she realized. The act could feel so beautiful and intimate. The minute it was over, she was nothing but a whore.

Tori trembled, cold seeping down to her bones.

"If you'll excuse me, I need to get cleaned up." Her voice shook.

"I'll take you home. We can leave here quietly," Callum offered. "Oliver, I'll talk to you in the morning."

"No, you're staying. You've got a speech to make in twenty minutes for your fundraiser," Oliver snarled. "Do your fucking job."

She wished they would both leave. "You have to go, Callum. If you don't thank the people for attending and donating, they'll remark on it. Given the bad press of late, it won't do the company any good."

He clenched his teeth and reached for her hand. "I don't want to leave you. You're rattled, vulnerable."

She couldn't touch him now or she'd throw herself into his arms and cry. He couldn't shelter her from Oliver's wrath. She had made a terrible lapse in judgment, and he couldn't save her from that. "I'll be fine, Callum. Just give me a moment."

His jaw tightened. "This isn't over, Tori. I'll see you in the ballroom. Oliver, why don't you come with me?"

The eldest Thurston-Hughes looked her up and down, lingering on her rumpled skirt and swollen lips. Tori felt three inches tall before they both turned and exited, leaving her alone.

She'd ruined utterly everything. Now, she had to hope she could leave with some smidgeon of dignity. She feared that asking for a sparkling professional reputation was too much to hope for. And she wouldn't even consider her heart.

With tears running down her face, she planned her escape.

* * * *

Oliver watched the conference room door. He wasn't a fool. Tori meant to run. No way she would choose any other path. As much as he seethed with anger, he didn't want her gone from his life. He might be a stupid bastard, but he couldn't abide the thought of her no longer near him.

A young woman in a daring evening gown stepped up to Callum and said something, rubbing against him as if she was in heat. His brother flirted back with ease. Oliver scoffed. So much for true love.

"What happened?" Rory moved in beside him, asking his question in a low tone.

"What do you think happened? I found Cal with his hand in Tori's knickers. He was two bloody seconds away from another paternity suit."

Rory sighed and leaned against the wall. "Hell. Where is she? Is she all right?"

"She's still in the conference room. I suspect she's pulling herself together, though she should really be here so she can see how quickly Cal moves on."

Rory frowned as he looked Callum's way. "What are you talking about?"

"The blonde. He walked straight out of Tori's arms and into hers. I don't know. Perhaps she won't care. Perhaps she'll do the same thing with the next man she meets."

Why had he thought she was any different? Why did he still care, for that matter? He'd caught her cheating on the man she'd promised to marry before they'd even exchanged vows. And here he was, loitering outside the conference room, hoping to catch a glimpse of her. He really was a self-torturing fuckwit.

He also had terrible taste in women. But at least now he knew what cloth Tori was cut from. No need to treat her with kid gloves anymore. If she didn't care about her fiancé and wanted a fucking on the side, why shouldn't he give it to her?

Something nasty took root in his gut, and it warmed him. Oliver welcomed the sensation because he'd been cold and almost numb for so long. Any change felt good, including the need to get a taste of what his brother had gotten—before she left for good.

"He's just being polite, Oliver." Rory's voice drew him out of his thoughts. "And now he's actively trying to escape her."

Sure enough, Callum was extricating himself from the handsy blonde. His brother turned away and began pointedly speaking to a portly member of parliament.

"Really, Rory. Give him time," Oliver drawled. "He'll be back to his old habits."

"No, I think you've got it wrong. He's serious about Tori and he won't give up. At this point, I understand completely." Rory hesitated. "You know I like Tori quite a bit, too."

He turned on his younger brother. They were all mad for the girl, and she would destroy his family if he didn't stop her. "You would have liked her even more if you had seen her a moment ago. She was spreading her legs for your brother while still wearing her engagement ring. Is that the kind of woman you want? Do you fancy Callum's leftovers?"

Rory's eyes narrowed. "Watch what you say about her. She isn't some object, and she isn't a whore. She's a woman and she has feelings. I understand that you went through something terrible with your first wife, but Tori isn't Yasmin. I don't know what happened between her and Cal tonight, but I'm willing to bet she got caught up in the moment because

Cal has more experience with sex in his little finger than she has in her entire body."

"She looked pretty experienced to me."

She'd also looked stunning, like a woman claiming her pleasure. Oliver had watched, and she'd been uninhibited and raw. Her beauty had shocked him. As soon as she'd caught sight of him, she'd utterly shut down, shame smothering her like a blanket.

He'd done that. He'd shut down her glow.

"Because you see everything through a set of pitch-black lenses, and I don't know that you're smart enough to ever take them off. I'm going to talk to Cal. Try to behave yourself around her. Just because you can't see how pure and kind she is doesn't mean the rest of us can't. If you drive that woman off, you'll have problems with more than Callum." Rory strode away.

Oliver watched him go, blinking, bereft. All this time, he'd believed he could count on Rory when the chips were truly down. He'd genuinely thought his youngest brother understood him. All his siblings had closed ranks around him after Yasmin had nearly destroyed him. They'd sat at his bedside and nursed him back to health and assured him that he wasn't at fault. But after a time, they'd fallen away as though they'd grown weary of waiting for the smiling, laughing Oliver again. Only Rory had understood that man was gone for good.

Finally, the door down the hall opened, and Tori stepped out, smoothing her gown around her. Oliver retreated to the shadows as she wiped at her eyes. When she glanced up, as if she sensed his eyes on her, he noted that most of her makeup was gone. She looked young and vulnerable and impossibly innocent.

Only he knew that face masked a cheating wanton.

Before she returned to the ballroom, he planned to have a talk with her. She would not jump beds from her fiancé's to his brother's. No matter what, he refused to let Callum fall into a relationship with a woman who would ruin him. Yes, Cal would be furious, but if he saved his brother future anguish, then Oliver could live in peace, knowing he'd served the greater good.

Of course in showing Cal the error of his ways, Oliver didn't mind if he got a little pussy for himself.

Tori turned and fled the opposite direction, not toward the ballroom—but the exit.

Damnation. He couldn't let her escape. He couldn't let her play the wounded bird. Callum would fall right into that trap, and Rory, who was already half under her spell, would follow.

"Where is she going? Is Tori all right?" Claire approached, wearing a concerned expression.

Naturally, his siblings would take her side. Perhaps they wouldn't when he proved she was nothing more than a doe-eyed hustler. "I don't know, but I'll find out. Help Callum get ready for his speech. Make sure his tie is on properly. He should be announcing how much money we've raised in the next fifteen minutes."

"Is something troubling you, Oliver?" His sister had always been able to see through him.

He schooled his features into a polite mask and placated her. "Nothing. I'll make certain Tori is safe."

From everyone except him.

He left Claire and followed Tori down the hall, the world getting quieter as they put distance between them and the glittery ballroom.

Ahead of him, she sniffled but didn't seem to notice anyone following. That didn't surprise him. She'd never once noticed when he'd followed her before.

She managed to wend her way to a hall that led out of the building. When she darted outside into the cool, humid evening, she took a deep breath, then sighed as though relieved to be free of the pomp and the people.

Oliver was relieved as well. Now he could hunt her down

properly.

Then again, she should be easy prey. She had no way back to her corporate flat. She'd come with them in the limo. Was she going to try to navigate the Tube in a designer dress that left her looking half naked and four-inch heels that would break on the first grate she stepped onto?

Absently, he wondered why she behaved with such maudlin desperation. She had Cal under her finger. All she had to do was bat her lashes and cry prettily. He would likely drop everything to take her home.

With a curse, Oliver texted his driver his location and continued following her on foot. When she got to the end of the street, she hailed a cab.

Luckily his car pulled up and he climbed in. "Follow the taxi, Charles."

It didn't take long before he realized she was heading back to her flat. Within minutes, the cab arrived in front of the building where Thurston-Hughes housed its visiting employees. Tori got out and turned to pay the driver with money she'd tucked into a clever pocket in her skirt.

The street was quiet at this time of night, though no part of London was ever really deserted. He watched as she stepped into the light under a streetlamp. She'd been crying again. It was there in the pink of her skin, the slight puffiness around her eyes.

Did she feel guilty now for cheating on her fiancé? Was she going to tell him that she'd been unfaithful or would she pretend it had never happened?

Tori made it to the door and swiped her card through the reader. The door popped open. He was about to tell Charles to pull away when a man dressed in head-to-toe black sprinted from the shadows and slipped in before the door closed behind them. A ski mask covered his face.

Oliver bolted out of the car. It looked like he would finally get that fight he needed after all.

CHAPTER FIVE

Tori sniffled as she stepped through the stark, contemporary lobby of her building, toward the lifts. Her heels clicked against the marble tile in the eerily empty space. She was alone. The hour wasn't late, but it seemed as if everyone was either tucked in for the night or out on the town. The building employed a maintenance worker and a manager, but not a doorman. She usually liked the privacy and tonight was no exception. The last thing she wanted was someone she knew seeing her walk of shame. Of course it wasn't morning, but slinking back here after running out on Callum felt wretched, both professionally and personally.

Her heels continued clomping against the floor, reminding her that she wasn't used to walking in anything so high. She usually wore practical shoes because she was on her feet most of the day, nothing like these princess shoes she was going to have to figure out a way to return.

Groaning, she reached down and pulled the shoes off. Her feet ached, but that was nothing compared to the rest of her. She was weary. Her whole bright future in public relations seemed to have vanished with one foolish act, and the biggest idiocy of it all? She would be damned for spreading her legs at a work event for one of her bosses, and she hadn't even gotten to have sex.

What did her virginity really mean if she didn't give it to

someone worthwhile? She loved Callum, and he would have made sure she enjoyed the act.

Maybe her virginity was holding her back. She'd come to that conclusion during the cab ride back to her flat. An experienced woman wouldn't have lied about her engagement because she was worried about being hit on. She would have refused the men she didn't want and dated the ones she did. An experienced woman wouldn't have stood in front of Oliver Thurston-Hughes and felt shame slither down her spine. She wouldn't have felt like a whore because she hadn't done anything wrong. Okay, maybe the timing hadn't been spectacular, but still... If she'd been a man caught with a woman's hands down his pants, there would have been a quick cover-up and a shrug.

When she returned to the States, Tori intended to find some decent guy, have some hopefully decent sex, get the virginity thing behind her, then move on with her life. After that, she wouldn't be the sort of girl who lived her life like a nun and turned into a puddle of goo the minute some hot man put his hands on her. Nope, she would be experienced then. She would take charge.

The plan seemed logical...but she didn't love it. Thankfully, she didn't have to unravel this mess and figure out her future tonight. She would chalk up her time in London as a lesson. She'd spend a couple weeks' vacation in Bezakistan and hold a bunch of babies and try to forget that she'd ever come to England. Back in the U.S., she'd start over professionally and romantically.

A little squeak behind Tori made her pause. It sounded like the rubber soles of sneakers on the marble floor. She whirled and saw a large man creeping up behind her, his face covered by a ski mask. He held a wicked-looking knife. Terror flooded her as she gasped. She thought about running but knew she wouldn't get far with her aching feet.

"Give me the jewelry," he snarled.

Tori took a steady breath to quell her shaking. Surely,

CCTV cameras lurked in the corners and someone would see what was happening. They would send help, right? She heard the ding of the lift and considered making a dash for safety. Maybe she could surprise him and get the doors closed between them before he caught her. She couldn't give up the jewelry. It was too expensive. She could never repay Callum if she lost it.

"Don't even think about it, bitch." Her assailant grabbed her wrist, wrenching it as he pulled her close.

His meaty fist tightened around her wrist. Pain flared. She tried to jerk free. "Help!"

"There's no one to hear you." He sounded snide. "I can already see this job will have benefits. I was told to have a little fun with you." He yanked her close and pressed the knife against her ribs. "I think it's time we take this party to your flat. If you scream one more time, I'll cut you. And I'll still have my way with you. I don't mind if you get a little cold."

Abject horror threatened to overtake Tori. Her entire being revolted at the idea, but before she could fight him, the man grunted and stumbled back, releasing her.

Tori heard the knife clatter to the floor, then turned to see the big attacker whirled around—and Oliver manhandling him.

Relief poured through her. She couldn't quite breathe. Oliver was here. He'd pulled her attacker away. She probably shouldn't be relieved that a CEO had come to take on a street thug, but she wasn't alone anymore. He was risking himself for her. They would defeat him together.

As Oliver punched up with an uppercut, she grabbed the closest thing she could, a solid-looking lamp next to a table beside the lifts. She picked it up and swung it around, plowing the base into the attacker's skull as Oliver kicked the thug in the balls.

The CEO didn't fight fair, it seemed.

Her assailant doubled over with a grunt, clutching his

balls.

"What the hell do you want?" Oliver growled.

The other man didn't answer for a long moment, just groaned like a wounded animal. As Tori wondered how badly they'd hurt him, he jumped to his feet, shouldering Oliver aside. He stumbled toward the door, grabbing his knife from the tile, then burst out onto the street. With a curse, Oliver started after him.

"Wait." Tori grabbed his sleeve.

He spun around to her. Blood trickled from his lip, onto his shirt. Breathing heavily, he swiped his thumb over the drop at the corner of his mouth and glanced down at the crimson smeared over his skin.

The savage look he wore made her take a step back. "Oliver?"

He sucked in a breath and seemed to force himself off the ledge. "You made me lose him. He's gone."

"What were you thinking, chasing after him? He could have killed you." Her pounding heart pumped adrenaline through her system.

Oliver pulled out his cell. "Or I could have killed him. Have you thought of that? What did he want?"

She touched her throat.

Oliver rolled his deep blue eyes. "Of course. You thought it was a good idea to traipse around London after dark, wearing a fortune in jewels. You got what you deserved for that foolishness."

Anger flared. He'd been determined to make her miserable all night. "Yes, well, he also wanted to rape me. I'm sure I deserved that, too."

Oliver clenched his jaw. "You should have let me kill the bastard. All I can do now is ring the police."

And then her well-meaning brothers-in-law would probably smother her with guards and take away her freedom. "No. Please, don't. We don't have a description of him. We don't have anything to go on. It would be a huge waste of time."

"And the sheikh would find out if you filed a police report detailing the attack."

Well, she'd never accused him of being dumb. "If he finds out something like this happened, I will likely find myself in the custody of the royal guard."

"Well, we can't have that." He pocketed the phone. "Do you mind if I clean up?"

"Go ahead." He could take the jewelry with him when he left and return it to Callum. Then she'd have one less thing to do before she left London.

She crossed the lobby to the lift, which still sat open. Her hands shook as she entered, still clutching her shoes, with Oliver following behind. She pressed the button for four. Her floor. Well, not for much longer.

"Do you have anything to drink?" Oliver asked after they'd ascended and the doors opened again.

"I have a little bottle of Scotch." Her neighbors had brought it over as a gift after she'd collected their mail while they were on holiday.

"Excellent." Oliver stopped in front of her door.

He'd never been here. How had he known what flat she lived in? She let it go. Why question it? It didn't really matter.

She pulled the key out of the hidden pocket in her dress, but she was still shaking.

Oliver wrapped his big hand around her own, warming her icy skin. "Give it to me."

He didn't wait for her reply, just took the keys from her. With steady fingers, he opened the door, ushering her inside.

The minute they were alone, he turned on her, charging into her space, and pressed his body to hers against the back of the door. "He could have killed you. He could have raped you and killed you."

He could have. And she would have lost something precious that should have been hers to give. A violent stranger could have taken it from her before he killed her, and she would never have known what it meant to lie with a man she cared about.

Oliver Thurston-Hughes had been a dick to her this evening, but it didn't wash away all the months of his kindness, his friendship. Maybe that should make her want him less, but it didn't.

As she stared at him, separated by only a few feet, their breaths rough, all she could think about was him and the regret she'd have if she let this moment pass and never knew what it felt like to touch this man she loved.

When his mouth descended on hers, the adrenaline that coursed through her body morphed into a desperate arousal. She softened against him, ready to have him in any way she could.

* * * *

"What do you mean she's gone?"

Rory looked at His Highness, the Royal Sheikh of Bezakistan, and wished the night would end. "Tori wasn't feeling well and she decided to go back to her place."

Talib al Mussad's eyes narrowed as though he'd detected a lie. "Without informing her sister? That seems very unlike Tori. She is always quite thoughtful about such things. Piper raised her, you see. She wouldn't leave without informing my wife. It's a bit of a habit. She rarely lets a day pass without informing her sister where she is and how she's doing."

"She wasn't feeling well." It was all Rory could think to say. It wasn't surprising that Tori was close to her sister, even though they lived in different countries. From what he understood, they'd always been very close, especially after their parents had died.

"As I said, Tori definitely would have sought out her sister."

If he didn't deal with the sheikh, the entire al Mussad

clan would leave this event and go straight to Tori's. And Rory would be shocked if those overprotective men didn't haul her off to the palace where he'd never see her again. "She wanted some time alone."

"Why? I can only imagine she would desire such a thing if she was upset."

It was time to start staking a claim, as the Americans would say. Callum had pushed the subject earlier. Tonight's debacle would affect all of them, so no one could pretend that Tori was merely a colleague or a friend anymore. Rory knew he had to push through. One way or another, Tori was going to belong to the Thurston-Hughes family, and it was time the al Mussads learned that.

"I believe she's weighing her options. My brother is very interested in pursuing something serious with Tori. He's quite in love with her and he expressed his feelings tonight." He'd nearly expressed his semen as well, but the sheikh didn't need those details.

Talib frowned and heaved a long sigh. "I believe it is far too soon for her to consider such a request, and I would need to speak to Oliver myself."

"It's not Oliver. Rather, it's Callum."

That had Talib's right eyebrow rising in aristocratic query. "I'm not a fool, Mr. Thurston-Hughes. Oliver is interested in Tori."

How to explain it? It was harder given the man's lifestyle. Rory shrugged. "Perhaps, but Callum has chosen to press his claim."

At least he didn't have to worry about Talib being offended by the use of that word. The man seemed to take a very old-fashioned approach to the women in his life.

"And what of your claim?"

"I don't have one."

The sheikh sent him a knowing stare. "But you want her."

Rory tried to shrug it off. "She's a beautiful woman. You

should know that I intend to treat her with every kindness and courtesy, as I would my own sister."

"I sincerely doubt you spend your nights dreaming of sex with your own sister."

"Of course not!"

"That is why the arrangement you speak of will not work and I will not give my blessing." He smoothed down his jacket, his decision seemingly made. "I thank you for your kindness to my sister, but I'm afraid I'll be taking her home with me tomorrow morning. I'll send someone from the palace to pack her things. Whatever penalty she incurs for leaving her job before the end of her contract, send the bill my direction. That will be all."

"Excuse me?" Rory might not be royalty, but he wasn't used to being dismissed.

The sheikh stared at him for a moment. "We're done here, so you may leave."

"I'm not going anywhere and, unless Tori consents, neither is she. This is the twenty-first century, and if you think for a second I'll do your bidding because some random bit of DNA landed you a sovereign role, you should think again. I won't let Tori go without a fight and you should know I don't always fight clean."

A little smile curled up the sheikh's mouth, and Rory wondered if he hadn't fallen into a well-placed trap. "Now I see a man I can talk to. I do not understand the stiff politeness of you British. When it comes to our women, a man should be a bit savage."

Rory certainly felt that way now, despite the fact that she wasn't his. "Tori will make her own decision."

"Tori is too shy and naïve to ask for what she wants. Until she learns, I will look after her. You and your brothers will either get on the same page or you will let her go."

"I am working on that." Callum's hotheaded moments aside, Rory had believed they were on the same page. "The plan has been to back Oliver's play. I'm afraid he waited too long, and now Callum won't step back."

"The fact that you call it a play urges me to remove Tori now. We aren't discussing a game or a pawn. This is her life. For the record, I wasn't talking about the three of you deciding which brother should have the woman you all love. The three of you should stop being selfish children and figure out how you will share her or stay away. If you and your brothers do not, you will leave her forever torn, and I won't have it. She has feelings for you all. Perhaps you are willing to martyr yourself for your so-called brotherhood, but think about her. By forcing her to choose, you ask her to give up pieces of her heart. You are right, Rory Thurston-Hughes, you have no claim. When you grow up and learn to put her first, you may call me. Until then, leave my sister alone."

"Do you think it's that easy?" He was getting really sick of being treated like a child. Talib couldn't know how much he'd sacrificed for his family, how far he was willing to go. "Have you had to watch your brother slowly kill himself? Have you watched as he endured something so brutal and world-changing that you were certain he could never be the same again?"

The sheikh paused for a long moment, and Rory thought the man would simply walk away. Finally, Talib skewered him with a dark stare. "I have not been forced to watch my brothers struggle, but I have been where Oliver is. I know my own brothers worried for my life and they prayed Piper could be the one to save me. She did, but if I had not had their support and encouragement, I would never have touched her. Your heart is in the right place, Rory. You are simply approaching Tori in the wrong way. I was a brutal man before my Piper. The violence and betrayal I lived through exposed me to a side of the world most men are never forced to see. Afterward, I was a wounded animal, much like Oliver. I was dangerous to Piper then, but my brothers were there to ensure I could not hurt her. Well, not too much. I still hang my head in shame at some of the ways I pushed our wife away.

95

Without my brothers, I would be alone in the world. If you love Tori, you will find a way to compromise with your brothers and work together to make her whole."

"We don't live in Bezakistan. Our world would never accept such a relationship."

Talib put a hand on his shoulder. "If you aren't ready to be the one to define what is and what isn't acceptable to your world, then you are not ready to love Tori. I wish you all well, but we will be collecting our sister. I require some time with my queen now."

He watched as the sheikh crossed the ballroom floor to stand with his brothers and their beautiful wife. They all welcomed him with open arms. Rafe moved to one side, ceding his place by Piper as though he understood his brother's need. Talib kissed his wife, their hands tangling together. She squeezed his hand, and though Rory could see him shaking his head as if to say he was fine, Piper's little frown said that she didn't believe him. She leaned in, as though she could give him her strength.

What would having that sort of love feel like, with a woman who knew him well enough to see through well-meaning lies? And what would it feel like to know that no matter what happened to him, his wife would always have his brothers to lean on, to share her life with?

Talib al Mussad was a lucky man and not simply because of his birth.

"That is one lucky woman." Claire threaded her arm through his as Callum headed toward the stage, notes in one hand, his public smile firmly in place.

"Funny. I was thinking the sheikh was a lucky man." He glanced at his sister. She was always so reasonable, so intellectual. "You don't think it would be hard to live in a way the rest of the world thinks is wrong?"

"Who cares what the world thinks, Rory? The world doesn't hold you at night. The world doesn't take care of you. So no, if I had the chance, I wouldn't give a damn what the world thought. I would choose love." She nodded to the stage. "Good. After Callum's speech, we can start closing this thing down. I'm rather tired after all the dancing. Say, have you seen Oliver?"

Yes. He'd seen Oliver stalking after Tori like a lion about to tear apart a luscious little antelope. "No," he lied. "I'm certain he's around here somewhere."

He had to hope Oliver wasn't ruining the future for all of them.

* * * *

Oliver pressed Tori against the door, his cock shooting to life. Months—years, really—it seemed as if the damn thing had been completely apathetic. Oh, it functioned for the most part, but only in an obligatory capacity.

Now, fire rained down and passion pelted him. His cock pulsed with life, strictly because of her.

He covered her body with his, pressing his chest against the softness of her breasts, dying to be inside her. He wanted tonight to last because it was all he would ever allow himself to have of her.

"I'm not going to play the gentleman like my brother."

"I don't want you to." The last thing she wanted now was gentle.

"Good, because I'm going to get inside you and I'm going to stay there for a good, long while." He would take her again and again. When he was fully sated, maybe this terrible longing to be near her would dissipate and he could get back to his real life.

And she would move on with hers. Away from him because after tonight, Callum would have to see the sort of woman she really was.

But he didn't care now. All he could think about was how soft she felt and how fucking sweet she seemed. He didn't care if all that was an illusion he no longer believed.

Right now, all that mattered was sinking into her for a few hours and forgetting anything else existed.

"Take it off. Now."

"My dress?" Her breath caught. "I can't reach the zipper."

"I meant the ring. I'm not making love to you with that bloody thing on your finger."

"I'm sorry." She gripped it with her right thumb and forefinger and tossed it away as if it meant nothing. He heard it ping on the hardwood floor as it rolled away. "I shouldn't have even tried it. I was very foolish. It's nothing, Oliver. It was a stupid idea."

Yes, marriage was a very stupid idea, especially with her. She was dangerous to his peace of mind, and he wouldn't marry again. His brothers and sister could do all the heir making for the family. He was through with silly notions of faithful love.

He pressed his hand up her body and cupped her pert breast. Even through the material of her gown, he could sense how soft that skin was going to be. Touching her was what mattered. Sex with her right now mattered. He could scratch his itch, then send her back to the idiot who planned to marry her. And if she thought she'd traded up... Well, he would make sure she understood the way of the world come morning.

He slammed his mouth over hers, taking possession with a slow grind of his hips timed to his moving tongue. She opened to him, softened under him, throwing her arms around his neck and clutching him close. Those pretty lips flowered open under his sensual assault and her tongue came out to shyly brush his.

Pure fire whipped through his system. He craved her, needed her—and that rankled him. He'd nearly lost her to a thug who'd meant to gut her with that knife. Now, he needed to drag her skirt up and shove his cock deep in order to remind himself she was still warm and alive.

He fumbled for the zipper at her back and jerked it down. He lacked all his usual grace and nearly ripped the designer gown off in his haste to touch her skin. Now that he was kissing her, giving in to his desire, he wouldn't tolerate anything between them.

She gasped as he tugged at the bodice of the dress, freeing her breasts. She raised her hands, covering the plump mounds.

He stepped back with an arched brow. Was she going to play innocent? "No games, Tori. You either want me or you don't. If you do, I want to see what you're offering me. Show me your breasts."

She hesitated, biting her lip and breathing hard. Her hair tumbled around her shoulders. Her blue eyes clung to him, almost pleading. But he'd told her what he needed from her— his stare on her body now.

When she didn't obey, he almost turned away. His cock practically howled at the notion, but he wouldn't get on his knees and beg and pledge his devotion. This wasn't about love. It was about possession. Obsession. He needed to take her once and purge the emotion forever.

"All right." Her voice shook. "But if you laugh at me, I'll kick you in the groin, and right now that looks like it could hurt."

Slowly, Tori lowered her hands, revealing her breasts. They weren't huge, just two perfect handfuls. Creamy ivory skin with pink-tipped nipples teased him. Those hard tips looked like they longed to be sucked and tormented with his teeth and tongue.

"Why would I laugh?" He sidled closer again. "You're fucking beautiful."

A confused little frown flitted across her face. "Earlier, I got the idea that you don't like me anymore, Oliver. I thought you only wanted me for revenge, though I don't understand why. I know I shouldn't have let Callum kiss me any more than I should let you."

Let? He wanted to growl at her to try to stop him, but that would make him no better than the bastard who had held a knife to her. "Why are you letting me then? I'm going to do a hell of a lot more than kiss you, Tori."

"I want to know how it feels to make love to a man I want. Maybe it's not smart, but it's honest."

He had to hand it to her. She knew exactly how to manipulate him. Everything about her—from the way her lip trembled to the innocent bat of her lashes—called to his long dormant protective streak. "This isn't love. It's sex. If you want love, you should call my brother. I'm sure he'll play to your fantasy."

"Oliver, I know you don't love me, but please, just promise me one thing."

Ah, here it was, the bargaining. He could have her in bed if he would just buy her this or that. He hoped she wouldn't go too far. He was willing to pay for his pleasure, but he wasn't going to promise her devotion or shackle himself to her for life. "What?"

"Be kind to me. I'm leaving anyway, so I'm just asking that you be kind to me for one night. You don't have to pretend to love me, but can you make believe you like me? The way you did before?"

He *had* liked her. Tori was smart and funny, and he felt alive when she entered a room. They'd spent hours going over strategy to fix the company image. She likely didn't know it, but he'd drawn those meetings out simply because he enjoyed being in a room with her. He'd liked her quite a bit until she'd proven herself to be just another faithless cheat.

Not all relationships were as bad as his, Oliver knew. Sometimes things didn't work out, and it wasn't anyone's fault. She'd been away from her fiancé for half a year and the bugger had never visited her. Could she be blamed for craving someone's touch?

Why was she asking him for the one thing she should

always expect from a lover? How had the men in her past treated her? "I do like you. I simply cannot love you, and that's a very good reason for me to walk away."

She released the dress and let it drop to the floor. His breath caught.

"I don't need love," Tori murmured. "I just want to feel something I've never felt before. I realized that if that attacker in the lobby killed me, I wouldn't have left this earth with very many precious memories. I would have lived all these years and experienced nothing joyful that really made me feel alive. I might regret this choice but... Make me feel, Oliver."

He needed to feel, too. It had been so long since he'd had a woman soft and giving against him, and after no more than a few kisses with Tori, he had to wonder if he'd ever experienced anything truly real before. Sliding her lush curves against him and delving into her sweet mouth was more visceral than anything he'd ever imagined.

At the realization, Oliver hesitated. He had the feeling that if he went through with this, if he lost himself in her now, he might never be found again.

She touched his cheek, fingertips gossamer soft. "Please..."

He couldn't refuse her.

Oliver wrapped his arms around her, drawing her to his body. She was completely naked, utterly vulnerable to him. He kissed her, tongue sweeping deep inside her mouth while he explored the smooth skin of her back with eager palms. He brushed his fingers down the graceful length of her spine, nearly down to that glorious round arse he'd dreamed about.

His cock nudged her belly, desperate to be free and to feel her. He was dying for her touch.

He sank his hand into her hair and gently pulled her head back. In the moonlight, her lips looked sweetly bruised by his rough kisses. For a night, he could pretend she was his to do with as he pleased. He intended to indulge to the fullest.

"Tori, undress me."

With a jerky nod, she raised trembling hands to his tuxedo coat and eased it off his shoulders. The second she touched him, Oliver's entire body jolted with electric desire. *Patience.* He forced himself to stand still as she hung the jacket on a nearby rack, then while her pink-tipped fingers worked his tie and unfastened each button down his shirt. She blinked shyly at him as she pushed the shirt off his torso.

His patience fled. He toed out of his loafers and reached for his belt. The minute his trousers were off he was going to start teaching her exactly how he liked to be pleasured.

With that thought, Oliver realized this was precisely what he needed. Why should he spend his time alone? Life was about negotiating the best terms of payment, and he could afford Tori Glen. He could train her to cater to his physical needs. In return, he could set her up in a much better flat. Her only job would be to satisfy him sexually.

He didn't have to love her. He could put her in a nice, sumptuously appointed box and they would both have what they wanted.

With unsteady fingers, she pushed aside his hands and unfastened his belt, and an unwanted compassion flitted through him. She'd had a hell of a night. If she needed to slow down and take a breath, he would make sure she did. "Do you need more time, darling? I won't force you to do anything before you're ready, but I will ask for what I want. And I want your mouth on me."

She tilted her chin up, her eyes widening. "You want a blow job."

He chuckled a bit because she whispered the words like a teenager afraid her mother would overhear. "Yes. I want that sweet mouth on my cock. I want your tongue to lick every inch of me."

Tori straightened her shoulders. "Maybe I want that, too. Except for you to put your mouth on my...down there." She frowned, looking like a curious little kitten. "On my...I believe you Brits call it a fanny, though that's not what it means in America, so I wish you would all stop laughing at me when I talk about a fanny pack."

He grinned, drawing her back to him, and he couldn't remember a woman who pleased him more. "I promise not to laugh at your fanny. Why don't we call it your pussy, darling? We'll make a deal. You learn how I want you to suck my cock, and I'll eat your sweet pussy."

She swallowed hard and nodded, her fingers back to untangling his belt. "I want to know how both of those feel."

Oliver had to hand it to her. Clever manipulation, intimating that he was the only man in the world she could possibly want and that sex with him would be so different. Of course it wasn't true since he'd caught her on the verge of fucking his younger brother, but he couldn't bring himself to call her on it. If he did, then he had to leave the fantasy, too, and there would be time enough for that in the morning. Now, he wanted to forget his earlier jealousy and pretend a bit. He liked the world she wove around him. As long as he remembered it wasn't real, it was safe to indulge.

Finally, she slipped his belt free, and he could feel his unruly cock nearly thumping against his trousers, desperate to get out. "Be careful with the zip."

It would be easier to do it himself, but he liked the idea of her preparing him before she got to her knees and served him.

With careful fingers, she lowered the zip and shoved his knickers aside. His cock bobbed between them, and the little sound she made soothed his ego.

Impatiently, he shoved everything off his hips and kicked it aside. "Touch me, Tori."

She stared at his cock and petted him softly, reverently. He couldn't take that.

Oliver gripped her hand and clamped it around his stalk. "Don't be gentle. I like it rough. Hold it tight and stroke it like this."

He had no idea why she was playing the innocent. From the doorway of the conference room at the hotel earlier, he'd watched her with her legs spread, luxuriating in his brother's touch and moaning. But suddenly she behaved as if she was so damn inexperienced that he had to explain how to stroke a cock? If this was another ploy of hers, Oliver would give her credit. She was a master.

Her hands trembled as he demonstrated exactly how he wanted her to handle his erection. She cast her gaze down, watching as he guided her to pump his cock in long passes that had his whole body tightening in anticipation.

Over and over, he guided her hand over his dick. How long had it been since he'd felt this good? This right? He should be thanking Callum for forcing the issue earlier in the evening. Now he didn't have to play the gentleman. He could take what he wanted and they could come to a proper arrangement—one that didn't involve either of his brothers.

Oliver wasn't an idiot. He knew Rory fancied himself in love with Tori and had been willing to sacrifice because he'd thought she would bring his oldest brother back to life. How would Rory feel about giving up the woman he loved when he learned Oliver wanted her as a mistress and nothing more? Would that finally break his youngest brother?

He shoved the guilt aside. After everything he'd been through, the universe owed him and he intended to take it from her. Of course he'd also make certain to drench her in pleasure, but he refused to sit around feeling guilty another second. She'd agreed to be his lover tonight. She'd tossed her ring aside like a piece of garbage.

She was fair game.

"Get on your knees. I want your mouth on me." He helped her to the floor. Seeing her beneath him, her hair flowing around her shoulders, he had to catch his breath. She was so beautiful he could almost buy what she was selling, likely would have had Yasmin not given him such a horrifically useful life lesson. His late wife had actually done him a favor. If not for her, he might have loved Tori with everything he had, and her eventual betrayal would have been worse than Yasmin's. He'd always kept a tiny part of himself from Yasmin that he doubted he could have managed with Tori. Now he could enjoy her properly, without surrendering his heart.

"Should I use my hands, too? Or just my mouth?" The husky but sweet sound of her voice made his cock tighten painfully.

He liked this game of hers. He could pretend she was new to all of this, that she'd saved herself for him. "Grip it like I taught you and lick the head as if it's something sweet you want to devour."

Her soft fingers encased his cock just before her tongue darted out for a taste. A sizzle slid down his spine. He groaned. God, it would be so easy for her to undo him. She swiped her tongue across the head tentatively, as though she wasn't quite sure what to do but was willing to try. He thrust his hands into her hair to steady himself while he fought the urge to shove his way deep inside her mouth.

"Like this?" Her tongue fluttered around the head of his dick, and he shuddered. Then she pumped his cock and sucked the tip inside.

"That's a perfect start." He closed his eyes briefly, letting his head roll back as the heat of her mouth flowed over him. "Now take more."

She immediately obeyed, opening her mouth to receive another inch of him. She stopped there and worked that bit of flesh, laving it with her affection. Oliver couldn't stand not to see her lips around his cock for another second. He opened his eyes and looked down, stunned by the sight of her devouring him. Her lush lips moved over his flesh, heating him to the boiling point. Her hand tightened and her mouth moved, his dick disappearing a little more with each pass.

Without even thinking about it, he gripped her scalp and directed her to take the rhythm he craved. She sucked him hard. The long passes of her mouth soon had him panting with the need to come down her throat. He could do it and still be ready to take her again in no time at all. That's how much he wanted her. She made him feel like he was bloody sixteen again and ready to rut at the merest hint of sex. He could fuck her all night and wake her in the morning to take his cock again.

"Harder. Take the rest, Tori. You can do it. Breathe through your nose and let it happen. I'm going to come down that soft throat of yours and you will swallow everything I give you."

She nodded around his cock and took another inch, softly growling against his skin. The sensation had him growling right back at her.

"Oh, yes. You feel so good, darling. I can't wait. Let me guide you."

She seemed to relax under his touch, and he thrust harder into her mouth. She spread her legs a bit wider and balanced herself, taking him deeper and submitting to him. This was what Oliver craved, her perfect willingness in the bedroom. He could see the appeal of the kink Callum had long embraced. He loved the way she looked on her knees in front of him, his cock moving between her lips as her breasts bounced in time.

His balls drew up, heat flaring across his spine as the head of his cock breached the soft opening at the back of her throat.

His heart thundered. Dizziness assailed him. Oliver groaned long and low as he let his eyes roll back. Orgasm roared through him. So good. Bloody amazing. Beyond pleasure.

He thrust past her lips again, forcing every drop out. She took it all, never stiffening or faltering. She just laved and swallowed and blew his mind. Could he ever give her up now that he knew how fucking perfect she felt?

After a long, dazzling moment, he released the tight grip

he had on her hair, groaning again as she licked her way up his shaft and sat back on her heels.

"Was it good?" She sounded breathy, and when he looked down at her, he saw how flushed her skin was, how aroused she'd become while sucking him off.

"Very." He leaned over to kiss her, the faint salty taste of himself on her tongue.

Yes, she would make a perfect mistress.

CHAPTER SIX

Tori could still taste him on her tongue. The act had been a revelation, but then the whole night had been. Getting to her knees in front of Oliver had aroused her more than she'd thought possible. Whenever she'd fantasized about making love, she imagined gentle caresses and warm embraces. Oliver's touch was nothing like that. He incited a wildfire in her blood. It sizzled under her skin, seeped into her skin, and left her aching.

He loomed large over her. Even as he softened, he was still a big man.

Once he released her mouth from his hungry kiss, Tori returned to her ministrations. She licked at his cock, loving the taste and the intimacy of the act. She'd never felt as close to a man as she felt to Oliver now. Well...except for the moment she'd shuddered in Callum's arms and he'd shown her that every pleasure she'd felt before had been nothing compared to the ecstasy he could give her. Being in his arms had been different than the feelings Oliver's embrace roused, but she'd loved them both the same.

Tori sucked Oliver's cock and wished Callum were here. And she ached at the thought of Rory's intent stare directed on her as she pleased the others before she turned her attention on him. She could imagine moving between the three of them, giving them all her devotion because she loved them. Choosing just one of them was impossible when she yearned for them all.

It wouldn't happen. She'd seen plainly that they would never share her. Tonight would be all she had of the Thurston-Hughes brothers. She would leave with her sister tomorrow and try to forget them.

She wished she'd kissed Rory just once.

"Stand up." Oliver commanded, dragging her from that fantasy.

Oliver assisted her up, helping to steady her wobbly legs.

"Did you like that? Because I certainly did. You have a gorgeous mouth, darling. It was meant to suck a man's cock. My cock." He smoothed her hair from her face before lowering his restless hands to her hips. "Now it's my turn to get a taste of you."

When he reached between her legs and slid a single finger through her labia, she gasped.

"You're so wet," he said, clearly pleased, as he explored her tight sheath with his finger. "Don't move and don't be shy. Spread your legs wider for me."

The Thurston-Hughes brothers had the demanding thing in common. When they turned those dark voices on her, she couldn't help but obey. In real life, she would fight and argue, but here she wanted nothing more than to trust these men with her heart and her body. She knew sharing a love with them was out of the question, so she yielded her will to Oliver now.

Pleasing him thrilled her, and she figured that would extend to the other two as well. Too bad that would never happen.

Oliver pushed his fingers into her pussy gently, delving deep. She couldn't help but squeeze around it. "You enjoyed sucking my cock. The act made you wet. I could take you right now."

He was probably right, and she was eager to feel him moving inside her, but he'd promised her something else.

Tori knew she'd have only this night with him so she wanted to make it last before she had to face reality again.

She needed more time with him. Desperation made her bold. "You promised."

His lips curled up in the sexiest smirk. "I promised you what?"

He seemed to like to hear her say dirty things. "You promised you would taste me."

She wanted to know what his mouth on her sex would feel like. There were a million reasons why this was a bad idea. It seemed far too intimate and what if she didn't taste good? She would be mortified, but she shook those worries off. She had one night and she wasn't going to waste it on insecurity. He'd already seen her body with all its imperfections and his cock had gotten hard as a rock. He hadn't turned her away. So she was going to be brave in a way she hadn't been before and ask for everything she desired.

"You want my mouth on you? You want my tongue drilling into your sweet cunt?"

She didn't like that word, but somehow he made it sound sexy. Her whole body tightened, nipples turning tender and sensitive. She needed Oliver to touch her or she might explode. "Yes."

"Then take me to your bedroom. You'll get on the bed, your arse on the edge and legs spread wide. You won't hide from me. You'll touch yourself and show me where you like to be licked and sucked."

Tori whimpered. His words sent another rush of moisture pooling between her thighs, deepened the ache of need for him.

She took Oliver's hand and led him back to her small bedroom. She'd brought the comforts of home with her so she had to move her big pink dragon off the bed. She tucked the stuffed animal into the closest, then shut the door behind it.

"A pink dragon?" If Oliver felt any self-consciousness at

being naked in her bedroom, she couldn't tell. Of course if she looked like him, she wouldn't feel a moment's regret at tossing her clothes aside, either. He was tall and broad with abs that could grace any Hollywood action film. There was a scar on his torso where he'd been injured by his late wife. The palace residents told the story often. Yasmin had tried to kill Princess Alea and hadn't cared if her husband had gotten in the way. She'd simply tried to end his life, too.

"My dad won it for me when I was a kid." She didn't want to talk about her parents. The intimacy Oliver intended to give her wasn't emotional. It never would be. That scar on his chest served as a reminder that she couldn't fix him. After all these months of becoming friends, the minute they dropped their clothes, he seemed far more like a stranger.

She wasn't arrogant enough to think she was the woman who could make the world right for him, but at least they could share this night of pleasure together and part on good terms.

He'd promised.

She crawled onto the bed, hoping she hadn't ruined the moment. It was time to leave her childhood stowed elsewhere. That meant her girlish innocence, too.

"I want your ankles apart, legs splayed."

"That position sounds awkward," she ventured.

"I find it quite stunning, actually." He disappeared from view, but wasn't gone for more than a moment before she felt his heat. He pressed her thighs wide with big, hot hands as his mouth hovered over her most sensitive flesh. "Whoever did your wax job was very proficient. This skin is perfection."

Oliver stroked her thigh and palmed the mound of her pussy, letting his heat sink in.

Tori forgot about the awkwardness and raised her head from the bed. She looked down the length of her body to find Oliver staring at her pussy like it was some work of art. "My sister talked me into getting it lasered."

Piper had given her the appointments as a gift. Yes, little

bee stings on her hoo haw had not felt like a gift then, but now she was grateful because Oliver seemed fascinated with her smooth flesh.

He leaned in, breath hot, and bestowed a gentle kiss on her clit. She had to swallow against a rush of desire that made her dizzy and hope that her heart didn't beat out of her chest. "You're beautiful, Tori. A woman like you deserves pleasure and more."

She wouldn't get the "more" from him and she didn't have time to mourn that fact now. She couldn't risk losing whatever experience he was willing to give her. "Touch me. Kiss me again. Please, Oliver."

"You really know how to stroke a man's ego, darling. You know exactly what to say and how to say it. You make me believe I'm the only man in your world. I would do a lot to keep that. We're going to talk in the morning, you and I."

A little sliver of hope broke through, but she quashed it. Even if Oliver was willing to try a relationship, it wouldn't work because she was in love with his brothers, and he'd already shown that he disapproved of their hands on her.

Her yearnings were selfish, she knew. Most women were happy to find one man to love, but Tori knew if she tried to take the traditional path of choosing just one Thurston-Hughes brother, she would always long for the others.

She pushed the thought aside. Tonight wasn't about regrets. "Please, Oliver."

He dragged his tongue through her pussy, making her whole body ping with a fresh swell of need. She writhed under him.

"Don't move or I'll stop. Be very still and let me enjoy you." Another long stroke of his tongue had her grabbing the comforter with both hands, fisting the soft material.

She lay vulnerable and naked to him. To remain still, as he'd demanded, took so much of her control that she had to give elsewhere. Tori felt her grip on her emotions slipping. She shouldn't even consider talking to Oliver about a relationship, but as he tortured her with the sweet sensation of his tongue, she wondered... Was she giving up on them too soon?

Maybe she should fight for what she wanted. Her sister certainly had.

"You taste so sweet." He growled the words against her pussy, every syllable rumbling and flowing over her. "But this is the sweetest part of you."

With one finger, he gently pulled back the hood of her clitoris and she watched his blond head descend to her. He kissed the pearl softly, then sucked it into his mouth.

Tori's whole system overloaded with pleasure. She couldn't breathe, couldn't speak, couldn't do anything but moan and ride out the pleasure as it gathered and swelled, then crested into a wave that had her twisting, crying out, and dying the most beautiful little death inside.

Oliver laved her all the way through the exquisite sensations, his tongue a torture all its own. Finally, as the sensation dissipated, she sagged against the bed. Before she could make sense of the feelings coursing through her, he moved her onto the middle of the bed, sliding her back across the sheets, and covered her body with his own. He pressed her legs apart with strong thighs and made a place for himself there.

"You're going to feel so good." Oliver groaned, and she felt the broad head of his cock prod against her. He hovered over her, propping his torso up with his elbows, pressing their lower bodies together. She stroked a palm across his stunningly muscled chest. All she could think about was how perfect it felt to be close to him, in his arms with nothing between them.

She already felt good. Her body was humming from orgasm, the world seeming hazy and pleasant. She would enjoy sleeping in his arms someday. But the thought fled once she felt him move between her legs. He wasn't through with her yet. In fact, he was hard again, and she remembered what he'd promised. He wouldn't leave her sex unfilled like Callum had. The erection he nudged against her said he intended to have her.

"Oliver, I need to tell you something." She hadn't meant to mention it, but now that they were so close, she needed him to know that he would be her first. Maybe it wouldn't thrill him, but she wanted him to hear that he was special to her.

Before she could confess, he thrust hard inside her, shoving his way through her tight tissue. She felt something tear—along with stabbing pain. She couldn't help the strangled scream that came from her throat.

How was it possible that he'd had to break her hymen? She'd been really active in sports in school. Shouldn't her hymen have imploded before now? Hell, he was so big, and he'd pushed in with such force. He'd filled her so completely that she couldn't take another breath.

All the earlier pleasure dissipated, and she clutched Oliver, praying for relief, balance…something to make the agony go away. She dug her nails into his shoulders and tried to hold back tears.

"What the hell?" Oliver froze over her, his face twisting in dawning horror. "Tell me that wasn't what I think it was."

The hard tone of his voice forced the last of her pleasant fog away. She shifted, struggling to get used to the feel of him taking up all the space inside her. She tried not to let his words hurt.

"Don't," Oliver ordered in an almost desperate voice. "Don't fucking move. I can't…."

Tori couldn't help it. He was too big. She felt him way too deep yet still had to somehow accommodate his breath-stealing girth. She gritted her teeth. Tears blurred her vision as she writhed against him.

His whole face tightened. He groaned, his hips flexing as he thrust in again and again, as though he couldn't help himself. Slowly, the pain lifted. Heat began to wash over her.

Tingles sprang to life between her legs, making her gasp. It was happening. Oliver was inside her. She couldn't wait to feel the sense of connection, like they were two people becoming one.

He buried his face in her neck and picked up the pace, faster, faster. A minute later, he grunted long and low, then pressed deep inside her, his body shuddering. Something warm coated her insides.

He rolled off and stared at the ceiling. "Damn it." His chest heaved. He gritted his teeth and dragged his hand down his face. "What the fuck was that?"

Tori struggled to suck in a deep breath, not to cry in the face of his biting anger. She rolled over, wishing they'd pulled the comforter down so she had something to cover up with. The best she could do was turn onto her side so he could only see her butt. She calculated her odds of dashing to the bathroom without him stopping her. "I think you should go."

After feeling packed full just minutes ago, Tori hadn't expected to feel so empty...so used. She hadn't really expected him to notice her virginity at all, much less be angry that she'd still possessed it.

"There's blood on my cock. Would you like to explain that?" Ice dripped from his words.

She felt him move, the bed shifting under her. She sat, her feet hitting the floor. Carefully, Tori kept her back to him because she felt too naked now. Somehow she hadn't envisioned lovemaking ending between them this way.

But it hadn't been lovemaking. Just sex.

She wasn't stupid. She'd known her first time would be uncomfortable, but Oliver had prepared her and the penetration should have been easy. It could have felt fabulous. They both should have been satisfied. She should be lying in his arms right now, feeling adored. Instead, she was cold and naked and alone. "I told you to go."

"I'm not going anywhere until I get an explanation." He launched to his feet, his hands settled on muscular hips.

"Tori, tell me you weren't a virgin."

She stood up and started for the bathroom where her robe hung. She wasn't having this conversation with him, especially not while she was naked. Something between them had gone very wrong. Until she figured it out, she was covering up and not getting naked for a man for a very long time.

An ache pulsed low in her pelvis. Moisture seeped from her sore sex, onto her thighs. Oh god...

She spun around to send him an accusing glare, complete horror threatening to take over. "You didn't use a condom. Damn you."

Tori couldn't stay naked and near him without falling apart. She strode across the room and toward the bathroom.

He caught her before she could escape, gripping her elbow. "I wasn't thinking straight, but then I assumed that, since you have a fiancé, birth control wouldn't be an issue, Torrance. I believed I was having a mutually pleasurable encounter with an experienced woman. Wasn't that what you wanted me to believe?"

He was accusing her of something but she couldn't quite grasp what. "I only wanted a night to make some good memories with you before I leave in the morning. And you want me to tell you I wasn't a virgin. Neither of us got what we wanted."

"You're not going anywhere now." He released her elbow suddenly as if he couldn't stand touching her. The look of utter disdain on his face sent a chill through her. "I should have seen this ploy coming. You're quite good. Tell me something. How long did it take you to set this scam up? Who was the original target?"

"Scam? Target?" How could she possibly be standing here with him, vibrating with anger, crushed by such hurt, when moments before she'd been shuddering in pleasure beneath his mouth? The abrupt shift felt surreal. She'd been more intimate with Oliver than she'd been with anyone in her life, and now he felt like a stranger.

"Yes, target of your scam. That's what we are to you, isn't it? Or perhaps you prefer the word mark. What do con artists call their victims?"

He might as well have slapped her. "Con artist?"

"Gold digger, in your case. So tell me, if I hadn't interrupted you and Callum at the hotel, would he be the one reeling with the notion that he might have knocked up a lying little virgin?"

Oh, she was so done with him. Tori gritted her teeth. She should have listened to her sister, to her brothers-in-law. Oliver Thurston-Hughes was a wounded beast and he didn't want to be healed. Deep down she'd known it. She simply hadn't listened to the instinct that told her he could lash out like a predator and rip her apart.

"Get out." She turned away and ran to the bathroom, slamming the door shut and locking it with shaking fingers. Tears rolled down her face.

"I'm not leaving until we get a few things straight," Oliver shouted through the door between them. "If you think for one second you can use a child to manipulate me, think again."

"I'm not Yasmin," she cried back.

She knew his story. Sadly, everyone in the world did. Yasmin's infidelity and the fact that she'd manipulated him with pregnancies she'd later terminated and called miscarriages had been on the front page of every tabloid in Europe after her death. Stupid. Tori realized she'd been so stupid to think Oliver could be fixed, even for a single night.

"You're not Yasmin, and I'm going to bloody well make sure you can't play her games. Get out here because I have a few things to say to you."

"Just go away, Oliver. I'm leaving so you don't have to worry about seeing me again. Keep your nasty words for the next fool who thinks she has feelings for you and that you're worth the risk." More tears scalded their way down her cheeks. She felt hollowed out, as if someone had taken an ice cream scooper, carved out all the happiness, and left a sad shell.

She stared into the mirror. She'd wanted to be as happy and as brave in love as her sister. That was all. She'd wanted to be adored and she'd thought for a moment she'd found something special. Those men needed a woman to become the center of their world like Piper was for her husbands. Tori realized that wasn't going to be her.

Too late, Tori remembered why she'd protected herself, why she'd held on to her virginity. She'd thought it was a gift to be given to one of the men she loved. She hadn't remembered that gifts could be opened, found wanting, and rejected.

He'd been quiet for a few moments, and she hoped he'd gotten the hint and left. She wouldn't call him or write him. If she was pregnant she'd know soon and she would prep for life as a single mother because Oliver was toxic.

With a weariness she'd never felt before, she dragged her robe on and opened the bathroom door and peeked into her bedroom.

Oliver was gone. His big, angry, sexual presence lingered but the man himself had left. She was alone, thank god. She felt empty. Her apartment felt empty. Her future...yeah, empty. She was ruined both professionally and personally. God, she couldn't even cry anymore. She would do it when she got to the palace. She would sit and hold her nephews and would find a way to purge the Thurston-Hughes brothers from her heart.

"You bastard," a familiar voice shouted from what sounded like her living room. Callum. What was he doing here?

There was a muffled reply, followed by a crash.

"Stop it, both of you." Rory's shout sounded loud and clear.

Anger exploded like a bomb detonating. These men were

forever fighting, and now they were using her as an excuse. Not that they needed one. Her body ached, but that was nothing compared to the pain she felt deep inside. It was good to put both aside and let the rage flow.

Tori intended to make it very clear that she was done with them. Now and forever.

* * * *

Stunned, dazed, Oliver shuffled away from her bathroom door before he did something extremely stupid like kick it in, throw Tori over his shoulder, and take her home with him. He'd behaved badly. He accepted responsibility for that, just as he would take responsibility for the manipulative little thing, but he wouldn't give her whatever she sought.

He found his slacks and forced himself to step into them. What the fuck had happened? He could scarcely wrap his brain around the fact that she'd been a virgin. He should have suspected something when he first put his fingers inside her and felt the spectacularly tight grip of her cunt. He'd wondered if her fiancé had a tiny penis. Then the thought of James Fenway's dick inside Tori incited particularly nasty thoughts, which had prodded him into thrusting hard and fast into her before sense prevailed and he could talk himself out of touching her. The need to make her his had overwhelmed him.

Well, she was his now. His and only his. No other cock had ever enjoyed that tight pussy. Certainly no other cock had possibly gotten her pregnant. What the hell had he been thinking? He shoved his feet into his socks and searched the room for his shirt. He hadn't been thinking at all. He'd been delighting in her sweetness, how soft and pliable she was for him. He'd been thinking about how Callum liked to tie women up and spank them and fuck them. He'd been considering that Tori would look delicious all wrapped in rope like a gift, waiting for him to unwrap and enjoy her.

He shrugged into his shirt and wondered how the hell he should deal with this mess. A little sparkle on the floor caught his eye.

Her ring. He leaned over and picked it up.

Poor sap. Somewhere in Texas, a man waited for his perfect little virgin bride. That man was about to find out the world wasn't fair.

Oliver had taken her. She was his responsibility now. Perhaps he'd even marry her, but by god, he would watch her like a hawk. He wouldn't allow her the tiniest bit of leeway that she might use against him.

The one bright note? He could have the children he'd dreamed of. They wouldn't erase the ones Yasmin had terminated, but maybe these new precious ones would ease some of the ache and guilt in his heart.

He pocketed the ring. Her engagement—former in his mind—was just one of the matters they needed to discuss after she finished her sulk and exited the bathroom.

You are the world's biggest prick, Oliver Thurston-Hughes. Sulk? You took her virginity without being remotely gentle and gave her not an ounce of pleasure in return. She surrendered to you, and you screamed at her, accused her of all manner of perdition, and then have the gall to say that she's sulking. You promised her kindness and the minute you were through you gave her bile and vitriol. You don't deserve her.

His inner voice often made too much sense for his well-being. He looked back at the bedroom door. He'd closed it because he wanted space between them. He'd told himself it was so he didn't wrap his hands around her pretty throat, but that was a lie. He needed the doors closed so he didn't walk back, fall to his knees, and beg her forgiveness.

He couldn't do that. No matter how poorly he'd handled the thing, he couldn't give her that kind of power over him.

Why not? You gave Yasmin the power to ruin your life for eternity. She wins, you stupid prat. If you let Tori walk out

*of your life, that bitch wins. You should have just allowed her
to kill you.*

He really liked it better when he simply hated everything
and everyone and wished he had died that day in the palace.
But no. All of that had begun to change when Tori had
walked though his door in her bright colors, smiling that
sunny smile he knew so well.

She'd made him start to want more.

*So return to her bedroom and start over. Knock on the
door and beg her to talk to you because you really do care for
her. Confess that you've handled everything horribly. Talk
her back into bed and hold her, give her everything she
deserves—kindness, intimacy, warmth. Do it.*

As much as he wanted it, Oliver found the prospect
horrifying. If he followed that voice in his head, he would be
so vulnerable to her. He wasn't ready for that yet. He didn't
know if he ever would be.

But he couldn't walk away if she was pregnant. He
wasn't ready to leave his child defenseless again.

He was stuck, but then he had been stuck since he'd
learned the truth about Yasmin and had to face his negligent
complicity. He simply hadn't believed her capable of such
evil. Now, he was stuck and he had no idea how to break free.

He looked at the door between them and wished he'd met
her when he'd been younger, when he believed in all that love
shit, when he could possibly have given her what she needed.

And he turned away because that ring of hers was
burning a hole in his pocket.

What was he thinking? The fact that she'd possessed a
hymen didn't make her innocent. She'd cheated on her fiancé
twice in one night with two different brothers, and yet he
stood outside her door mooning over her like an idiot.

Perhaps he hadn't learned as much as he'd thought he
had from Yasmin.

A knock on Tori's front door drew him from his
thoughts. Oliver glanced down at his watch. It was after

midnight. Who would call on her at this hour? He crossed the space and opened the door, only to be confronted with the one person in the world he would have given half his life not to deal with tonight.

"Callum, go home," he ordered wearily.

"What are you doing here?" Callum glared, somewhere between shock and anger.

Rory put a hand on Callum's arm. "I think we should go, Cal."

Oliver winced. Now he could see what a massive mistake this whole evening had been. He should never have followed Tori at the fundraiser, never gone looking for her in the first place. Then she wouldn't have fled. Callum could have been the one to find himself in the trap. No doubt his younger brother would have been thrilled. Now he had to face the fact that he'd taken not only what should have been her fiancé's prize, but he'd also fucked his brother's crush.

"Tori left early and I escorted her home."

"And then you took your clothes off?" Callum accused, scowling at his unbuttoned shirt. He pushed his way into the room, and his gaze dropped immediately to the floor. He bent and picked up the designer gown Tori had been wearing earlier. "And hers."

Oliver's gut knotted. He'd hoped Tori was simply another in his younger brother's long line of flirtations, but the devastated look on his brother's face said that Callum fancied himself in love with her.

Apparently, he'd started a shit storm.

"Callum, I can explain."

"Where's Tori?" Rory asked. "Tell me she's not asleep and that you weren't trying to sneak out of her bed."

He hadn't had the opportunity to sneak out. Not that he'd wanted to. He'd planned on talking to her in the morning about setting her up as his mistress. If she turned up pregnant, he would make her his wife. Now he could see plainly how that plan would go over with his brothers. Callum wasn't the only one who thought he was in love. Rory did, too, and Oliver could see he was going to be the villain in this piece. "I think we should all sit down and talk this out. I made a mistake tonight. Unfortunately, it's not one I can take back."

He might have tied himself to Tori. He might even be able to keep her, but if he did, he stood a good chance of losing his brothers.

Rory's face had flushed a vibrant red. "Tell me you were gentle with her. She's not experienced."

"How did you know that?" Now he could feel his own fury building. "Callum wasn't the only one who got caught with his hands in the honey pot?"

"Don't talk about her like that," Callum said through clenched teeth.

He didn't like the possessive tone in his brother's voice. Callum needed to understand what had transpired tonight and what would happen tomorrow because of it. Oliver had made his bed with his impatient dick. Now they would all have to lie in it. "I'll talk about her any way I like. I took her virginity, so she's my responsibility now. You two will keep your hands off her."

"You can't treat her like she's property, Oliver," Rory shot back, grinding his teeth.

"I can and I will. If she turns up pregnant, I'll be forced to marry her and she'll be your sister-in-law. That episode in the conference room will be the last such incident I'll abide."

"Pregnant? You might have gotten her pregnant?" Rory breathed the words like they were some sort of secret that could kill them all. "Don't you carry condoms?"

Of all the things he was ashamed of, this ranked among the highest. "I imagined she was on the pill."

He couldn't tell his brothers that while he'd been in her arms he hadn't thought about anything except her. Nothing else had existed except her arms around him, her body against his. He hadn't been smart enough to don a condom.

"You bastard!" Callum shouted and ran for him, a

threatening fist cocked.

Oliver took a punch hard to the jaw that almost had him seeing stars. Pain exploded through his head. He fell to the ground before he knew it.

Callum pounced on top of him and reared back again, fist at the ready. "You ruined everything."

"Stop it, you two." Rory tried to shove his way between them.

Across the room, he heard a loud crash. "Out!"

Tori stood stiffly, the remnants of tears streaking her face as she shouted at him. Could this bloody night get any worse?

Callum rolled off him, perched on his knees. "Tori, love, we need to talk. I don't care what you did with him. It was his fault. He tricked you."

"I didn't trick her." Rubbing at the ache in his jaw, he got to his feet and was stunned by the utterly delicious sight of Tori standing in her living room, holding an umbrella like a damn female warrior. Her eyes were lit with fire and her robe gaped open the slightest bit, exposing creamy skin. Despite everything, his dick flared to life again at the sight of her.

"Get out." She stood her ground, her stare falling on each of them as if assessing her enemies.

"Tori, I agree my brothers need to leave, but you and I have to talk." It was time to tone down the emotion and get reasonable. Oliver knew he'd been a bastard to her. No matter what she'd done, she deserved to have her first sexual experience be more memorable than a couple of thrusts, followed by her lover railing at her because she'd been a virgin. He'd made a hack of the whole thing. Once Callum and Rory were gone, he would talk to her, apologize, make it up to her.

"I meant you, too. Get out of my apartment."

If he left her now, he doubted he would be allowed back in. "Don't you think we should talk about this here, rather than at the office?"

"I quit. Get out. All of you."

"Love, I don't know what he did but I'll fix it. I'll make you happy," Callum vowed.

"You can't quit," Rory said. "We've already talked about this."

"Bill me, assholes. Now, out. All of you," Tori insisted, her voice firm.

The situation was spinning out of control. If only his brothers hadn't shown up, he might have been able to salvage it. "Both of you leave now."

"*All* of you," Tori snarled. "This is my last warning."

Like soft little Tori was really going to hurt anyone. Oliver shook his head and stepped toward her. "I'm not leaving, darl—"

Before he could finish speaking, she whapped him with the umbrella. Suddenly, he was stumbling across her flat and trying to find his footing. The pain wasn't bad, but Oliver found himself scrambling to get out of her way. He stumbled toward the door, and his brothers followed suit as Tori bore down on them, weapon in hand.

She swung a few times, her eyes wild, and backed them into the hallway before any of them thought to fight back against the petite brunette whom they each outweighed by four stones of muscle.

"Stay out. And don't contact me again." She slammed the door in their faces, and Oliver heard the distinct sound of the deadbolt sliding home.

He blinked, stunned that he was stuck in the hallway in the middle of the night without his shoes. He rather believed that if he knocked and asked for them, she might try to shove them up his arse. He was staring at the door when one of his brothers grabbed his arm and whirled him around.

"I'll kill you for this." Callum's eyes had gone so cold.

Rory stepped between them. "That won't fix the situation. You're both idiots. I'm going down to Cal's. He's already moved in three doors down. I'm going to get into his Scotch and figure a way out of this mess. If you two kill each other, all the better for me. I'll take the company and Tori for myself. I'm the only one of us who hasn't fucked her over. You're both pathetic. Talib was right. We don't deserve her." He turned and walked away without looking back.

Oliver felt more vulnerable than ever. Even as he'd lain on the floor of Bezakistan's royal palace after Yasmin had done her best to kill him, he hadn't felt this wretched. Tonight, he'd ruined something good, something pure.

Callum jerked away, snarling in his face. "You hurt her."

"I didn't mean to." He really hadn't. He'd meant to…god, he didn't even know what he'd meant to do at this point. "I didn't like the fact that she seduced you while she has a fiancé."

"You haven't figured it out yet? She doesn't have a bloody fiancé. She made it up to keep men like us away. She's alone and you've made sure she'll stay that way. And don't you dare try to say that what you did to her tonight had anything to do with me. I hate you."

Oliver watched his brother walk away, slamming the door behind him.

As he followed his brother down the hall, he kind of hated himself, too.

* * * *

Callum thought seriously about murdering his brother. He knew how he would do it. He would wrap his fingers around Oliver's throat and squeeze until his head popped off. Then he would kick the thing around like a football.

As Rory loitered by the door, Callum shoved his key in the lock, bitterly aware of the fact that he was now three doors away from the woman of his dreams and she wouldn't speak to him. He thought about closing the door and locking them all out, but Rory shoved his way in.

"Are you all right?"

"No thanks to him." Callum pointed a thumb at Oliver.

His oldest brother shuffled inside, looking a bit stunned. "She really doesn't have a fiancé?"

Callum shut and locked the door. Thea had been waiting for him outside the hotel. She'd managed to sneak into the car park and had been lying in wait for him. All in all, it had been a fairly terrible night.

With the singular exception of watching Tori Glen come apart in his arms.

She'd been so beautiful, so unselfconscious. She hadn't been pretending. Her eyes had gone wide with wonder as he'd stroked her and sent her over the edge. She'd been a woman finding her sensuality.

"No, she doesn't. The investigator's report is on the bar if you don't believe me." He crossed to the utilitarian kitchen and grabbed the fifty-year he kept for special occasions or days when the world seemed coated in dung. It had been both today, so he poured three fingers. And then a second glass because Rory hadn't been a bastard. He slid it to his brother.

"I believe you." But Oliver was already opening the private investigator's report. "I could use a drink."

"Then go home and get one," Callum shot back stubbornly.

"No one is leaving until we figure out what to do," Rory said decisively. "We must fix this situation."

"What is there to do?" Oliver ran a hand through his hair. "She quit. She's leaving tomorrow."

"Well, we can choose not to accept her resignation, for starters." Rory took a sip and sighed. "I don't believe she truly wants to leave."

"She seemed fairly certain she did when she attempted to eviscerate Oliver with her umbrella." Callum wished she'd gotten in a good hit. "I'll be surprised if she shows up for work. I'm going to be at her doorstep first thing in the morning. I'll convince her to let me go with her. You'll have my resignation in the morning, too. And you won't talk me out of it."

He knew one thing in the world: He wanted to be with her. And after talking to Thea tonight, perhaps leaving London for a while would be a good thing. She'd been off, and not simply zany, the way she'd been before. She'd actually convinced herself they were a couple. Claire had called the police, but not before Thea had made a terrible scene.

He could lay that at Oliver's feet, too. His older brother had taken the limo, leaving the rest of them to find their own ride. Luckily, a friend had dropped them home after the nasty row with Thea. She'd accused him of sleeping with whores. Had she been talking about Tori? What did she know about their relationship? The last thing he needed was Thea confronting Tori, though after seeing Tori's fierce anger, Callum wasn't quite as worried. Unfortunately, her fury had been aimed at him and Rory—the wrong brothers.

"You should go with her." Oliver nodded. "She needs you. I don't like the thought of her out in the world on her own. Trouble seems to follow her."

"Both of you are idiots, and I'm only going to have the rest of this conversation because she deserves to get what she wants. Though I have my worries that she no longer wants any of us." Rory set his glass down.

"What are you talking about?" The truth was, Callum didn't want to leave England. This was his home, but he couldn't see a way out of it now. He certainly couldn't see them being one big happy family.

"She won't run off with you, Cal. I know you think she will but she won't separate or hurt this family. She's got too much integrity. It's exactly why she hadn't given in to any one of us until tonight. Callum, how did you get her alone? I seriously doubt she jumped you in the conference room."

He felt himself flush. He wasn't proud of what he'd done. He'd thought she simply needed a little push to give into her desire. Once she had, she'd responded beautifully. "I might have told her I would exchange my silence about the false engagement for a kiss, and things might have escalated from there."

"You blackmailed her." Oliver's lips thinned to a judgmental line.

"It was only supposed to be a kiss. I was giving her the nudge she needed."

"To fuck you? At least I didn't blackmail her," Oliver snapped.

"So how did it happen?" Rory asked.

Oliver's eyes tightened, a sure sign he was feeling guilty. "I told you, trouble follows her. She was attacked as she walked into the building. We're lucky I have a key card."

Callum's gut knotted. "Attacked?"

"Well, she was walking around wearing ridiculously expensive jewelry, thanks to you," Oliver pointed out. "Though she had nearly been attacked recently, too."

"Are you serious?" Rory demanded.

"Like I said, trouble finds her. She must look like an easy target." Oliver shrugged. "Tonight, like last time, I fought the man off. When we reached her flat, the adrenaline kicked in. We ended up in bed. Everything was fine until…"

"You found out she was a virgin," Rory stated flatly.

"How did you know?" Oliver asked.

"She was really a virgin?" Callum could scarcely believe it. She was so beautiful, so sensual. How had she remained untouched all these years? Were American men idiots? Had he known her as a teen, he would have spent all his time trying to get into her knickers.

"Do you two know her at all?" Rory shook his head as though tired of the lot of them. "She obviously inexperienced. I wasn't sure she was a virgin, but I knew she hadn't had more than one or two men in her life. After her parents died, she tried not to be a burden or create problems for her sister. She never got into the kinds of trouble other teenagers do. She went to school and she worked a job to help out Piper financially."

"How do you know this?" Callum demanded. He and Tori had talked about a lot of things, but mostly current events and things like movies she enjoyed.

"Because I asked her. I like her. That's a foolish thing to say. I love her." Rory looked as resolved as he sounded. "I wanted to know everything about her."

Another brother he had to compete with. "Yet you're willing to give her up for Oliver?"

Rory shook his head. "Not anymore."

"So you two will battle it out?" Oliver's shoulders drooped wearily.

How long had it been since he'd managed a decent night's sleep? Years, Callum would bet.

Before he or Rory could answer, Oliver sighed. "I told you she would tear us apart. It's why I tried to stay away from her."

"That's not the reason, and you know it." He was sick of his older brother's denial. "You stayed away from her because you're convinced every woman is Yasmin. I bet she wasn't a virgin when you took her the first time."

"No, she wasn't and she was also a liar. She claimed she'd had one lover, though now I'm sure it was many more. I didn't care. I don't care about virginity. It isn't some prize to be claimed. Though I think in Tori's case it was a gift she gave. I fear I rejected it quite harshly."

Rory clapped Oliver on the shoulder, a gesture both soothing and threatening. "You made a mistake. You can apologize for it."

Oliver shrugged. "Do you know what I was really angry about?"

Callum could bet. "That you may have gotten her pregnant."

An unwilling sympathy flared through him. Callum didn't want to feel for Oliver, but he knew how those lost children haunted him. Perhaps if he and Yasmin had made the decision together that they weren't ready for children, Oliver might have forgiven himself. But the bitch had convinced him that she'd wanted those babies. She'd sworn that she had miscarried, and Oliver had blamed himself for not seeing through her.

"Tori would never deceive me the way Yasmin did. If she found herself pregnant, she would talk to me. Even I'm not that stupid," Oliver said. "I know intellectually that Tori is as far from Yasmin as a rabbit from a rabid tiger, but in the moment, I reacted poorly."

"All right, then we huddle up here until we come up with a plan of action," Rory suggested.

Callum was a bit worried Rory would ask him for a white board and dry erase markers and turn this entire thing into some weird business meeting. "What kind of action can we take?" The enormity of the situation hit him. They really were fucked. He loved Tori. Rory loved Tori. Oliver would never admit it, but he loved her, too. "No matter what we do, she gets hurt. Two of us do, as well."

Could he actually battle it out with his own brothers? That hadn't seemed like a real possibility until tonight. Now Callum wasn't sure he had the right to take her from them…or them from her.

"Or we do this together like we should have from the beginning," Rory cut into his thoughts. "We go after her as brothers looking for a wife. We treat her with respect and love."

Though he'd just been thinking the same thing, Callum recoiled. "That sounds terrible. Especially the 'respect' part. That sounds very much like none of us will be getting any."

Rory stared at him, a single brow arching over his left eye. "I put forth a plan, and the only problem you have is with the word respect?"

"I can respect her and still sleep with her." Callum was actually shocked to find he was okay with everything else.

Perhaps they could share her, share the intimacy. Share the responsibility. Lift each other when they were down.

Become a team to create a truly cohesive family.

Yes, he didn't mind that concept at all, but the no sex bit wouldn't work. Ever.

"As it happens, I agree with you," Rory assured. "I think we should take her to bed as soon as possible. When I talked about respect, I meant we have to think about her needs. We have to respect that she might need a bit of time to get used to the idea. We definitely have to respect the relationship we're attempting and one another. So no plotting behind my back to run away with her. I will hunt you down. You might be the athlete in the family, but I was the marksman."

Callum grinned, feeling something ease inside him. "Don't run off with our girl or I'll shoot you like that fox at Benedict Pine's eighteenth birthday party and beer bash. Got it. Hey, I just thought of rule number two. Never mention anything that happened at Benedict Pine's eighteenth birthday party. Tori is surprisingly sensitive for a girl from Texas. She'd be upset about the fox. Well, and the strippers."

Oliver slapped at the bar, gaining Cal's attention. He scowled. "What is wrong with you two? It's not going to work. Cal, do you understand what he wants?"

"He wants to share Tori."

"You do know he's not talking about a time share. You're not going to sign up for custody of the wife and pass her off when your turn is up. He's talking about all three of you in bed together. Do you understand what that means?"

"It means we're going to have to learn to communicate so our balls don't ever touch. I'm serious about that, Rory. Perhaps we'll come up with a series of hand gestures."

Rory rolled his eyes. "Certainly. We'll get right on that." He stopped and smiled at Callum in a way he hadn't in forever, as if they were young and had a secret. "We're going to give her what she needs. She needs all of us."

Oliver stood. "You're insane if you think that will work. What will you tell Claire? How will our sister handle this ménage of yours?"

"It will be a marriage," Rory corrected him. "And Claire is the one who made me see I was being a ridiculous prude. She'll stand by us."

"What about when the tabloids start questioning your and Callum's sexuality?" Oliver pointed out.

Callum couldn't care less. "I've got about a thousand women who will testify to my intense heterosexuality." That actually sounded quite bad. He winced. "Rule number three— never mention our 'number' to our wife."

He liked the idea of calling Tori "our wife." It sounded right.

"I don't give a damn what they say. I'm Rory Thurston-Hughes and I don't follow society. Society can follow me, and if they choose not to, they can go to hell. I'm not living my life by their rules anymore. We'll set our own."

Damn, Callum was suddenly proud of his brother. They'd all suffered in the last several years. It was past time to come out from under Yasmin's dark cloud and back into the light. "Besides, we're marrying a publicist. Tori can spin the whole thing. She's good at that. We'll be honoring her Bezakistani heritage."

"She's from Texas," Oliver pointed out stubbornly.

"Well, then, she can shoot anyone who thinks to soil our reputations." Callum couldn't help but grin. He felt lighter than he had in years. "We're going to do something completely crazy and it's going to work. She's not going to be able to resist the three of us."

"Correction: the two of you," Oliver said. "I won't be a part of this. I've hurt her enough already. I won't make a mockery of her."

Naturally Oliver had to be the one to put a damper on things. Callum got between his brother and the door. "Then you'll work against us?"

Oliver's eyes met his. "No. I'll stand by you if you decide to go through with this insanity."

"You know you want her, too, Ollie," Rory pointed out,

his voice low and coaxing.

"I do, but I'm smart enough to know I shouldn't want her and I care enough about her to know she damn well shouldn't want me. I hope she doesn't refuse you because of anything I've done. I should have known better than to lose my head tonight." He sidestepped Callum and made it to the door. "Try to take care of her. She really does get into trouble."

And he was gone, closing the door behind him quietly.

Callum stared after Oliver for a moment. "I don't know how he'll handle it. Do you really think he'll manage all right having Tori for a sister-in-law?"

"Absolutely not. It's going to drive him mad, and we'll rub his nose in the fact that we're making love to her at every opportunity." A look of satisfaction crossed Rory's face.

He agreed with Rory's assessment. Oliver wouldn't be able to hold out forever. All it had taken was one adrenaline-fueled event, and he'd forgotten to don a condom. What was he going to do when he could hear her moan all night, then had to sit across the breakfast table from her the next morning?

"I thought you believed in the gentle method of repairing his ego," Callum challenged.

"Well, we've seen how effective that approach was." Rory poured himself another glass. "He'll come around. We'll let him in when he does and pray Tori doesn't take another umbrella to his arse."

"And if he doesn't come around?"

"Then we move on with our lives and we make sure our wife is as happy as we possibly can. I've tried to force him to see that what happened with Yasmin wasn't his fault, but he's insisting on this self-flagellation. He'll have to realize the truth himself. He's right about her getting into trouble though. We'll need to keep an eye on her. I hate to think what could have happened if Oliver hadn't followed her home tonight."

The thought chilled Callum to the bone, but he had other questions. "She took a cab and Oliver was following her. He thinks it was about the jewelry. But why would someone wait outside this building on the off chance that a woman wearing enormously expensive jewels might happen by?"

Rory thought for a moment. "It's an exclusive building."

"But it's filled with contract workers. They're more likely to be carrying briefcases and laptops than wearing jewels. Most of the tenants in this building are single men, and that's reason enough to get her out of here." He didn't like the thought that the attempted armed robbery wasn't random.

"We won't let her wander about at night by herself anymore."

He needed to get his investigator on Thea. He wouldn't put it past her to try to eliminate the competition. "And if this has something to do with Thea? Should I be close to Tori while that psychotic bitch is still after me?"

"You're not pushing her away now. We'll protect her if the need arises. Now think fast because we're going to be on her doorstep in a few hours. We must have a plan to stop her from both quitting and leaving."

Callum meandered to the window as the ideas flowed. He and Rory spent the hours before dawn plotting and planning—and it was all for naught.

When they knocked on her door at seven a.m., she was already gone.

CHAPTER SEVEN

"How are you doing?" Princess Alea asked as she walked into the room. Alea was a lovely woman with sun-kissed skin and blue-black hair. She grinned down at her son and got to her knees to give the toddler a kiss on the forehead.

Tori looked up and sighed. Everyone asked her that question. It was the most popular query in the palace these days. Since that morning two weeks before when she'd snuck out of her building in the early morning hours and gone to her sister's flat in London, it seemed the royal family had made it their hobby to worry about her. "I'm good."

She was physically fine. Her period had come and gone, and with it any hope of having a piece of the Thurston-Hughes brothers.

She tried to tell herself that was a good thing.

Alea sat on the floor, picking up a block and setting it down in front of her son. All three of the royal boys were crawling across the playroom floor, though the youngest, Michael, was just starting out. He did that super-cute baby thing where he managed to roll over and then push himself up to his knees, then he pulsed back and forth like he was going to take off any minute and it would be so cool.

God, she loved those babies and she worried she would never have her own. She would forever be their sad maiden aunt because she loved three men who were too stupid to live.

She dreamed about beating some sense into them, but then the dream always turned carnal and she woke up aching for them.

"I don't believe you," Alea said with a frown as she petted her son's head. "I know heartache when I see it and you've got it written all over your face. You haven't even tried to ditch your guard once while you've been here. That's my first bit of evidence."

"Shouldn't a smart girl know the guard is there for a reason?" She could still remember that robber in the lobby of her building telling her what he intended to do to her.

But every time she thought about that, she thought about Oliver rescuing her...and the act that had led to. For all the pain it had caused her, Tori was glad that her first time had been her choice and no one else's.

"I don't know. I still try to ditch my husbands every now and then. They drive me crazy. Love you, baby." Alea winked Landon's way. He was standing by the door, a forbidding look on his handsome face.

"I'll remember that when you want me to change diapers." His lips curled up in the sweetest grin and he winked his wife's way.

No one would wink her way. Tori was alone and she would remain that way unless she could find some way to move on. "Well, when I go back to the States next week, I won't have to worry about guards."

She had plenty of other things to worry about. Like a job. Where she would live. All of her things were in storage, and she'd given up her apartment when she'd agreed to work for a year in London.

She also had to figure out how to pay back her brothers-in-law for the large check they had undoubtedly written to Thurston-Hughes, Inc. because Tori had been too impatient to read her contract. Wherever she was going to be living, it would have to be cheap.

"Tal wants to send two guards with you when you return

home." Alea helped her boy stack some blocks.

"I've told him no and I meant it." She wasn't going to be caged in. She understood why Piper needed a guard. Why Alea needed one. But Tori wasn't royal. Once she returned to Texas, no one would even know her name. There was no reason for her to have a dedicated guard who would curb her personal freedom.

Not that it mattered. She wasn't sure when she would be ready to try dating again.

"My cousin usually gets what he wants and he wants you safe," Alea explained. "You might find yourself with an at-distance guard you don't even know is there."

"As long as they stay away, I don't care."

Alea sighed and seemed to change her tactic. "Have you thought about meeting my al Bashir cousins?"

Tori shook her head vigorously. "Absolutely not. I can't handle five men. No way. No how. I thought briefly about trying with three and that blew up in my face. I can't try it with five brothers."

She hadn't even figured out where she would put five men. During sex, that is. Oh, she'd quite vividly figured out where the Thurston-Hughes brothers would go, but five seemed out of her grasp. She was a traditionalist when it came to her fantasy ménage.

"Sometimes people from outside our world don't understand it." Alea's eyes were wide and sympathetic.

"I'm not from your world. I don't always understand it, either." She definitely didn't understand how to make it work in the real world. Real was a crappy word. Bezakistan was real. It just wasn't the norm.

"What don't you understand?" Landon hovered a hand over the gun attached to his hip, but his expression looked non-threatening.

"I don't know why I can't love only one of them. Why am I so selfish? Why can't I compromise?"

Alea smiled as she rubbed a palm across her son's head.

"That's not the question you should ask. Perhaps the better question is, why should you compromise? Do you really believe they wouldn't be better off sharing you? Are they not close?"

That was a good question. "I know they love each other, but they fight a lot."

"Sharing you would bring them closer."

She glanced up at Landon, who smiled indulgently at his wife and kid. "Did you always know you wanted to share?" She felt her cheeks flame in embarrassment. "I'm so sorry. That was rude. Please forgive me."

He was working. She didn't have any right to ask such personal questions of him.

Lan stepped in closer, his hand coming off the P-90 he wore over his chest like a vest. He dropped to one knee beside his wife. "There's nothing to forgive, Tori. You ask all the questions you need to. No one here will be offended. And no. I didn't always know. I'll be honest, I didn't really think about the future until I met Alea."

His wife leaned into him. "Neither did I, my love."

He kissed her forehead with one arm wound around her shoulder and the other ruffled his son's hair. "Men don't think about these things the way women do. When I did meet her, I realized she was far too much woman for one man to handle." He chuckled lightly. "I know there might have been some alternate world where it could have been just the two of us, but I like how we work. I like having brothers to rely on. Loving a woman, starting a family, it's a real responsibility and the reassurance of knowing Dane and Coop will carry on if anything happens to me is worth gold, in my opinion. I also like the fact that there are two people in the world who know what it means to love her. I don't feel alone."

Wistfulness washed over her. What would it feel like to not be so alone? She'd known for the briefest of moments. When she'd been with Callum and then Oliver, she'd been able to fool herself that all things were possible. She'd been able to dream that she could have the life she wanted.

But she knew reality now and she was going to have to make some hard choices soon. She had a couple of options to consider. She'd already decided against staying here. Besides, being coddled and cloistered like a nun, if she remained at the palace, she would likely find herself dating the infamous five cousins at some point, and she wasn't sure she could handle that many Bezakistani men. So she'd go somewhere in the States and start over again. She had friends in New York. Los Angeles was also an option. It was a hot spot for a person who knew how to handle a scandal. Or she could be safe and go home to Dallas.

Tori couldn't stop thinking about London and how awfully she'd left. She'd snuck out in the middle of the night. She'd packed her bags, called a cab, and shown up on her sister's doorstep right before dawn. If she'd stayed even until morning, one of them would have shown up. Callum or perhaps Rory. Oliver might have torn through her again with his damage and demands.

But they were out of her life now. The day she'd gotten her period she'd sent Oliver a text so he wouldn't worry about it. Then she'd promptly changed her number because the last thing she wanted was his reply. It likely would have been full of curse words.

"I'm glad you all have each other." She smoothed down Sabir's hair. How long would it be before she had babies? Would she ever have them? Even if she did, would she always long for little blond-haired British boys?

"Is it really over with Oliver and his brothers?" Alea asked.

"They can't share. They can barely be in the same room with each other."

Alea frowned. "That's not the way I remember them. Oliver was very close to his brothers once. He was very much the head of his family and he cared for all his siblings. They would come to the palace, and it was where I first worried that Yasmin wasn't right for him. She hated the fact that he would bring his siblings with them. She wanted all of his focus on her and she was nasty to anyone who took it away."

"Why did he marry her?" As far as Tori could tell, Yasmin had been pure evil.

"She was lovely," Alea explained with a sigh.

"She was also super-aggressive sexually," Lan said. He immediately turned a nice shade of pink and coughed a little. "Not that I would know."

Alea's eyes rolled. "She hit on everyone, but she was careful that Oliver never saw. She played him very differently. She went slowly with him. She teased him and kept him at arm's length."

"Though she'd likely already slept with most of the men at their wedding." Lan stood up. "I'll shut up now."

"Poor Oliver. He really liked Talib, respected him. She used that relationship to move him toward marriage and did a number on him. I do get that. I guess she knew exactly how to play him." Apparently Yasmin had known him better than Tori did. The woman had figured out that her best move was to play coy with him. Tori hadn't, and he'd made it pretty plain what he thought of her that night. Her virginity had only infuriated him. He certainly hadn't been about to propose marriage.

Well, she didn't have to worry about that anymore. Nope. She was definitely not a virgin now and she'd already survived her first pregnancy scare. Yay, her. She'd always been an overachiever.

"I remember Oliver before he married Yasmin," Alea said with a sad smile.

"Douchebag," Lan coughed.

Alea rolled her eyes. "Don't listen to him. He doesn't like the fact that Oliver once had a crush on me when we were young."

Tori didn't much like that fact, either. So Oliver's type was stupendously wealthy, stunning royal women. She did not fit that bill.

"You're jealous." Alea reached for her hand. "There's no reason to be. Oliver and I never even kissed. He married Yasmin because she told him she was pregnant. She conveniently had a miscarriage shortly after. That's the story she told him anyway. After she nearly killed the both of us, Oliver discovered bills for clinics around London. Apparently she'd gotten pregnant twice and dealt with the problem herself, telling Oliver that she miscarried. She kept him in the dark, and when he finally emerged, the truth blinded him. He was devastated. He hasn't been the same since, except I saw him smile the last time I was in London. It was just for a moment and I don't think he knew I was watching. I was about to cross the street to meet Callum and Rory to talk about their company sponsoring a charity event."

"I remember that visit."

"Oliver was standing in the lobby, staring out the window, and the loveliest smile transformed his face. I had to stop and stare at him because he looked like the Oliver I knew. He was young and happy in that moment. I wondered what had put that grin back on his face."

Tears threatened because she'd never seen Oliver smile like that. He'd always been polite, always scrupulously in control. Except that night when he wasn't, when he'd taken her in his arms. "What was it?"

"Oh, darling, it was you. You were wearing a blue skirt and a white cardie and you looked like a little bit of sunshine walking down the street. By the time you walked into the building, he was suitably dour. But for that moment, he was Oliver again."

Tori sniffled a little and was grateful Sabir chose that moment to sit in her lap. He cuddled close and she took comfort in his warmth. "Well, I'm afraid he changed his mind."

"He's a fool then." Lan kissed his wife briefly before getting to his feet. "You can't let the past rob you of a future.

That's one thing my wife taught me. You've got two hours before the ball. Alea, my love, we've got to get ready to go."

Tori sighed. Another ball. She'd proven she was no Cinderella. "I'm going to stay far away from the ball and get in my PJs and watch Disney movies with the babies."

"No, you can't do that." Alea let Lan help her to her feet. "It's been announced you'll be in attendance. If you don't come there will be gossip that you and your sister are at odds."

"Why would they think that?" This was the part of her sister's life she couldn't comprehend. Even when she was working for the Thurston-Hughes brothers, she'd struggled with the idea of being the target of all those vultures. She knew how to work them. She had no problem being the spokesperson or the woman behind the scenes plotting to get a client out of a sticky situation, but the idea of her life being under a microscope made her ill.

Which was another very good reason she should stay away from the Thurston-Hughes brothers. They were a bad idea all around.

"They think that because the tabloids here use any excuse to pit the royals against each other. It doesn't help that we've had two cousins try to kill us," Alea explained. "You have to come. I believe Piper said arrangements had already been made for your gown."

The last thing she wanted was to be in another borrowed gown. PJs sounded so comfy, accompanied by a nice gallon of mint chocolate chip ice cream. "You could say I was sick." She coughed a little. "I definitely feel an illness coming on."

"Oh, if we say you're sick, they'll report that you're pregnant and bringing shame on the sheikh. They really enjoy the bringing-shame-to-the-sheikh headlines. Those sell out in record time." Alea picked up her baby and cuddled him to her chest.

Lan flashed a devastating grin. "You're caught, Tori. That's what happens here. One minute you're happy in your comfortable fatigues and the next someone's sticking you in a monkey suit and telling you to dance like it's freaking 1805."

"At least you don't have to wear heels," Tori complained.

"Perks of manhood." Lan winked and whisked away his wife and baby. Piper's nanny came to take her boys as well.

She was alone again. Well, except for the next guard on duty who opened the door and took up sentry.

Tori sighed. It really was time to go home.

* * * *

Rory stepped into the sheikh's office beside Callum with his head held high. It was located in the business wing of the palace. Tori was likely in the residential wing, but he would have to talk fast to even be permitted to walk those halls. The fact that the sheikh had chosen to use his formal office rather than the private one reserved for gatherings with family and friends told him a lot. Of course, so did the look on his face.

Talib al Mussad looked like a man in a bad mood. He sat behind his massive desk, wearing an impeccable three-piece suit, and when they were introduced he nodded his regal head and gestured to the chairs in front of him.

"Gentlemen, you may sit." The words were polite, but Rory was fairly certain Talib would be excruciatingly polite even as he delivered a death sentence. How did they dispatch people who committed crimes against the royal family in Bezakistan? He was fairly certain it wasn't pleasant.

"Thank you for agreeing to see us," Rory said.

"And for letting us in the country, but you need to talk to your security people. I don't think that full body cavity search was really warranted." Callum had been unhappy with the extra security protocols that had been put in place since the last time they'd visited.

Yes, Rory was fairly certain the very intrusive personal search had been just for them.

144

The sheikh's lips curled up the tiniest bit. "You can never be too careful these days." His smile faded and he leaned forward. "Now why don't you explain to me why you've come to my country. I know it can't be because you've come to enforce the contract you had my sister-in-law sign. I believe I sent you a check for the full amount, and the jewelry you allowed her to borrow has been returned. Unfortunately, her dress was torn. I added that expense to the check."

If words were ice, Rory would have frozen where he sat. "No, Your Highness. We didn't come here to demand anything."

"And the jewelry was a gift. I'm not cashing that check," Callum insisted.

"A gift? For what?" Talib's hawk-like glare settled on Callum.

His brother might not be the world's most diplomatic man, but he wasn't a coward either. He held the sheikh's stare. "For the woman I love."

"From what I understand you didn't present it to her as a gift. You chose to trick her into thinking she was purchasing the items herself."

"I didn't think she would accept it," Callum said, finally starting to squirm the tiniest bit.

It was time to save his brother or this was going to go poorly. Unfortunately, Talib was the gateway to Tori. If he couldn't be moved, there was no telling when they would see her next. If she chose to stay in the palace, they might not see her at all. "I believe what my brother is trying to say is he couldn't stand the thought of Tori not having a wardrobe and jewels to match her beauty. You know how British society can be. She's stubborn. She won't accept handouts and he couldn't stand the thought that she would walk into that room and be mocked for having to purchase last season's fashions. She deserves more."

Talib's eyes narrowed. "You should do most of the talking."

"Of that, I am very aware, Your Highness." Rory settled in, secure they weren't getting tossed out yet. "As for Tori's contract, consider it null and void. I only brought it up in an attempt to keep her close. I certainly wasn't going to demand payment. We've made mistakes with her, but we care very much."

"We love her," Callum said. "And I didn't take back the jewels. They're hers and they're waiting for her."

"You said 'we.'" Talib sat back, regarding them both now. "I thought Callum was the only one willing to stake his claim."

"I've always wanted Tori. I knew the day she walked through the door that she was the one for me. The others are slow," Callum explained.

"Oliver isn't with you," Talib pointed out.

No, and that weighed heavily on him. Oliver had talked them into giving Tori a few days to think, though Callum had been packed and ready to go thirty minutes after they discovered she was gone. Unfortunately, receiving clearance to visit Bezakistan hadn't proven quite as simple as it once had.

During those awful weeks, Rory had written her an e-mail he was fairly certain she hadn't read. He'd sent her a few texts she hadn't returned.

And then her number had been disconnected.

Luckily, they'd known exactly where she'd gone since the tabloids had published pictures of the royals entering the palace. There in the background had been a somber Tori, following after her sister, a grim look on her face.

Oliver had announced that his idiocy wasn't going to come back to haunt them, then he'd left the office, not to return. Shortly thereafter, he'd sent Rory a note. Oliver intended to take a vacation. Since he hadn't taken one in years, Rory should have been thrilled. If he'd thought for an instant that Ollie was on some tropical island, he would have been. But his brother was somewhere brooding, and that wasn't good for any of them.

"I'm afraid Oliver isn't ready." Rory worried Oliver might never be. "But if we don't move soon, we're going to lose Tori. We can't wait for him. How much do you know about what happened the night before she left England?"

Talib shook his head. "Very little. From what the guards have overheard, she spent the night with Oliver and it did not go well. I was pleased to discover she wasn't pregnant. Oliver should be pleased as well."

"I don't think he was actually." Callum seemed to miss the "or else" inherent in Tal's tone. "I think he hoped she'd conceived so he would have to marry her. Oliver can't allow himself happiness. That's the problem. But we think if he sees enough of it, he won't be able to stop himself from joining in."

"You have the guards listen in on the women's conversations?" It was actually quite brilliant.

"It's a hobby of mine. But seriously, you will find that women like to keep their secrets. I learned long ago I can't protect the people I love if I don't know what's happening. In a place this large, a network of well-meaning spies is required to ensure happiness. You will find that a woman oftentimes expects a man to sense what she is feeling. As I am not psychic or even particularly sensitive, spying works. When I find out my wife has had a bad day, I am able to magically show up with her favorite flowers and a sympathetic shoulder. There are tricks to being a husband."

And if Talib couldn't be there, one of his brothers could. He never had to worry about Piper being alone.

He did, however, have to worry about Oliver being alone, but it was time to look past his guilt. Guilt wouldn't solve the situation and it would only make everything worse. Guilt would keep Oliver distant from her.

"We are serious about Tori, Your Highness, and we've come to ask your permission to court her."

Talib's fingers steepled under his chin and a long

moment passed. "You are willing to marry her in the Bezakistani fashion?"

He'd already figured all of this out. "Yes. Once she agrees, we'll be married here. I've studied some of your laws. If Oliver turns around, we can return and file with the courts to have his name placed on our marriage license."

"Interesting. That law was put in place for brothers who happened to be off fighting wars when the marriage took place, but I cannot see any reason why it wouldn't work," the sheikh agreed.

"Oliver's fighting his own war." Sometimes Callum showed depth. "We want him to know he's welcome when he's ready to come home."

Tori was home. He knew that now. "As for the legalities in England, we've decided Callum will file a marriage license with her there, though my personal will shall be altered to reflect that she is my heir and the company would be divided between our sister and Tori should anything happen to us."

"And how will you handle the press? The British tabloids will go wild."

Callum shrugged. "It's never bothered me. They've run every story imaginable on me. I impregnated an alien, according to one."

Talib's eyes narrowed. "I am not concerned with the alien."

Callum's hands rose as if in self-defense. "I have not touched the Palmer woman in over a year. She's lying about me."

"I came to the same conclusion. I had a private investigator follow her and watch her house. She is not pregnant. Though I find it distasteful, my PI tipped off the tabloids to go through her garbage for proof. I believe the story will run tomorrow. I thought Tori at least deserved to know you weren't a complete bastard."

Callum's head fell back. "Thank god that's over."

"We are deeply appreciative, Your Highness." Rory was

a little in awe of the sheikh's devious mind. He certainly hadn't thought of that and he should. "With regard to the tabloids, you should know I will ruthlessly protect my family with everything I have and I vow to learn from you. I don't care what they think. I'm going to be happy and they can shove it up their tight arses if they don't like it. I'm done playing by their rules. The people who care about me will accept the relationship."

"After a while, we'll be boring," Callum explained. "Rory here will lose his hair and no tabloids will take pictures of that."

His brother could really get on his nerves. "As you can see, my brother has plans."

Talib smiled, the first genuine happiness Rory had seen since they walked into the room. "You should replace his shampoo with Nair. I did this to Kadir once. It was very amusing. It's good to see you behaving as brothers should."

"Oliver was once the joker," Callum said quietly. He shook his head as though clearing it. "Sorry, it's hard not to think about who he was before his last visit to the palace. I worry a bit that one of the reasons he won't admit he wants Tori is because she's so connected to this place. I don't think he'll ever walk through these doors again."

Rory worried the same thing. "One day, Cal. Your Highness, we're formally asking permission to court your sister-in-law. Do we have it?"

"As long as you promise you will never tell her this meeting occurred," Talib said, getting to his feet. He strode to the small bar he kept near his desk. "Tori can be very independent. The idea that a group of men sat in an office drinking incredibly expensive liquor while deciding her future would likely rankle. Scotch?"

"Please. After the two-hour interrogation by your airport security, I need it. Did you know they set bomb-sniffing dogs on our private jet?" Rory gratefully took the tumbler.

"And drug-sniffing dogs. One of the German shepherds

buried her head in my crotch. I was fairly certain I would lose my manhood then and there," Callum admitted.

Talib threw back his head and laughed. "You have Rafe to thank for the greeting. He took great joy in torturing you. Now, I have something to tell you. Oliver is here."

Rory sat up straight. "What do you mean? How?"

"By plane, of course." Talib passed Callum a drink and made one for himself. "Though he came on a commercial jet. He arrived yesterday and asked my forgiveness for the manner in which he treated Tori. I knew what you were going to ask me because he's already pleaded your case. He intends to talk to Tori tonight and ask her forgiveness as well."

Oliver was here? Rory had to take a moment to wrap his mind around the fact. "He didn't tell us."

"I doubt he wanted you to know. Tori has no idea. He's sequestered in a private room, and I don't think he's left, so only Rafe, Kade, and I know he's here. I'm actually about to tell my cousin I want her to speak with him."

"Alea." Rory remembered the kind princess. They had met when they were younger, before Oliver married Yasmin. "He always liked Alea."

"Should we talk to him, too?" Callum asked. "I don't want to surprise him. He doesn't like surprises. Well, not anymore."

At one point, adventure had been Oliver's middle name. Before Yasmin, he'd been the one to try everything. Rory had to pin him down to get him to work because he'd wanted to see the world. Rory had taken care of most of the day-to-day operations of the company and he'd definitely held the purse strings. He'd always wanted less responsibility, but the reasons Oliver had finally assumed responsibility had always bothered him. Oliver used the job to hide. "I don't think it would do any good. Our presence here might unsettle him."

"I think you should meet with him. However, I will leave it up to you. He claims he simply wants to talk to Tori and will then return home. I believe he's trying to be a good brother. He doesn't understand that the sacrifice is unnecessary. It's up to her to teach him. It's something a man learns from a woman or not at all. I hope Tori can get through to him. As for the two of you, I suspect you have an uphill climb. She's not happy with any of you. What's your plan?"

Rory knew what his plan was. "We corner her at the ball and show her how good it can be to have two men who care for her."

"But with respect," Callum said.

"God, I hope not too much," Talib said with a groan. "Really, you should bed her as soon as possible. Courtship is overrated. Get her into bed, muddle her mind with pleasure, and before she knows it she'll find herself with a ring on her finger. It's the best plan of action. You'll find your bedrooms are fully stocked with everything you could possibly need. A woman like Tori has to stop thinking and feel. That is your job. And if you don't marry her quickly... Well, it's been a while since we've had an execution."

Yes, this was going to be his brother-in-law. He was glad he fully intended to treat Tori like a queen. "Thank you for everything."

Rory looked to Callum. His brother sent him a hopeful grin. Tonight they claimed their woman.

CHAPTER EIGHT

Callum took a deep breath and knocked on the door, hoping this wasn't going to end in blood. Lately, all of his encounters with Oliver seemed to culminate in someone throwing a punch.

He wouldn't do that today. Well, he wouldn't throw the first one, at least. If Oliver punched him, naturally he would be forced to defend himself.

And then he would ruin his perfectly good tux. Maybe he should have changed for the gala after this meeting.

The door opened, and Oliver reared back, eyes wide. "Well, I suppose I should have expected this. Rory is here as well?"

"Indeed. He's getting dressed for the ball." When Oliver stepped aside to admit him, Callum entered. It looked as if Rory wasn't the only one running behind in his preparations. Oliver had apparently shaved and showered already and had dressed in slacks and a snowy white shirt. His tie hung loose around his neck. He'd slung his tuxedo jacket negligently over a chair. "I was surprised to learn you were here."

Oliver closed the door. "I wanted to talk to Tori. I also need to speak with Alea."

That surprised him, too. "You haven't talked to Alea in years. You duck her phone calls."

A faint blush stained Oliver's cheeks. "Yes, that wasn't

well done of me. We used to be friends. I'm going to apologize to her for that."

"Are you going to apologize for anything else?" Since the moment Talib mentioned Oliver's visit, Callum had suspected his brother had several motives. He'd always been a multitasker.

Oliver crossed his arms over his chest. "As a matter of fact, yes. I'm going to say some things I should have said long ago."

A chill settled over Callum. "Are you planning on committing suicide?"

Oliver's jaw dropped in shock. "No. Why on earth would you say that?"

"Knew a bloke who offed himself. For three weeks, he made amends to everyone, apologizing for things he'd done years before. At the time we thought he was just trying to be less of an arsehole. Then he shot himself through the head the night before our game with Liverpool Football Club. The next day the press came forward with a story and some pictures, outing him for being gay. It's funny what people think is worth dying over."

The clubhouse could be a cruel place at times, but Callum couldn't imagine the choice his teammate had made. The one he was afraid his brother might make. He hadn't even been able to talk to Rory about it. But from the second Talib had mentioned Oliver's visit, Callum had feared this possibility.

Oliver stared at him for a long moment. "I remember that incident. I've no plan to kill myself. I promise you on my honor."

Something inside Callum's chest eased, but he wasn't done. "It isn't enough to not kill yourself, brother. It's time for you to start living again."

His older brother groaned but at least he wasn't tossing him out on his arse.

Oliver crossed the room. "I came nearly three thousand

miles to avoid this lecture."

Callum followed. "I thought you came here to apologize to Tori and Alea. By the way, I get Tori. You completely owe her an apology because you were an asshat."

Oliver turned. "What?"

"Asshat. It's an American phrase. Tori uses it a lot. Apparently hats are made infinitely more terrible if they're on an arse. Who knows why Americans say anything, but you have to admit they come up with some colorful insults. You were also a douchebag and a douche nozzle. Really, anything that can attach to a douche."

Oliver was still for a moment, then he burst out laughing. "I will try not to be attached to a douche again, I promise. I do owe her an apology and I wanted to clear a few things up with her tonight. As for Alea, I have my reasons for apologizing. Do you want a drink? The sheikh stocks his bars well."

"No, I want to go into this evening with all my faculties."

He would need them. Tori might not be happy to see them. Who was he kidding? She wasn't going to be happy. He hoped there were no blunt instruments lying about when she found them.

"You've grown up, Cal."

"Sometimes I don't act like it, but I really am ready to be the man Tori needs."

A wistful smile crossed his brother's face. "I'm glad for you. So you and Rory have figured everything out? You know, where Tori is concerned?"

He hadn't expected that question, but he was pleased Oliver was opening up a bit. "Yes, we've discussed it and I'm going to take her backside. I've got more experience with anal than Rory, so I think I'm the man to do it. Rory will practice, of course, and then we'll flip positions occasionally."

Oliver's jaw dropped for the second time. "That is not what I meant."

Callum sighed. "Oh, sorry. I suppose that was a lot of information."

Oliver had gone pink and he strode toward the door that connected the parlor to the bedroom. "Yes. That was quite too much information, but I'm glad you've given it such thought. Now have you made any plans to marry her before you start perverting her?"

"You know you used to be quite perverse before that stick lodged up your arse." He wasn't going to let Oliver's newfound prudishness make him feel ashamed. What he was planning to do was a beautiful act between two brothers—who would try very hard not to glance at each other's junk—and the woman they loved.

Oliver stepped back out into the sitting room, working at the tie around his precisely buttoned-up collar. "I'm not the only one who thinks it's out of the norm. How are you going to protect Tori from the tabloids?"

"If we behave normally, our marriage will be front page news for exactly three minutes. I was thinking we announce the marriage, have the sheikh release a few official photos, along with his endorsement of the marriage. Then we'll go on a nice long honeymoon in the country. While we're having weeks and weeks of depraved sex with our wife, everyone will lose interest. Do you think our choices will hurt the company?"

"Of course not. We're solid. We can weather any storm. I'm not worried about the company. I'm worried about Tori."

"She handles this kind of thing all the time." She was brilliant at deflecting negative press.

"Yes, for other people. She's never been in the eye of the storm herself, and I don't think she'll handle her own scandal well. She nearly broke down when I found you with her. She was ready to walk away from everything because she didn't want to face us again. She walked away from everything rather than deal with the fallout. Her embarrassment was more important than her job, it seems."

"Maybe it was her broken heart. You hurt her with your terrible accusations and she probably couldn't think of a single reason why she should stay and hear more of your contempt." Callum offered an alternate suggestion with a sardonic lift of his brow.

Oliver gave him a half-shrug, as if admitting that his younger brother might have a point. "I think you're going to have a hard time convincing her she can handle the pressure."

Put like that, her actions concerned him. "Do you think she believes we're not worth it?"

"I'm not certain she's figured that out yet. I worry she won't allow herself to. I suspect she intends to leave for America soon."

"How do you know that?"

"I don't. But I know how to run away from a problem, Cal. I'm an expert at it. Why do you think I'm here? I'm looking for closure so I don't make the same mistakes again. I hate myself for what I did to Tori that night. I don't want to hurt another woman the way I hurt her."

"How are you going to handle it once she's married to Rory and me? I know you doubt it's going to happen, but I can't live without her. I'll do whatever it takes to make it happen."

"To be honest, I don't know." Oliver sighed. "That's another thing I'm trying to figure out."

"There's always a place for you with us," Callum offered, hoping that Oliver truly listened. "Just think about it. You wouldn't have to worry about who would take care of Tori if something happened to you. You also wouldn't have to worry about her suddenly turning into Satan because I obviously have better taste in women than you."

"You think so?" Oliver laughed. "I will point out your fling with Thea."

Callum couldn't argue that. "Yes, but I've come up in the world. Tori is nothing like Thea."

"She's not Yas, either. I know that. I simply don't know

how I would feel about sharing her. I can be possessive."

Holy hell. They were talking about it. Oliver was actually talking about the possibility of sharing Tori. Callum wasn't sure what his older brother had been doing whilst he was away, but it seemed to have done Oliver a world of good. "Rory and I are both figuring it out moment by moment. We want the same thing out of life. That's a start."

"Well, it seems all the good places are taken." Oliver deflected his seriousness with a smirk.

"Oh, we rotate, brother, and that girl has a saucy mouth."

Oliver's grin widened. "You're quite creative when it comes to penetrating a woman."

"It's a calling." Callum winked, thinking that maybe Ollie wasn't the only one who needed to apologize. "I'm sorry about the fight we had. I should have talked to you before I decided to claim Tori. I knew both you and Rory had a thing for her. I was being selfish. I hadn't thought it through."

"I'm sorry about the fight, too. I lost my temper."

Callum paused, looking for the right words. "You know… I truly think sharing Tori is a good solution for all of us."

"I'm not certain of that. I'm not certain of anything except that I need to talk to her."

"Do you still want her?" Callum asked.

"Yes, more than I want my next breath, but I'm not sure I'm good for her."

It was a start. "That's the beauty of this relationship, brother. We bolster each other's weaknesses. She's always got the three of us."

Oliver seemed to ponder that for a long moment. "I hadn't thought of it that way."

The door flung open suddenly, and Rory dashed inside, his eyes wild. He'd put on his tux, but his tie was undone and it looked as if his hair had endured a windstorm.

Rory stopped short, staring at the two of them. "You're

not fighting." He sounded shocked. "I realized Cal was gone and I figured he'd come here."

Oliver sent Rory a deeply superior stare. "Callum and I are adults and we get on quite well."

It was good to feel like they were on the same side. Rory could be very bossy.

"That's right." Callum nodded.

Rory frowned. "I don't know that I like you two putting on a united front."

But he was smiling, most likely since it had been such a long time since they'd been united on anything. Not since before what had happened in this room.

This very room. Callum hadn't recognized it before. The whole place had been redone, but now he could see this was the room where Oliver had nearly been killed.

Was he back to wallow in the past? Or had he truly come back for closure?

"Rory, come here. You've made a complete mess of that tie." Oliver took over while their youngest brother fussed back at him.

One way or another, Callum would get his family back together. Starting tonight.

* * * *

"Is it time, Your High Ass?" Tori kind of coughed the last couple of words. Shortly after her sister had married the al Mussad brothers, Tori had taken a class on protocol and been told that she must always refer to her sister as "Your Highness." That had not gone over well.

Piper looked utterly luminous as she turned and smiled her way. "Oh, how I've missed your smart mouth. I almost thought it was gone."

"Never." She was going to miss being on the same continent as her sister. And her nephews. Life wasn't the same without them. "My sarcasm goes on and on."

Piper slipped her hand into Tori's as they ascended the stairs. At the top, they would line up to step down into the magnificently elegant ballroom. The space really consisted of several rooms used for entertaining on a grand scale, including a massive formal dining room, the grand ballroom, and a large reception hall for splashy entrances. All of the guests, including many members of the press, were in the reception hall on the first floor of the public wing, waiting for them. These rooms were far from the other two wings of the palace, one each for business and residential purposes. All led to the amazing gardens that surrounded the palace. Tori planned on smiling and waving, then running straight for the shelter of the magnificent greenery outside.

She would give it an hour before she disappeared to cozy up in her PJs and whatever ice cream she could find. She would turn on the satellite dish and try to find some juicy TV. Anything to make her forget about the three men she'd left behind in England.

"You both look lovely." Kadir stepped up and winked her way. "You know my cousins are here."

That was so *not* happening. "Please tell them I would love a dance."

She would be gone by the time the music started.

"Liar," her sister whispered.

"I will tell them. They'll be very excited." Kadir turned to Rafiq, who was walking up with Talib. All three men looked resplendent in their formal wear. She couldn't help but remember how the Thurston-Hughes brothers appeared so masculine and gorgeous in their tuxedos.

Rafe winked her way as he tucked Piper's hand into his own. "Abdul will be thrilled. He's done nothing but talk about Tori since he first saw her picture. He's told his brothers that you're the one."

Unfortunately, there was no one for her. Even if she could have the three she wanted, she shouldn't. She couldn't handle the complexities of that kind of relationship the way her sister did.

Tori stepped away and took her place at the back of the group.

"A thousand Euros says she dances with none of them this evening." Talib gave his brothers a superior grin.

They started up the stairs. Ahead, she spotted Princess Alea and her husbands being announced. They entered, Dane leading the way. On either side of Alea, Landon and Cooper surrounded her. She was protected by them.

Her sister's husbands would enter in the same formation, Talib in the lead.

And Tori would bring up the rear. Alone.

"I'll take that bet," Kade said.

"I don't know. I think Tal knows something we don't. Do you think our visitor will be a problem?" Rafe asked as they moved toward the top of the stairs.

"Visitor?" Tori asked.

"We have many visitors," Tal explained. "Tonight we will celebrate Bezakistan's founding. It should be a wonderful occasion. And very entertaining. Shall we? The boys are downstairs with their nanny. We'll greet the party and let them make a brief appearance."

She so hoped her nephews pooped on a dignitary. Or the press. That would be fun. Maybe all her clients from now on should be babies. They were sweeter than most of her clientele and they rarely made as big a mess. Michael and Sabir's dirty bottoms had nothing on a Thurston-Hughes scandal.

She followed her family up the steps. At the top, they were presented to the guests with all appropriate pomp and circumstance. As they descended into the ballroom, guests clapped and cheered in support for the royal family. Tori hoped no one noticed she was struggling with her shoes. Piper had picked out a gorgeous strapless Gucci gown in a luscious cream color and to-die-for Charlotte Olympia shoes, but the dress was slightly too long, the heels definitely too high. And Tori wished she had a wrap. She was showing a lot more cleavage than she ever comfortably revealed.

Breathe. She tried not to look out over the glittering crowd. During times like this, she realized how far her sister had come. Piper was regal, gracefully managing each step while she smiled and nodded to the crowd. She was at ease with their attention and the three men who made up her world. Tori bet her sister would have handled the situation with Oliver and Callum differently. Piper was strong. If she'd been caught in that conference room with Callum's hand on her hoo haw, she wouldn't have stood there in shame. She would have told Oliver to stop whining and join in or get the hell out and let her enjoy her time with Callum. Piper would likely have walked right up to Rory and kissed him, then laid out the law to all three of them.

Piper could also weather the storm that would follow.

No. She'd decided. She was going back to Texas. She would accept the Black Oak Oil job she'd been offered not an hour before. Eventually, she would find a nice guy and live a quiet life. That was her speed. No cameras. No paparazzi. No crazy headlines. Just her and a nice man and some very normal children.

She made it to the edge of the last step, focusing on the back of Kadir's shoulders rather than the waiting sea of faces, when she released the side of her dress. Then she somehow stepped on her hem. As she lost her balance and started to topple over, she heard the gasps of the crowd. Flashbulbs flared, and Tori could see the headline: *Royal Celebration Ruined by Clumsy Sister.* She was going to break a leg. She couldn't watch. Her ankle was twisting as she went down.

Right before she hit the floor, muscular arms surrounded her, cradling her from the fall. She opened her eyes ready to thank whichever al Mussad brother had caught her.

"Are you all right, sweetheart?" Rory's stare delved hers.

Rory was here? Or had she taken a header down the stairs and conked her skull? Was she now seeing things?

Maybe she had a concussion. Could those cause realistic visions?

"Love?" Another familiar voice hit her ear. Callum.

Flashbulbs popped again. Whispers and gasps all around them resounded.

"Mindy, what happened?" Piper whirled around to her, then sent a warning stare to Rory and Callum. "What are you two doing here?"

At least her sister hadn't known.

Tori tried to get to her feet, but Rory's arms tightened around her.

"They are my guests." Talib took Piper's hand. "And they seem to have the situation in hand. Gentlemen, I suggest you take her someplace private for a chat. This reunion does not require gawkers."

Talib had known, damn him. She pushed her way out of Rory's arms, struggling to find her feet in the tight dress. "Your guests? You invited them here?"

"Tori, please. The press," Piper whispered.

She glanced around. Everyone was staring. Oliver shouldered his way through the crowd, wearing a fierce frown. The whole gang was here. Yippee. They would all get to witness her humiliation.

Oliver stepped in front of her and reached for her bodice.

She slapped at him. "What are you doing?"

"Slipping your nipple back into your dress. I think the press has more than enough photos," he explained matter of factly.

"Oh, my god." When she'd fallen, part of her right breast had slipped free.

"Please, Rafiq, have the orchestra begin as soon as possible," Talib murmured.

Piper tried to pull away from him. "I need to help my sister."

Tal leaned in, his voice quiet, but Tori could hear him. "The reporters will follow you, dear. Your sister has help.

Allow her men to do their jobs. This is a request, *habibti*. Don't make me command what you know is right."

Piper nodded and sent Tori a small smile. "It's going to be okay." She turned back to the crowd. "I think it's time we gathered the princes for a photo op."

The minute she waved her hand, the nanny brought the two princes forward. Sure enough, everyone's attention immediately went to the adorable royal babies. Her sister and Talib held the boys for pictures as Rafe and Kadir started on damage control.

"I'll try to secure the images, but I can't take every camera." Kade headed for the reporters.

She'd messed everything up.

Tori turned to start back up the stairs. If she were her own client she would tell herself to straighten her dress and paste on a smile and dance with her head held high. It was better to laugh off a mistake than to let the public see you cry. Maybe she could have done it if she'd had any experience with that personally and no one had seen how gauche and graceless she'd been.

Rory gripped her hand. "You're not leaving."

Anger flared through her. Leaving was better than suffering horrible humiliation. "You don't have a say in what I do."

Callum was suddenly at her side as though ready to stop her should she climb any further up the stairs. "Darling, we need to dance. Smile and talk to the reporters. Nothing happened to you that hasn't happened to every starlet in Hollywood. You had a wardrobe malfunction. It's not the end of the world."

"It's not your boob that's going to be plastered all over the papers tomorrow," she hissed back.

Callum's eyes went arctic cold. "Like hell it's not. Now, stop acting like a brat or I'll throw you over my knee and give the press a real story to report."

Oliver stood at the bottom of the stairs, watching them.

163

"While that might be amusing, I think we should spank her privately. Do I have a vote? We haven't talked about it. Is this a democratic ménage?"

What was Oliver talking about? "Callum can't spank me."

He leaned in, his voice right against her ear. "I can and I will. I already owe you for lying to me about your engagement in London. You'll thank me when it's over. I can be deeply indulgent, but I also know when to take control. You might be clever, love, but I can play a rough game and I always play to win. I might do it with an idiotic grin on my face, but that's a mask. You keep pushing me and you'll meet the real man."

A shiver went down her spine that had only the tiniest thing to do with fear. The rest was pure arousal.

"Come on. We'll put in an appearance. Then the four of us will go somewhere to talk," Rory commanded. It wasn't a suggestion.

The hardness of his tone shocked Tori…but perhaps it shouldn't. After all, Rory had taken over the company when their father died. Sometimes it was easy to forget that Rory had steered the ship while Oliver had gotten married and Callum had played football. He'd been the glue, and when Oliver needed something to occupy his mind after Yasmin's betrayal, Rory had been strong enough to relinquish some of his power to his eldest brother.

"We don't have anything to talk about." But she allowed Rory to lead her off the steps. She was still shaky. At least her ankle was feeling solid. She hadn't sprained anything except her ego. "My brother-in-law sent you a check."

And she'd be repaying him until the end of time.

"Which I promptly tore up," Rory explained, looking so sleek in his tux. If he had a martini in his hand, he would remind her of James Bond. Sophisticated, gorgeous, and dangerous. He threaded her arm through his, stabilizing her. "Those shoes are lovely, but you're going to break a leg in them. You'll need to take them off before we dance."

"I can't take them off. I can't walk around here without shoes."

"Of course you can," Callum said.

"Why do you think it's a problem, Tori?" Oliver asked. "And while I'm asking questions, why does your sister call you Mindy?"

Why was Oliver acting so calmly? And why had he mentioned the word ménage as if it included him?

Rory helped her into the grand ballroom where the orchestra was starting up. "My sister calls me Mindy because it's my first name. I thought Torrance sounded more like a publicist. And I can't go barefoot because it's rude."

"Who says it's rude?" Rory steered her to one of the tables that formed an elegant *U* around the dance floor.

A waiter with a tray of champagne strolled by. Callum snagged a glass and pressed it in her hand as Rory gently sat her down.

She took a long sip of the bubbly. Tori suspected she was going to need it. "Everyone knows you don't go to a formal ball barefoot."

Callum sat down opposite her and before she could protest, he pulled her right foot into his lap and eased the shoe off, the warmth of his big hands sliding over her aching foot. She bit back a moan as his thumb slid up the arch of her foot. "Relax, love. The worst is over. Once we prove everything is normal, they'll stop watching us."

"Normal?" She kept her voice low because the ballroom was filling up and sure enough, now that the royal princes were leaving, everyone began looking their way. Rory sat beside her, his hand on her shoulder while Oliver loomed over her like a watchful sentry. "There is nothing normal about this situation. I'm sure they're already gossiping that you three and I are..." She shook her head. "Let go of my foot."

"Only so I can move on to the other one." Callum

4

Shayla Black and Lexi Blake

exchanged her right foot for her left, giving it the same attention.

"Do you need another drink?" Oliver asked. "Perhaps some food? When was the last time you ate? You look a bit pale."

God, Callum knew how to rub a foot. She tried to focus. "It's none of your concern."

His thumb dug into her arch, nearly relaxing into a catatonic state. "Love, I want you to think about how good this feels. The spanking won't feel like this. Nor will you like it when I put those sweet little nipples in clamps."

"You brought nipple clamps?" Oliver asked, his voice going husky.

"We brought two kits, and the sheikh has promised that he can provide anything we need," Rory explained. "I don't believe Oliver has ever gone to a club, but I've been training with Callum for the last six months. I began when I realized what a firm hand you'll need."

Tori's head was muddled. She still wasn't sure she wouldn't wake up any minute and realize all of this was a surreal dream. Part of her prayed she would do just that because she wasn't sure she could refuse them when they came at her together. "Training?"

Rory couldn't be talking about what she thought he was talking about. But a glance at his face said otherwise. Her heart sped up. She didn't want or need BDSM. Her sister played with her husbands. They hadn't discussed it much beyond Piper assuring her it was consensual. Tori hadn't understood the point, so Piper had equipped her with a stack of romantic BDSM novels. These fictional lovers explored and indulged their darkest desires. They played hard and loved well.

Tori wasn't certain she could handle that from them.

"Do you understand where you and Oliver went wrong?" Callum kissed her foot, then set it aside.

"I opened my bloody mouth," Oliver said with sigh.

166

She nodded. "Yep. He opened his mouth."

"Not precisely. Neither one of you said enough. Ollie, you said all the wrong things at the wrong time. Tori, my love, did you bother to mention that little gem you were gifting him with?" Callum asked.

Her virginity. She didn't want to talk about it, but somehow she didn't think Callum would let it go. He seemed so much more serious and confident than usual. Callum was often an adorable goofball. Except when he'd gotten her alone and practically stripped her down and gave her the sort of orgasm she'd dreamed about.

She should tell him it was none of his business, but for some reason she found herself answering him. "No. I tried, but things moved too fast."

"I wasn't listening and I didn't ask," Oliver admitted. "And I was very surprised to learn the truth." He knelt beside her, taking her hand into his. "Tori, I'm sorry for the way I treated you. I've got no excuse except that I was upset. The whole time we were together, I told you it was only one night, but I was already thinking of ways to keep you. I wanted to make you my mistress. When I realized you were a virgin, I suspected you would say no to that."

Anger flared again. "Yes. I mean no. I mean yes, I would have said no to that." She pulled away and started to stand. This chat was over. "I think I've made enough of a fool of myself for one evening."

"Oliver, step up." Callum instructed, looking to his brother. "Top her."

The eldest brother flushed and she wondered why. After surviving the fallout from Yasmin, he'd always seemed utterly untouchable. "I don't know if that's a good idea."

"Then this won't work." Callum shook his head.

Why was she sitting here as if waiting for their permission? She could make a clean getaway now before they hurt her again. Tori grabbed her shoes.

"You have to help her, Ollie. Tori's pride is telling her to walk away as fast as her sore feet will carry her," Rory explained. "She's hesitating because she doesn't actually want to leave us. If she did, she'd already be halfway out the door. If you top her, you'll help her past her pride so the two of you can talk."

"I do not need anyone to top me. I know what I want," Tori blurted. Then she paused.

Perhaps she was being incredibly stubborn. She was thinking with her pride and didn't know how to get around it without making herself vulnerable. They'd ripped her apart once. She wasn't sure she could handle being crushed again.

But maybe if she was careful with her heart, she could have a night with them. *Just one*, that voice in her head whispered to her, luring her like an addiction. One more night, and she could move on.

If she listened to that voice in her head, it would lure her to doom. She was saving herself.

Tori jumped, scanning the room for the nearest exit.

"Oliver?" Callum prompted, his tone deeper and darker than she'd ever heard.

Suddenly, Oliver grabbed her hand and led her to the dance floor.

She struggled against his hold. "Let me go."

"Not until we've talked," Oliver insisted. "If you still want to leave here alone, I'll let you go. I can't speak for my brothers. I think they'll hunt you down and persuade you, but if you tell me plainly you don't want me, then I'll leave."

"I don't want you." She didn't. Not really. How could she want him after the way he'd treated her?

The orchestra played a slow song, and she found herself in Oliver's arms, against his body. "I said *after* you listen to me. This behavior doesn't suit you, Torrance."

"What behavior?" She wouldn't let him shame her. She hadn't torn his heart to shreds.

"You're acting like a spoiled brat." His hand tightened on her waist, pressing her against his body. "My brothers are certainly right about that. I've come thousands of mile to apologize and make amends. Are you telling me I don't deserve a few moments of your time? We were friends once."

Okay, maybe she was going to let him shame her. She couldn't forget the way he'd faced down a thug with a knife for her. And yes, they had been friends. "Fine. I'm listening."

"Are you?" He kept moving, his long legs graceful as he led her around the dance floor. "I'm starting to think Callum is smarter than I gave him credit for. You and I should have talked, especially before anything happened between us. But neither of us wanted to do that."

"I was caught up in the adrenaline."

"Are you telling me it was only adrenaline?" he challenged. "It wasn't for me. I used that as an excuse, but I wanted you very badly and I jumped at the chance to have you, no matter the cost. I was passionate about you, but passion isn't the most forgiving mistress. It's easy to give in to passion. It's harder to care for someone and take responsibility. I should have taken care of you. And I'm deeply sorry."

She softened against him, her body finding the rhythm he set in time with the music. It felt good to be in his arms, even if his logic hurt. He was completely right. "I took the chance. I knew I shouldn't have waited to tell you about my virginity or tried so halfheartedly, but I didn't want to stop. I knew if we talked…"

"If we'd talked, we wouldn't have done it." He slowed, his cheek resting against her temple. "And that is how we made a horrible mistake. We should be able to talk, shouldn't we?"

"Did you really think I would be your mistress?"

He chuckled, the sound caressing her skin. "I wanted a way to make you mine without having to love you. So that's where my thoughts went." He pulled back slightly, tilting her head up. "It's not you, Tori. Please believe me. You are the single most lovable woman I've ever met, but I'm hollow inside and I don't think anything can fill me up again."

She laid her head against his shoulder with a sigh. He'd told her as much. He'd never said it in so many words, but she knew what his wife had done to him and she'd known he considered himself damaged beyond repair. "I think one day you'll meet the woman of your dreams and you won't feel so hollow anymore."

She wished it could have been her. It was better this way, she told herself. She couldn't live in the same world as the Thurston-Hughes brothers. Tonight had proven it. She wanted to be behind the scenes, liked blending in and helping people. Being in front of all those cameras and enduring the constant scrutiny? Not for her. Still, knowing that their separation was for the best didn't make her heart ache less.

"You *are* the woman of my dreams, Tori. I just can't wake up from my nightmare. God, I wish I'd met you when I was twenty." His hand smoothed down her hair. "I'm not a good man."

"You are. I've seen you. You can be kind when you want to be."

"I don't want to be most of the time. I'm also not a strong man. I know it's best if I step aside, but I don't want to. I think that makes me selfish."

"What are you saying, Oliver?"

"I'm saying my brothers want you and they're willing to let me play. I would be faithful. I wouldn't have any other lovers. I promise I would take care of you this time."

She blinked up at him, suddenly stopping in the middle of the dance floor. Of all the reasons they could be here, she hadn't even considered this one. "Are you saying Rory and Callum want to share me?"

His lips curled up in the most delicious smile. "You hadn't figured that out? Yes. They're serious about it. They've spent the last couple of weeks negotiating."

"Negotiating?" Her mind was humming. It was a horrible idea. Right? Horrible. She might tear the brothers apart, so the idea was only, like, ten percent interesting. Twenty, tops. The other eighty percent of that idea was pure stupidity.

Unless… Could they keep it quiet? Could they be secret lovers?

"I think it's what Doms do. I'm not sure. I haven't really been to a club, though my brothers have explained the philosophy. I'm afraid Callum might talk you to death before he drags out all those toys he likes to use. Either way, don't expect they'll let you go without a fight. They're willing to let me in. I'm asking if you'll let me, Tori. I don't know what will happen between us precisely. I can promise that I'll respect you and care for you. I'll always be your friend. No matter what your answer is. I'm always going to be a man you can count on."

For anything but love.

Then again, she wasn't looking for love. She couldn't afford it. By the end of the week, she would be back in Dallas and moving on with her life. No matter how intrigued she was by everything Oliver and his brothers plotted, she knew she couldn't handle this life.

"I don't need a pledge of devotion, Oliver."

"But you deserve one." He frowned, his eyes crinkling as though he was attempting to figure out what to say. "I'm trying, Tori."

She'd been so angry with him these past few weeks, but that was a useless emotion. She'd figured out a long time ago that a person had to want to be saved. Her father hadn't wanted it. He'd given in to the grief of losing their mother. Nothing his daughters had said or done made him want to live again because he'd no longer had the will. Nothing would alter Oliver's outlook unless he wanted to change.

Sorrow for what might have been weighed on her. The best she could do was give him some peace.

"I forgive you," she murmured. "We've both made mistakes. I suspect going to bed with you again would be another."

He sighed and leaned forward, kissing her forehead. "I hope you reconsider. I think my time is up. Tori, if I could change anything in my whole life, do you know what it would be?"

She could imagine. "Your first marriage."

He shook his head. "No. I deserved that. I was careless and stupid and I married for all the wrong reasons. I would change what happened between us. I would go back and be gentle with you. I would make it good for you. Whatever happens, know that it's not supposed to be like that. Your lover should make you feel like the goddess you are. I wish I had shown you that."

Tears blurred her vision and she gripped him when he started to move away. "Why do you think you're a bad man, Oliver? Yasmin did those things to you. They weren't your fault."

A shadow seemed to cross his face. "My father used to say you don't know what kind of a man you are until you face death. How you face it is the sum of your soul. I don't have much of a soul, I'm afraid. I don't have much to give you and I don't deserve you. I'll be honest, if it weren't for my brothers I would never have considered touching you again. Not because I don't want to. I want you so badly I ache with it, but I care about you. I'm not good for you, but Callum and Rory won't let me hurt you, so I'm being selfish. If you decide to give them a go, I'd like to be there. I need one good thing and I think bringing you pleasure could be it."

"May I cut in?" Rory stepped up.

Oliver released her, moving her hand into Rory's. "Of course. Where did Callum go?"

"He went back to our room to prepare a few things. Tori has made her appearance at this event. I spoke with Talib and he's still trying to get all the photos from her mishap. He's already dealt with the local photographers. There won't be any pictures of her in Bezakistani newspapers," Rory reassured.

"It will get out." She'd been doing her job for too long to be naïve about her chances of the incident going away.

They would run a blurred photo of her. Now that she thought about it, maybe she'd made a big deal out of nothing. She was the sister of a royal. The press preferred Piper. So she'd had a tiny nip slip. Maybe, given the dim light and the thick crowd, the wardrobe malfunction had barely registered in a photo. The press would blow it out of proportion and put a huge star over her barely-there nipple and the world wouldn't end.

Talking to Oliver had put a few things in perspective.

She had no idea why he thought he'd seen his soul and found it wanting, but she knew a man in pain when she saw one. He'd changed since the night he'd taken her virginity. This was a different Oliver, more contemplative. More thoughtful. More in need than ever.

"I'll go help him." Oliver nodded and walked away.

She found herself in Rory's arms. Quiet, polite Rory. She could handle him. Truly, Rory would listen to reason and she could move forward with her plans for a very quiet evening— and a very quiet life—alone. "What is Callum preparing?"

"The bedroom for our play," he said matter of factly. He could have been talking about the weather. "Do you know how to waltz, love? The next song is a waltz."

Her head spun, and she shook her head. "No. I don't."

"Put your feet on top of mine and relax. I paid the orchestra to ensure the next song is a waltz. You see, I'm the only one of the three of us who paid attention in dance class. Oliver was too busy ogling the teacher and Callum, for all his athleticism, has horrible rhythm. Really, this will be our thing. I'll teach you to waltz first. Eventually, we'll tango. That's my favorite."

Tori squirmed in his arms. The notion of them sharing a dance thing was sweet but... She would have to let him down gently. "I'm sure you're very good, but I don't really want lessons."

"That's why you're going to stand on my feet and I'm going to do all the work."

"I'm too heavy. Rory, if you have something to say, can't we sit down and talk?"

Those polite blue eyes hardened, turning to steel. "Darling, I'm through talking. I've talked to you for months and all it got me was sent to the back of the line. I was acting like a self-sacrificing martyr, but I'm done with that. I'm afraid you're going to have to deal with me."

"I don't understand." The whole world seemed to have tilted and she wasn't sure where she stood anymore.

"I'm well aware. You didn't fully know me before. I let Oliver take the reins of the company because he needed the work to occupy him and he needed to feel in control. So I stepped aside from the CEO position and took over legal. When he's ready for another role, I'll assume the helm again. I'm the shark, Tori. I've buried that part of me because my brothers needed someone to hold us all together, but I've always been the shark. So you're going to have to deal with me and I'm not going to politely sit down and listen to all the reasons you think this won't work. I'm going to dance with you and lay out my rationale. You'll listen because I haven't even had a kiss out of you yet."

Heat zipped down her spine. Tori had been fooled by his gentlemanly façade, but she now sensed his ruthlessness underneath like a living thing. He didn't play fair. For some reason, that turned her on. "How is that my fault? I didn't even know you wanted to kiss me."

"Didn't you? I suspect you did. Here's the thing, darling. You can dance with me or I'll take that kiss here and now in front of everyone."

She flushed. She could feel her skin turning pink. He wouldn't. She glanced up at him through her lashes and changed her mind. He would—absolutely. He would lay his lips over hers and claim her lips in front of everyone so there would be no mistaking that she belonged to him.

The orchestra began the waltz and she decided to not start another scandal. Very gingerly she stepped onto Rory's dress shoes, her right hand in his as she placed her left on his shoulder.

"Good choice." He wrapped his free arm around her waist, and she felt his strength as he pressed her against his body. "Typically we would keep a bit of space between us, but I don't feel like playing by the rules this evening. A good dance is a lot like making love. It should be two bodies in complete sync, trust and joy marking the movements. Hang on to me."

She gasped as he took off. The ballroom whirled around her, but Rory held her firmly and he wasn't letting her fall. After a moment of panic, complete exhilaration took over. She'd never danced before. Not like this. Rory held her tight, twirling her across the parquet floor. She relaxed and let her body flow against his.

He led her effortlessly. This was what he was offering her. He would assume control. He and Callum, and if she allowed him, Oliver, too. They would take control, surround and protect her. All she had to do was hold them tight and let go of everything else.

Tori wasn't certain she could manage that in the long run, but for a night… Yes, she could have her night with them.

The music invaded her soul as she let Rory steer them around and around. The rest of the world seemed to fade away as he swept her into euphoria. Tori felt safe with his arms around her. Nothing else mattered—or existed—except Rory and the cresting music enveloping them. A thrill went through her like nothing she'd felt before. She couldn't help but smile because he was so beautiful and he made her feel alive.

The music began to wind down, and Tori wished it would lilt on longer. As Rory started to slow, she realized everyone stared at them. The people on the dance floor had stopped to watch her and Rory. But he didn't pay them any mind. His eyes were steady on her as he finished the dance with a flourish. The crowd around them applauded.

Piper stood nearby, grinning broadly. When she caught Tori's eye, she winked. More flashbulbs burst in the dim room. The speculative whispers started all around them again. Tori tensed.

"Relax. Smile." Rory eased her off his feet. "They're watching us because we're lovely and I'm a brilliant dancer. Could have gone pro if I wanted to, but I decided one full-of-himself celebrity in the family was enough." He grinned, then nodded to the crowd. "Thank you."

"That's not a nice way to talk about your brother." Maybe it was a stupid thing to say, but talking about Callum was better than acknowledging all the stares on them.

"It's true. Did you know that one year he gave us all signed footballs for Christmas?" Rory started to lead her off the dance floor.

Her heart still pounded, her mind whirling from the excitement. And her nipples were hard just from being so close to him. She hoped no one noticed. "I'm sure he simply didn't have time to be more personal."

His fingers laced through hers. "He makes the time now. I shoved that damn thing up his arse, and now he's more thoughtful. You'll have to be that way with Callum from time to time. He doesn't always think. Put him on his arse when he requires it and everything will run smoothly. Outside the bedroom, of course. He won't take orders when you're intimate, but you'll have a good deal of control with him in the real world. It's Oliver you'll have to worry about. He's the one who'll tell you everything is fine when his world is falling apart."

She had to protest. "But I'm not—"

"Don't let him get away with it," Rory kept on as if she hadn't spoken at all. "Fine is like his safe word. When he uses it, everything needs to stop."

"Safe word?" She knew that meant a word the submissive used if she'd had too much of a punishment or got scared.

Rory stopped and turned, looming over her like a gorgeous Viking god. "Yes. I was joking about Oliver's— mostly. But you should choose yours. You'll need one very soon."

Her dress suddenly felt way too tight. "I don't think any of this is a good idea."

Heat and desire lit his blue eyes as his fingers tightened around hers. "Don't be scared. Everything we'll do to you is designed to bring you pleasure and draw us closer together. I've trained for this day."

"But you... I-I didn't know you wanted me."

"I fought like hell to hide how I felt. The first time I went to a club, I thought I could rid myself of my desire for you. I followed Callum, seeking a sub who looked like you. I planned to purge myself so I could help Oliver find his way. I found a pretty sub with hair like yours and I trained with her. I learned everything necessary but I felt almost nothing because she wasn't you. I couldn't muster any desire whatsoever to touch her in a sexual way because the minute you walked in the door, I belonged to you. I don't know why or how, but I haven't looked at another woman since we met. I know Oliver hurt you, but I can't help but be happy because it forced Callum and me to come to terms. I think in the end, that's exactly what Oliver needed to be comfortable with our marriage."

"M-marriage?" She squeaked out the word.

Tori didn't ask if he was serious. His weight and the heat of his dark stare told her he was.

"Yes, don't think for a second that I'll settle for anything less. I love you, Tori."

She so wasn't ready for that. She didn't know how to believe it. Sex was easier. One night with the three of them was something she could conceive of. "I'm not thinking of the future. I'm honestly not thinking of anything at all, Rory. I can't. I'm not staying here."

"I know you're not."

A hand touched her elbow. "Torrance? I am Abdul al Bashir, cousin to the sheikh. May I have this dance?"

She turned and saw a stunning man. With golden skin and fathomless dark eyes, he was dressed in an immaculate tux and smiled down at her with a flash of white teeth in a stunning face. Oh, he was one of the five cousins she'd absolutely planned on avoiding. No matter how delicious he was, he came with four extras...and her heart belonged elsewhere. Not that she could handle the three currently propositioning her. Not only that, Abdul and his brothers were Bezakistani men. They'd been known to steal the bride they wanted.

Still, it might get her out of temptation's way if she danced with him.

"I'm afraid not. So sorry," Rory lied as he began to tug her away.

Tori stood her ground. "Mr. al Bashir—" Then she squeaked. "What the hell!"

One minute she was talking politely and the next she found herself in Rory's arms, being carried out of the ballroom. Staid, very British Rory Thurston-Hughes picked her up and carried her toward the exit like a pirate with a particularly thrilling bit of booty.

"Rory, what are you doing?" she demanded.

He was supposed to be the reasonable one, but he'd proven that looks could be deceiving.

Rory kicked opened the door to the hallway. Kicked it open. Yeah, nobody noticed that and it certainly didn't make her ovaries melt at all. Nope. She didn't like this side of Rory. Well, no part of her except those softening pink bits and maybe her heart.

"I'm taking charge." He strode down the hall. He didn't pause or hesitate. When he walked past reporters, he didn't bother to look their way. He was a man on a mission.

"Put me down! You can't carry me off. I thought I was supposed to smile at the press and make my nip slip go away." Though she'd actually planned to be long gone by now, Tori realized it was too early to leave.

"I don't care about that. Your breast looked stunning. If it ends up on the front page, I'll make a poster of it. I don't care what other people think. I'm done with that and you need to be done with it, too." He stopped when they passed a security station. The guards allowed them into the palace's private family wing. One even grinned as he opened the door for them.

Once the door closed, they were alone in a grand foyer. The heavy portal blocked the sounds of the party. Now that her surroundings were quiet, she could practically hear her heart pounding.

Finally, Rory stopped, and she found herself on her feet again. Tori tried to catch her breath as he pressed closer and invaded her space. "This is too fast."

His fingers brushed her jawline. He dipped his head low. "No. We've dragged this out for months. I won't slow down. Now that I've made the decision, I can't wait any longer."

His mouth descended on hers in a slow slide. He clutched her hips, pulling her into the cradle of his muscular thighs. His lips took hold of hers, molding in a dominant glide. Her whole body went soft and she was grateful for his arms around her. They held her up when all she wanted to do was drop to her knees.

Rory was kissing her. Finally. Callum had mentioned topping her. She knew what BDSM meant to well-meaning Doms. It meant they cared about her. It meant they protected her and watched over her. She might be naïve, but that was what it meant to her sister and husbands. BDSM didn't guarantee a happily ever after, but it should mean she got a say in whatever happened. If they were going to this much effort, surely she meant something to them.

Tentatively, she let her hands roam Rory's shoulders and back as his tongue plunged inside her mouth. There was no questioning lick. He dominated, delving deep. His tongue slid along hers, luring and tempting Tori.

Every cell in her body seemed to soften, and she felt her pussy growing slick and wet. Heat burned through her flesh, and she slid her left leg against his to get closer. Rory answered with a groan, pressing her against the wall and pushing his erection against her. He felt so big, so hard. Tori writhed against him, trying desperately to rub herself against his cock and satisfy her growing ache.

His forehead pressed to hers as he took a long breath, trying to calm himself. "Keep doing that and I'll prove to you I don't mind risking a scandal. I'll pull up this skirt and fuck you right here."

She had to be the sensible one. "I don't think this will work."

"The sex will be divine. I already know it."

Tori had no doubt of that. "I meant anything more."

"We'll make it work, sweetheart." He brushed another kiss against her lips.

All the reasons it couldn't work pressed on her. The Thurston-Hughes brothers were overwhelmingly possessive men. How could they share? They fought. Would they fight over her? She'd seen Callum's anger at Oliver and she'd wondered… "Why were Oliver and Callum fighting the day the reporter came to the office?"

Even as she asked the question, her hands roved over Rory's hard form. The woman inside her wasn't sure she wanted the answer right now. That part of her craved what these brothers could give her. She might have been a virgin until Oliver, but she wasn't stupid. He could offer her more. They all could, and she wanted to feel the pleasure she'd been denied her first time.

He kissed the line of her jaw, then his tongue found her pulse point, making her shiver with desire. "You, of course.

You didn't see the very nice punch I landed. We were fighting over you, but that's not going to happen again. We've talked in detail. Now we're a united front."

For how long? If she only wanted a night, it didn't matter...but deep down, Tori suspected she wanted far more.

Every cell in her body quaked as he kissed her neck. "Rory, I don't know."

"Yes, you do. You've always known." He took a step back. "But I'm going to give you a choice. If you're scared, walk back into that ballroom and I'll consider the matter finished. I'll talk to Callum and Oliver, and we'll court you in a more proper fashion. We'll be polite and escort you out and take turns like gentlemen. But if you walk into that room with me, there won't be anything polite about the way we take you. I won't be a gentleman. I'll be a Dom. *Your* Dom, and you'll know what it means to be utterly possessed by three men who can't breathe without you. We'll start preparing you because we're going to take you in every way a man can take a woman. Think about this because you're selecting the path we travel. Polite and proper? Or as wild as you can handle it? Do you want to know what it means to submit to men who love you?"

"Yes." The word was out before she could think about it. It didn't matter. Despite all the reasons she shouldn't do this, she couldn't walk away.

"Then come with me." He grabbed her hand and strode down the hall.

Tori hurried after him, knowing nothing would be the same again.

CHAPTER NINE

Oliver stared at his brother as he pulled out a pink plastic plug and laid it on a towel on the bar. Callum had turned the bar into a buffet of sex toys. He wasn't sure he knew what some of them were for. Still, even he knew that was an awfully small plug if it was supposed to serve the purpose he supposed. "I'm bigger than that plug, Cal."

It was a bit surreal to be standing in his brother's room laying out sex toys and talking about how they were going to seduce their woman. He'd never been a big planner when it came to sex. He went with the flow and now he was wondering if that wasn't his problem.

Callum snorted as he pulled out a bottle of lube. "Of course you are, but she's got a little tiny virgin arsehole. It's got to be trained to accept a cock. This is a training plug. When she's used to it, I'll move her up to something bigger. It's going to take a while."

The thought of her virgin backside made him wince as his cock hardened painfully. "How did you get into all this stuff?"

He had to admit he was curious. His brother was so happy-go-lucky. He wouldn't have believed he could turn into a Dominant male, but he could see the change now. Callum wasn't the cheeky boy he knew. He seemed dark and commanding.

"A teammate introduced me. So much of my life was out of my control. I spent all my time reacting—to rivals, to coaches, to fans, to the press. I needed a place where my control was absolute."

Oliver had never thought of it that way. He'd seen Callum as a charming playboy, jetting all over the world and playing a game. He'd never considered that his brother's life had likely been highly regulated by someone other than himself. He would have been told when to practice, when to play. Everyone would have wanted a piece of him. Callum likely had to constantly deal with women like Thea who wanted him for his money and fame and would do anything to get it. No wonder his brother had been determined to seize control where he could.

Oliver thought he had taken back his control when he'd assumed the helm of the company, but now he wondered. Had he pursued the wrong kind of control? "And you think Tori will submit to you? That she needs to?"

Callum started to unbutton his shirt, his jacket and tie gone the minute they'd left the party. "I know she does. I've seen her work. She's excellent at her job, but she's also the kind of woman who tries to please everyone around her. She struggles to say no, and the world is filled with people out there who take advantage of her."

Oliver nodded. "She takes on far too much because she doesn't want to disappoint anyone. I don't see how taking more choices away helps her."

"Because you don't understand the philosophy. I'm not taking a single choice away from her. Every time she obeys in the bedroom, it's because she chooses to. It's because she trusts us with her pleasure. She can always say no and walk away, but I intend to teach her that she never has to. I intend to teach her that she's worthy of being pleased and that her choices matter. Gradually, I hope that she'll learn she can say no to people because she's got a strong core of self-confidence and trust in her family. We'll be the ones who matter."

Oliver frowned. "But—"

"We take control or Talib will do it," Cal cut in. "Tori might think she's going to go her own way, but I know her brother-in-law and he'll make sure no one can take advantage of her. If we don't do something, she'll end up working here in the palace again and Talib will maneuver her into a relationship he feels comfortable with. I happen to have heard he was planning on introducing her to his cousins tonight."

The hell he would.

Callum pointed at him. "There. Tell me what just went through your head. You look quite fierce right now."

"Talib has a woman of his own. He should stay away from…" *Mine.*

He'd been about to call Tori mine.

Callum's lips curled up in obvious satisfaction. "Just because you don't say it doesn't make the facts less true. We can top her or Tal and his brothers will quietly do it until they give up the role to men of their choice. They care about her and she needs someone to watch out for her. It won't work because she's a stubborn little vixen and they can't spank her properly."

"If they try, I'll kill them." He was surprised at how savage he felt at the prospect of someone coming in and organizing her life. She might need it, but he would be damned if he let someone else see to the task. All his good intentions seemed to be flying out the door. He'd intended to apologize and give Tori over to his brothers. After all he'd heard, Oliver wasn't sure he could leave the room tonight if his life depended on it.

"Now you're talking like the brother I know. You always were a possessive arse. And yet you let Yasmin run around with whomever she wanted."

His stomach turned at the very mention of her name. "I don't want to talk about her."

Callum held his hands up, placating him. "I'm merely

pointing out that you never acted possessive with Yasmin. Because you never really loved her. You got caught in her mess. Tori is different. You've been a prick since the day you met her. You tried everything you could to keep the rest of us away."

"And yet here I am."

"Because now you're being a reasonable prick and all you have to do is change one little pronoun. Not my woman. Ours. She's ours. And the good news is if someone needs an arsekicking because they've done our woman wrong, we've got our own gang."

Callum made it sound so easy, but Oliver wasn't sold yet. Oh, he was sold on tonight. He simply wasn't certain it could work long term.

Then the door opened, and he couldn't think about anything but her.

She hurried in behind Rory. A gorgeous flush made her skin glow. Her hair was mussed in a way that made Oliver's dick throb. Rory had gotten his hands on her at some point.

Callum stood beside him. "Fuck, she's gorgeous. Did you finally kiss her?"

The look of satisfaction on his brother's face was nearly palpable. Rory was always so buttoned up and proper, but now his hair was messy, his jacket wrinkled from whatever he'd been doing with Tori, and he seemed so much happier for it. "Not as much as I would have liked, but I believe she understands the situation now."

Tori's gaze moved between the three of them, her eyes wide and her lips swollen. "He's wrong. I don't understand anything."

Oliver was in the same boat. He didn't understand... but he was curious. "Show me how you kissed her, Rory."

He needed to know if he could handle it. The idea of it didn't make him want to murder his brother the way he would have thought. Yes, he'd been furious at Callum for fondling Tori during the fundraiser, but mostly because he'd assumed his younger brother meant to keep the girl for himself. Now Oliver had to know if he could handle his brothers touching her without going into a rage.

A slow smile slid across his brother's face and he reached out to draw Tori in. She gasped, the little sound making Oliver think of a kitten who got caught by a lion. She was small compared to Rory, delicate, but not fragile. Oliver knew from experience how solid Tori was. She wouldn't break. She could handle them even when they were total bastards.

Rory's fingers tangled in her hair as he tilted her head up before his mouth descended on hers. He wasn't soft or sweet. His brother devoured her, and Tori responded. Her whole body softened against his, her breasts crushed to his chest. He watched her, watched how readily she responded to Rory's dominance. Her arms wound around his neck, her hips cuddling his.

She wanted Rory. Did she want him, too?

"Feel the need to rip her away from him?" Callum asked, his voice low.

Oliver shook his head. The truth settled deep inside him. He didn't try to dodge it or rationalize it. He just accepted it. "I like watching her."

She was beautiful and he wouldn't get to see her like this if he was the man doing the kissing. He wouldn't be able to watch how she responded, to really study her. He would be driving toward his own pleasure and now he could see that would be a mistake. Her pleasure would heighten his own. He wanted to give her as much as possible.

Callum stood beside him, his stare all over Tori. "You can really get a sense of what she needs from watching her with someone else. I wouldn't allow this with anyone but the two of you. I couldn't take her to a club and share her with someone else just to watch her. This only works between us. Rory won't run off with her. He won't try to steal her from us."

Rory sighed and gave her lips one last kiss before letting her go. "I couldn't handle her by myself. She's far too much woman for any one man."

Tori flushed, and her lips curled up. Dominance followed by tenderness. She needed both. Was it possible she needed him, too?

"Tori, you know what I want, right?" Callum stepped up, moving into her space.

"Sex," she answered quietly.

Callum loomed over her. "So much more than sex. I want to play with you. I want to share you with my brothers. You'll be the center of our world and we'll give you more pleasure than you can imagine, but you have to obey me if you want it. That's the exchange."

"I want a night with you," she said, biting her lip. "And as you all know, I don't have much experience so following your advice seems logical."

Callum caught her chin, forcing her to look him in the eyes. "This isn't following advice. You'll obey or you'll face the punishment."

She stared up at Callum. "Punishment? You'll really spank me?"

The thought of watching his brother slap her gorgeous arse nearly unmanned Oliver. He needed to get himself under control or he would be no good to her.

"I'll definitely spank you," Callum answered. "You're going to lay yourself over my knee and accept my discipline for lying about a fiancé, running away like a frightened little bird, and forcing us to track you down in order to settle our differences."

A frown turned her lips down. "That's not fair. I didn't know I could get spanked for doing that. And I wasn't a frightened little bird. I was mad as hell."

"I can attest to that." Oliver quipped.

Where had that come from? Was his sense of humor finally coming back after all this time?

Callum kept his gaze steady on her. "Make your decision, Torrance. You will be spanked if you stay in this room. Tell me you're not curious about it. Tell me that pussy of yours isn't already wet and aching at the thought of my hand on your backside. You might not have experience, but you know what you want. You also know that anything worth having requires courage. Can you be brave?"

Tori nodded. "I want it. I want to try everything."

Callum placed a very chaste kiss on her lips. "That's my girl. Now go over there and kiss Oliver. He's as inexperienced in this particular form of play as you are, and I think he's feeling out of place. Can you forgive him for being a wretched arse?"

He was feeling out of place. He was wondering if it wouldn't be better to leave her with Callum and Rory. Did Callum have to point that out just now?

She swayed across the room to him, her body moving with unconscious grace. Oliver found himself caught in the gaze of those somber eyes. She was so beautiful, and he'd treated her so poorly. She'd deserved the world, and he'd given her hell. If she slapped him, he'd endure it. If she wanted to rail at his injustices, he would listen to every word.

"I'm sorry, Tori." He could never apologize enough.

She reached up to him, bracing her hands on his chest. Their gazes met. "I want to erase that night."

That wasn't what he wanted. "I only want to erase the end. I want to go back and hold you, make it good for you."

"Then do it tonight, Oliver." She rose to her tiptoes and brushed her lips over his.

This was what he'd missed for weeks. Oliver caught her in his arms and pressed his body to hers. Her sweet gasp thrilled him. He felt powerful and perfect for her as he took her mouth. Their first time had been too fast. It had become a blur in his head, a rapid-fire rush to pleasure, like all of his encounters since Yasmin. After her, he'd rushed through and taken what he needed, getting his lover off, then running away as soon as possible.

Not this time. He was going to indulge in Tori. He was going to learn every inch of her skin. He would know her touch and taste and how she looked when she came.

Callum might call it play, but it was going to be a long, decadent discovery for Oliver.

She softened for him, her mouth readily opening to accept the thrust of his tongue. He caressed his way down her body, memorizing her curves through the fabric of her dress. He loved her hourglass figure, how her small waist flared to womanly hips. While their tongues played, he pressed his hips in, letting her feel the hard line of his erection.

Every little mewl and roll of her hips told him she was ready, but he refused to fuck and run again. He was following his brothers' lead, and that meant they were both in for some torture. He wanted nothing more than to sink into her, but he was determined this would be a night she couldn't forget. It was their first real night together. From here on out, he would change.

Maybe he could be a better man. Maybe he could do it for her.

Oliver broke off the kiss with a gentle brushing of their lips. "I'm so glad to be here with you, Tori."

She hugged him, her cheek pressed against his heart. "I am, too. I need this. I need to be with you all just once."

"Once won't be enough." He could admit deep down that he wanted forever with her. He simply wasn't sure he deserved it. But tonight wasn't about fixing his tormented soul. It was about giving her the pleasure and adoration she deserved. He glanced at Callum and Rory, who were watching. "What should I do now?"

Rory worked the buttons of his shirt and tossed it aside, revealing a torso packed with hard muscle. Oliver was happy he'd never stopped going to the gym because both his brothers were built like brick shithouses.

"I think it's time we saw what she has to offer us." Rory

turned a burning stare on her. "Since you've already had the pleasure of seeing our lovely sub naked, you can do the honors. Undress her for us, Oliver."

Tori shivered in his arms but he could tell she wasn't afraid. Her body was still languid against his. She was a sensual thing, and the idea of being presented to his brothers seemed to arouse her.

"I want to show them how gorgeous you are," he whispered to Tori. "Will you let me?"

Oliver wouldn't proceed until he knew she agreed to his brothers' request.

She nodded against his chest, and that was all he needed. He slid his fingers along the back of her beautiful dress until he found the zip, then eased it down, brushing along the line of her spine all the way down to the two sexy dimples he knew sat at the small of her back.

He looked down at the swell of her beautiful breasts. "I don't like the fact that you're not wearing a bra."

"I couldn't find one that worked with the dress." She blushed as she clutched the dress. "Believe me, I wish I'd worn one, too."

The pictures. Oliver wanted to beat every person with a camera, but he wasn't going to waste time on anger now. "Turn around."

She seemed to gather her courage and nodded. She turned but pressed her back against him as though she needed the connection.

He needed it, too. Gently, he stroked her arms, coaxing her to let the dress go. "Show them how pretty you are. Show them you're ready to take everything they have to give."

She released the pretty silk. The dress pooled around her ankles.

Oliver cupped her breasts, offering them up to his brothers. Now he was quite happy he didn't have to deal with her bra. Those breasts were too lovely to be hidden. Round and firm, with perfect pinkish brown nipples made to be licked and nibbled on. "She's soft and warm and so fucking gorgeous it's nearly impossible to imagine. Her breasts are sensitive. These little nipples respond beautifully when you suck them."

He rolled them between his thumbs and forefingers, enjoying the way she fidgeted and arched against him. Her backside brushed his erection. Tiny silk knickers covered her. All it would take was a twist of his hands around that delicate fabric to see her bare.

"That's not the only beautiful thing I see. Tell me, Oliver, before you fucked everything up, how did it feel to be inside that tight pussy?" Callum asked, his voice hoarse.

Arousal flooded his system, making the world seem hazy and a little surreal. He was talking to his brothers about fucking the woman of his dreams—the woman he was about to share with them—and it seemed oddly natural. It was definitely natural to let his hand slide down to that pussy his brothers were staring at. He ran his palm over the silky scrap of fabric covering her and found it soaked. "Why do you think I fucked everything up? She felt too good to be true."

He dragged the knickers down her legs, and she obediently stepped out of them.

Callum dragged in a rough breath.

"Fuck me," Rory muttered thickly, staring at her cunt.

On his knees, Oliver was so close he could smell the citrus of her body and the strong spicy scent of her need. His fingers slid over her labia, finding her already coated with arousal. She was ripe and ready and he wanted to taste her again. He wanted to eat that pussy until she couldn't shout out his name anymore.

She moved against his fingers, silently begging for a pet.

"Don't move," Callum commanded. "She's trying to sneak in an orgasm and she doesn't get one until she's had her spanking."

She leaned back against him. "I wasn't trying to steal anything."

"Then let's get this over with so we can move on to the pleasant portions of the evening." Callum took a seat on the edge of the bed, patting his lap. "Over my knee."

* * * *

He couldn't be serious. Tori had never felt more vulnerable than standing there in Oliver's arms as his brother ordered her to lay over his lap and take her punishment. They were all dressed...and she was completely naked. What was she thinking? She was naked and aroused and Callum wanted to spank her. How could she be this aroused?

She just was. And knowing Oliver's and Rory's stares would be on her only turned her on more.

"Please, Tori, he's being a stubborn bastard, but I don't think he'll let us move on unless you obey," Oliver whispered into her ear. "And I'm dying here."

He pressed that massive erection into her backside. Tori held in a secret smile. Of course she was going to give in. She wanted what Rory had promised her—the three men she loved surrounding her, pleasuring her. Somehow knowing Oliver was as green at this kind of play as she was settled her. After their first time together, she hadn't been sure how she would react to Oliver, if she could trust him to make her body sing. But being with him felt right. Perfect. Oliver would support her, show her off to the others, and make her feel like a goddess. She had no doubt this would be a night to remember.

Too bad his brother was so serious about the whole discipline thing.

"I'm scared of the spanking," she murmured, eyes downcast. "I've never had one."

"Not even as a child?" Rory asked.

She shook her head. "I spent a lot of time in the corner, though. I got grounded a few times, but no one ever spanked me."

"I knew there was a reason you're such an incorrigible brat." Callum winked her way. "I'm glad I get to give you your first spanking. I'll teach you the first lesson. The longer you make me wait, the worse it will get. If you come to me now, you can expect an erotic spanking. Then we'll call the slate clean. If you make me wait, I'll need more from you."

"Do it, sweetheart," Rory encouraged. "Or I might need a few swats myself."

She hurried over because an erotic spanking really sounded better than a spanking spanking. Callum looked like a decadent dream sitting there wearing nothing but his dress slacks. He was covered in lean muscles. All three of her men were powerful, stunning, virile. She could practically swim in the testosterone floating in the air.

Her men. They were hers for the night. She couldn't think past the next few hours and she wasn't going to waste them feeling anxious. She wasn't really afraid of Callum. He wouldn't truly harm her. Yes, it might sting, but even the thought of his hand on her bare butt... No denying that turned her on more.

"All right." She gave him a shaky nod.

Callum held out his hand to steady her. "Excellent. Choose your safe word. If the sensations become too much, you say that word and everything stops. Do you understand?"

She wasn't sure she wanted anything to stop. Despite her reservations, she was rapidly discovering she liked having them stare at her, intent and focused and on edge. She felt more powerful giving them her submission than she ever had. Her mind whirled as she tried to come up with some odd word that she wouldn't normally say in an intimate situation. "Football."

Callum tugged her close with a grin. "Perfect."

Tori managed the awkward climb over his lap. She had to force herself to breathe. His cock prodded her belly as his hand settled on the small of her back. The other rested between her shoulders. His hold might seem casual but she wasn't getting up until he allowed it. Suddenly, she felt cool air—and their hungry gazes—all over her ass. Had she ever been so vulnerable? Defenseless? She couldn't do anything to defend herself in this position, yet she still felt safe.

"This is the most gorgeous backside I've ever seen." Callum stroked her curves with his big hand, spreading heat through her system. He trailed his fingertips down her thighs, then teased his way back up again, brushing so close to the juncture. She gasped.

The waiting was going to kill her. He was stroking her butt, gently petting her and making her insane. She needed more than this slow discovery. Her pussy was clenching with need, and Callum was taking his sweet time.

Rory knelt beside her, cupping her chin and forcing her head up. He skated his thumb along her bottom lip. "This is a foolish question, but I'll ask it anyway. Has anyone fucked this luscious mouth?"

She flushed. "Oliver."

"Naturally. It's my turn then. I want your mouth on my cock, sweetheart," Rory said, his voice a low, sexy rumble. "I've had dreams about it."

Tori wanted to taste him, to know what it felt like to run her tongue across his sensitive crest, suck her way up his stiff shaft, and feel him shudder with need. "I want that. I want it all."

"I think it's safe to say we'll push some boundaries," Callum said. "Starting now."

She heard the smack before she felt it. The sound hit her ears, short and sharp. A second later, pure fire licked along her flesh. She squealed in protest, then squirmed on Callum's lap. It stung like hell. Where was the erotic in that?

Another hard smack. "Don't move. Give it a minute before you spit out that safe word."

She shivered, tears blurring her vision as he smacked her ass again, and she writhed, trying to worm away from his next blow.

"I don't think she likes it," Oliver said.

"It takes a minute." Callum's hand was still on her ass, rubbing hard, settling fire under her skin. "If she'll let it, the pain will become pleasure."

Was he for real?

Tori took a deep, coping breath and tried to manage the hurt that flared where he'd already spanked her. Callum's hand came down again, and this time she didn't fight it. She opened herself up and let the pain rush across her nerve endings and sink into her senses. He struck her again, and the agony blooming under her skin suddenly morphed into a deep heat. He rubbed into her with the flat of his palm. It settled in her core. A rush of fresh arousal made her shudder.

"I think you should let her up. This isn't working." Oliver sounded concerned.

Before Callum could reply, she lifted her head. Oliver needed to let her have this moment with Callum. Nothing would work between them if they didn't respect each other's boundaries. "It's working fine, Oliver. Be quiet. I can't think when you're talking."

A much sharper slap to her already sore rear cheek made her gasp. Callum had meant that blow. "No disrespect. Even when one of us is acting like a prat. But there's my girl. Pretty sub. I knew you were there." Another smack, this one lighter. "You like this."

"I don't know yet." She couldn't admit it that quickly.

Smack. Harder again. Louder. Callum hit her ass dead center, right between her cheeks. "I think you're lying."

She probably didn't want to know what he would do if he knew she was. "I-I do like it. I'm just not used to it yet."

He peppered another volley of little smacks across her backside.

"How can you tell she likes it?" Oliver asked, stroking a soothing hand over her calf.

"Show him," Rory ordered.

"Touch her. Her mouth might lie, but her pussy never

will." Callum spread her legs.

Before she could protest she felt Oliver's big fingers sliding through her sex.

"She's quite wet." Oliver's voice deepened as he worked two fingers inside her. He rotated them and it was all Tori could do not to move against him.

"And she's obedient." Callum's hand on the small of her back held her steady. "Is it hard to be still, love? Do you want to thrust back and fuck those big fingers of Oliver's?"

She wanted to scream in frustration, but managed to hold still—barely. She was determined to win this little game Callum played. "Yes. That's exactly what I want to do."

Callum's hand tightened on her back. "So the spanking got you all hot and bothered and ready to fuck."

She wasn't the only one. She could feel his cock practically pulsing against her belly. "Yes, but I'm not going to steal an orgasm. I've never stolen anything."

She was well aware that she sounded far more prim than any woman who was naked across one brother's lap while a second finger fucked her and the third waited for his blow job should, but it was true. She wasn't a thief and she wouldn't start now.

"Then consider this one freely given, love," Callum offered. "Oliver, let's get her in a better position for this."

She nearly cried when those fingers pulled free. Empty. She'd been close to release and now she was tight and empty again. Callum maneuvered her until she was sitting upright on his lap. He shifted, moving his knees wide, which spread her legs as well, opening her completely to Oliver and Rory's gaze.

"Do you see how helpful having a partner or two can be now, Ollie?" Rory asked. He squeezed her shoulder before brushing his way down to cradle her breast while Oliver moved between her legs.

All three men had their hands on her. She was caught between them and she'd never felt more cherished in her life.

It suddenly didn't matter that she was naked and they weren't. She felt strong as Oliver kneeled down. Her whole body thrummed in anticipation.

"It is extremely helpful. Hold her down, brother. I need a good taste of this." He bent toward her, and Tori felt the heat from his mouth on her pussy.

"Get her ready because we're not stopping until we've all had our fill." Callum's deep voice vibrated in her ear as he rolled her nipples between his thick fingers. "Enjoy this because you're serving Rory next."

She glanced at Rory, who was shoving his slacks off, exposing the gasp-worthy length of his body. He was stunning. Every inch of his body was muscled and cut, from his broad shoulders to a lean and tapered waist that led to strong legs. She had to catch her breath when she saw his cock. He watched her gape at him, his big dick in hand. He stroked himself, clearly impatient for the moment she took him into her mouth. She had no idea how she would get that cock all the way in, but she was more than willing to try.

She had one night and she was going to make the most of it. She planned to make as many memories of these men as she could.

Oliver licked around her folds, teased her opening, then laved her clit. Pure fire roared through her system. Callum chose that exact moment to pinch her nipples, and she couldn't stop the pleading groan that came from her throat.

Oliver worked her with his clever tongue, flicking all around and keeping her off balance as Callum played with her sensitive crests, engorging them with more blood. She couldn't move, couldn't do anything but ride the growing wave. Oliver dipped his fingers inside her again, curling the digits up and rubbing just the right way as his tongue found the nub of her clit and stroked it relentlessly.

Tori stiffened under Oliver's ministrations, arched, dug her nails into Callum's thighs, and turned a pleading glance to Rory.

"Come, sweetheart."

Rory's soft command somehow set her off. Orgasm exploded through her system, and she couldn't contain her keening cry, and pleasure jolted her entire system, tightening every muscle and rendering her absolutely helpless under their touch.

Oliver kept at her, licking and stroking like he was a starving man, and she was his first meal in weeks. The euphoria rose higher, and she shouted as the sensation shot through her again. Her whole body seemed swept up in an endless charge of bliss.

Finally, the tension fell, seeping out, leaving satisfaction in its wake. She slumped against Callum's chest, her blood pounding even as Oliver's tongue softened and he pressed one last kiss on the pad of her swollen pussy.

He rose and bent to her, his lips hovering above hers. "That was perfect. I'll never get the taste of you out of my mind. I'll always crave you."

Then Oliver kissed her mouth, his tongue tangling with hers, and she could taste herself on his lips. This was intimacy beyond anything she'd imagined. Shockingly, desire began to swirl and gather inside her again.

After a long moment, Callum helped her to her feet. The ache made her press her thighs together. Tori wanted them so badly, she felt willing to beg. She couldn't be in a room with these men and not want them.

"Drop to your knees and present yourself." Callum held her hand and helped her to the floor. "Spread your knees."

She was so wet. "I think I need a towel."

Callum knelt beside her, plucking at her nipple. He twisted it to the right side of pain. "You don't need anything I don't give you. You're beautiful. Rory, are you offended by the sight of her slick pussy?"

Rory's stare was glued to her pink folds as he slowly stroked his cock. "You know I think she's gorgeous, but that is the prettiest pussy I've ever seen. Do you know how gorgeous you are when you come? I almost joined you."

"It was a close thing," Callum agreed. "So keep those legs open and stop worrying about what's right or proper. When we're alone like this, all you have to worry about is pleasing your Masters, and watching you come truly pleased me."

"Me, too." Oliver touched her head, stroking his big palm over her crown. When she blinked up at him, she was shocked to see how calm and present he looked. There was always a piece of Oliver that seemed to be somewhere else, but now he was relaxed and in the moment.

She'd given him that. She'd given him a little respite from the demons in his head. The thought made her sit up straighter, her spine lengthening as she spread her knees wide.

"That's my girl." Callum's hand softened on her breast. "Now kiss me. You haven't kissed me yet. My turn."

Finally she heard something of the man she usually knew. Sweet Callum lurked under the hungry Dom. She had to admit she found the two sides of the man utterly fascinating. He was willing to let his brothers lead when it came to business, but they followed him in this room.

She turned her lips up to meet his, surprised that he didn't immediately take over. He kissed her softly as though she was infinitely precious. His lips molded to hers and when he was finished, he pressed his forehead to hers. "Thank you for trusting me. I've wanted this since I first met you. I won't let you down, Tori."

Her heart constricted because she wanted to believe him. She wanted her fairy godmother to wave her magic wand and say that she could have the Thurston-Hughes brothers now and forever. Maybe her love would be enough.

She let the thoughts go. No decisions now. For tonight, she resolved to live in the moment. Just be.

Then she turned to Rory, determined to give her men what they needed.

CHAPTER TEN

Rory wasn't sure how long he'd last, but he vowed to feel that sweet mouth on his cock. Watching Tori writhe and moan under his brothers' hands had sent his thoughts reeling. He and Callum had worked with submissives together before but this was new territory. This was something he could never picture again without her. He'd never wanted to share a woman sexually with his brothers before, but this felt right. Meant to be.

He was in love for the first time and he finally understood what that meant. He intended to give her anything she needed. She needed the three of them and what they could provide. Nothing else mattered. Society didn't matter. The tabloids meant even less. Her needs. Her desires. Her love. That was what would rule him here and forever more.

There was such freedom in knowing where he belonged and with whom.

And right now his place was in front of her, his cock about to touch those perfect lips.

Tori held her back straight, her body in a lovely submissive position. She'd spread her knees wide, and it was hard to take his eyes off her cunt. That soft flesh had swollen a vivid pink. Cream coated her labia.

"Let me taste you first." He had to know. He wanted that taste in his mouth when she took him into her own.

"You want me back on the chair?" She bit her lip, looking a bit disappointed, as though she'd actually been looking forward to sucking his cock.

"No," Callum said. He sprang to his feet again, his hand dropping to the belt at his waist. "He wants a taste of your pussy. Something to tide him over. Use your finger. Offer it to him."

She hesitated.

Rory knew it was time for him to step up.

He tangled his hands in her hair and pulled just enough to make her scalp sting with the tension. "I said I wanted a taste, sweetheart. Are you going to give it to me or should I spank you?"

He wanted a turn at that, too. He wanted to use his hand to make her squirm and squeal.

Tori dipped her hand between her thighs, and he watched her eyes widen when she ran a finger over her clitoris, then between her labia. She raised her drenched finger, offering it up for his pleasure.

Her pink-tipped finger gleamed with evidence of her arousal, and Rory didn't hesitate. He grasped her wrist, bringing that finger to his lips. With a little growl of anticipation, he sucked the digit inside.

Sweet with a hint of tang, she was as spicy and hot as he'd expected her to be. He licked the arousal off her finger with a long groan, then it was his turn.

"Take me." He didn't have to pretend to play nice. She knew what he wanted and he could see from the way her nipples pebbled and her eyes dilated that she wanted it, too. She didn't need sweet and soft. That would come later. For now, she needed to obey.

She leaned forward. As he felt the press of her lips on the tip of his cock, his eyes nearly rolled in the back of his head. She kissed him, an oddly innocent gesture. He stood there, offering himself to her as she explored.

Her lips slid all over the crest of his cock, moving down

to the stalk and the base before laving back up. They were like butterflies on his sensitive flesh, descending and then flying away again, awakening his senses to her touch.

He groaned when the first swipe of her tongue hit. One teasing lick from her, and he was ready to blow.

"Talk to her. Tell her how you like it," Callum said. "She's only done this once."

Rory groaned. No fucking way could he speak now. He glanced at his eldest brother.

Oliver grinned. "I don't suspect I could talk very much if I were in your position, either. Hold his cock in your hand, Tori."

"Yes," Rory gasped, willing to cede a little control to Oliver. "Do what he tells you to."

He'd spent two years trying to coax his brother back to life. All they'd needed to do was find one woman they all loved and share her. Kink had been the way to get Ollie smiling again. They'd all wasted the last six months, but Rory refused to waste another second.

Tori hesitated.

Rory pulled his head together enough to threaten her. "Or Oliver will spank you good."

"You guys are very quick with the spankings," she said as she gripped him in her small fist.

"You look gorgeous with a pink arse, love." Callum shifted behind her, caressing the flesh he'd flushed with impact. "And you liked it."

Her eyes sparkled with amusement. "Yes, which is why the threat doesn't seem to be much of a threat."

A loud smack blasted through the room. She gasped. Rory felt the delicate hand around his dick tighten.

It felt so fucking good.

No more games. He surged forward, hips thrusting as he pumped his dick against her lips.

"Was that a threat, love?" Apparently, Callum had a tiny streak of sadist.

She moaned and shifted, trying to press her thighs together. "You know it was. It hurt, but now it feels like heat and I like it. Tell me what to do next. Should I suck on the head?"

Her words went straight to his dick. He was fairly certain all of the blood in his body had pooled in his cock and he would pass out at any moment.

"Grip him harder," Oliver commanded. "He won't break."

Pleasure sizzled up his spine as she tightened her hold. Yes, that was what he needed. Her hand began to work his cock.

"Tell me what you want to do, Tori." Oliver's voice turned deep, and Rory wasn't surprised to see his eldest brother shucking his slacks. There was really no more need for clothes between them. "What does instinct tell you to do to that big cock in your hand?"

"Lick it. Suck it into my mouth. I want to know what it tastes like." She stared at his cock and swallowed hard.

"I want that, too," Rory groaned.

Her little tongue peeked out and teased him with a long, slow laving. She dragged it over the head of his dick where pearly fluid already leaked from the slit.

"Lick him all over," Oliver ordered. "Take care of him or Callum will stop what he's doing to you."

Rory looked to his side and found Callum stroking her, rubbing her clit in slow circles. "Is he making you feel good?"

Tori whimpered against him, the sound rolling across his flesh. Rory shuddered as need pooled. His balls drew up. He started to sweat.

"If you like it, please me, too." He felt desperate. "Suck me, Tori. Suck my cock and suck it hard."

"If you want another orgasm, you make Rory come and you drink down everything he gives you or Callum will stop what he's doing." Oliver crouched down, drawing closer, watching the scene in front of him with seeming fascination. "You give me a show because I want to watch you. I want to see my beautiful girl sucking a dick and loving it. Can you do that, darling?"

Her reply was to suck the head of his cock right into her mouth. Rory groaned deep in his throat. *So good.* Her mouth was warm and soft as she worked the head of his cock, inching down, only to suck her way back up.

"Move it in time with your hand. Squeeze him and find a rhythm," Oliver said.

Rory would have clapped Oliver on the back if he hadn't been so damn close to orgasm. His oldest brother seemed to know exactly what he needed from Tori. If he wasn't careful, Rory feared he would come far too soon. The need was right there, and it went beyond mere pleasure. For the first time in his life, he wanted to mark a woman.

He'd been careful with his relationships. He always kept them casual, always somewhat cool. He'd selected women for their beauty and their desire to use him to further their own careers. Always models or actresses. Always women who would move on from him at some point.

Tori was their exact opposite. Tori didn't want fame. She couldn't care less about their money. And he could never move on from her. She was his endgame.

"Yes... That's exactly what I want." He tightened his hands in her hair to guide her as she squeezed and moved her mouth in a sultry rhythm.

He watched her carefully for a moment, studying her movements. She showed zero signs of distress. She groaned around his cock and took him deep. He wanted to enjoy this with her. She was turning out to be far more adventurous and pliable than he'd expected. He'd thought they would have to coddle her and gently move her along, but she took to the pleasure—both giving and receiving—quickly. She'd been a virgin, but her first foray into Dominance and submission seemed to be turning her into a hungry vixen.

This was what they all needed—her. So many times he'd felt compelled to do whatever it took to keep the family together, but Tori was the glue that would bind them. Love for her would cement their bond.

She worked him, taking more and more of his cock with every pass. Her mouth was small, but she seemed determined to take all of him. He wasn't about to protest. There was nothing more he wanted than to find that soft spot at the back of her throat and give her everything he'd pent up for her.

Whatever Callum was doing to her made her whimper. The vibrations hummed along his cock.

"Do that again. She liked it," he gasped. "I fucking loved it."

"She responds so well," Callum said. "Do you want to come, love? Do you want to come while Rory's cock is in your mouth? Let's see if I can get the timing perfect. You like it when I touch you here."

She hummed again, a sound of panicked passion, as if she sat on the razor's edge and Callum held her in his ruthless hands. Tori swallowed more of his cock, and he watched his inches disappear between her lips. The sensation made his spine bow as he felt his balls begin to draw up.

"I'm almost there." He used her hair to roughen his thrusts between her lips. He couldn't let her have control a second longer. "Just relax and let me fuck your mouth."

She did as he asked, but her little whimpers were getting stronger as Callum apparently hurtled her toward climax. She moaned around his cock, her mouth softening as she took him deeper. He thrust in and pulled out, only to have her lips tighten around him, drawing him back in. Over and over, he gained precious ground until she'd taken him balls deep.

Her tongue whirled, and Rory couldn't stop himself from letting go. Her body swaying, her head bobbing, her tongue rubbing, and she hummed hard as she came. He slammed inside her mouth, and a groan tore from his chest as she took his cock to the back of her throat. There was no way to hold it back. He shot into her mouth, pumping himself again and again between her swollen lips.

She sucked him hard, cupping the cheeks of his ass. She leaned in, swallowing, taking every bit of him.

"Sweetheart...ah," Rory groaned. "Yes. Fuck. Yes!"

Pure joy suffused him as the world seemed to go soft and hazy. His whole body pulsed as he watched her lick him clean. She wore a radiant smile, glowing with pride and joy, when she finally looked up at him.

He was utterly lost. He loved her and he was never going to let her go.

* * * *

Callum was on fire. Tori's heat had definitely singed his fingers. He'd always known she had a burning sensuality inside her. She might look sweet and she might be as innocent as the day was long. He wasn't a man who equated innocence to virginity or virginity with goodness. Tori had been in a state of virginity because she was picky and there was nothing wrong with that, but her innocence had nothing to do with her hymen. It was all about her gorgeous soul.

She smiled as she toppled back. If he hadn't been there, she would have hit the floor, but she must have known that he would catch her. He would never let her down.

Callum stared at her, her weight so perfect in his arms. He remembered that moment he'd first seen her smile at him. The sight had been a revelation, like the heavens had parted and left him the sunny gift of her beauty after days of rain, and he'd known he'd found his reason to live. His woman to love.

For so long, his purpose had been about not letting his team down. His life had been about a sport. This was real. She was real. Loving Tori Glen could be the rest of his life.

It was everything he wanted. He even wanted this freaky turn his life had taken. Somehow it felt right to have his brothers here.

"Did you enjoy that?" He'd loved watching her blow Rory while he'd gotten her off with his fingers. He'd never had a woman respond so readily and beautifully to him. It was like she'd been made for him, made for his fingers and mouth and cock. Made for them—for the Thurston-Hughes brothers.

"I loved it." She turned her face up to his, making it easy for him to capture those lips he was so obsessed with. He gave himself a moment to memorize her. She would change over the years, but he would always see her like this, his sweet love just learning about the power of her own sensuality.

Callum knew he needed to enjoy her now because the minute she realized her power, he would be lost. He was already her slave, but at least in their bedroom, he was the Master. When he'd found BDSM, a piece of his soul had clicked into place. Now he knew why. He'd been born to be Tori's Dominant.

He stood, cradling her in his arms.

"You don't have to, but I love how you carry me around." She laid her head against his shoulder, her blue eyes dreamy. "It makes me feel delicate."

"You are compared to me." He didn't even notice her weight, but he definitely noticed her delicate softness in his arms. And his cock was rock hard at the thought of what he was about to do. "Rory, do you want to hold our sweet sub down?"

His younger brother was already tossing himself down on the bed. "I would love to."

They'd discussed how they would do this if they had the chance. Weeks of endless talk had brought them here, and Callum found his hands shook a little. He'd had sex almost every way possible, but it had never really mattered before. He'd never had it with a woman who mattered. He wanted her to enjoy it, to feel worshiped and loved. This was the start of their lives together.

He settled Tori against his youngest brother, her back to his front. Rory cuddled their woman and it was easy to see how she gloried in the affection.

Oliver crawled on the bed and leaned over to kiss her. Their mouths melded in a show of pure desire.

Fuck it all. This could work. This could really work. Hope settled in his heart. Through the tribulations of the past few weeks, he'd tried to stay positive, but in the back of his mind he'd wondered if any future with Tori would really work without Oliver. Now he knew how much Tori needed him, too. Callum would move heaven and earth to keep Oliver by their side—for her.

"You're so beautiful, love." Oliver kissed the tip of her nose, then sat back. His eyes were dark with desire, but his face held tenderness, too. "She's very small. Go easy with her. I hurt her the first time."

Tori tangled her fingers with Oliver's. "I'm fine. I want this."

And she would have it. She was surrounded by them, connected to all of them, so now he could take her. "I want this more than you can imagine. And if you're sore tomorrow, I promise to carry you around and treat you like a princess. But right now, I'm going to worship you my way."

After sheathing himself with a condom, he spread her legs and made a place for himself. Anticipation pounded through him. One day, he wouldn't wear a piece of latex. One day, he would have the right to spill inside her body. He couldn't wait.

Watching her intently, Callum lined up his cock and started to press inside. He concentrated on her and tried not to fixate on the fact that she was so tight, so hot, so perfect.

Her eyes widened and she let out a sexy little gasp.

"You're such a goddess," Rory whispered in her ear. "I can't wait to be the man inside you. Do you know how long I've waited?"

Oliver squeezed her hand. "Relax and let Cal take over. It won't hurt this time. He's going to be careful."

Callum inched his way in, sweat on his brow. Control was the key. He had to resist the insane urge to plunge inside her again and again, to mark her with his cock. She deserved more and he was determined to give it to her.

"It doesn't hurt, but he's so big. I'm so full." Her free hand drifted up to his waist, stroking toward his backside.

She was going to be more full. He gained another inch, moving in and out in short, controlled motions. He gradually opened her up, letting her get comfortable around him. He was anything but comfortable. In fact, Callum was sure he was going to die of pure pleasure. Her pussy pulsed around him, tempting him to let go.

He worked until he was finally deep inside, their bodies flush. He leaned over and fused his mouth over hers, enjoying that moment when they were finally together, finally connected. This was what he'd waited for.

"I love you." He'd never said it to another woman and now the yellow-brick road to happiness stretched out before them. It might be enough time for him. Maybe. "Are you all right now, love?"

She nodded. "I want to move."

He had to. Callum pulled out and slowly thrust back in. Every second was torture and pleasure and heaven. Another long, slow thrust had her skin flushing a delicate pink. Her nipples peaked as she wound her legs around his waist.

Her pelvis tilted up and somehow he slid even deeper inside. He could feel his balls rubbing against her backside. They drew up, a tingle starting to build in his spine.

He worked over her, thrusting harder and faster, letting her feel every inch of his cock. Feminine muscles squeezed tight around him. He couldn't last. She was too hot and tight.

"Come for us. You scream out. Don't hold back," Oliver commanded, his brother sounding more confident than he'd heard in forever as he toyed with Tori's nipples.

Her eyes flared, her whole body flushing as she screamed out her pleasure. There was no artifice or falsehood. There was no act. Callum felt her tighten, pulse, shudder as she came, her nails digging deep.

He couldn't hold out a second longer. He fucked her hard. He let his cock have sway, thrusting in and out, following the primitive rhythm he'd set. In response, Tori slammed her hips up, offering more and more, and he could have sworn she came again and again as he moved inside her.

Orgasm overwhelmed his senses as he spilled himself into her. The world seemed to fall away around him except...all he could see was Tori. All he could feel or hear was Tori. The world narrowed down as he ground against her, giving her everything he had.

He cradled her body to his. He let his hand find her breast and through the softness, he heard the pounding of her heart.

The world seemed a perfect place and only one thing could make it better.

The night wasn't done. He looked up at her and winked. "I think it's time we introduced our gorgeous girl to the anal plug."

Her eyes widened and joy suffused him.

Finally, his world was perfect.

CHAPTER ELEVEN

Tori woke with a start, panting. She forced herself to slow down her breathing, to drag in longer breaths. Fear tightened her whole body. Tears streamed down her face. She blinked in the shadowy dark, finally recognizing it as a bedroom in the palace. Her men lay sleeping all around her.

She'd simply had a nightmare. Her body sagged with relief. But the visions kept playing out in her head.

She'd had a version of this dream before, many times since she was thirteen. She'd been on the couch with her sister watching TV when the doorbell had rung. She'd followed Piper, and the sheriff had been standing there. He'd told them about their father—except he hadn't been talking about her dad this time. Fat tears had rolled down her cheeks. Suddenly, she'd been an adult and the sheriff had told her that Callum Thurston-Hughes had been killed by an unknown assailant

Instantly, she'd known Thea was the killer. Tori had run toward his body and that was when she'd seen Oliver and Rory locked in combat. They'd gripped bloody knives in their big hands. Red dripped down their torsos. They were fighting over her.

When they'd stabbed at one another again, she'd awakened with a start.

Now she looked around and panicked. What had she done? The night before had been perfect and now her heart was racing for a different reason. She lay cuddled between

Rory and Callum. Both men had their hands on her and she couldn't breathe.

She loved them. She loved them down to her soul—and that terrified her beyond anything. What if she lost them, really and truly? What if she woke up one day and they were all gone? It had happened to her before and she hadn't been able to do anything about it. She'd been utterly helpless to do anything except bury the two people she'd loved most, her parents.

If history repeated itself, she wouldn't survive.

And she couldn't take that risk.

To anyone else who hadn't suffered such a loss as a kid, it would probably sound stupid, but the towering swell of dread sucked the air out of her, stained her blood with icy fear. She panicked completely at the notion of losing them.

Tori pushed back the covers and managed to haul herself out of bed. The night before had been magical. She'd opened herself up and surrendered herself to them. Somewhere in the middle of the night, she'd given up the notion of leaving them. She wanted them. She wanted to be the center of their worlds.

But she couldn't do it. She couldn't risk her sanity and soul like that.

A sob nearly tore from her throat. Tori carefully extricated herself and crawled out of the bed. What had she been thinking last night? She'd been focused on pleasure, on the drugging bliss of the touches, on their protection and adoration and…everything else that would disappear in the snap of a finger if something happened to them.

If? Try when. Life wasn't forever. People died. She couldn't stop that. Besides, if she stayed with them, she would eventually tear them apart. They could handle sharing her for a night, but they were possessive. She'd seen how they fought. What happened if one of them wanted to get married legally? Or she became pregnant? How would they deal with that? Cohabitate in the same house or bed for years?

No, she would eventually tear them apart and if she didn't, she would likely be taken apart by the tabloids

"Sweetheart, where are you going?" Rory whispered.

She managed to clear the tangle of sheets and arms. Oliver was asleep on the other side of Callum. They all looked so gorgeous. Last night, they'd been so devoted. Tori had to bite back a cry. She couldn't let Rory know she was upset or he would be all over her. She needed a few moments to herself. Everything that had happened in the last twelve hours had all been too much.

"Just to the bathroom. I'll be right back," she said, happy that her voice betrayed none of her whirling emotions.

"Hurry."

She heard him settle back on the bed. When she glanced again, his eyes were closed and his chest had taken on the rhythm of sleep once more.

As quietly as she could, she grabbed a robe in the wardrobe and dashed to the outer rooms, refusing to look at a guard manning the hallway. From there she found her way back to her own quarters.

Inside, Tori locked the door and tore off the robe. She made it to the shower before the sobs hit. Too much. Everything had happened so quickly. She'd closed herself off for too long and now the emotion hit her like a hurricane. She let the hot water blend with her tears and prayed she could find the strength to make the right decisions.

* * * *

Two hours later, Tori stared at herself in the mirror and wondered why she was such a coward. She'd woken up surrounded by the three men she loved. Her body had felt deliciously sated and she'd been so warm. She'd never slept the whole night with another body at her side. When she'd been a child, her parents sometimes cuddled her in between them when she was scared or sick. She remembered looking up at them in contentment as they kissed her before turning out the lights. Even as a young kid, she'd felt their love. With them, she'd been safe and warm.

And she'd never imagined it could be over so swiftly.

The terrible nightmare she'd had brought it all back—the feelings of loss, helplessness, anger, and despair. One nightmare, and she remembered all too well how easily her happiness could end.

This was why she was a coward. She could still remember her father standing over her mother's grave, still feel her sister's hand in hers as they both stared with dry, aching eyes. From that moment on, they'd only had each other to count on. For all practical purposes, their dad had died with their mom. He'd just walked around for a few years more.

She should still be in bed with the Thurston-Hughes brothers, but she'd told Rory she'd only be a minute. Then she'd dashed to her own room like a scared rabbit. This felt like junior high all over again. She intended to barricade herself in the bathroom and stay until she figured out how to handle them.

She took a long breath and forced herself to relax. She would have to be calm with them. "Thank you for last night. It was wonderful. If we ever have time, I would love to do it again."

Good. Now she was the Emily Post of the ménage world.

Maybe casual was better. "Hey, guys. How'd you sleep? Good. Catch ya later!"

That would not go over well.

She groaned as she sank down to a waiting chaise. Naturally, her bathroom at the palace was bigger than her London flat and came complete with a sitting room.

As she turned to throw herself across the padded cushions, Tori winced at the soreness. She'd always been an overachiever, but three men in one night was a new high.

Images of the previous night assaulted her. After Callum

214

had tortured her with that damn plug, Rory made her forget how awkward it was. He'd taken her into his arms and before long, he'd been working over her. He'd kissed her while he'd thrust in and out, taking her over the edge again.

And Oliver. Oh, Oliver had been so patient and careful as he'd possessed her body utterly. The whole night had been a long, sensual feast. One of them had always had a hand on her. One of them had always been kissing her or delving into her depths with his big cock. And when she'd fallen into an exhausted slumber, she'd done it with their arms around her. In that moment the world had felt perfect, like everything had finally fallen into place and she couldn't ask for more.

Until she'd had that nightmare... That terrible slap-in-the-face reminder that nothing was perfect.

Yes, she and her men had survived one incredible night. But there was no way they could make it work in the real world. If they never left the palace again, maybe, just maybe, they could be happy for a while, but they would want to go home.

And then all hell would break loose.

She'd been lucky to have this one magical night the world knew nothing about. She couldn't possibly push her luck and ask for a lifetime.

A knock on the door jolted her out of her depressing thoughts and took her straight into some terrifying ones.

She wasn't ready to face them. Not at all.

"Mindy?"

With a sigh of relief, Tori leapt to her feet and opened the door. Piper stood there with a breakfast tray in her hand and a smirk on her face that told her someone in the palace filled her in on what had happened last night.

Tori's cheeks went up in flames. "I don't want to talk about it."

Damn the palace gossip mill. That guard who had let them into the private wing likely had a big mouth.

Piper strode in. She was still in her casual but chic

loungewear. She set the tray with coffee and Danishes on the counter. "Too bad because I want the scoop."

And Tori really needed coffee. Well, maybe telling her sister would be good practice. She sighed and poured herself a cup. "There's no real scoop to be had. It was a nice night. Someone should have told me about the plug though. I wasn't ready for that."

Brazen. That's what she'd be. She would plow her way through with confidence.

Piper's eyes lit up. "Oh, the plug never ends. Damn Doms. They really know how to get to a girl. Which one is the alpha Dom? It's Rory, isn't it?"

"Callum." Everyone had followed Callum's lead. It had been a revelation to see that side of him. "If I had to put them in order, Rory's next. Surprisingly, Oliver is the softie."

Piper grabbed herself some java. "I would never have guessed. So tell me what's up with the Little Miss Jaded act?" She frowned. "Tell me you're not going to pretend it meant nothing."

Her sister knew her too well. "It can't mean anything since I'm not going back to England. I've decided to take a job in Dallas."

"You're taking the Black Oak job? That will bore you to tears. Those men are solid pillars of the business community. They don't need anyone cleaning up their scandals because they don't have any."

The James brothers were happily married to their wife, Hannah. They were extremely careful and private. They were living a life that should make headlines. How had they managed it? Maybe keeping their secret would be part of her job.

It shouldn't be too hard because the James brothers got along. They were happy together. She would bet they'd never thrown a punch or gotten into a fight. They were a cohesive unit and the Thurston-Hughes brothers were a gorgeous, super-hot mess. And she loved them so much, her heart ached.

"I know. It's a peach of a job." She schooled her features. The last thing she needed was Piper to think she was lying. "I can concentrate on the company and not the employees. It's going to be good to get back to Texas."

Away from the three men she would spend a lifetime trying to forget.

Piper gracefully sat on the settee. "Do they know you're planning on leaving them after one night?"

Somehow her sister managed to make that simple question seem very accusatory. Or maybe Tori responded to her own shame. She didn't want forever with them. She didn't want forever with anyone. Not anyone she loved with her whole heart. Losing them after a lifetime of love would be too horrible. She'd already endured that moment when she'd felt as if her life was over. She would never choose to go through it again.

God, she was lying to herself now. She wanted everything Oliver, Callum, and Rory could give her, but she wasn't brave enough to take it.

"I never promised them a thing." Her appetite was gone. She wanted to go to bed. Her own bed. She would pull the covers over her head and try to pretend she knew what she was doing. She would try to forget that dream where Callum had been taken out by his former lover while Rory and Oliver nearly stood over the corpse and killed each other over her.

"They came together for you," Piper said quietly.

She shook her head. "It was just sex."

It was all she could allow it to be.

Piper stood and set the coffee mug down. It looked like her sister talk wasn't going the way she'd planned. "I don't understand what's going on and I don't know that I even want to, but I'm going to ask. Are you ashamed of me?"

What? Tori could barely fathom the idea. "How could you say that? Piper, I love you. You've been everything to me. My sister, my mom, my best friend. Why would you ask me that?"

"Because I can't figure out why else you wouldn't want to be with them when it's so obvious you love them. I think it has to be that you don't approve of the life I lead." Tears shone in her sister's eyes. "It's not like I haven't heard it before. I have. I've seen the tabloids. I've been called a whore many times."

Rage welled up. "I sued the holy fuck out of some of those tabloids."

Piper nodded. "But still you don't want it for yourself. I'm trying to understand why."

"Because I'm not sure I want one husband I love, much less three."

Piper frowned. "You don't want to get married? There's nothing wrong with that, but I always thought you wanted a family."

"I do. I do want a husband and kids. I simply don't want to lose my soul to some man. I don't want to die if he leaves me or something happens to him, and I'm really afraid that's how things would end with those brothers. So I think I should walk away."

"Do you love me?" Piper asked in a quiet, almost halting voice.

"Of course." Did she even have to ask?

"But in a distant way, right? You hold yourself back so if anything ever happens, you won't miss me too much."

Tears welled in Tori's eyes. How could she make her sister understand? "That's not true."

"I think it is, at least a little bit," Piper said with a sad sigh. "Now that I look at it, I can see how you hold yourself back. You do the same with your job. You train people how to handle the worst, how to put on a good face and move on. But you deal with the superficial, smoothing things over so no one has to see the truth underneath the façade."

"The truth is rarely as pretty as we want it to be." And the truth was, she'd made a mistake. She'd thought she could have one night with them. She'd thought she could sneak around the whole love thing.

If she never loved anyone, she never had to lose them.

Had she held her sister a bit at arm's length? Had she treated her more like a role model to worship and less like family?

Piper stared, shaking her head gently, as if she had no idea who Tori was. "Don't have children, Torrance. It's not fair if you can't love them with every bit of your heart and soul. If you can't give them your all, you'll ruin them."

It was the first time her sister had called her by her professional name. Tori felt the distance she'd always tried to maintain widening between her and her sister. And it terrified her.

"I love my nephews." Her stomach was in a knot. It was so much less painful not to think about the depth of her relationship with Piper. Couldn't they just be friends? Did they really have to talk about profound stuff?

Wasn't it enough for her to be kind to the people around her? She didn't have to be tangled up in their hearts and their lives if they were just "friends."

Piper narrowed her eyes as she studied Tori. "Do you? I think you think they're safe because they're young, but children can die, too, and if you think for a second you wouldn't be utterly destroyed by losing one of your babies then you haven't thought this plan out."

God, she'd never thought about it. She'd thought about being friendly with a husband—she could get by without really *needing* a man—but she'd always wanted kids. The idea of anything bad happening to little Sabir and Michael flattened her with agonizing grief—and they weren't even her babies.

The world could be a terrible, sometimes intolerant place. No one was guaranteed forever. No one was guaranteed joy and happiness. What happened if something unspeakable happened to one of her children? How could she go on living? How would she endure the pain?

"Are you all right?" Piper asked.

She shook her head. "No. I'm not. I can't stand the way you're looking at me. Please, Piper. I'm not some kind of monster."

Piper crossed the room and hugged her tight. "I love you, but you have to figure out what you want and how much of yourself you're willing to risk to have it. You have to look at what happened to our parents through different eyes. You're still seeing it like a child would."

"I don't understand." She didn't understand anything.

The night before had been so beautiful, and now she felt as if she stood in a maelstrom of emotion. She wanted the Thurston-Hughes brothers. She ached with terrible desperation, yet that very ache told Tori that she should walk away now. If she didn't, she could be left in pieces someday. Already, she could feel tears of sorrow and loss rolling down her cheeks. If the worst happened and she started crying, would she ever stop?

Piper slanted a gaze her way, compassion in her blue eyes. "You are taking that loss as the sum of their lives. You aren't looking at all the joy they had before. I don't believe Dad killed himself. He was mourning her, but eventually he would have come out of it. He would always have missed her, always have loved her, but he would have found a life again. I get that you're scared, but it's time to move past it. You don't honor them by living a life where nothing and no one can touch you. You were blessed with two parents who loved each other. Learn from them. Grasp love and joy and happiness with both hands. God, Mindy, you have to let yourself feel because there's no life worth living that doesn't also involve loss. If you don't ache sometimes it's because you have nothing inside."

So much for avoiding the profound conversation.

Tori tried not to flinch. "I don't know if I can do it."

Her sister took her hands. "You have to try or you will

lose them. And you will spend your life alone, regretting their loss every day. Would you rather lose them now, without ever really knowing what their devotion feels like, or what kind of husbands and fathers they would be, or how they would hold your hand through the good and the bad? Or would you rather lose them after years of storing treasured memories you could recall on a rainy day once your hair is gray and you're surrounded by your grandchildren?"

Piper's words hit her like a blow to the chest, and Tori wasn't sure she could breathe. Could she walk away now and never feel them again?

"And consider this," her sister added softly. "They're taking a chance on you, too. They're willing to love you now, knowing loss may come someday. They're willing to trust you with their hearts. Maybe you think that's easy for Callum and Rory. But for Oliver..."

After what Oliver had endured with Yasmin and her betrayal, she couldn't have blamed him for being the most hesitant of all. Yet here she was, holding out on them.

Tori sent her sister a glance filled with uncertainty, fear, and shame. But she didn't know what to say.

"I raised you with love." Regret filled Piper's voice. "I thought I taught you better."

"Piper? Are you here?" a masculine voice called out.

The moment was broken, and Piper wiped her eyes as she turned. "Rafe? We're in here."

Tori took a deep breath and tried to hold back tears. She didn't want to cry in front of her brother-in-law. In front of anyone.

Rafe stepped in. "I'm glad you're here with your sister. We need to talk."

"What's happened?" Oh, the look on his face told Tori it was bad. Her hands started shaking. Had something happened to Callum or Oliver or Rory? Oliver had been through so much. He couldn't handle any more. Callum could be reckless. Rory drove too fast sometimes.

She couldn't breathe. Her whole body felt stiff with anxiety. This was what it would be like. She would always worry. "Are they all right?"

"Who?" Rafe gave her a puzzled frown.

Piper raised a brow. "The Thurston-Hughes brothers."

Rafe shrugged. "As far as I know, they're fine. What I wish to talk to you about is this." He held up a paper. "The British tabloids picked up the story of your fall. I'm sorry, Tori. We did everything we could to stop it, but apparently someone took video and it's on the Internet."

She looked at the paper. She'd told herself it was only a little slip and it wouldn't be a big deal. Deep down, she'd convinced herself that it would go away. Talib had a lot of power, but apparently nothing was as big as the Internet.

One look told Tori the images were worse than she could have imagined. It wasn't a single shot but a collage of her gracelessness. There was a shot of her looking grim as she walked down the stairs behind her luminous sister. The second shot showed her tripping, her face contorted in the ugliest way possible. In the third, she was nearly on her ass. The last shot revealed her breast, the mound on full display. It wasn't a mere nip slip. No, this was pretty much her whole boob. The shock on her face somehow looked an awful lot like a smile, one that suggested she'd meant to "trip" and expose herself to be the center of attention.

Bezakistan Shame: Queen's Younger Sister a Graceless Gold Digger.

The headline said it all. Tori wished the floor would open up and swallow her whole.

She glanced at the article. The scathing write-up was worse than she could imagine. Not only had someone captured those pictures, but they knew she'd been behind closed doors with the Thurston-Hughes brothers all night long. Knowing a video existed for anyone on YouTube to watch only demoralized her more.

She'd helped a starlet once who had a sex tape go viral.

The woman had been humiliated, called every kind of name. Tori hadn't intentionally made a sex tape. And who would want to hire a publicist who caused a scandal? No one. These images could kill her career. Once that was gone, she wouldn't have anything left.

She especially wouldn't have the men she loved.

Panic threatened. Dizziness washed over her. She reached out for anything to balance herself but found nothing. No one.

"Mindy, this is not a big deal," her sister said. She felt a hand on her shoulder. "Why are you crying?"

Her nephews would see this one day. Her prospective employers. Her friends. Her men. Nothing ever went away on the Internet.

Maybe Oliver would read the words and think she was just as bad as his ex-wife.

Tori feared she would spend the rest of her life defending herself from rumors and allegations. She loved the people in her life—especially the three Brits who had captured her heart—but she couldn't handle this.

Her heart was pounding as if it was going to come right out of her chest. Her feet went numb. Everything else tingled as if she'd swallowed a jar of bees.

"I think she's having an anxiety attack." Someone was speaking. She thought it was her brother-in-law.

"Mindy, calm down. Take deep breaths. Rafe, I think we need a doctor."

Why did her sister sound so far away?

It didn't matter. Her brain was whirling. As she stared at the newspaper, the pictures and words seemed to swirl together.

She heard someone shout as the world became a blissful black.

* * * *

Rory stared at the paper. He'd read it twice and the words still didn't make sense.

The pictures of his lovely Tori could only be described as humiliating. At least he was sure she would see them that way. He thought she was cute, and damn he loved that breast. He just wished the rest of the world wasn't seeing it.

However, the piece written by one particularly vicious bitch had been picked up by more than one British paper. That article made him want to gut someone.

The "journalist" had described Tori as a gold-digging whore out for a perverted version of the love her sister had found. They'd even talked to Callum's ex, who implied that the former footballer had left her for Tori in order to please his brothers, who were under her spell. Thea had lied to the reporter, saying that Callum had asked her to marry him, and as a result, Rory and Oliver then threatened to cut him off from the family wealth. She claimed Tori had been behind the recent stories that her pregnancy was false and she was out to bilk her baby's father.

"We have to be certain Tori never sees this," Callum said, his face ferocious.

Oliver shook his head. "I'm sure she's already seen it. The press office of the palace receives newspapers from across the globe and they'll definitely inform the sheikh. He won't allow her to walk around ignorant. He'll sit her down and tell her what's happened."

"Surely he'll tell us first." But Rory suspected he wouldn't. Talib al Mussad would likely keep up his responsibilities to his sister-in-law until the moment they put a ring on her finger.

After a cursory knock, the door to their suite opened, and Piper stepped through followed by Rafiq and Kadir. She was pale and wore what looked like elegant pajamas, which were much more casual than he'd ever seen her.

Her eyes went straight to the papers. "You've seen it, then."

Oliver stepped forward. "Yes. Where's Tori? When we woke, she was gone."

"She told me she was going to the bathroom. She never came back," Rory explained. "It's been over two hours."

Rory feared she'd run away like a scared rabbit. He'd thought they'd settled things last night, but it looked as if they still had issues. Now he had to deal with the tabloids as well.

He swiveled a glance at her sister. If anyone knew how to deal with Tori, it was Piper. "Where is she?"

"In her room resting," Piper explained. "She didn't handle the news story well."

Rory could only imagine. "Why did you show her the article?"

"There was no way she wouldn't learn the truth," Rafe explained. "You don't understand how bad it is. These pictures come from a video."

Rory swore. "Which is all over the Internet by now."

"Yes," Kade affirmed. "Every tabloid has added its commentary. It's even made the news in some of the U.S. rags. She had to be told. We couldn't leave her to discover the news alone."

"Telling Tori should have been our responsibility." Callum stared at the al Mussad brothers. "She's ours."

Rafe launched into some ridiculous story about how they hadn't wanted to disturb the sleeping brothers, but Rory was watching Piper. She'd winced, turned pink. He'd worked in business long enough to know how to read a person. Rafe and Kade would never give anything away, but Piper's reaction told him she had something to hide.

"Your Highness, what do you know that we don't?" Rory would be polite, but he meant to get to the heart of the matter.

Kade stepped in front of his wife as though shielding her. "She didn't make this decision. The sheikh did, and we back him. Tori isn't your wife. Until such time, we assume responsibility for her."

"You'll have to forgive them," Piper said, trying to move

around her husband. "They never left the Dark Ages. For them, a woman goes from her father—or in this case, her brothers—to her husbands."

Rafe shook his head. "It's not quite as bad as that, but in our world, Talib is the head of the family. Tori is a member of that family. We feel she requires someone to watch after her. She's obviously a smart girl, but there's more at stake than her own reputation. This trashy article, despite the fact that its origin is about an innocent fall, has the possibility to harm us all. We have to protect our own."

"Then you won't mind turning Tori over to us. That way, she won't be your problem anymore," Rory growled more harshly than he intended, but he meant every word. He didn't appreciate the idea that the royal family now viewed her as a publicity liability.

Callum stepped beside him, presenting a united front. "She's a person, not some figurehead. I won't have her hurt in order to save the people who should love her a few problems. The palace can go to hell for all I care. She's the one who matters here."

Piper smiled, but there was a wealth of sadness behind it. "I'm very grateful you feel that way. I knew you were all good men."

"But?" Oliver stood. He'd stayed out of the circle of conversation, holding himself back. It was something he did frequently, so Rory hadn't thought much of it. Now he could see a chill settle over Oliver. His eyes had gone positively arctic as he looked at the queen. "I assume there's a but somewhere in that sentence."

Oliver was shutting down right in front of him. The night before he'd been so open, like the Oliver he'd known before Yasmin. With every second that went by, Rory watched his brother rebuilding his walls again.

Worse, he suspected Oliver was correct. "Where is Tori?"

Callum shook his head. "The wedding ring is a formality

at this point. We decided last night. She belongs to us. Piper, we'll take good care of your sister. We love her. I don't understand why there's a guard posted outside her door."

That was news to Rory. "When did you go looking for her?"

Callum shoved a hand through his hair, the gesture rife with frustration. "When I woke up and she was gone. The guard wouldn't let me in. Then when I found the paper, I went into problem-solving mode and I forgot to tell you. Obviously, Tori is embarrassed, but there's no reason for her to be. None of this was her fault. The press is being vicious, and we'll sue every single paper that runs a story disparaging her. And I'll beat the living shit out of the reporters."

"She fainted," Piper explained. "The doctor was with her when you came by. I actually think it was more than a fainting spell. I think she had an anxiety attack. These last few weeks, especially last night, have been too much for her."

Dread rolled over Rory at her words.

Callum immediately started for the door. Dane and Cooper stepped in front of the entrance to the hall, blocking the path that would ultimately lead them to Tori's suite. Callum stopped and turned around, his eyes wide with surprise. "What is the meaning of this? I want to see my fiancée. I have the right to make certain she's well. For god's sake, you would want the same thing if we were talking about Piper."

"But we aren't talking about Piper. We're talking about Tori." Oliver picked up the small bag he'd brought with him the night before and stepped toward Kade. "Is she going to be all right? Physically, I mean."

Kade nodded. "I think so. She was quite emotional when I saw her. We'll watch her and take care of her."

"If she needs anything, please contact me. If not..." Oliver nodded toward Piper. "Please give your sister my best and tell her I won't bother her again. She's free of all obligations to Thurston-Hughes Inc."

A tear slipped down Piper's cheek. "I'm sorry it's ended this way, Oliver. For what it's worth, I thought you were good for her."

His lips curled up in a half smile that contained not an ounce of amusement. "Tori is a smart girl. Perhaps she's emotional now, but...she knows a good thing when she sees it. And obviously, she knows how to quit while she's ahead."

Rory stared at his eldest brother. What the hell was he doing? "Oliver, she's just had a shock. Give her a bit. We should be supporting her through this debacle, not walking away."

"He's right," Callum argued. "Don't be a barmy fuck. She needs us."

Oliver's face hardened to sharp lines. "Do you not see those two?" He gestured to the guards. "They aren't protecting us. They're here to make sure we can't see Torrance. They're ensuring she doesn't have to see us again. And in case you haven't been listening, she was hysterical at the thought of having to be around us."

Piper shook her head. "That's not what I said."

Rory ignored her. "Why? I told her what we wanted last night. I made it very clear."

"I told her I loved her." Callum looked back at him. "She didn't say it back. I thought she was simply being shy."

This couldn't be happening. Rory stumbled back, the moment smacking him in the face. He felt sick. "Something's wrong here. I made it plain to her that if she came to the suite last night with us, we were starting a relationship. I told her I love her, too. I explained that we wouldn't settle for less than marriage."

Had she not believed him? Somehow misunderstood him?

Oliver sighed as though Rory's naiveté was too sad to contemplate. "And she took what she desired anyway. She wanted us physically. Obviously, Tori never sought more than sex. Just because she was a virgin doesn't mean she's incapable of lying to get the orgasms she wanted."

"But I love her." Callum seemed caught, all that confidence from the night before dissolving in the face of the truth.

"I told her we had marriage in mind," Rory insisted.

"We don't always get what we want, brother." Oliver stepped toward the door, his shoulders slumping. "You've led a charmed existence, so maybe you weren't aware. Welcome to what the rest of the world knows. Just because we love someone doesn't mean they'll love us back. Does the fact that Tori doesn't want three broken bastards really surprise you?" He scoffed. "When does our flight leave?"

"Our flight?" Rory hadn't arranged the return trip.

"I'm almost certain we've worn out our welcome here." Oliver glanced back at the al Mussads. "You've readied our plane to whisk the unwanted lovers away, correct?"

Rafe's lips pursed in a tight frown. "Your jet will be fueled and ready for you this afternoon. We ask that you stay in your rooms until then to avoid any uncomfortable situations."

"She's kicking us out of her bed after one night?" Callum dropped into a chair, his expression incredulous.

"They've been explaining that in some detail, yes. She's had what she wants from us and she's done," Oliver explained. He turned back to the guards. "Could you escort me to my rooms? I need to pack."

"Oliver?" Piper began.

His oldest brother held out a hand. "No need to explain, Your Highness. I wish you luck with the rest of your life. You'll understand if I don't see you again. I'm afraid your family has done enough to me. I'll stay away from now on."

Cooper looked to Kade, who nodded. The sentry escorted Oliver out.

The guards really were barring them from seeing Tori. She really didn't want them anymore.

"This makes no sense," Rory argued. "She's not a selfish

girl. Something's scared her. Piper, I have to talk to her." He refused to let them end this way. If he could sit down with her, he could talk some sense into her. He could figure out what she was really afraid of.

"I'm sorry," Piper said as she clutched Rafe's hand. "She's overwhelmed now and not terribly rational. I think maybe if this whole thing with the tabloids hadn't gone wrong, you might have been able to get through to her. But as it stands, this is too much for her to deal with. I think she's hidden it well until now, but she's damaged, too."

"Damaged how?"

"Our parents...they were madly in love. Then my mom died, and everything went to hell. Tori was a kid. She didn't understand how many wonderful years came before the tragedy. She only knew that one day everything was perfect and the next her world crumbled. Our dad took it particularly hard. Tori saw him fading. Then he was killed in a car accident. She never had the chance to see him embrace life again. In her mind, love leaves people an empty shell. It's something to avoid at all costs."

In other words, anything resembling love would threaten her, and she would run. Like she had. She was putting up wall after wall between them, locking doors and protecting herself with guards because she cared too much.

The chemistry between them had always been undeniable. During their months together in London, their friendship and respect had blossomed into so much more. She'd known how he felt when she'd taken his hand last night. He suspected she'd known quite well what was in her own heart, too.

A hot dose of anger surged through his system. "So she was never going to give us a real chance. Why would she go to bed with us when she knew what we wanted and that she would never give it to us?"

"Because I think deep down she wanted to try. She loves you. I think she didn't want to go through the rest of her life not knowing what it meant to be yours, even if it was only for a night," Piper said. "She's had a shock. If you give her time, she'll recover. I'll talk to Talib and ensure that you have an invitation to come back in a few weeks for Sabir's birthday. I believe she'll attend. Once the tabloids have calmed down, I also think she'll be able to see reason and will come around."

Kade nodded to his brother. "Now, Her Highness has had a rough morning. Why don't you take her back to our rooms, brother?"

Rafe led Piper out, and Rory felt more fury spark his system.

Kade moved to stand in front of him. "You can't take anything Tori does right now too seriously."

"I have an engagement ring for her." Callum shook his head as though trying to clear it. "We were going to formally ask her tonight."

"Don't give up," Kade advised. "She's confused and overwhelmed. This kind of life can do that to a normal person. This is the first time she's been at the center of the storm, and it's a nasty one. Couple that with the fact that this being her first time to really be in love, and I think she's so overwhelmed she can't function. What she needs is to get out of the palace, go someplace quiet so she can think about this. I don't claim to truly understand what Tori's going through, but I know Piper was in shock when she first became involved with my brothers and me, as well as a target for the press."

"How did you break through?" Callum asked. He stood again as though even the thought of having something active to do restored his energy.

"Tori doesn't want us to break through," Rory pointed out.

She'd lied. She'd played them all for fools. Rory felt doubly foolish because he had instigated the very incident she'd used to get what she'd wanted. She'd danced with him, taken his hand, and agreed to everything he'd asked for. And that had included giving them a chance.

He wondered now… If Oliver had given her pleasure when he'd taken her virginity, would she have even bothered to sleep with the rest of them? Maybe she'd only wanted a night to ensure that she experienced the pleasures to be found in sex. Now that she had, she obviously no longer needed them.

"Of course she does." Callum was always the optimist. "She's scared and she needs us. Just because the palace wants us to return to London doesn't mean we have to."

"I don't know. Talib was fairly adamant. After he talked to Tori, he made the decision to ask you to leave. I think for now it would be best for you all to lay low," Kade said.

"I didn't say we wouldn't leave Bezakistan. We could return to England. We've got a country house. It's isolated and peaceful, but you're insane if you think I'll go along without Tori." Callum stared at their host. "Tell her she'd better not ever leave the palace again because I won't be pushed away. I'll do whatever it takes to make certain she doesn't forget me."

Kade smiled. "That's the resolve you'll need. And she won't stay in the palace forever. I believe I overheard her talking about Dallas."

"Excellent. I'll be waiting for her there. Tell her that if she makes me hunt her down, I won't be happy. She'll be much better off if she simply agrees to talk to me now." Callum's Dom had risen to the fore again.

Rory stared at his brother. Either that threat would prove to be the stupidest move in history…or the most brilliant strategy ever.

Kade bowed slightly and left them alone with Dane standing guard outside. Rory suspected Alea's other husband, Landon, was watching over Torrance, ensuring she didn't have to deal with the men she'd promised the world to the night before. Oh, she might not have said the words and that was his fault. He should have insisted. He should have suspected she'd run.

He should have known white lace and promises with Torrance wouldn't work.

"So we'll tell the pilot to take us to Dallas," Callum was saying. "I want to be there when she lands."

Rory couldn't fathom why Cal thought that was a good idea. "Why? So she can call the police and take out a restraining order?"

"No, so I can put her over my bloody knee, spank her, then give her the hard fucking she deserves for pulling this shit. Afterward, I'll figure out what's going on in her head and fix it."

"All you'll do is get yourself thrown in jail for attacking her."

Callum stopped. "She doesn't want to be alone. She's upset and confused, embarrassed and overwhelmed. She needs a reason to trust and embrace. We're going to give it to her."

"Are you mad?" Rory asked. "Did you forget the part where she's locked all the doors between us? She doesn't want a reason to stop because she's already got one: She doesn't want us. She's told us flatly that she's done."

Callum tensed his jaw, his face set in stubborn lines. "No. She ran because deep down she thinks we'll abandon her like her parents did."

"Her parents died."

Callum paced, his mind obviously going a mile a minute. "Either way, they left. I didn't say it was rational. Our feelings, our motivations, they aren't always logical, either. She's terrified, and not just of having her world fall apart again. My god, I don't know a single woman worth loving who wouldn't be afraid of us. We're asking her to be the center of three worlds. We can pretend that we'll live in harmony, but we're human. There's going to be conflict, and Tori will have to deal with it. She's young and inexperienced and she's not handling things as perfectly as we would want her to. That's no reason to leave her completely alone. Don't you see? Being alone is what she really fears most. She just has to realize it."

Rory tried very hard not to punch his brother. "Would you open your eyes? She left us. She's done."

Callum rolled his eyes. "Grow up. You and Oliver always think you've had it so much harder than I did because I played football. You know what I learned because I wasn't in some ivory fucking tower either learning how to run a business or allowing people to run it for me? I figured out we've all got it rough because we're human, and every person ever born went through bad shit. The only way to survive is to hold on to what you love with both hands. She's scared and I love her, so I won't let her be alone. Your problem is you don't think she's worth loving if she can't love you back the way you demand it. That's fucking selfish. I'm going after her. Until she tells me her life is worse for having me in it, I'm going to make her world better. You and Oliver can cling to your damage like some shield."

Callum charged away, and Rory could hear him in the closet. He was packing. The minute the plane touched down in London, Callum would hop on a flight to Dallas. Being a professional athlete had clearly taught his older brother never to give up. And somewhere along the way, his brother had learned to love with his whole heart.

Rory stared out the window. Somewhere out there, Tori was alone. Had she lied or had she not understood how she would feel the next day? Had she meant to deceive them or been inundated by fear in the cold light of day?

He took a deep breath and made a decision. Life came down to decisions. He'd taken responsibility for her the night before. The Tori he knew would never mean to hurt anyone, and nothing that had happened this morning changed his view of her or how he felt. She belonged to them, and it was time to show her what that meant.

Even if he had to go all the way to Texas to do it.

CHAPTER TWELVE

Oliver stared at the spot where he'd almost died and he put a hand on his chest. He could still feel the bullet pierce him, feel his knees hit the marble floor, smell the coppery scent of blood fill his world.

And he could hear her.

I've set everything up so it looks like you killed yourself and poor dumb Oliver.

Yasmin had prowled around, stalking Alea who had always been her target. That day, he'd discovered she'd married him under false pretenses and every moment of their life together had been a lie. Still, that wasn't what hurt the most.

His brother already thinks very little of him. When he hears about this, he'll think even less.

Of course she'd been talking about his made-up affair with Alea, but that wasn't what haunted him all these years afterward.

He was fairly certain Rory thought less of him for being so weak, for allowing himself to fall into that relationship, for being so pathetically blind.

And now he knew what Tori really thought.

For one brief moment, he'd thought it could work. Oh, he'd certainly intended to be in the background. He didn't deserve to take control. A company was one thing, but a woman as fragile and priceless as Tori? Never. He wasn't that man, but any time at all with her had seemed better than none. Now he knew what heaven tasted like.

It hurt to be sent back to hell.

"Tal told me I would find you here," a familiar voice said. Alea. "You know I moved to a different part of the palace after I married. I haven't been in here in a while."

Ah, Talib was sending in the troops to make sure there was an orderly dismissal. He'd been surprised the sheikh had so readily accepted him into the palace in the first place. He'd shocked himself by asking to stay in the very rooms where he'd almost died. Then again, he'd come here looking for insight or closure—something that escaped him now. He'd thought he needed to walk this room again, remember…and try to forget.

He'd needed to see that the room had moved on even if he hadn't.

All he'd really learned was that none of it mattered. He couldn't change what happened here. Staying in these rooms, making love to Tori—those things didn't fix the truth he'd learned about himself.

"I don't blame you for moving. I would have, too," he said quietly to Alea.

This was the first time he'd been back to the palace in years. He'd stood outside for long moments the day before, looking up at the elegant structure, unmoving. Rafe had finally come out and escorted him inside.

"I did it for practical reasons. This space wasn't big enough for all of us. I always loved this room. It was my safe place after I was first rescued." She walked around the room, a little smile on her face as she took it in.

Alea had been taken prisoner thanks to his late wife. She'd arranged for Alea to be kidnapped and sold to a bordello. The princess's life had become a living hell because Yasmin had been jealous. All the bad things in his world had flowed from that woman and her black heart.

How could he have been married to the devil and never seen it?

"It was safe until my wife tried to kill you here."

She shook her head. "The place itself was always safe. Sometimes the wrong person walks in and we have to deal with it. It doesn't make the place itself less beautiful. It doesn't erase the fact that I came back to life in this room. No one but me can erase those things, and why would I want to do that?"

He looked at the vibrant woman she'd become, remembering the sweet girl she'd been and also the hollow soul who had returned home so broken. Alea had changed and grown and survived. No. He survived. Survival was the simple process of breathing, walking, and sleeping every day. Alea thrived. She'd been through the crucible and found peace, happiness, and love. She'd discovered her true soul. Unfortunately, so had Oliver.

"It's good to see you. I came to Bezakistan, in part, to talk to you. But first, I want you to know that I won't give Tori any trouble. I'm already packed. I'll leave quietly this afternoon." He would go back to London and try to figure out what to do with the rest of his life.

"I thought you might say that. Talib really doesn't want to send you away, you know."

"No, but Tori does and she has the right to feel comfortable." Most women didn't have the luxury of spending the night with three men only to forcibly ship them out of the country the next morning.

"Tori is making a dreadful mistake. Tal feels guilty that he wasn't able to keep her mishap out of the papers. Did you read them? They were particularly nasty."

He'd only really needed to see the headlines to know how devastated Tori must be. It was proof that she wasn't ready to handle the gossip of being with three men, even if they would have stood by her until the end of time. Clearly, she'd never wanted them much. "They're always nasty."

"Something I've observed over the years... Women don't react like men. Most men would get angry, even downright furious, about something like that. Then they'd shrug and move on, do something more active. Women aren't quite as able to compartmentalize. Tori feels like a laughingstock. I understand. I had to deal with lies the press told about me, too. I think women, especially ones with tender hearts, can really let something like that drag them under." She stepped up to the balcony. "I jumped from here, you know."

He could barely make himself step outside. He wasn't afraid of heights, but he was afraid of being seen. The last thing Tori needed was to have any quiet walk in the garden she might be taking disrupted by the sight of him. So he stayed just inside the French doors. "I was told. I didn't see it."

"You were busy dying, Oliver."

Yes, he'd been on the floor, his lifeblood draining away while Alea had fought for her life. From what he understood, Yasmin had chased her out to the balcony, and Alea had been forced to choose between taking a bullet or hoping Landon Nix would catch her. "I'm sorry you had to jump."

And during all that, Oliver had been useless, a mass of pathetic humanity lying on the floor.

"I'm happy I had the chance to. If you hadn't fought as hard as you did, I wouldn't have."

"What are you talking about?" There'd been no fight. He'd taken a bullet and he'd gone down.

She turned to him quizzically, eyes wide for a silent moment. "You don't remember?"

"Of course I remember." How could he ever forget that day? It was ingrained on his memory, every horrible moment of it. "She shot me. I fell. I didn't get back up."

"Oliver, she shot you more than once," Alea said quietly.

He knew that. He felt the scars every day. "Yes, my wife tried to be thorough. I went down and she kept shooting."

"No." Alea hurried back into the room and put her hand in his as she led him to the couch. "I can't believe you don't remember what really happened. I mean, the event was traumatic, so it stands to reason. I just assumed you knew the truth so I never told you."

He sat beside her, feeling so much older than his thirty-one years. They'd never talked because he hadn't wanted to. He'd never wanted to trek down this memory lane again and remember what a mess he'd made of things by being weak. "There's nothing to tell. The scars prove everything."

She leaned forward, her midnight eyes steady on him. "Scars are what you make them, Oliver. They're reminders of the things that happened to us, but yours are lying to you. I was there, and I didn't have a bullet in me so I remember everything with perfect clarity. Yasmin walked in, called me a bitch whore—I don't know where she got that mouth—and shot you. She then talked for a really long time. Do you not remember that? She told me everything. In fact, she couldn't wait to tell me she'd been behind all of it."

Sometimes in his dreams, Yasmin kept talking while the pain in his gut had him praying for death just to put a stop to her incessant chatter. "She loved the sound of her own voice. I learned to tune her out or go mad."

Alea leaned forward. "The whole time she was talking about what she'd done, you were getting up. I kept her attention on me because I didn't want her to see that you still had so much strength."

He didn't remember that at all. He shook his head because her words didn't make any sense. "I was on the floor over there."

He pointed to a spot on the other side of the room.

"That's where you ended up, but that's not where you fell. You fell ten feet that way." She nodded to a place in front of the sofa. "If you look at the crime scene photos, you'll see a large pool of blood there. It's yours. I'm sure Tal has them buried somewhere in the records. She shot you the first time right there. You went down, but you didn't stay there."

He stared at the spot, reality shifting deep inside him. The scenario Alea described didn't match his memories. He remembered being weak and helpless and soft. He hadn't fought. He'd just lain there and waited to die like some hapless prey. "How did I end up on the opposite side of the room?"

Alea took his hand in hers. "You ended up there because you got to your feet and you attacked her. She was busy threatening me. It would have been easy for you to get to the door. At that point, you only had one bullet in your body. That wound wasn't life-threatening. The second shot was. You could have left me and saved yourself, but you didn't. You got to your feet, told her she wasn't getting away with it, and you wrapped your hands around her throat."

Her words sparked some memory in the haze of that day. Some little whisper that told him Alea was telling him the truth he'd forgotten in the thickness of shock and pain.

I disagree, bitch.

That day was beginning to come back to him. "She said she wasn't going down for your abduction or my death. She intended to blame everything on you and me."

She said those things and he'd replied with *I disagree, bitch.* He remembered his mouth making the words. He'd had to force them from his throat.

Alea nodded excitedly. "Yes. She did and I tried to keep her attention on me so you could make your move."

"You didn't think I would run?"

"I knew you wouldn't. The minute I saw you forcing yourself up, I knew you would fight her. And you did. You're the reason I made it to the balcony. You're the reason I'm alive today, Oliver." There was a sheen of tears in her eyes. "I know you came here, at least in part, because you had some misguided notion that you should apologize to me. There's no need, but there is something left unsaid between us. Thank you. Thank you for being as strong as you were. Thank you for fighting."

Memories like flashes of lightning sparked through him as more of the terrible incident came back to him. He stood suddenly because the world blurred. Shock steamrolled him. "Thank you for coming. I need to be alone for a bit."

He knew he was being terribly rude, but he couldn't help it. A dam was about to open, and he couldn't contain it another second.

As she hurried to leave, he shut the door between the parlor and the bedroom. It seemed like forever before he reached the bathroom. He locked himself in and fell to the floor, cool marble beneath his hands.

He'd been wrong. For the last several years, he had been about deriding himself for his weakness, for his inability to fight, but now the day came back with righteous clarity, like a dream he'd forgotten but that lay beneath the surface of his consciousness. He remembered how hard it had been to stand that day and fend off his own wife. His legs hadn't wanted to work, but he'd forced them to. It flooded back, the sights, the sounds, her voice. The pain. And the rage. It had pooled and boiled inside him. He'd been a volcano of fury. But above the anger, there had been something else. He'd been dying and he'd refused to let Alea die, too.

As much as he'd hated his wife, it had been the thought of an innocent woman—his friend—dying that forced him to his feet.

He hadn't been weak after all. He'd made a choice, so he'd fought. And he'd won. Now he knew the truth: When his world had shattered, when death had been whispering along his spine, he'd told it to go to hell. He'd tried to do the right thing even at the cost of his own life.

He rested his cheek against the floor, the shock of revelation bringing him full circle. He was once again on the floor, his body weak with memory, but now there was a difference.

Oliver Thurston-Hughes knew he would get up again. He would fight.

His father had told him once that a man didn't know the sum of his soul until he faced death. He hadn't been measured and found wanting after all. He'd fought for himself and for Alea. He'd only survived since because he hadn't really decided to start living again.

That changed now.

When he got to his feet, he felt like a different human being. Some weight had been lifted, and for the first time since that terrible day, he could look at himself in the mirror with pride.

He'd fought. He was a fighter.

And now he had something worth fighting for.

Tori.

He washed his face and calmed, some peace and confidence settling deep inside him. The trouble was, he didn't just have to fight for Tori. He had to get around Talib and all those doors she'd locked between them.

Luckily, he knew a little bit about being a sneaky bastard.

Once he'd been a man who knew how to get what he wanted. He wanted Tori Glen. She would be his prize for fighting and coming out victorious. For finally moving on.

He straightened his shirt and walked back into the parlor. Alea was standing at the door, talking to her husband. Ah, his guard. The first hurdle. He knew how to handle the guard.

"I need to speak to my brothers," he said politely. He never yelled when politeness would work.

Landon Nix frowned. "I'm sorry. I'm supposed to keep you in here until it's time for your plane to depart. It's only a few hours. Do you need something?"

He glanced Alea's way. "Please. I won't try to speak to Tori. I simply need to be with my brothers. Talking about that day…" He drew in a shuddering breath. "I need their company."

She took his hand and started down the hall.

Lan cursed and followed, but he didn't try to stop them again.

All the while, Oliver's brain churned, his heart hammering because he had the solution—and it was so simple. Tori had done them the favor of coming to the palace. Oliver intended to use that in order to help her past her pride and facilitate the ending that would make them all happy.

They were in Bezakistan, and the rules were different here. Tori really should have remembered that. Likely, she'd thought he and his brothers were polite Brits. But Oliver had been married to a Bezakistani national, so they'd granted him dual citizenship. That made him Bezakistani, too.

He had rights here that sweet Tori might not be aware of. He doubted she would believe he'd ever exercise them. But oh, he intended to.

She would belong to him and his brothers again because they would take her—with Talib's blessing. Because the sheikh would never violate or refuse the laws of his own country.

Lan opened the door to Callum and Rory's suite.

Alea hugged him. "I hope you find some peace, Oliver. I know it didn't work with Tori, but there's a woman out there for someone as kind as you."

He schooled his expression into something suitably bland. He needed to play the pathetic, depressed Oliver for a few minutes more because he didn't want to tip anyone off about his plans...just in case.

"I hope you're right." He managed a broken murmur.

Alea kissed his cheek as though he was fragile and promised to call. Then she left, and he was alone with his brothers.

"I know you're upset with Tori, but you have to listen, Ollie." Callum came at him, pure willpower shining in his eyes.

Why had he ever thought his brother was laidback?

Callum was only laidback when he didn't care. When something mattered, he pursued what he wanted with a singular purpose.

"No, I need you to sit down."

Callum clenched his jaw. "I'm not going to listen to reasons why we should leave her and walk away from Tori. I'm going to Dallas. That's where she'll be."

"I'm going with him." Rory nodded, his decision made.

Thank god. He'd thought he might have to convince his youngest brother that Tori was the woman for them, but it looked like Callum had done that job. "None of us are going to Dallas."

His brothers began to argue.

"Stop! We're not going to Dallas because Tori won't be there. She'll be on that bloody plane to London with us. How much rope do we have? And dear god, tell me we have some sort of gag because I don't think she'll go quietly."

Callum's jaw dropped. It was good to know he could surprise his brother. "What the hell are you saying?"

"I'm saying that I'm a Bezakistani citizen and I have rights in this country. We're not going to Dallas on our hands and knees. We're not going to beg. Tori chose to hide in Bezakistan and I'm going to claim my right. Brothers, we're going to steal our bride."

* * * *

Tori looked out over the gardens and wondered if the three brothers were on their plane back to London yet.

Her heart ached at the thought. She would never see them again. Never touch or hold them or even talk to them. Their chats had always been the best part of her day. She'd loved working at Thurston-Hughes. The dynamic environment meant there'd always been something happening, and she'd enjoyed the challenge of dealing with the British press.

Except when the press was after her. She stared out into

the night and tried to tell herself she'd done the right thing. She couldn't handle being the center of attention. She couldn't handle their high-profile lives. There was a cost that came with the money and fame. She didn't mind the money, but she loathed the fame. She wanted a quiet life. They couldn't give it to her.

And she couldn't give them what they deserved. She couldn't give them a whole heart because she was too afraid.

"How are you?" Piper asked as she walked out onto the balcony.

At least her sister was still talking to her. She was fairly certain Talib wasn't. When she'd asked him to send the Thurston-Hughes brothers home, he'd become frustrated with her, pushing her to tell him what had really happened. She'd cried until he'd given in but she could tell he'd been deeply disappointed in her.

"I'm fine. I'm ready to head home." Her bags were packed. She'd leave for Texas in the morning mere hours after the best men that ever happened to her got the boot from the country. She wondered if they hated her now.

"Is it really home? I'm not there. You don't have any friends in Dallas, do you? So why is it home?" Piper seemed to feel the need to ask her hard questions today.

But her sister was right. Dallas wasn't home. Tori wasn't even sure she had one. Home was where the people you loved live.

God, home was England, and she would never go back.

"I'm going to make it my home." Tears threatened, but if she showed Piper a single sign of regret, her sage sister would be all over it.

"Tell me why you sent them away. And I swear I will scream if you tell me that they meant nothing to you beyond sex and you're over them."

At least she could answer this one. "It wouldn't work. It was good for a night, but it can't work long term."

"Why not? It works for me."

Tori sighed. "But that's the norm here. The law. Not so much in London."

"You didn't even try to make it work," Piper pointed out.

She fisted her hands at her sides. "I don't have to try. I've watched those men for the last six months. They can't share, not long term. They fight too much. Last night was a moment out of time. It was great...but it wasn't reality. I know you think I'm making a mistake, but I believe everyone going their separate ways is the right thing. London just isn't like here. You saw how the press tore me apart for falling down the stairs. Can you imagine what they'll do if we actually got married?"

"Every marriage has its issues. You won't ever have to worry about money. And don't discount the beauty of that. You'll have every need met. Is there a tradeoff for that? Yes." Her sister leaned against the banister. "But I think you have a skewed view of the world. I'm kind of shocked that I never saw it before. You're very good at hiding it."

"I have a realistic view of the world, Piper. I live out in it. You're the one who's sheltered." She lived in a palace surrounded by guards and loving husbands.

Piper's lips turned up. "Am I? Do you know what I did two weeks ago?"

"I'm sure it was fabulous."

"I visited the border. We have refugees streaming in from the Middle East and we have to figure out how to house them and feed them because we can't turn them away."

The border was dangerous. Though Bezakistan had some cushion from the fighting happening all over the Middle East, it was still dangerous for anyone, let alone a royal. "Did Tal know? He would never let you go in there. Is that why there wasn't any press?"

"There wasn't any press because it wasn't a photo op," her sister said firmly. "It was an intelligence-gathering mission. I can't know what they need unless I talk to them myself and they can't know that the sheikh and I care unless we walk in, hand in hand, and show them. Talib understands that I won't be a figurehead who only poses and looks pretty and gives birth every now and then. He, Rafe, and Kade picked me and they can't change me. I'm going to do what I can to help my people."

"Piper, you could have been killed." The thought brought tears to her eyes.

Piper wiped them away with a tender swipe of her fingers. "It's good to know you care, but I'm going back in a few days. I'm helping to build temporary shelters. I won't leave those displaced people to the butchers of this world and I won't turn them away because they weren't born here. They've survived so much. I think I'm more scared when my husbands go than I am for myself."

"Yes, because you would be devastated if anything happened." And yet her brothers-in-law wouldn't hide and protect themselves. It went counter to who they were as human beings. Tori wanted to beg her sister to never go back, but she knew it wouldn't work. Piper was who she was. If she believed in a cause, she wouldn't back down, especially if someone needed her.

Suddenly Tori's life seemed the slightest bit shallow. She helped pretty people do pretty things and hide all the ugliness under the surface. She'd chosen a profession that masked the real issues of the world in glitter and glitz. "I understand why you didn't take the press with you, but having a campaign around the refugees could bring light to their plight. It could do them good."

"I know. I have someone working on it."

"Why wouldn't you ask me?" She was afraid she knew the answer.

"I don't know how you would handle walking through those camps. You hold yourself apart, and they need people who are open."

She did hold herself apart. Tori knew it now. She erected walls so she would stay safe.

Piper risked her life for people she didn't know. Tori wouldn't even risk her heart for three men she loved.

Love. She was starting to wonder if she even knew what the word meant.

"I've put something in your suitcase," her sister said. "After I packed up the old house, I sold it with all the furniture. I thought I'd cleaned out everything personal, but apparently I missed some nook in Dad's office. It's crazy but the people who bought the house have been trying to find me. Imagine their surprise when they discovered I was now a queen. Such a nice family. They could have sold those things to tabloids for a fortune, but they wanted us to have them. They sent me a box last month. I found Dad's journal and two old photo albums. I want you to spend the next month studying your childhood with adult eyes."

Her father had kept a journal. She knew that. She'd assumed it had been lost after he died. "I would love to read it. I don't know how much time I'll have though with moving and settling into a new job. I'll try to read it before I come back for Sabir's birthday."

Tori needed time and space to process things. Maybe in a few weeks she could write to one of the Thurston-Hughes brothers. Or all of them. Maybe they could find a friendship eventually. She couldn't stand the thought of never seeing or talking to them again.

Or never feeling their hands on her body, warm breath caressing her flesh.

The night air suddenly seemed warmer than before and she wondered if she would spend the rest of her life longing for them.

"Oh, I think you're going to have plenty of time." A secretive smile crossed Piper's face. "I really hope you can understand that we have traditions in Bezakistan that must be honored."

"Of course." She'd sat through many a bizarre dinner because ritual demanded it, though she refused to eat the fried goat balls everyone seemed crazy about. "I always try to honor my in-laws' traditions."

"Ah, but now they're your traditions, too. You see by Bezakistani law, you aren't merely an in-law. When I married my husbands, you became their sister. It's why they issued you a passport. Therefore, you have dual citizenship."

She understood that. It's one reason she had the right to travel here freely. "What are you trying to say?"

"I'm trying to say that while I had no real say in what's about to happen, I'm kind of glad. I never got this part. My men were sneakier than yours. Yours are taking the traditional, more aggressive approach." Piper stood in front of her, smoothing down her clothes. "Do you want some gloss? This occasion is usually marked with some photos."

"Occasion? Photos? I was getting ready to go to bed."

Piper just smiled. Something was afoot.

Before Tori could further question her sister, the door to her suite burst open and the Thurston-Hughes brothers strode in looking super-gorgeous and supremely satisfied. Why they looked so pleased—almost smug—she had no idea. Tori only knew that expression mirrored on their three faces scared her to death. She backed up, but had nowhere to go.

Talib, Rafe, and Kade sauntered in behind them, followed by Alea and her husbands.

Thank god. The royal guard was here. Dane, Cooper, and Lan were in their normal uniforms. They were big protectors with nice-sized guns.

Why weren't they dragging the brothers out? Not that she wanted to see them hurt, but they did have orders not to come near her. She'd been terrified that if someone forced her to speak with them that she'd give in. Tori felt sure that would be a very bad idea, especially before she had time to think. But god, they were beautiful. She hated to see them leave again.

"Dane, be gentle with them," she implored. "Don't hurt them."

The big sentry arched a single brow. "That's not going to be a problem."

Piper smiled as she kissed her sister on the cheek. "I'm so happy for you. Just remember that one day you'll forgive me. And don't forget about the stuff I put in your suitcase. Oh, I also included all your favorite hair products. They're hard to get where you're going."

In Dallas? But Oliver, Callum, and Rory's confident expressions told her she wouldn't be stepping foot in Texas.

"What's happening?" Tori clutched her sister's hand.

"Perhaps you should explain, cousin," Talib said, looking pointedly at Oliver.

Cousin? She'd never heard Tal refer to Oliver as his cousin, but Piper's husband was clearly making a point with that form of address. Tori's mind whirled. Bezakistanis took the family stuff seriously. She was proof of that. When a Bezakistani married, the rest of the family claimed the new spouse. Not as an in-law, but as a true child of the family.

Oh, god. Oliver had been married to Talib's cousin. Surely that didn't mean…

"By my rights as a Bezakistani male and a member of the royal and ruling family, I claim my bride. And by the rights of all males of this land, I choose to share her with my brothers." Oliver sent her a sizzling stare, and Tori felt as if he saw straight through the pajamas she'd put on only an hour before. They were soft and warm, and she'd thought about the fact that nothing had felt better against her skin than their hands. Nothing ever would.

Now she felt stripped and bare.

"What's going on?" she demanded again.

Talib ignored her, choosing to stand in front of Oliver. Maybe now her brother-in-law would explain that whatever Oliver thought he was doing wouldn't work.

Talib laid a hand on Oliver's head. "In lieu of your father, I will stand in his stead and I also stand for my sister. Take her with my blessings. As is our law, you have thirty days to convince her. Our brides might be stolen, but they are no slaves. The bride of a royal must be wooed and won in the allotted time or released to find a more suitable mate. I suggest you use this time to brand her with pleasure and chain her with affection."

"I don't want to be branded or chained," Tori protested. This had to be some weird dream. It couldn't be happening. "I'm a girl from Texas. We don't get stolen. Well, if we do, the law tends to object. You can't expect me to go with you because there's some outdated, barbaric ritual that shouldn't apply to me."

"The laws of this country very much apply to you, sister," Talib said as Kade and Rafe stepped to either side of her wearing smirks that infuriated her.

Was she being herded toward the Brits? "This is a joke, right? You people know it's the twenty-first century and this is technically a crime."

Talib stepped forward. "Not in this country. And you'll find now that Oliver Thurston-Hughes and his brothers have full Bezakistani citizenship. I believe they intend to take you somewhere private for your concubine period."

"My concubine period?" Holy shit. They were serious. According to law—ancient and slightly barbaric law—a Bezakistani royal was allowed to steal a wanted bride. She then became the concubine of the bride-thieving brothers and they had one month to use just about any means necessary to convince her to stay with them. If she chose to leave at the end, her wishes would be granted and she suffered no social dishonor.

How did they convince the bride? With pleasure. With sex. With long nights of seduction.

Everything about this idea was horrible. A terrifying joke. She was in love with them. If she gave them thirty days of intimacy, she would never be able to leave.

"You decide, but I hope you make the right choice. I hope you choose love over fear." Piper hugged her, then stood beside Talib. "I wish you well. And smile because the photographer is right outside. Private only. I know I wish I had pictures, but they never did the whole tying me up thing."

Talib smiled down at his bride. "I've made up for it, my love. I tie you up as often as possible. I believe our sister is going to do something foolish now."

Hell, yes, she was. She made a break for it. If she could get to the bathroom, she could lock herself in. Pure panic threatened. She sprinted toward the bathroom, her bare feet pounding across the marble.

Before she could make it, a strong arm banded around her middle, pulling her back against a hard, muscled chest.

"Give me a chance, darling. Give me ten minutes alone with you and if you don't agree with everything I have to say, I'll let you go. You can spend your thirty days here and we won't bother you again," Oliver vowed, his breath against her ear.

She breathed in his scent. Spicy and male and clean. It had been less than twenty-four hours since she'd touched him, and she'd missed him like they'd been apart for years. Her body betrayed her, folding back against him. The arm around her middle tightened, and she found herself leaning on his strength. "You can't steal me, Oliver."

"I can, but I won't. Give us ten minutes. You owe that to us."

Shame washed over her. He was right about that. Tori wondered if she'd made a terrible mistake. She was so confused, but was she making it better or worse by shutting them out? "All right. But you have to promise you'll let me go at the end."

"If you don't drop to your knees at the end and ask us to take you away, we'll leave you here. The concubine period will expire in thirty days, and this trial marriage will be over. You can tell Talib you refuse the suit and go on with your life."

"We can all go on with our lives," she said.

"Not us," Oliver replied. "I don't know what we'll do, but we'll love you until the day we die."

She turned, squirming her way out of his arms so she could see his face. "You don't use that word, Oliver."

He sighed. "I must. There isn't another word that comes close. I didn't know what it meant until you. Until now. Not really. But I realize love means being brave. Love means taking a chance. I love you. If you leave, I'll lose the best piece of myself."

"If you leave, I'll wait for you to come back," Rory promised. He moved in behind her. "I'll wait however long it takes because there's only one woman in the world for me."

"I'll move to Dallas." Callum put a hand in her hair. "You'll have to see me every day and know that I'm waiting for you to wake up and take what I offer you. What I will only ever offer to you. Look me in the eyes and tell me last night meant nothing. Then maybe, just maybe I can walk away, but I won't be whole again because last night was everything to me. Last night was the night my life really began."

This was why she'd guarded her door. She'd known they would say things to make her melt. To weaken her defenses. To persuade her to take a chance on them—and love.

She would have thirty days to figure out if they could make the marriage work. Thirty days to find out how brave she could be.

Tori dropped to her knees. "I don't need ten minutes. Take me away, Masters. I can't promise that I'll stay, but I will promise that I'll try."

As they smiled down at her, she wondered if she hadn't just sealed her fate.

CHAPTER THIRTEEN

Callum stared at the screen of his tablet, wishing he could reach through it and strangle whoever dreamed this shit up on the other side. The limo moved through the small village on the edge of their country estate. It wouldn't be long before they arrived. The flight from Bezakistan had taken them to a private airport where they'd been met by the limo currently whisking them to their solitude. Claire had already arrived and was preparing for their stay.

He suspected his sister might be their ace in the hole. For the next month, he and his brothers were supposed to be spending time convincing their new bride this marriage could work, but he rather thought Tori would enjoy having another woman to talk to. She'd grown up with a sister. Claire could be like another.

Unfortunately, Claire couldn't clean up the disaster that had been waiting for them when they'd arrived back in the UK and hit the tarmac.

The press had been out in full force. He'd hoped that since Tori's "exposé" had run the day before, the tabloids had found someone new to torment. But Tori was front page news again. Someone had snapped a picture of her at the palace ball wearing an angry sneer while he and his brother surrounded her. The headline read: *Gold digger mistress to three of Britain's elite?*

How could she be a bloody gold digger? She was the sister-in-law to three of the world's richest men. She had wealth at her fingertips.

Of course, the article wasn't much nicer to the rest of them. It recounted the trouble from Oliver's first marriage and hinted that he was after the al Mussad fortune for revenge. Callum wasn't sure why anyone thought Oliver needed the money or how both Ollie and Tori could both be perceived as greedy. Naturally, the tabloid also accused Callum of heartlessly choosing Tori over the mother of his unborn child. Despite Talib's best intentions, the Thea story was still causing damage and likely would for many months to come. If she was pregnant—and he didn't believe she was—Thea would play the role of jilted lover up to the birth. If not, he could bet she would claim a miscarriage brought on by all the stress.

The time had come to deal with her head-on. He hadn't given a damn before, but now he had to think about Tori.

Rory leaned over, keeping his voice as low as possible. "I'm hoping Tori doesn't see that. Once we get to the country house, we can turn off the Internet and tell the staff to keep the papers away."

He looked across the car to where Tori was asleep, her head on Oliver's shoulder. From the moment she'd dropped to her knees and asked them to take her away, one of them kept a hand on her at all times. They'd decided to put off her punishment and any play until they arrived safely in the country, but they weren't foolish enough to give Tori a moment alone.

"You're the only one who comes out of it all right," Callum murmured.

Rory's eyes rolled. "You're joking, right? They imply I'm the idiot who's giving into your lust and Oliver's greed because I'm too stupid to think for myself. Ridiculous. The more pressing concern is Thea."

Callum sighed and pushed the tablet away. "As much as I

hate it, it's time to pay her off."

"We tried it before," Rory warned. "Perhaps if we raise the payment, she'll bite. She must know that we won't be throwing Tori over for her, especially after we've just traveled to Bezakistan to bring our girl home. Maybe that's the shot of reality Thea needs. I know you hate paying her for something like this, but it's the quickest way. She signs a nondisclosure, and we still get our paternity test. If the child is yours, we agree to pay child support, but she can't ever talk to the press about you or your family again."

"We won't owe child support." God, Callum hoped they at least believed him about that.

"I know, but we'll have to put some language like that in the contract. I'll be honest, I think she's a bit unstable. We need to treat her as if her story could be true. Once she signs that document, she won't be able to discuss the incident and it will be over."

Callum nodded. They had more important things to talk about.

"What do you think happened to him?" He gestured Oliver's way.

Their older brother seemed like a different person. Not the Oliver before Yasmin, but not the shell he'd been after, either. This man had walked through the fire and forged a new strength. He'd certainly taken charge of Tori. He hadn't backed down or blended into the background.

A ghost of a smile crossed Rory's lips. "Alea happened. I talked to her before we left. Apparently Ollie didn't remember the night as well as he believed. He thought he'd given up."

"I can't imagine that," Callum muttered.

He'd never read the reports. They were too bloody, too real. He hated thinking about that day. He'd gotten the call in the locker room and walked out on a match. It had been the only time he'd missed one for anything other than injury. But he'd walked away because his brother needed him. That flight had been the longest of his life. He hadn't known if his brother was alive or dead.

"At least it appears that he's stopped believing Tori is anything like Yasmin. Not that the latest news cycle is going to help."

"What are they saying now?" Tori yawned sleepily. "You two aren't as quiet as you think you are."

Oliver stretched as she sat up. "They never have been. Cal's indoor voice resembles most people shouting."

Callum winced. Maybe that was something he should work on.

"Come here, love." He patted his thigh and found his lap full of soft, sweet woman in no time at all. Tori wrapped her arms around his neck and cuddled against him. He had to ask the one question he wasn't sure he wanted the answer to. "Are you going to use these thirty days to fuck us out of your system?"

She stiffened but didn't move off his lap. "Not intentionally."

Rory huffed. "I thought this was over."

The little minx actually cuddled closer to him. "I need time to figure a few things out."

"What are you afraid of?" Oliver moved to a closer seat. "I don't understand. We've made our intentions plain. You can't think we're using you for sex."

"I'm beginning to suspect *she's* using *us* for sex," Rory accused.

She shook her head. "It's not like that."

"What is it like, then?" Callum was determined to get to the bottom of whatever stood between them. "Because from where I was sitting, it looks like you used us. You were ready to leave."

"And I was already thinking about ways I could get back in contact with you." She closed her eyes for a moment. "I don't know that I can handle the intensity of what I feel for you. If anything happened to one of you, I would be devastated."

"That's ridiculous," Rory said. "Sweetheart, anything can happen at any moment. You can't live your life trying to avoid pain. You avoid joy and happiness, too. It's no way to live."

"That's what my sister says. I'm trying to...assimilate her advice. Believe it. I also can't stand the thought of my life being plastered on the pages of a magazine. I've seen how that affects people," she explained. "And I doubt the papers will leave us alone. There was another story today, right?"

Callum smoothed back her hair, his stare delving into hers. "If we don't comment and act as if nothing is wrong, they'll let it go. Some other scandal will crop up. I've been in the public eye since I signed my first contract at eighteen. When I act up, they come out like locusts, and for a while, I can do no right. Eventually, if I lay low, they go away. It's not right, but it is true. They will get bored with us. We'll live quietly and all of this will fade. Yes, there will be questions, and some people won't approve. But I don't care about them. I care about you."

"And if we ever have children?" Tori asked.

"We'll cross that bridge when we come to it." He worried about it, too. "But we wouldn't be the first with an unusual relationship."

"They could get teased."

"Love, every child gets teased for something. Are you saying that just because he or she might encounter heartache at some point, that's a reason to not bring him or her into the world?"

She sniffled a little. "I don't know what I'm saying. I simply know that loving the three of you scares the crap out of me and I don't know if I can handle it. When I left your room yesterday morning, I just needed a few minutes to myself. But I began to realize how much I cared, then I saw the papers and..."

She'd shut down. Callum held her tighter.

"I've been thinking. What if I become your very quiet mistress? I might be able to handle that. If no one knew, then they couldn't judge."

And she would be able to keep her distance. As much as she seemed to want that, Callum knew he and his brothers couldn't allow it. "Their judgment means nothing. Tell me why you think it does."

She shrugged. "I grew up in a small town. After my parents died, Piper had to be absolutely above reproach. Everyone thought she was too young to take care of me. She had to walk a very straight line because everyone was watching, waiting for her to screw up or for me to do something foolish. They thought I should go to foster care. A couple of women even reported us to CPS to have me removed from Piper's care."

Ah, so that explained one thing. "No one can take you away now."

"They could fire me," she said logically.

"Who?" Callum frowned. "My brothers and I employ you."

"And if we ever break up?"

Oliver shook his head. "You never have to worry about money again. And don't think for a second that money isn't power. If your sister had money back then, they wouldn't have dared to challenge her. They had small minds and too little to occupy their time. This argument makes no sense. You're an adult now and those tabloids, while annoying, can't really harm you. There would be plenty of clients who would hire you because you'd made headlines."

"I don't like people watching me, judging me." She'd gone stiff in his arms.

"No one does. Well, no one sane." He'd had teammates who loved the limelight for a time. But once it became invasive, everyone wanted a break. "I'm asking you to suffer it for a bit."

"Once it's obvious we've settled down, no one will find

us fascinating," Rory assured her.

She took a deep breath. "All right. Like I said, I want to try. I'm just not sure if the three of you can get along for thirty days."

Oh, she thought she would have a loophole out that way? No. He and his brothers intended to make certain they didn't give her a reason not to face her fears. "You have no idea, darling." He rested his hand on her knee. "We were a team when we were younger. I used to beat up all the bullies who went after my brothers."

"When we were in boarding school, the others quickly learned not to mess with us. Our unity was unbreakable," Rory said with a fond grin.

"Until Yasmin." Oliver frowned. "But that's over, and you should understand we've talked about this. We understand that in order to make you feel safe, we have to form a cohesive unit that not even your sweet smile can corrupt."

Tori sat up. "I don't know if I like the sound of that."

"Brat." She looked so sweet Callum wanted to eat her up. Now that she was here with them, that hole in his gut seemed repaired. She couldn't possibly stay with them for a month, then walk away. "You don't like the idea of not being able to manipulate us."

Tori shook her head. "I prefer to think of it as being able to reason with you."

"We're all out of reason here, love." Rory winked her way. He looked out the window. "We should take her fishing. There's this lovely spot on the river right outside the carriage house. We used to sit there for hours and hours during summer."

"Until Mum sent someone to find us," Callum concurred. "The gardener told us if we were very quiet, the fairies would come out. When we were little, we really wanted to see those fairies."

He fully intended to tell his own children these stories.

Their children.

"We were never quiet enough," Oliver said with a laugh. "Well, I was, of course. I was perfect. Cal always had gas. I swear his flatulence drove all the fairies away."

Callum sent his brother a rude hand gesture, but he couldn't help smiling. Whatever had happened to Oliver at the palace before they'd left seemed to have worked wonders. Oliver had joked more in the last day than in the last three years combined. And since their Bezakistani ritual, he'd been all over Tori. Callum made a mental note to train Oliver on the finer points of topping their girl or she would walk all over him with those pretty pink toes of hers.

"Oliver, don't be mean to your brother," Tori said with a stern look.

Ollie grabbed one of her feet. She'd kicked off her shoes the minute they'd climbed in the limo. He brought her delicate foot to his lips and kissed her arch. "I'd rather be mean to you, darling. Just a little."

Tori giggled. "That tickles!"

"Not as much as this." Callum ran a firm hand over her ribs.

She struggled to get away. "No!" She reached out to Rory. "Help me!"

He cradled her head in his lap and gazed down at her. "I thought you wanted the three of us to play nicely together. Don't you like how my brothers and I share our toy?"

Tori giggled as Callum and Oliver worked her over, while Rory cheered them on. Her feet kicked, her laughter trilled, and joy suffused him. They should play and love well and find happiness together. They should be a family.

"Stop!" Tori shouted.

They finally let her up but only to kiss her. Rory bent to her, his lips caressing hers in a slow glide. Watching intently, Callum cupped her breast. He loved how soft she was. He wanted nothing more than to pull off her blouse and attach himself to those perfect pink nipples. He could suck on them until she was screaming for release—which they'd grant her. In fact, he suspected they would all feel better if they found some relief. Twenty-four hours was way too long to spend without being inside her.

Rory eased a hand down her shirt, molding to her other breast as his tongue plunged deep. They could have her naked in no time. They could command her to her knees and she could move between them, sucking their cocks before they made her scream.

"What the hell?" Oliver leaned forward and pressed the button that connected him to the driver. "Lyle, is that what I think it is?"

Callum helped Tori sit upright. Rory turned in his seat and cursed soundly.

The driver's voice came over the intercom. "It looks as if the press is waiting in front of the gate to the house, sir. I spoke to the housekeeper. She said they've been there all morning."

Tori went pale and tried to scramble off his lap. Callum caught her. He wasn't about to let her retreat. Her fear couldn't win.

"It's fine." He stroked a hand down her back. "Think of our situation as a job, love. You're good at this. I've watched you handle the press with one hand tied behind your back."

"Never when they were after me." A fine tremble shook her hands.

"What do you tell clients when you first meet them? The ones whose image needs rehabbing? Pretend this situation has nothing to do with you."

She took a deep breath and calmed a bit. "I ask them how they want to be seen."

This was what she needed. She needed to think professionally. "All right, how do you want to be seen?"

"I don't want to be seen at all." She frowned. "Since that's not possible... I guess I want to be seen as a smart, competent woman."

"Then show them you're that woman. Pretend you're your own client. Advise yourself." If he could get her to look past her emotion and view the problem logically, she would see it wasn't so bad. Oh, they were in for a few nasty moments, but it was a storm they could weather.

He saw the instant her intellect took over.

She sat up straighter and her eyes lost that frightened look. "The best way to get rid of them is to make a statement. We should be honest. We explain we're in our concubine period and request privacy while we're working out our relationship. I ask my sister and her husbands to release a statement that they stand behind the potential marriage and my brothers-in-law thank you three for honoring his culture and values. We move the press away from the salacious aspects of our relationship. We focus less on anything that encourages this 'mistress' business and talk more about the potential of another semi-royal wedding."

"That's perfect." Rory breathed an obvious sigh of relief.

Oliver brought her free hand to his lips. "I think that will work beautifully, love. We'll still have some trying to take photographs, so no outdoor sex. But the reporters should leave us alone for a while. The very fact that we're isolated will help."

This time when Tori moved off his lap, he helped her. She was back in control. She reached for her bag as Oliver informed Lyle they would stop and speak with the press. Tori brushed her hair and smoothed on a bit of gloss. Either way she looked gorgeous.

"Callum, they're going to ask you about Thea," she instructed.

"What do you want me to say?" Callum asked.

Her lips quirked up in the sweetest smile. "I thought you were the boss."

"Only in the bedroom, my love. Or when you need it. Right now, I think you'll find we'll follow your lead. We didn't pick a doormat of a woman. We picked someone smart and competent. In this, you are our leader."

A sheen of tears made her eyes a little watery. "So we're a team?"

Had she not realized that? Callum reached for her hand. "The three of us were a team for months, but we got a bit lost. We needed you to bring us together. We're always a team. We always back each other. That's what a family is."

She leaned forward and kissed him. "You know what to say, Callum. You run the old 'on the advice of my lawyers' line and don't say a thing about Thea. When they ask you about the baby, say only that you look forward to being a father one day and that any child of yours will have all your love. Oliver, don't frown. In fact, everyone smile unless the question warrants somberness. When they ask about our sex lives, and you know they will, smile and tell them we like to keep our private lives private."

The limo rolled to a stop right outside the estate's big gates. Thick trees hid the house and the river beyond from view, affording them privacy. Callum wondered briefly if they should just drive on. Or if they should simply head straight back to Bezakistan. But running their business from another continent for thirty days without any advance planning would be somewhere between ball-busting and impossible.

When Lyle opened the car door, Rory stepped out and reached back inside to help Tori. She winked Cal's way before exiting the limo.

Oliver sent a bolstering glance his way, too. "Don't let them get to you. Five minutes tops, then we won't be dealing with these people for a whole month. And you handled her beautifully."

Oliver stepped out and then it was Callum's turn. He was well aware he was the real fuck-up of the group. The press might have been interested in three wealthy brothers sharing a bride, but it likely wouldn't have been as huge a story without him. He was one of the chief reasons they were swarming.

He'd been the bad boy of football for years, and now that was coming back to haunt them all.

But they needed him, too. All he could do was smile and follow Tori's instructions. Eventually, they would see that he'd settled down.

He followed Oliver out of the car, and the cluster of reporters immediately assaulted them with questions.

"Ms. Glen, how do you feel about stealing a pregnant woman's man?"

"Torrance, do you think your sister is embarrassed by your recent nude display?"

"How does the sex work? Do you all take turns? Can none of you find a woman of your own?"

Every word turned his gut. They were locusts. Callum fisted his hands and anger roiled through his system.

"Don't. Their words don't mean a thing," Rory whispered in his ear. "Let Tori handle this."

He tried to calm himself. It was one thing for these prats to heap this humiliation on him, but quite another that they dumped it on her. The fact that he couldn't protect her burned him.

Tori smiled, something serene and professional. "First, I've never stolen any woman's man. Callum was perfectly single when we began our relationship. Second, my sister has never teased me more than the night of my wardrobe malfunction. In turn, I teased her about greeting the press wearing nothing but her husband's shirt the day after her marriage. What can I say? We're not debutantes but strong women who've faced a lot of adversities in life. I can safely say that, given the amount of turmoil in the world, my right breast having its own Twitter feed is of no consequence. I promise to wear more sensible shoes in the future. Obviously, I'm not suited to wear five-inch heels."

"With regard to our private lives, we intend to keep the details to ourselves," Rory said, his hand at her back, providing support.

Callum had been good at dealing with these vultures once. He could do it again.

"I believe someone asked if none of us could find our own women." He stepped up on the other side of Tori. "The truth is, we don't want other women. This one is more than enough for the three of us. We intend to marry in the Bezakistani fashion of our fiancée's sister and our cousins. Expect a statement from the palace no later than tomorrow. We thank you all for taking such kind interest in our lives and now ask for privacy while we follow the traditional month of bonding before our wedding."

Tori gave him an encouraging smile, but his gaze snagged on a man in black who stepped out from behind one of the massive oak trees that dotted the property. Callum looked up in horror as the stranger drew a gun and began to shoot.

He threw himself in front of Tori and felt a bullet tear through the flesh of his arm. He heard a scream, then the world faded away.

* * * *

Rory paced as the local magistrate prepared to leave. "So you have nothing on this man?"

The magistrate shrugged. "No. Our working theory is he was making a statement against the royal family. We've been in touch with the sheikh and he says that threats against them have risen since the country started taking in refugees. Unfortunately your...Ms. Glen is an easy target. You're very lucky your brother is so quick on his feet or she would be dead."

"You're absolutely sure she was the target?" Oliver asked, his stare straying toward the back of the house where Callum now rested after the doctor had treated him. Thankfully, the bullet had clipped Callum's left arm rather than hitting anything vital. The wound had barely required two stitches and some painkillers.

Since then, Tori had refused to leave his side. After she'd cried, she seemed to distance herself. Rory didn't like the blank look on her face. Yes, she sat beside him, holding his good hand. She was kind, but she seemed as if she was running on autopilot. A loved one dying was her greatest fear, and today's attack had been a trigger, sending her back into her protective shell.

The magistrate nodded as he picked up his briefcase. "Yes. From where the man was standing, the trajectory of the bullet was straight to Ms. Glen's torso. She was his target. We'll take a look at the video footage some of the reporters took. Unfortunately, we don't have much. Many scattered when he started shooting. We're lucky he ran. Some true believers would have simply stayed and shot until she was dead. We'll have officers patrol around the grounds."

"I also have security of our own. They'll be here before dark." Rory had immediately requested a detail for the house and grounds. He had no doubt Talib would send someone tomorrow. The sheikh had been upset to say the least.

The magistrate promised to be in contact, then he headed for the door, leaving Rory alone with Oliver.

"Are you thinking what I'm thinking?" Rory asked. He couldn't get Tori's last night in London out of his mind.

"Of course. This isn't the first time. It can't be a coincidence that someone tried to attack her before she left. Now that I think about it, it might have been the same man all three times."

Rory felt his eyes widen. "Three times? Are you talking about Peckham?"

"Yes, I was about to ask the same thing." Tori stood in the doorway, her skin pale and that haunted look in her eyes. "Callum is asleep. Claire is sitting with him. I was going to ask if you thought what happened in London is connected to the shooting. Now I'd really like to know what you mean by three times."

Oliver winced and sat on the sofa. The curtains were drawn, despite the fact that sun still shined brightly. "I followed you one night."

"Creepy stalker," she said with the first hint of humor he'd seen from her since the shooting.

Oliver shrugged. "Perhaps, but I wasn't the only one. According to Claire, a man followed you off the bus. I jumped him in an alley when he pulled a knife."

Her eyes narrowed. "Your last 'bar fight,' I presume."

Oliver held his hands up. "The very last. I assure you I'm through with the fight club mentality. Unless I get my hands on the shooter. Then all bets are off."

Tori frowned. "So I was visiting a friend, you were following me, and Claire was following you. The creepy stalker thing must run in the family."

Oliver leaned forward. "This feels more personal than someone with a political agenda. Besides, even with Tori's ties to the royal family, someone with an ax to grind against the Bezakistani way of life probably wouldn't have targeted her before today. I want to know where Thea's been."

"It certainly wasn't a female who shot at me today. I saw him." Tori crossed her arms over her chest.

"That doesn't mean a thing." Rory actually thought that idea made sense. "He behaved more like a hired hand than a terrorist."

"He was after me." Tori turned toward the door. "It doesn't matter why. Callum nearly died. The only plan that makes sense is me leaving."

Rory had worried she would retreat emotionally since the thug had fired the gun. He hated to be proven right. "Where would you go?"

She shrugged. "It doesn't matter."

It did. Rory crossed his arms over his chest. "Absolutely not."

Her greatest fear was loss, and Callum had nearly played out that story earlier.

Oliver frowned and agreed. "You're not going anywhere. We have security. It's going to be all right. We'll protect you."

She pursed her lips and turned toward the hall. "I'm not worried about me. I'm giving you notice now. Someone— fate, maybe—doesn't want us together. So in thirty days, I'll be leaving. No one will have to take a bullet for me again."

Rory wasn't about to let that lie. In three steps he was at her side, his hand wrapped around her arm. "That's not how it's going to go, love."

She looked at him, that blank stare nearly ripping him asunder.

"Don't look at me as if none of this matters. Everything about you matters to us, and you need to understand that. I know what happened this afternoon scared you, but Callum is fine. He's a tough one and he's going to be perfectly fresh by tomorrow. He won't even remember he's been shot."

"I'll remember," she promised.

He tried to drag her into his arms. She stood still, stiff. "Tori, Callum did what he had to do. Any one of us would have done the same."

"You shouldn't have had to do anything at all," she said, her voice flat. "This is ridiculous. I'm not married to royalty. Why would they come after me?"

She was already erecting walls again. Every time he managed to tear through the last barrier, she started building another. He had to prove to her that there was no wall that he and his brothers couldn't break down.

Rory squeezed her tight. "I don't know, but I will find out. I've got a call in to a London security agency that investigates things like this. I'm also going to put an end to the thing with Thea."

"Callum's baby mama?" Tori rolled her eyes.

Ah, there was his first hint that she wasn't as unemotional as she pretended.

"Does it bother you?"

She shrugged. "It's not my business."

Oliver stood, coming to Rory's side. "Really? You don't care who Cal has sex with?"

Those sweet lips of hers flattened into a stubborn line. "No. I can't. Can't you see this won't work? The press won't leave us alone and now someone is trying to hurt me. Callum could have been killed. Do you get that?"

Tears welled in her eyes again. She needed to cry and purge those emotions, but she held tightly to her control.

It was time to strip that from her.

Rory tangled his fingers in her hair, twisting lightly so she was forced to look into his eyes. "Cal could die on the road. Any one of us could get into an accident at any time. No one is guaranteed tomorrow. I won't allow this irrational fear of yours to come between us."

"It's not irrational," she argued. "I've seen it. It's happened to me before and now it's happening again. On top of that, someone wants me dead. Why can't you see that it's more logical to let me go? I don't want to put everyone in danger. I couldn't stand it if one of you died because of me. Please let me go, Rory. I can be back in London in a few hours, even farther away by tomorrow."

He tightened his hold, relieved when her breath hitched. He could see the way her nipples peaked under her thin shirt. She was already responding and he'd hardly touched her. Did she honestly think she could walk away from this? He knew damn well he never would.

Oliver moved in behind her, crowding her until she was between their big bodies. "We're not letting you go. You can beg all you like but you're not leaving this house."

"You can't keep me here." The words came out on a breathy gasp as their bodies collided. One manicured hand came up to touch his chest. The other moved back to Oliver's hip. "Just because the sex is good doesn't mean this is a good idea."

Tal had been right. The only way to break through Tori's

defenses was sheer intimacy. They would be inside her so often for the next thirty days that she would feel empty if one of them wasn't making love to her.

"The fact that you only call it good sex shows me how naïve you are and how little you understand. It's not sex. I've had sex. I've had so much sex I got bored with it. We don't have sex." Rory cupped his free hand around her breast. She seemed to swell around his fingers, forcing him to take more into his hand. "What we do is make love and I've never made love to another woman."

She arched a brow at him. "I seem to remember a couple of models who would disagree."

"Ah, that was sex. It was an itch I could scratch with anyone. This is more. I hunger. I crave, and only one person in the world can satisfy me now. You. Only you." It had been that way since the moment he'd seen Tori. Only she mattered now. Only Tori could fulfill his needs.

"I thought I'd been in love," Oliver whispered. "I thought I knew everything. Then my whole world got ripped out from under me."

Tears formed in her eyes. "Then you should understand why I can't do this."

Oliver didn't let up. "I understand that you're scared. I've been the same. My fear caused me to lash out and hurt you, but I won't ever do that again. I'm stronger now."

"What happened to you, Oliver?" she asked.

Oliver kissed her cheek. "You happened, love. I went back to the palace for you and I found myself again. I'd been lying on that floor dying for years, but I got up and I won't go back down again. I'll fight. You wanted to see the real me. Well, this is who I am, darling. I'm going to fight for what I want and that's a family with you and my brothers. Give in now. Make it easy on all of us because there is only one acceptable outcome and that is marriage. A life together. I'll accept nothing less."

She shook her head, but she shifted between them as

though she couldn't decide which way to turn. "I can't handle it."

"You can and you will. I'll make sure of it. We'll all help you." Rory took her mouth with hungry dominance as though his lips and tongue could brand her.

She softened under the onslaught, and he could feel her tears against his face. He refused to let up. She needed to cry, needed to feel. She closed herself off from everything and he was beginning to understand that she only seemed open to people who didn't matter. She was terrified of letting anyone in who she really cared about.

Rory intended to change that because he intended to be one of the men she loved more than life itself. All that passion and love was trapped. It was up to them to set it free.

Words didn't seem to work on her so Rory was going to try something far less verbal.

He let his tongue dive deep, playing along hers. He tugged at the hem of her shirt. "You don't need this, sweetheart."

Then Oliver was undressing her, and Rory assisted.

Life was easier with a couple of partners. He never had to stop kissing her yet his older brother continued to peel away her layers. Before too long, they revealed her warm flesh. With a twist, her bra came free and her breasts fell between them, begging for his attention. He ended the kiss with one last swipe of his tongue over her bottom lip and studied her.

"How do you do this to me?" Her guileless eyes had clouded with desire.

There was an easy answer to that question. "I'm passionate about you. I love you with my whole heart and soul. Tori, you're never going to find this again. We all click. We fit together. Oliver, have you ever wanted another woman like you want her?"

"Never. I didn't know I could want a woman the way I want her." Oliver cupped her chin, tilting her up toward him.

He brushed his lips against hers. "And I've never had such pleasure from a woman. It doesn't work like this with other people. You won't find this with another man. You have to settle for only having the three of us."

"Another man? I can't handle the ones I have. You three don't listen to good sense." She arched back, her mouth against Oliver's while her breast filled Rory's hand. "You make me forget to think."

"There's no need to think right now. Just feel. Give over to us. We need to be together. I need to be close to you. I know you're afraid, but so are we. We don't want to lose you. Not to a bullet or to your own fear." He lowered his head and licked at the tight peak. It tightened further, begging him to torment her even more.

He glanced up and Oliver was kissing her, their mouths fused in passion. It made his dick harden to the point of pain to watch as she submitted to their desires. She wasn't thinking about the potential of loss now. She was thinking about pleasure and love and what they could give her.

He sucked the nipple into his mouth. This would be hard and fast. It couldn't be any other way. Later tonight they would inundate her with long strokes of their tongue and hands and cocks. Hopefully, Cal would be up to joining them. But after the events of the day, Rory needed to be inside her.

Now.

He tugged at the waist of her pants, dragging them down and dropping to his knees. Oliver kept kissing her, his hands wrapping around to tweak her nipples. Her body moved with unconscious grace, sensuously rolling between them.

"Step out," he commanded her as he pulled her knickers down as well, revealing perfect feminine skin and that lovely pussy he couldn't wait to make his again. He could scent her desire. She was already getting wet and ready for them. The evidence of her need glistened on the folds of her pussy.

He leaned over and nosed her, gathering the sweet smell of her desire around him. He loved how quick she was to respond. When it came to sex, she didn't prevaricate or play games. The honest, open need she displayed threatened to send him over the edge.

He wasn't going until she went with him.

Rory dragged his tongue through her labia and right over her needy clitoris. He stopped for a moment and suckled the nub between his lips.

Tori squirmed and gasped, calling out his name even as Oliver tweaked her nipples.

He found a deep satisfaction in knowing his brother was right there, holding her down for his pleasure. And hers.

Rory moved in, giving that sweet clitoris a hard suck as his fingers found her pussy and slid in. He curled them inside her and found her sweet spot, stroking as he sucked. Tori came all over his fingers. She soaked him with her release. It was perfect and gave him leave to move to the next phase.

"Hands and knees," Rory commanded.

Oliver helped her slip to the floor. Tori's whole body was flush with orgasm. She looked up at him and Rory realized there were no walls between them now. This was the only place he could be utterly sure of her. He needed to broaden their safe places.

Oliver moved in front of her, shoving his slacks down and freeing his cock. She didn't need prompting. The minute he was in position, she sucked the head between her lips. Oliver hissed and thrust his hands in her hair. "You should do what you're going to do. I can't last too long. That little tongue of hers is a killer."

Rory shoved out of his pants, snagging a condom before tossing them aside. He rolled it over his hard-as-nails cock and settled in behind her. Her ass swayed invitingly and he promised it wouldn't be too long before he felt that sweet hole around him. On the plane, they'd instructed her to wear a plug for several hours. She'd balked at first...then she'd complied. In a few days, she would be ready for them to take her together. But for now he would be satisfied getting her between him and Oliver.

"Spread your knees wide," he commanded. "Don't stop sucking Oliver, but prepare yourself for me. I'm going to fuck you hard while you take him. Suck him deep. You can do it. You can take him and me. Eventually, Callum is going to fuck this sweet arse of yours. You'll be so full. There won't be an inch of you we don't explore."

She hummed, wiggling her backside.

Oliver cursed. "Fuck, that feels good. Just a little more. Take every inch."

There was no way his brother would last much longer. Rory knew exactly how good it felt to be balls deep inside that hot mouth. If they were going to go together, he had some work to do. He lined his cock up with her soaked pussy and started to press inside. She moved to accommodate him, tilting her pelvis up toward him. So tight. She was so perfectly tight and hot. He pressed in, ruthlessly forcing his dick into her channel. He pushed forward, gripping her hips to hold her still.

She wriggled and squirmed as she kept sucking Oliver's cock. She was caught between them, a precious bundle of femininity. She was theirs to protect and love. And she was definitely theirs to fuck.

He thrust until he was flush against her and then held himself still for a moment, enjoying the deep connection he felt every time he immersed himself inside her. This was intimacy unlike anything he'd ever experienced before. She was the right woman and this was the right time.

He moved one hand around to find her clit as he began a pounding rhythm. He held nothing back. She was strong and not just physically. He was going to prove it to her, but for now all that mattered was the sound of her mouth sucking Oliver and the feel of her pussy tightening on him.

He stroked her clit and felt her spasm. Oliver groaned and thrust hard into her mouth.

Rory felt her quake and gave in. The orgasm made him

shudder, but he kept thrusting, stroking her to greater heights. She sucked furiously and finally let go, having taken everything Oliver gave her. She thrust back and cried out his name as she came all over his cock.

He forced his way inside her one last time before sheer exhaustion felled him. He cradled her as he moved to her side. It didn't matter that they were in the parlor where his mother used to have teas. This was their home now, and they would love their wife how they saw fit. He kissed her ear. "I don't want to hear anything further about leaving. You belong here with us."

She reached out for Oliver, taking his hand as she rested her head back against Rory's chest. "Do I have a say?"

"Not in this." Oliver tenderly kissed her palm. "Not when your safety and happiness are at risk. You can't live away from us forever. We have to figure this out."

"Together," Rory said with finality.

"It's a mistake." But she brought Oliver's hand to her breast.

"Then it's our mistake." Rory thought the only real mistake was being apart. Everything else would fall in place. Once they'd taken care of Thea, the press would die down a bit and they could focus on finding the man trying to kill Tori.

A shadow darkened the door. "I go to sleep for twenty minutes and this is what I find you doing?"

Rory looked up and Callum was standing in the doorway, a glower on his face.

"You snooze you lose, as the Americans say," Oliver taunted.

Tori sat up, scrambling to get to her clothes. "You're supposed to be in bed."

"He barely needed stitches. He's played with a concussion," Rory grumbled as he got to his feet. It looked like his playtime was at an end.

"My arm hurts something fierce, and I think the drugs the

doctor gave me are affecting me." Callum looked at Tori like a sad little boy. "I woke up without you."

Tori picked up Rory's shirt, abandoning her own clothes. She hurried to reach Callum. "I won't leave you alone again." She took his good hand and started leading him out to the hallway. "I'll take care of you."

Just before he disappeared, Cal looked back, giving his brothers a triumphant grin.

"Bastard," Oliver whispered with a shake of his head.

"Well, that's Cal for you. Leaving us with the rough work." He started for the bathroom and heard a scream.

"Did I forget to tell you the maid's already here?" Oliver asked. "We're going to have to warn the staff."

Rory grabbed his slacks. This definitely wasn't his father's staid home anymore.

And hallelujah for that.

CHAPTER FOURTEEN

Two weeks later, Tori sat in front of the fire, staring down at the pages of her father's journal and wondering if she'd ever known the man at all.

Her father had been a calm, sweet man. He'd been a great dad. And he'd been so passionate about their mother.

He'd written page after page about how much he'd loved her, wanted her, needed her. He'd met her when they were seniors in high school and he'd scrapped his idea of going into the Army and followed her to college just to be with her. It had taken him three years to convince her to go out with him, but they had almost twenty years together.

She hesitated to turn the page because she knew what came next. Her sister had given her three journals filled with their father's words. She'd made it through the first two. Now she was halfway through the last one, but she knew the remaining pages were deceiving. Journal three had a lot of blank space, the symbol of a life cut short.

She closed the book and stared at the fire. Did she even want to know? Did she really want to know how her father felt when her mother died? Did she want to know how that love and passion had turned to ashes?

When Tori closed her eyes, she could see that man pointing the gun and firing at her. She'd felt time slow and watched as blood bloomed on Callum's arm. In her nightmares, his arm hadn't taken a bullet but his heart. In those terrible visions, she'd held him while the light in his eyes dimmed...then extinguished. She'd known beyond a shadow of a doubt that his death was on her conscience.

The past two weeks had been a revelation. Not since childhood had she felt so secure and loved, but she knew that didn't always last. Sometimes love could be torn asunder by something like a tiny tumor.

"I wondered where you were." Her sister-in-law stepped into the room.

No, her name was Claire, damn it. Tori had to stop thinking of the woman as family. This was the insidious part of the Thurston-Hughes brothers' plan. They'd tucked her away in the isolation of the gorgeous English countryside and insisted they play house. It was far too easy to forget she wasn't actually married. Her concubine period still had another two weeks. Then she had to decide if she was going to move forward...or move on.

"I'm hiding out. I don't want any part in what's happening with those lawyers."

"Callum thinks you're mad at him."

She sighed. "I'm not. I just don't want to incite a riot. I heard she insisted on being here."

Claire nodded shortly. "She refused to sign the papers if she didn't get to talk to Callum one last time."

Thea had become the bane of Tori's existence. She'd gone on every talk show possible, chatting endlessly about how Tori had stolen the father of her unborn child. She'd even blamed the fact that she hadn't gained any weight on the stress of being apart from her lover.

She believed Callum. They all did. Cal had never loved Thea. She even believed Talib's report that the woman wasn't pregnant at all, so the idea of paying her for bad behavior rankled.

And she knew the news vans with their reporters were still camped outside the gates. They would still be there two weeks from now, waiting for her to tell the world whether there would be a royal wedding or a split.

"I don't think Thea should have had a choice." Tori hated the fact that the woman was in her house. She stopped. In the Thurston-Hughes's house. It didn't matter that she'd started to love this place. That still didn't make it hers. She'd even gotten used to the staff smiling at her and giggling at times. At first, that had been disconcerting. They knew she had sex with three men. She'd gotten the evil eye from some of the older staff members, but she'd overheard them talking in the kitchens. They didn't dislike her for her morals. They simply couldn't understand why she needed thirty days to decide to marry the brothers. According to them, any woman who needed that much time to decide didn't have the sense to become their mistress.

They were simply protective of the masters.

"Have you told them that?" Claire asked, sitting down beside her.

"It's not my place." She wasn't certain she had a place.

"All right, then. I'll deal with it myself." She stood abruptly and straightened out her skirt.

"Deal with what?"

Claire didn't turn. "This is woman's work. My brothers need someone to guide them. As it obviously won't be you, I'll see to this nasty Thea business. I'll take care of them, as I have ever since my mother died. Apparently, I'll continue to take care of them once you're gone."

Tori wasn't sure what had gotten under Claire's skin. "I haven't said I'm leaving at all. I simply don't know that I have any business dealing with the problem."

"What do you think a relationship is? You know I like you, Tori, but I've come to believe you're cold. You pretend to be this super-sweet woman who cares about everyone."

"I do care." This conversation was running dangerously close to the one she'd had with Piper. Only she suspected Claire would be less understanding.

"Only if it doesn't cross some boundary in your head. You care...but not too much. You're going to leave them in the end, so you should know I'll do everything I possibly can to find the right woman for them."

Tori should have been happy that Claire was giving her blessing to leave if that was her choice. It should have pleased Tori to know that Claire would take responsibility for these men.

But Claire was their sister, not their wife, and her words prodded a sore spot Tori hadn't even known existed. It was her place to deal with Thea because Callum obviously hadn't done enough to let the woman know she wasn't wanted. When it came to matters of the heart, there were some things only another woman could explain.

Tori saw plainly that Claire meant to take her rightful place.

Claire stared at her for a long moment as though hoping Tori would do something. Instead, Tori felt glued to the chair. She was at a crossroads, and the idea of deciding the rest of her life within a handful of days was daunting. It was all happening way too fast. She wasn't ready. She might never be ready.

"All right, then," Claire said with a sigh. "I wish you wouldn't stay the rest of the time. They think you'll choose them. Obviously, you won't. You'll use them until the time comes. Then you'll crush their hearts when you walk off to your safe little world."

Every word seemed like a kick in the gut. "The world isn't safe. I should know that better than anyone."

Tears glistened in Claire's eyes. "I lost my parents, too. I also lost the man I loved. I never talked about it with my brothers. I met him at university. I dated him for over a year. He was killed walking home one night. Some idiot tried to rob him. He didn't have any money. My parents would have been horrified, which was why I didn't talk about him. Now I wish I had. I regret that they never knew him. That's the hardest part. I have no one to talk to about him because no one knew him."

Then Claire could understand. "You still feel his loss? It's still an ache in your heart, right?"

"Of course. It's always going to be there." Claire put a hand to her chest as though she wished it would stop.

"Don't you wish it would go away?" Tori asked.

She shook her head. "That would mean I never loved him. I wouldn't trade that for anything. I'm a better person for having loved him. You think you can hide from loss, but all you'll get at the end of your days is a meaningless existence. When you look back, do you really think you'll be happy you never loved? Never really loved. Do you think you'll die with a smile on your face because you never felt anything? No, you'll die alone and bitter because you chose to. Go home, Tori. There's no place for you here and you only hurt them by staying. They need a woman, not a frightened little girl. I'm sorry if that sounds harsh. I really do wish you all the best. I'll see what I can do about saving my brother from that awful woman."

She strode away, and Tori felt something break open inside her.

God, what was she doing to her men? How could she ever possibly leave them? How could she even think about walking away from them?

She looked down at the book in her lap. Would her father have done it differently if he'd had the chance? Would he have taken back the years of joy to avoid the horrific pain?

She flipped to the back because she had to know. She had to know what he'd been thinking in those last days. Had he said good-bye to his girls with every intention of ending his pain?

With trembling hands, she turned to the last page. Unlike the rest of the journals, which he'd written to himself, he seemed to have written this to their mother after she died. These pages read like letters to his lost love.

The final entry was two days before his death. Two days before she'd lost her father. The words blurred as Tori read them.

Dearest Wife,

It's been years. I could tell you the exact time to the second, but I'm going to stop that now. My heart aches, but I realized that I can't mourn forever. I love you. That will never stop, but I have to get up in the morning and move forward. Not because I love you less, but because I realized all the best parts of you are here with me. They're sleeping two rooms over and I'm failing them. Every moment I spend wishing I'd gone with you is a moment I lose with them and god, they are spectacular. Piper has your sweetness and your smarts. And Mindy. Oh, our Melinda Torrance has your guts. Nothing scares her, but losing her mother seems to have thrown a shadow over her brave soul. So tomorrow, I'm going to wake up and make them breakfast and we're all going to learn how to live again. We'll do it together because the last thing they should think is that we should mourn for the rest of their lives. So I'm ending this journal because I think it holds me back. I'm going to talk to them from now on. Good-bye, my love. Until we meet again...

Tori remembered that morning he'd awakened her and Piper early for breakfast. He'd been more energetic. He'd even talked about their mom. Before that, he'd been silent about her for so long. When Tori had looked back at that morning, she'd assumed he'd merely been preparing to see her mom again. Never once had she imagined that Dad had decided to live once more.

Fate had changed everything.

She put the book down.

She'd once been brave. Her parents had often worried she would die while investigating a sewer drain or climbing a tree she'd had no business climbing. Her sister had been the practical one, always pulling her back from the edge. Tori hadn't feared anything. Somewhere along the way, she'd learned to be afraid.

Maybe it was time to learn how to be brave again.

Would she really push away three men who loved her—whom she loved desperately in return—so she didn't have to feel pain? Did she really think that if she left them tomorrow that choosing to be without them would hurt less than fate making the choice for her? Either way, she would miss them for the rest of her days.

Tori let out a trembling breath. Until now, she'd taken everything they had and given them very little in return. She had to change that.

It was time to take her place beside them.

She didn't need two weeks. In fact, she didn't need another moment. She loved them and they deserved more than the safe part of her heart. They deserved for her to grow the fuck up and be the woman she was meant to be, the woman they needed her to be.

The woman her parents had raised her to be.

With a silent thanks to her sister for once again showing her the way, Tori stepped out into the hallway. They wanted the real her? Well, everyone was about to see her—starting with that crazy bitch who needed to understand that no one came between a Texas girl and her men.

* * * *

Callum took a long drink. He was definitely going to need it. The crackpot was in his house. Just a short walk down the hall sat the bane of his existence. He'd rather thought he wouldn't have to see her again, but naturally Thea leveraged what power she had and got her way. She was trading one last meeting with him for a million pounds and the promise never to speak his name again. The very thought turned his stomach, but this torture would be worth it if she went away for good.

Unfortunately, he was fairly certain she wasn't the only one who was going away for good. No matter how he tried to reach Tori, she seemed further away than ever.

They made love to her every night, pushing her boundaries a bit more, preparing her for what they all wanted. She was loving and giving when they stripped her down, but the moment they donned clothes again, the careful distance she always maintained snapped back in place.

Callum was beginning to ask himself if he could truly breach her walls. Given the rate of her progress now, two more weeks didn't seem like enough time to win her.

"Ah, you need fortification, too, I see." Rory sighed and grabbed a glass. "Her lawyer alone is enough to drive a man to drink. Do you think she found him on a list of the most despicable solicitors in Great Britain?"

Thea's solicitor was a cadaverously thin prat with dark eyes that made Callum think of the Grim Reaper. "I hate all of this."

Rory poured himself two fingers of the fifty-year-old liquid. "It'll be over soon."

"That's what I'm afraid of."

Rory's jaw tightened. "Don't be. I was talking about Thea, not Tori. It's going to be all right."

"How can you say that? She's no closer to becoming our wife than she was before. She won't talk about the future."

"She's skittish, but she's also smart. She'll make the right choice."

"Or we'll kidnap her again." Oliver strode in. "We're going to need more Scotch to get through this day." He clapped a hand on Callum's shoulder. "We're going to take care of the Thea situation. Maybe then the press will settle down."

"We promised her. We told her if she would give us thirty days, we would let her go if that's what she still wanted." That vow haunted him, kept him up at night. But he was a man of his word.

Oliver shrugged a shoulder elegantly as he poured himself a drink. "We promised her she could leave if she gave it a real shot."

Rory nodded. "Good point. She hasn't done that. She's enjoying the sex and holding herself apart the rest of the time. So our deal is off. I say we give it the thirty days, then we put her on a private plane back home. But, oh, it got diverted. That's so sad. I'm thinking of that little island we own in the Bahamas. It's quite lovely."

His brothers were ruthless. He might dominate in the bedroom, but they had the devious minds. "I don't know if that will do anything but make her angry."

"She'll relent after a few years. Also, oops, we accidentally left the condoms behind. After we impregnate her a couple of times, she'll settle right down," Rory explained.

Callum had to laugh. "What century are you living in?"

"The one where we get the girl and we're all happy," Rory shot back. "I intended to play fair, but she's not, so why should we?"

Oliver leaned against the bar. "All of this is a moot point. I've handled it. We won't have to risk prison or try to find a sneaky way to impregnate her. I think she'll fall into our hands quite smartly soon."

A little flare of hope sparked through Cal. When that look filled Oliver's face, it meant he knew something the rest of them didn't and he thought his next card would win the game.

Before Callum could speak, the door swung open and a somber-eyed Claire walked in.

She was dressed casually, but a determined look flashed through his sister's eyes. "I'm here to help now. I think it would be best if Callum made himself scarce for the rest of the afternoon."

He would love to, but there was a problem with that scenario. "If I don't make an appearance, Thea won't sign the documents. That's the entire point of this meeting. She swears she'll sign the nondisclosure agreement. If she manages to fake her way through a whole pregnancy and produce a child, I'll take a paternity test. It will be administered by a doctor of my choosing and processed at a lab she can't bribe. That's the agreement."

Claire shook her head. "No. We're not going to reward her poor behavior. And she won't stick to it. She'll simply switch to feeding the tabloids through 'sources' and it will continue on. There is no negotiating with a woman like her. She believes she can have whatever she wants because up until this moment she's been dealing with a bunch of men. I'm going to take charge and absolve her of those ridiculous notions. She'll learn quickly that I won't be moved by false tears or promises of sexual favors."

Rory frowned down at his sister. "I wasn't promised sexual favors."

"I was," Oliver admitted with a sigh.

"When?" That was news to Callum.

"Back in London. She stopped by the office, tearful and pleading, trying to get me to talk to you." Oliver looked all too calm for a man whose world might fall apart in fourteen days. His lips even curled up like a cat who'd managed to steal all the cream. "I wish I'd taped the meeting. She even got down on her knees, begging me to think of my nephew. The position was perfect for oral. I think she was trying to get me to marry her to save her child. She's read far too many novels." Oliver turned to Claire. "You're right. I don't think we should be dealing with her. I suspect she'll be far off kilter if we make her deal with another female."

What the hell was Oliver doing? Thea hated all other females. She never listened to anyone, especially a rival female.

Claire's jaw tightened. "I know Tori should be stepping

in to end this nonsense but…"

Callum looked over Claire's head to eye his brother. Rory did the same. Had Oliver persuaded their sister to step in and take over? Why?

Oliver took Claire's hand. "It's all right. We know Tori isn't as invested as we'd like."

"Well, I had a talk with her," Claire admitted. "I explained that if she couldn't find the strength to take care of the men in her life, then I would have to do it for her. She can sit and read that bloody journal of hers all day. It doesn't solve the problem. I always thought American women had more backbone than this."

"You should point that out to her," Oliver agreed.

Claire's chin came up stubbornly. "I shall. After this is over, I'll 'chat' with her. You've obviously allowed yourselves to be used for sexual purposes, and if no one else is going to explain to her how wrong that is, I suppose that task falls to me. I won't allow her to blatantly use my brothers and toss them away like so much rubbish."

Oh, dear lord. Did Oliver know what he was starting? Did he understand what could happen when two women decided they had the same place in a family?

Would Tori even care?

"You always watch out for us." Oliver squeezed her hand. "Let us know if you have trouble with Thea. I, for one, am so much happier now that you're in charge. You're right. We were making a terrible mistake."

Claire nodded, then turned to Callum, pointing at him with a very judgmental finger. "You stay away from that woman."

He watched with wide eyes as she walked out the door, her shoulders squared.

"What the hell just happened?" His sister had always been so quiet and retiring. "Did you pit our sister against Tori?"

Oliver sighed. "I simply talked to Claire about how

vulnerable I've been feeling. You have to admit, Tori is using us shamelessly."

Callum rolled his eyes. "She's thinking. She's not using us for sex. She's scared."

Rory smiled. "I like the way Oliver thinks. And he's simply given her something else to ponder. Tori is a very responsible woman. She's also competitive. She's not going to like another woman taking her to task."

"She definitely won't like another woman assuming her role." Oliver took a sip. "But I also seem to have unleashed a tigress in our sister. I wasn't really expecting that. I might have miscalculated a bit there."

The door flew open, and Tori hovered impatiently in the doorway. "Where is she?"

Callum had to stop himself from taking a step back. Tori looked the tiniest bit wild. Her hair looked windswept, as though she'd gone for a walk in a storm. That was when he noticed she was carrying a riding crop in her hand. "Love, maybe you should sit and have a drink."

She didn't budge. "Naturally you're all hiding in here drinking. Well, you can stay right here, but I need to talk to your ex, Cal. Also, I need to talk to our lawyer. Is he here, too?"

Rory held a hand up. "I'm acting as our solicitor in this matter."

"Good, you should probably witness this. Is she in the dining room?" Tori glanced to her right, toward the room in question.

Oliver tipped his drink her way. "Yes, but Claire is taking care of everything."

Her eyes narrowed. "No, she isn't. I'll be having a talk with her, too." She pointed the riding crop. "You three stay out of my way."

Callum couldn't help it. This decisive side of Tori not only got him a little hot, it also brought out his Dom side. "Tori, I don't like the way you're talking to me, love."

She stalked right up to him and turned her chin up. "I don't like the way your slutty past has come back to haunt us all, but I still have to deal with it. And you can spank me later, Master, but you need to let me handle that bitch now. I need to do this. She's coming after my men, and I won't have it. I certainly won't hide behind you. If she wants you, she's going to come through me. And she won't like how I handle her."

He stared down at her. His brothers seemed perfectly fine with sending Tori in to tame the Thea beast.

If Tori had her spirit back and she was calling the three of them her men, Callum was all for it—with one caveat. "I'll let you handle her as you see fit, but there's no way I'm sending you in alone."

"She doesn't get to see you." Tori's blue eyes went hard.

Oh, he was going to enjoy this evening. "I want to spank you. I'm going to tie you down and spank that saucy arse of yours, and then I'm going to ease my cock into that tight little hole. Do you understand?"

Her breath hitched. She wasn't unaffected.

"Are we negotiating?"

"Yes." He brushed his thumb across her lower lip. "I'll stay back here and let you handle the situation if I can do wicked, nasty things to you later on that will make me feel like your man again."

"Done." Her eyes sparkled with mirth. "But I suspect I'll have to take Oliver and Rory with me. Am I right?"

Such a clever girl. "Exactly. You do your thing. Then you come back to me and present yourself. Tonight's play starts early."

She nodded, suddenly somber. "I'm done running away."

He pressed his forehead to hers. "I can't tell you how glad I am to hear that. I love you. You won't regret this."

"I'm done regretting things. I also won't regret this." She kissed him one last time and turned away, still clutching that riding crop in her hand. "Let's get this bitch out of our lives for good."

As Oliver followed her, he leaned toward Callum. "You're welcome."

"I'm not thanking you. You made a monster." Cal smiled as he said it.

"Well, I'm thanking you, Ollie. Damn uncomfortable not knowing whether Tori intended to stay or go." Rory hurried after them.

Callum was fairly certain their woman was about to cause trouble. And he was going to be a good boy and let her do it. Then he would have his revenge on her sweet ass.

He poured himself another Scotch and wished he could see his woman in action. He was sure she would be spectacular.

CHAPTER FIFTEEN

Tori paused outside the dining room. She could hear voices inside, and her sister-in-law was definitely out of her league. She didn't stop to correct herself. Claire was going to be her sister-in-law and it was time Tori taught the woman a few things.

"I'm advising my brothers to not make any kind of a deal with you." Through the slightly open door, she saw Claire sitting across from the platinum blonde. Thea was decked out. She wore more bling than a hooker looking for a "date." It fit. Thea was the sort of girl looking for a man to pay her way through life and wasn't above using her body to get it.

She was done preying on Callum—or any of the Thurston-Hughes brothers.

"I don't care what you advise your brothers to do," Thea said in a nasally voice. "I only care about Callum and what he promised me. When we made this baby together, he promised me we would be married. I need to talk to him, to remind him of how good we are together."

Claire shook her head. "I think it's best if he doesn't see you again."

"Then you should be prepared for me to write a tell-all book about how your family works and how that whore took my husband. I'm not stupid. I know the great and almighty publicist hates her real face being shown to the world." Thea's overly long nail tapped against the conference table.

Tori wondered if Thea would sound so confident if the woman knew what Callum had done to her on that very table. It had involved some rope, an anal plug, a paddle, and some screaming hot sex. Oliver and Rory hadn't been shy about joining in.

The world hadn't ended when her nipple graced the cover of the tabloids, and she would survive the Thea mishap, too. Somehow since that moment she'd read her father's words, she'd found a strength that she'd been missing for years.

"Not at all. Tori simply wouldn't lower herself to be in the same room with you." Sweet Claire. Even as angry as she was, her future sister-in-law hadn't thrown her under the bus.

It was time to save Claire. A good publicist knew that a client should always stay calm, always face the event in question with grace and dignity.

She wasn't a publicist today. She was a wife—and not a very happy one.

"If you make her bleed, get her off the rug. It's antique Aubusson, worth a fortune, and stains like that are hard to remove. Best to kill her on the hardwoods," Oliver said without a hint of teasing in his voice.

She turned to him. "I like the new Oliver."

"He's actually just the old Oliver. Bloody sarcastic," Rory pointed out. "Actually, the hardwoods are original. Do you know how much they would cost to replace? Maybe you could end her outside. I'll help you carry her."

It was good to know she had backup.

"I'm going to get everything I have coming to me, Claire," Thea taunted. "You poor thing. I feel sorry for you. It must be difficult to be the wren among peacocks. Your brothers are so handsome and you're such a pathetic nothing. Even that fat bitch they're playing around with is prettier than you."

Oh, Tori was so done waiting.

She shoved the door open, slamming it against the wall,

and stared at her rival. She'd seen Thea in pictures but had tried to stay away. She could see now that had been a mistake. "Hello, Thea. I'm glad you could make it today. We've needed to talk for a while. I will say that being nasty to my sister-in-law isn't going to help your case."

Claire looked up and smiled. "It's good to see you."

"I'm sorry I'm late. I would have been here much sooner, but sometimes…we all need a swift kick in the pants to get us going. Or three." She cupped Claire's shoulder. "I think you're gorgeous. Plastic Sally over there wouldn't know real beauty if it bit her in the ass."

Thea huffed, then glanced at Oliver and Rory as they entered the room and seated themselves as far away as possible. She stared at the opening, as if longing for Callum to walk through.

The woman's lawyer sat at the end of the table, shuffling through papers. If he was upset by the scene, Tori couldn't tell. He raised grim eyes and sighed as though he'd rather be any place other than here. "Ms. Glen, I don't see what you bring to the proceedings."

"It's Mrs. Thurston-Hughes," Rory corrected. "By the laws of Bezakistan, she's our wife unless she chooses otherwise."

"I'm your wife, babe. I've already made my choice. I don't need two more weeks." She winked his way.

Tori took a moment to enjoy their shock while Thea simply pouted. "Where's Callum? He can't possibly have any interest in this odd marriage. He won't take his brothers' leftovers when he can have me."

"He's not coming." She needed to make that plain.

"What?" Thea's eyes softened, her mouth twisting. Somehow she forced out a pretty tear. She stared at the door as if certain her savior would appear any moment.

Tori rolled her eyes. Claire had been correct. Only another woman could properly deal with her. "He has no interest in seeing you."

Thea bit her bottom lip. "I don't believe you. You're hiding him from me. Do you get more money if you marry all three brothers? Is this some weird foreign deal you've made?"

"No, I'm marrying them because I love them. And before you accuse me of chasing them for their money, my brother is one of the richest men in the world. I'm not hurting." She'd wanted to make it on her own. Now, Tori saw that was still possible. This time, she'd follow her own definition of success. She would follow Piper's lead—be grateful and help the people around her. Tori realized she'd been given an opportunity to make a difference in the world, and she was done shirking her responsibilities.

"He's your brother-in-law," Thea said with venom. "He's trying to pawn you off on someone else so he doesn't have to deal with you."

"I would love to see you make that statement to the sheikh," Oliver said, his eyes narrowing. "You should understand he views Tori as his sister. He takes his family seriously. He's very protective. We had to work hard to get his permission to court her. She's precious to him, and anyone who threatens her should expect to feel the wrath of the al Mussads."

"And the Thurston-Hughes family," Rory added. "We're not without some power ourselves."

Thea dropped the innocent act. "We had a deal. I won't sign anything unless I get to talk to Callum. So if you want your precious deal, you better produce my boyfriend."

Tori dragged the riding crop across the table once or twice. She didn't miss the way Thea's eyes widened. "I found this in the stables. I was looking for something else, but I think the crop will do nicely. Callum will probably be happy I found it later."

Rory winked her way. "Oh, I'm sure he'll deeply enjoy using it on your backside, brat."

"Callum would never. He's a gentleman," Thea said, her

face going red.

Tori scoffed. The woman didn't know Callum at all.

"Not if all that screaming at night is any indication," Claire said blandly.

"We'll attempt to keep it quieter, dear." Oliver tipped his head toward his sister.

Thea glared at Oliver, clearly stunned, as if she was just realizing that she'd meant nothing to Callum. She'd been a midnight hookup when he was at loose ends. It was obvious now that Thea had feelings for him. Tori actually felt a little bad for the crazy lady.

"If you don't know this side of Callum, then you don't know him at all. Dominance and submission occupies an important part of his life. If he chose not to share it with you, I'm not sure how much the single encounter meant to him."

Her eyes narrowed. "Single encounter? We were lovers for a year."

Not by Callum's count, but she wasn't about to argue. It would only feed Thea's fire, and that was something Tori really wanted to put out.

"It doesn't matter. He's with me. We're getting married according to British law. In the eyes of my sister's family, we're already married. You should know I'm not going to kick them to the curb in two weeks. We'll have a lovely royal wedding that I will absolutely allow my brother to pay for."

Rory gave her a thumbs-up. "Excellent, sweetheart. Charging Talib for our super-expensive wedding is the best idea ever."

"Well, he agreed to let you kidnap me. He can pay for my flowers, at least. I want lilies." She looked back to Thea and decided honesty would serve her best. "I don't care if you're pregnant. If you are and the baby is Callum's, then I will love and adore that child because that baby is a part of my husband. If you think his past is going turn me away from him, you're quite wrong. We'll be married within the month, and I'll be a very good stepmother."

"She's not pregnant," Oliver said with a sigh.

"I don't care. Callum matters. If there's a child, we'll welcome him or her with open and happy arms and we'll give that baby some siblings to love very soon."

Rory gazed at her with a soft look in his eyes. "Do you mean it?"

She'd done a number on them. It was time to let her men know how serious she was. "I mean it. I won't hold your pasts against you if you'll do the same for me."

"Darling, you don't have much of a past," Oliver reminded.

"And yet I let it almost ruin us." She wouldn't again. She would be what a wife should be—steadfast, loyal, deeply in love. "I won't let that happen and I definitely won't allow Thea to have any influence on what we do in the future. I'm going to love Callum no matter what. So the deal is off. If Thea can prove the child is Callum's, we'll make sure the child has the best we can provide. Until such time, I choose to believe my husband and he couldn't possibly have fathered your baby. You may leave."

Thea leaned forward. "I'm not giving up. I won't let you take him from me. I'll grant an interview to every reporter who will listen. I'll trash your reputation. I'll tear you apart."

Now that she'd calmed down, Tori really did see things from her sister's point of view. She needed to use her assets. "Try. My wedding will be a royal affair. Every paper who wants those pictures will understand that I'll cut them off the moment they take your side. The same holds true of our subsequent babies. And if they want access to my sister and her family, they will not print anything negative about me or my husbands."

Thea stopped, her eyes flaring. "You can't do that."

"I can," she said softly.

"They'll listen to me." She'd gone a nice shade of red. "I'll tell them everything."

"And some of them will publish whatever you say, but

the important papers will want access to the royal family. The truth of the matter is, all we have to do is wait you out. If you're pregnant, we'll get the DNA test and clear everything up. If you're not... Well, I'm sure you've got plans for that. But the story will blow over. The world will continue on. My husbands and I are going to be happy."

"I have to advise my client to stop negotiating if the original agreement is now moot." The lawyer stood up, collecting his paperwork. "You really should decide what you want, girl. You're wasting everyone's time."

Yes, Thea had done that for a good long while. Tori was done with it. "I know exactly what I want and that's never to think about your client again. I'll thank you to take her with you as you leave."

Thea stood. Tori didn't believe that a child could possibly be growing in her super-skinny belly. "I want to see Callum. I deserve to see him. He told me he loves me. He made a child with me."

A hint of madness lurked in her eyes. Somewhere in her brain, Thea believed what she was saying. Again, unwelcome sympathy welled in Tori, but she couldn't back down. "And he married me. Like I said, we'll sort it all out after you've had the baby. Until then, you do what you need to do."

"I'll ruin you. I swear to god, I'll make sure you pay. You're keeping him from me." Her lips turned down in a nasty sneer. "You'll see. I'll take care of you. You can't hide forever."

She strode out with her lawyer.

Oliver followed and murmured to his brother. "I want someone watching that woman. I want a PI looking into everything she does."

Rory nodded. "Yes. I think we should look into her finances."

"Do you suspect she's behind the attacks on Tori?" Claire asked. "You think she paid someone?"

"The police believe it's a political act." Tori didn't agree.

Could Thea be crazy enough to hire someone to kill her rival?

"I don't think so. If this was a political act, the perpetrators would look for press. This person is trying to hide his identity. I'm not even sure if it was the same person every time. If it's Thea, I think she's hiring various thugs to attack you." Oliver pulled out his cell phone. "I'm going to contact the private investigator and get an update."

Rory turned to her. "Why the riding crop?"

She grinned a little. "I would never go into battle unarmed."

Claire's eyes widened. "Do I even want to know what that means?"

"Let's just say Oliver angered our wife one night and he won't do it again." Rory winked her way.

"Oh, I'm sure I'll do it again," Oliver acknowledged. "I'll simply make sure I get rid of all the umbrellas, riding crops, and cricket bats before I do. Tori has a terrible temper."

Claire stepped in front of her. "I'm so glad you've decided to stay."

Tori hugged her sister-in-law. "I am, too. Thank you for kicking me. I promise not to forget my place again."

"Good, because it turns out I'm quite terrible at confrontations. That woman was horrible. What was Callum thinking?" Claire asked.

The door came opened, and Callum stood waiting, staring straight at Tori, a dark light in his eyes. Oh, she was in serious trouble. The Dom had been pacing, seething and impatient. He wanted his due. Tori shivered at the very thought. When Callum decided to top her, she knew she was in for hours and hours of pure pleasure.

"Callum wasn't thinking at all," he said of himself. "I was on the road, and Thea was easy. She found me in a pub and told me all she wanted was one night. I was single and rather easy myself at the time. Is she gone? Am I allowed to come out of the corner now?"

He might have let her take over, but he obviously intended to shift the power now.

Tori needed to play this very carefully if she was going to come out of today without a red ass.

She approached him, hips swaying, and softened her voice. She cast her gaze down as submissively as she could. "Thank you for indulging my jealousy, Master."

He gripped her hips, and Tori risked a peek up to see his gorgeous lips ticked up in a playful smile. "Is that how you're going to play this?"

She rose on her tiptoes to whisper in his ear. "I would be on my knees naked in front of you if your sister weren't here. I know how much you hated not being in that conference room with me, but we couldn't give her what she wanted."

"And why is that?"

She cupped his face. "Because you're mine."

"And you're mine, sweetheart. So take that riding crop you found and go to our bedroom. You will take off your clothes and be in the proper position to greet your Masters. Don't expect to leave there for the rest of the day." He kissed the tip of her nose, but his voice was deliciously dark. "Understand that I expect perfect obedience for the rest of the night."

She might get that red backside, but that wasn't all. She would also feel the joy of being with her men. She would finally have them all.

Tori stepped away and grabbed the crop. It had seemed like a nice little prop to intimidate Thea. She hadn't really imagined that Callum would turn it on her. *Uh-oh.* With as much submission as she could muster, she left the room.

The minute the door closed behind her she practically skipped down the hall toward the stairs that led to the bedrooms. There was no stopping them now. She was married and she was keeping her husbands. Yes, they would have crap to deal with in the future, but who didn't? She'd been wrong to hold herself back and she couldn't wait to show them that she would never do that again.

Starting now.

When she reached the bedroom, she opened the door and tossed the crop on the bed. She wouldn't be the one using it. As she turned and began unbuttoning her blouse, a cold chill ran across her skin.

"You know the old saying, don't you?" Thea stepped out of the shadows, a gun in her hand. "If you want it done right, you better do it yourself. Open your mouth even a little and I'll shoot you right here."

Tori put her hands up. It looked like her future would have to wait.

* * * *

Oliver hung up with the PI. The minute he had any kind of proof, he would have the police move in on Thea. There had to be something to connect her to the attempts on Tori's life. He hadn't spent much time with the woman, but the few minutes he'd been in her presence this time made him believe Thea was unhinged—and that the woman wanted his future wife dead. Oliver wasn't about to let that happen.

"That bitch is utterly mad," he growled.

Callum held a hand up. "You're not telling me anything I don't know."

Claire stared at Callum like he'd grown two heads. "I don't understand any of this."

"It was dark," Callum complained. "I'd had a couple of pints. I couldn't see the crazy eyes. Men aren't always intelligent creatures, dear, but you should know I intend to only sleep with Tori from now on. Her crazy eyes aren't insane. Thea was a terrible mistake, and she's come back to bite us all in the arse. I can't apologize enough."

Somehow Oliver didn't think Claire was talking about Thea. "We're not going to hurt Tori. Not really."

Rory turned to Claire, concern furrowing his brow.

"We'd never hurt our wife. Everything we do is consensual. We can explain it to you."

Claire rolled her eyes like the brat Oliver was always sure she could be. "I'm not talking about bondage. Only a complete moron could look at Tori and think she's an abused woman. Besides, I read quite a bit. I even know what an anal plug is and what it's used for."

Callum went a little green. "I don't think I needed to hear that."

She was their sister after all. Oliver wasn't sure he wanted to hear about her sex life, either. He'd rather hoped she didn't have one. Since she'd gotten out of school, she lived like a nun it seemed. "I'm deeply sorry if we've been too loud or too indiscreet. I promise we'll keep it down. I'm happy you've been here. I think you were the one to really get through to Tori."

She waved him off. "I don't care about the noise. I'm not a prude. I'm just confused as to how Callum seemed to grow two inches and his voice went all...not very Callum-like. Who on earth was that? Because he wasn't my goofy brother."

Rory snorted a bit. "There's only one place Cal truly takes control and that's...well, that's in private."

"Are you telling me my football playing brother is the Dominant?" Claire shook her head and held out a hand. "I don't want to know. It's actually quite horrifying. I don't even want to think about it."

Poor Claire. He had to fix that for her. If there was one person he knew who could use a Dom, it was his sister. "Talib al Mussad is the Dominant male in his marriage. His brothers top their wife as well, but Talib takes control in the bedroom. Keep that image in your head and I'm sure the one with Cal will go away."

She sighed. "Thank you. The concept of a Dom is now back to being sexy."

He was glad to help. "Now, I think we should talk about

how we're going to keep our wife safe until we can pin all of this on Thea and have her thrown in jail."

Rory sat back down. Cal did the same, propping his feet up and leaning back with a sigh.

Claire looked between them. "But didn't you just tell Tori to go and wait for you?"

"Yes, and she should be naked and kneeling by now," Callum said with a satisfied little smirk. "She can keep her lovely arse there for the exact amount of time she made me wait in the kitchen. She thinks she can top from the bottom? Not likely. She can think about what I'm going to do with that crop."

Claire sighed. "On that note, I'm going to tell the cook that dinner will be served in our respective rooms tonight."

His sister did know how to run a house. After their mum died, Claire had taken care of the day-to-day workings. Oliver was grateful but didn't think he'd ever said so. "Thank you, dear. And thank you for being so understanding about this."

"Yes, there are a lot of sisters who wouldn't understand. I know we've put you through a lot, but you've been the best, love." Rory nodded her way.

Callum stood and enveloped their sister in a hug. "Love you, Claire."

There were tears in her eyes as she stepped back. "I love you all. And I will always stand beside you. That's what we do. Of course I understand, Oliver. You're in love. You don't shove that aside because it doesn't look traditional. You reach out and hold on to it. Now I shall enjoy my dinner and some telly. You should make some babies. I need nieces and nephews to hold."

"Only until you have your own," Rory said.

She took a deep breath. "Sometimes that plan doesn't work out, you know. I think I was born to be the maiden aunt. Good night."

She stepped out into the hallway.

"Perhaps it's time we did something about Claire."

Callum stared at the door.

Oliver raised a curious brow. "And what would that entail, Master Callum? Do you have a Dom you want to gift her to?"

Callum shuddered. "Again, let's not talk about our sister having sex. She has had sex, right? I mean she's not...she went to university and everything."

"So did Tori, but she managed to come out of it a virgin," Rory pointed out. "I don't know, but something or someone definitely hurt Claire. She never dates. I'm not sure how to fix that. Perhaps Oliver's right and we should find her a husband. I've got a couple of good candidates."

Did his brothers think at all? "I'm sure she'll be thrilled to find herself back in the medieval period where it's acceptable for her brothers to sell her off like chattel."

"I'm not trying to do that." Rory's fingers drummed along the table. "I just don't like the idea of her being alone. Now that we're with Tori, who will she take care of?"

"Rory's right. Claire's a born caregiver. I can't imagine her without a family of her own." Callum looked back at the door. "Maybe we should look into what happened to her those years she was away at university."

Oliver had zero problems with intruding into his sister's life. She'd taken care of him for years. It was time to do the same for her. "I'll get someone on it. But for now, I think we've made Tori wait long enough. She's naked by now. I, for one, am ready to celebrate the fact that we're getting married."

He was getting married. He'd never believed he would do it again. He'd been absolutely certain he would never try to love another woman, but Tori had gotten under his skin. She'd been the catalyst for everything. She'd been the reason he'd gone back to Bezakistan and faced his past, the reason he'd learned that it wasn't everything he'd believed. She was the reason he was strong again and it was far past time to devote his life to her.

The door rounded open and slammed against the wall. Claire rushed in. "I was on my way to the kitchen when I found him."

A sharp jolt of dread flashed through Oliver. Claire's eyes were wild with terror. Her hands were shaking. He reached out and grabbed them, hoping to steady her. "What are you talking about? Who did you find?"

"The solicitor. That man she brought with her," Claire stammered.

Callum was on his feet and Rory pulled out his phone.

"I need a security check," Rory said immediately. "I want to know when Thea and her solicitor left and I need confirmation they are no longer on the grounds. I'll wait."

"You saw the solicitor leaving?" Oliver asked, though he was fairly certain it wasn't true.

Claire shook her head. "I think he's dead. He was just inside the foyer. He's not moving. I-I don't think the guard has patrolled that way yet."

Rory shook his head. "He has now. He's called an ambulance. The solicitor was struck on the back of the head with one of our mother's antique fireplace pokers. Thea must have picked it up as they walked through the parlor. He's still breathing, but he's definitely injured."

Oliver's heart started to race. "Please tell me she stole his car and left."

Callum looked out the window. "It's still in the drive. Thea is here and she's going to look for Tori."

"Or you." There was no question she wanted Callum more than anything. But she may have descended into madness and convinced herself that if she got rid of Tori, Callum would be hers.

"She's in my bedroom." Callum started out the door. "I bet Thea looked in my bedroom, and that's where I just sent Tori."

If Oliver let him, Callum would rush in and possibly startle the crazy bitch into shooting. Instead, he caught his brother by the arm, slowing him. "How does she know where the bedrooms are?"

"It isn't hard to figure out they're upstairs," Callum shot back.

Rory followed. "I'm getting a hunting rifle. I'll coordinate with the security team."

Callum struggled to get his arm loose. "You have to let me go. I've got to save Tori."

Oliver needed his brother to think clearly. "Think for a second. We can't run in. Chaos is the enemy. She'll shoot first. You need to be calm. Let's head to the bedroom. She might have overheard us telling Tori to wait for us there. I'm sure she's read the articles about this place. If she's as obsessed as she seems to be, it would have been easy for her to find all the information about this house. Mother used to talk about the architecture and how she decorated all the time. One of the magazines even included blueprints. She knows where the bedrooms are. We have to go in as if we don't know anything is wrong."

"I'll set up outside." Rory nodded toward the door. "There's got to be someplace with a view of the bedroom. If I can take her out, I will."

Two of the security guards were already striding toward them. Rory caught up with them and began talking.

They had very little time. Oliver rather thought the guards would try to take over. "Let's go. If they understand what's happening, they might try to hide us somewhere safe until they have the situation under control. I don't trust anyone but us to squelch it. You must talk Thea down."

They started toward the stairs, jogging beside each other.

"Mr. Thurston-Hughes," the guard from the front of the house called out. "We have a situation. I need you and your brother to come with me."

"Take care of Claire. We'll be down in a moment," he said to the guard nearest him, hoping the sentry would comply.

Claire helped out. She gave a little sigh, then winked Oliver's way before going into an absolutely perfect swoon. The guard caught her before she hit the floor.

Clever girl. The man wouldn't leave her now.

Callum picked up the pace. "I'll never forgive myself if something happens to Tori. This is all my fault."

"Don't. That's exactly the type of thinking that cost us months with her," Oliver argued. "You didn't ask for Thea to go off her rocker. You didn't ask for her to drag your name through the mud. I've been there and I've finally figured out that guilt helps nothing. We go in there and we do anything we need to do to save our wife. I mean anything."

"I'll do whatever it takes." Callum stared at the door.

"Stay calm. We'll enter and act as if we don't know anything is wrong. If Thea isn't there and Tori is waiting alone, we pick her up and run like hell and let the guards search the house."

"She's naked. If she's alone, she's naked. I ordered her..." Callum took a deep breath, clearly shoving down his fear.

At least Callum was a damn fine listener. He'd obviously pushed aside his guilt. They had no use for it.

As Oliver and his brother approached the door, he prayed he would have the chance to carry his naked wife kicking and screaming out of the house. They'd get a robe on her once they reached safety, but he wouldn't risk her life for anything.

"This isn't going to work." Tori's voice floated through the door, thready and thin. Afraid.

Shit. Oliver looked to his brother. Callum had paled, but he knocked on the door after clearing the fear from his face. Oliver tried to do the same.

"Tori, Oliver and I need to talk to you about Thea. Are you decent?" Callum asked.

After a long pause, Tori spoke. No doubt, Thea was forcing her to speak, maybe at gunpoint. The idea made Oliver's fists clench. "What about her?"

"I've been thinking, and I don't know if I'm doing the right thing. She's carrying my child."

Oliver could see how hard it was for his brother to say the words. He rested a soothing hand on Callum's back. Surely Tori wouldn't believe him.

"You said she wasn't. You promised me the baby wasn't yours." Her voice sounded ragged, desperate.

Callum's eyes closed, his hand on the door as though he could connect with her, make her believe. "I lied. She's the mother of my child. I've been with you because my brothers pressured me into it. I'm so sorry, but knowing she was here today and that you all kept me from seeing her, it made me change my mind."

He heard Tori cry out, heard her bite back a sob.

"You're a bastard, Callum." Her voice shook.

"I know," he said hollowly. "I need to find her. Can I come in? I need to pack a bag. I'm going to stay with her from now on."

"Yes," came the tense reply.

Callum glanced over and Oliver nodded, then whispered. "We go in slowly. Try to get her to the big window. I left all the windows open this afternoon because it's so warm, but the one on the right is likely where Rory will set up."

Callum nodded, then turned the doorknob.

Oliver caught his breath. Tori was standing in the middle of the room, her hands raised in the air. Obviously, she was terrified and shaking. Thea was standing behind her, using her as a shield.

"Callum?" Thea said, glancing over Tori's shoulder. "Did you mean it?"

Yes, he saw the crazy eyes Callum had talked about. Thea was staring at Callum as if nothing out of the ordinary was happening, certainly not like she was holding a gun to his wife's back.

Callum raised his hands, clearly trying to go for the non-threatening route. "What are you doing here, Thea? I was going to come looking for you."

"What's he doing here?" Thea glanced Oliver's way, and it stopped his attempt to flank her.

He went still, lifting his hands as well.

"Oliver came to collect Tori," Callum explained patiently. "He and Rory are going to marry her."

Thea frowned. "I don't like her. She kept us apart."

"She's going to be my wife," Oliver said, his voice deep. "I won't be happy if you hurt her. Neither will Rory. Do you want to alienate Callum's brothers if we're going to be family?"

Callum seemed to take up his idea. He moved to her left, a couple of steps closer. They needed to back her into the corner, preferably near the east window. From that position, Rory would be able to see Thea through the hunting rifle. Their father hadn't believed in playing fair. When he'd hunted, he'd used a scope. Oliver could still hear his father saying if the buck wanted a fighting chance, the deer population should have developed technology. He hoped it worked on Thea.

"Thea, the last thing either of us wants is for our baby to be born in jail." Callum's voice was perfectly soothing.

Tori's face twisted up in a mask of rage. "You're a liar. You said it wasn't yours."

Oliver took over. "Tori, love, let's get out of here and leave them to it. It sounds as though they have a lot to talk about."

"Yes," Callum said. "Let Oliver take his wife. You and I will talk."

Tori's back bowed and she hissed as though in pain.

"I don't think you mean that, lover." Thea's lips thinned, and she pulled Tori's hair, tugging her back. "I think you're trying to save her."

"I'll be alone with you if you let her go," Callum pointed out. "Just you and me. For as long as you want. Thea, we can close the doors and nothing else will matter but us, just like old times."

"I hate you," Tori spat at Callum. "I really hate you. You lied to me. You bastard!"

She fought against Thea's hold, and Oliver could see her struggle was working. Tori was far stronger than ultra-skinny Thea. Unfortunately, their wife wasn't stronger than a bullet.

"Stop," Oliver commanded. In this case, Tori needed to wait for them. She needed to trust them to talk her out of this situation. "Be still."

Tori stopped. "I don't want to talk to him. He lied. He's an asshole."

Callum physically flinched. "I'm sorry. I was trying to do right by my brothers, but I have to do right by her. I have feelings for her."

While Thea was watching Cal, Oliver inched to her side.

She snapped the gun up to Tori's head. "You should listen to the one man here who loves you. It isn't Callum. He's mine. He always loved me. He always wanted me."

"Yes," Callum said. "You're the one I wanted all along. I got a bit put off by how you talked to the press. I'm very private. But I know you only wanted what was best for us. Our union and our baby."

"We can be private." Thea stepped back, keeping her hand on Tori.

Oliver noticed the way the gun in her other hand quivered. Thea was rapidly losing strength. Maybe her adrenaline was draining out or she never ate any damn protein to build muscle. He didn't care which as long as Tori survived.

The sun was filtering in behind the mad woman, temporarily blinding him. But that was all right because Rory could likely see Thea quite well. He needed to move her back a little more. The windows were open, allowing the sweetness of the summer afternoon to flood the room.

"Let me take my wife." If he could only get Tori away, maybe they could trap the bitch inside this room. He didn't want to leave his brother. They were a family. They weren't as strong if they weren't together. He was fairly certain Tori would kick his arse if Callum died. "Really, you two should talk."

He held his hand out as though it was his right. It was, damn it. Tori was his. She belonged to them and he was representing his brothers right now.

Tori sent him a pleading, tremulous stare, reaching out for him. "Oliver..."

"Stop!" Thea shouted. "You're not going anywhere. I don't know what to do. I want Cal, but I don't trust him."

"We have a baby, Thea," his brother tried.

She sniffled. "We should. We would make beautiful babies. Wouldn't our baby be gorgeous?"

"He will be." Callum was playing to her crazy, but he was doing a damn fine job.

Tori teared up.

Thea shifted, inching ever closer to the window. He needed her back just a little further...

Oliver leaned forward. "Thea, you can't have Callum if you kill her. If you're in prison, Callum won't have anyone to keep him warm at night."

"He needs someone. He needs me." Thea let go of Tori's hair, but the gun stayed at her back.

"I do." Callum took another step forward.

"He definitely needs you." Oliver moved with him and sure enough, Thea stepped back, almost to the window.

"I love you, Callum," Thea said.

Oliver saw a glint of metal in the background. It was almost time. Could Rory align the shot? Or were they too close to the mental wench?

Thea frowned. "I'm scared. I lost the baby, Callum."

Of course she had. Oliver knew this song and dance well.

Callum shook his head. "We'll have to make another one then, won't we?"

For a moment, Thea looked utterly tortured. He could

almost believe she was heartbroken. "I've already done something bad. I didn't mean to hurt him, but he was trying to make me leave."

"The solicitor? He's fine." Callum wasn't letting go. "I'm sure once we write him a nice fat check, he'll agree that it was all a misunderstanding. But I think my brother is going to have a real problem with you threatening his wife. If you'll let her go, I'm sure he won't call the police."

That gun was suddenly pointing his way. "I can make certain he doesn't call the police."

Tori chose that moment to raise her leg and kick back toward Thea. The woman shuffled at impact but managed to stay on her feet, then whirl around. She pointed the gun at Tori.

Oliver leapt forward. He didn't think about anything but that bullet coming for Tori. Thea wasn't going to take hostages. She wasn't going to put her hands up and give in. She was willing to kill Tori and possibly him. He had to give Callum the chance to save their wife.

Then Oliver heard the shot. The sound blasted through the air. He hit Tori like a freight train, and for a moment was terrified he'd hurt her. His velocity forced her against the bed and he heard a loud smack.

Then a scream. Tori yelped, screeched in terror, her lovely eyes wide. Oh, god, had she been hit?

The world seemed a little hazy, but he forced himself to move, to cover her. He caught sight of blood. God. His heart pounded. Where was she hit?

There was the sound of glass breaking and he tried to cover Tori.

More screaming. He tried to move, but his arm didn't seem to be working.

Suddenly Callum was standing over him. "Rory got her. She's gone. Tori, it's all right."

"No, it's not. He's been hit. You have to get an ambulance. He's losing blood." Tori was clutching him like she wouldn't let go.

"Who?" He looked down at her. She was getting fuzzy. "Who got hit?"

Tori stared up at him, clutched his hand tightly. "You. Please... Please don't leave me."

Well, this wasn't how he'd thought his day would end. Blood. It was his. Damn. "You all right?"

She nodded, tears in her eyes. "Fine. Oliver..."

In the part of his brain still functioning, he realized this was everything Tori feared. His wife was clearly terrified. He'd just found her. He couldn't leave her.

Oliver slumped down, his head too heavy to hold up anymore. Her warmth surrounded him, but so did the darkness.

CHAPTER SIXTEEN

Callum glanced over at Tori as they pulled up to the gates. She sat in the backseat with Oliver, fussing over him.

Oliver was a wimp. The bullet had barely grazed him, but he'd hit his head on the side of the bed and required an overnight stay at hospital. Callum knew all too well what concussions felt like, and he know Ollie's head was throbbing. Still, his brother was milking the injury for everything it was worth. Between the small bullet wound and the hit to his head, there had been enough blood to terrify their wife.

Actually, Tori hadn't been the only one scared. He'd seen all that blood and feared Oliver could die. Again.

Thankfully, Oliver was basking in Tori's attention like a conquering hero. Rory was the man who had saved them all with one shot. And Callum was the idiot who had gotten them all in trouble in the first place.

"More reporters." Rory sighed as he stared out the limo window.

"What did you expect?" Oliver asked. "'Brothers kill stalker in their own home is a big headline. Though I have to say some of the more offbeat tabloids are amusing. According to one, Thea was an alien and she was the leader of our sex cult."

Rory just shook his head. "Mad, I tell you."

"We're lucky Rory is a good shot," Tori murmured.

"And that Oliver's got such a thick skull," Rory replied, chuckling.

Tori's hand tensed in Oliver's. He gave it a squeeze.

They hadn't talked. He'd dealt with the doctors and the police, while Tori had stayed at Oliver's side. They still hadn't discussed what had happened. The past twenty-four hours had been a hazy mess of reports and waiting, and an aching feeling in his gut that he'd lost the love of his life.

"I've already put out a statement," Tori said. "It was a simple, please give us privacy while we deal with this tragedy. We pray for Thea's family and hope they find the peace they deserve."

"According to the reports, she didn't have much family," Oliver noted. Even from his hospital bed, he'd checked up on the investigators. "But she definitely hired two men to follow and kill Tori. They've been arrested in London. We shouldn't have to worry about them a moment longer."

"The coroner's report showed she'd never been pregnant," Rory said. "The papers are now reporting that she was lying about the pregnancy all along."

Tori gave Callum a wan smile. "That will help restore your image immensely."

He didn't care about his image. He cared about her. He cared about how she felt about him. He'd done what he had to, but he'd hurt her in the process. He was the reason Oliver had been shot. Because of him all her fears had bubbled back to the surface.

The driver made it through the throng of press at the gates and turned down the long drive.

Callum risked a glance at Tori. He had to get her alone. He needed to explain everything he'd said to Thea, make sure Tori wasn't spooked enough to leave them again. If he didn't, he feared she would build up those walls until they towered, unscalable. A bit less than two weeks remained in her concubine period. If she decided to leave them, he and his brothers would have no recourse. Talib would shut them out. She could well vanish inside the palace, and they would be unwelcome.

"When we get to the house, I was hoping we could talk, Tori," he murmured.

She frowned as though the idea wasn't pleasant. "I'm awfully tired. Aren't you?"

She hadn't slept much. Still, the idea of going to bed without resolving anything didn't sit well with him. "I think we should talk about what happened. I would like to explain to you."

She gave him a tight smile. "That's not necessary. I'd just like to pick up where we left off and move on."

He knew that wasn't possible. "I think there are things we need to say."

"Oh, Cal, leave the poor girl alone. She's tired. She's had a rough day. Let her get some sleep. We'll deal with all the fallout tomorrow," Oliver said.

"As you will." Callum turned to look out the window as the car stopped. Claire was waiting for them as the door was opened.

She wrapped her arms around Tori and then Oliver, fussing over him.

"What's wrong with you?" Rory asked as they walked toward the house behind the women and Ollie.

Callum glared at him. Was he kidding?

Rory slapped him on the back. "Fine. I'll reword. What's wrong, besides the fact that your psychotic ex nearly killed your brother and the woman we love? Because I, for one, am happy to have the whole situation resolved."

There was nothing happy about what had happened. "Don't you think all that shit will set Tori back? She's terrified of losing someone she loves. She would rather not love at all. She watched Oliver nearly die."

"And she's processing what happened. Pushing her on it won't make that better," Rory said as the front door closed, leaving them standing outside. "She's been good with Oliver, very affectionate. I think she's all right."

"You weren't there. You didn't see what happened." He wasn't sure he would ever be able to forget it.

Rory studied him for a moment. "I saw enough. I know something happened that made Thea decide to shoot. I know Oliver saved Tori. I know you tried to get to them. I shot her before she could get you. She had that gun aimed at you."

And in that moment he would have gladly taken the bullet if it would have spared his brother and their wife. He'd stared at that gun and known it was likely over, and all he'd wanted to do was hold Tori one last time.

"She said if she couldn't have me no one could. I think she meant to turn the gun on herself after she killed me. She wanted to be with me one way or another."

"She was crazy, Cal. The shooting wasn't your fault. Anyone who came in contact with her could have become the center of her psychotic fantasies. If it hadn't been you, it would have been an actor or some other man she viewed as wealthy and powerful. We're all alive and we'll be stronger for it."

"And if Tori decides to leave?"

"She won't." Rory sauntered to the door. "It's going to be all right. She gave us her word and she'll honor it. She's stronger than she seems. I think once she makes a decision, she doesn't go back."

"Even when everything goes to hell?"

"For better or worse." Rory clapped a hand on his shoulder. "Let's get something to eat. You'll see in the morning. She'll feel better once she rests."

They strode into the house, and Oliver was waiting in the kitchen, Claire pouring him a cup of tea.

"Where did Tori go?" She was nowhere to be seen.

Oliver gestured to the back of the house. "She was going to take a shower and get some sleep. I think we could all use some of that. I was going to have some tea and conk out myself."

"Are you feeling all right?" Callum worried his brother still looked a bit pale.

"I'm good. The doctor said I'm ready for anything." Oliver's eyes strayed to the back of the house. "Which is precisely why I think we should give her a moment, then cuddle up with her. When she's had some rest, I think we should debauch her thoroughly."

Callum wasn't sure he would be welcome at that event. "I'd like to talk to her first."

"I'd like to not hear this conversation," Claire complained.

Rory kissed her on the cheek. "You're right, dear. Oliver, finish up. We should go back to my room and have this discussion. I think Callum is still feeling guilty. If we don't fix him, he's going to fuck matters up with Tori."

His brothers were treating this like some kind of joke. "I already fucked matters up with her. Can't you see that? Rory, you have no idea the things I said."

"I heard every word," Oliver returned. "Tori is a smart girl. She spins stories to the press for a living. She understands damage control and spinning a good yarn for the audience." He set his teacup down. "Let's go talk to her. Callum isn't going to stop worrying until we settle this."

Finally. Callum didn't say a thing. He simply turned and strode up the stairs. He needed to change his attitude. He typically wouldn't top her outside the bedroom, but this was a different case. She was going to talk to him, damn it. It was better for both of them if they got everything out in the open. She'd gone through a trauma, and she wasn't leaning on them. She was doing her level best to take care of everyone else, but she wasn't letting them take care of her.

Callum intended to put a stop to that.

He walked past his door. They'd agreed not to stay there until they'd thoroughly cleaned and redecorated. Until they did, it could bring back bad memories. Once they'd torn down the wall between Cal's and Oliver's rooms and made a massive suite, they would be less likely to remember what had almost happened there. He already had plans to take what used to be his room and turn it into a decadent bathroom where he would lavish Tori with affection every morning. She would get used to not showering alone. One of them would always want to be with her.

Perhaps he should barge in on her now. After he'd had his way with her and shown her with his body how much he loved her, then she would be ready to talk to him.

Callum opened Oliver's door, ready to force the situation.

"Holy hell," Rory breathed behind him.

"I wasn't expecting that," Oliver agreed.

Tori was naked, kneeling on the soft rug. Her knees were spread wide and palms up on her thighs. She'd taken her hair down from the bun she'd tucked it into. Now it was a lovely brown waterfall caressing her shoulders and tumbling toward her breasts. Tight pink nipples peeked from under her hair. He stared at her for a moment, taking in how lovely she was. She'd bowed her head submissively. And her body. God, the beauty of her body made his pulse pound. His cock was suddenly full and erect as though the damn thing knew playtime had arrived. It pointed right where it wanted to go, to the apex of her thighs where her gorgeous pussy was on display. All he could see was her pretty pink flesh, begging for his attention.

Callum stepped into the room, his brothers behind him. He heard the door close. Someone engaged the lock. Good thinking. They didn't need interruptions. Dinner could wait. So could the rest of the fucking world for all he cared.

He let all the weight of the last twenty-four hours dissolve. This was his place of power. Most of his life it had been the football pitch, but he'd discovered something even better—being her Master.

He strode up to her, to a place where he was sure she

could see his boots move into view. She was a good girl. She kept her head down until the moment he reached for her chin, lifting it up. Luminous eyes gazed at him. "Tell me something, love. Don't lie because I'll know."

"Yes, Sir."

How much of a brat was she? "Did you know I was nervous? Did you know I thought you were going to reject me?"

She gasped a little. "Reject you? Why would I reject you? Ever?"

"Because of the things I said yesterday."

She rolled her eyes. "I'm not stupid, Cal. I knew you were lying. I was acting, too. I thought I was pretty good. I wonder if I missed my calling." She bit her bottom lip and softened. "I didn't know you thought I was going to reject you because that's very silly when I love you so much. I might have known you wanted to sit and talk. I didn't want to do that so I did this instead."

Such a brat. "I wanted to talk because we went through something terrible."

"And I wanted to pick up where we left off. Before Crazy Pants barged into your bedroom, I was supposed to kneel and wait for you. That's what I'm doing." She frowned. "If you really want to talk, I can get dressed."

Like that was going to happen. He might never allow her to wear clothes again. "So you decided to get your way, did you?"

"When you think about it, isn't this a good form of communication for all of us, Master?"

What was going to be so good for him was slapping her ass. "You know I owe you some discipline."

There was no way to miss the way her eyes dilated. "I know."

"Then stand up." He held out his hand.

She placed hers in his and stood with a sweet awkwardness. He was sure in a few months she'd be pure grace in motion, but he actually like the way she clung to his hand. He looked her over, brushed the hair back so her breasts were on full display.

"Damn but you're beautiful, Tori." Oliver was already stepping out of his slacks.

Rory moved beside Callum. "You are, love. I told you she wouldn't run."

"I'm not running." A hint of a smile drew her lips up. "I was scared and I'll always be scared when you're in danger, but I love you and that's worth the risk."

"I hope it's worth what's about to happen." His cock jumped. He had an awesome plan.

"I'm sure it will be, Master."

"Good, then lean forward. I want you to grab your ankles."

She bent over, leaving her backside in the air. He walked around her to inspect. So fucking beautiful. Her ass formed a gorgeous heart shape. He dragged his hand over the twin globes. Her skin was perfect porcelain and so soft he could barely stand it. She gripped her ankles and the position put more than her backside on display. Her pussy was right there for his pleasure, too. He let his fingers trace down the seam of her ass and to the edge of her already aroused flesh.

"Have you been thinking about us?"

"Yes, Master," came the breathless reply.

"What did you think about?" Oliver was completely naked as he moved to Callum's side. "Tell me in detail. What's got this pussy all ripe and juicy?"

"Thinking about being with all three of my husbands," Tori replied. "I've wanted it forever and you promised me it would happen. I want my men."

He wanted her, too, but he couldn't let her get away with such brattiness. He smacked her ass right down the center.

She made the sweetest little squeal.

"If we're going to take her together, don't we need to open that sweet arsehole up a bit?" Rory asked. "Should I get the plug?"

Callum held his hand to her flesh, keeping the heat against her. "Yes. I think we should fuck her with the plug before we take her. Do you want that? Do you want a big cock fucking that tiny hole?"

"Yes, Master. I want all my Masters."

"And you'll get them. Rory, we're going to need a plug and lube. Oliver, I think you should help me smack this pretty arse."

"She did put herself in danger," Oliver said.

"I didn't have much of a choice," Tori shot back. "She was waiting for me when I got to the room. After that, I did whatever I could not to get shot."

Oliver moved in. "Then why did you struggle against her? I had to order you to be still and you still fought her."

Oliver's hand reared back. He hit her with a loud smack. The sound hung in the air.

Her flesh flushed a gorgeous pink. Oliver drew his hand back, and Callum spotted a faint handprint on her backside. It was enough to make him growl and smack her himself.

"You don't put yourself in danger," he commanded.

She gasped and shuddered. "I was trying to help."

He slapped that sweet flesh again and then again. "There is no helping when you're in danger. None. You will obey us and keep yourself safe. You're the most important thing in our world. You don't get to play around with your life."

"I think that's my line." She yelped when he spanked her this time.

Oliver gave her a good smack just above her right cheek. "There's only one you. Only one wife for us. You must take care of yourself. We were lost without you before. We would absolutely be lost without you now."

Callum spanked her on the left side. "And no topping from the bottom. Don't you think I know when you're manipulating me?"

"You didn't realize it today. Apparently you thought I

was running away again." She groaned at the smack that quip earned.

Oh, she was going to be so much fun. He and Oliver traded turns spanking her until her backside morphed into a pretty shade of pink. Rory chose that moment to return with the plug. It was far larger than that little thing they'd started her out on, but over the last few weeks, they'd graduated her up. Tonight, they would give her the real thing.

"Move to the bed," he demanded.

She winced as she straightened out.

"Poor baby, is your backside hurting?" He rubbed his palm across her cheeks, satisfied by the way she shivered.

"You know it is and you know I like it that way," came her saucy reply.

Oliver moved in, clasping her face in his hands and kissing her. After a moment's sweet play, he picked her up and started for the bed. "The good news is, you don't have to walk anymore. One of us will always carry you where you need to go."

He laid her tenderly on the bed.

She looked so small lying there in that big bed. Fragile and delicate. It was all a ruse. His wife had grown to become one of the strongest women he knew. And she definitely wasn't going to break, despite life with three British bastards.

"Hands and knees," Callum commanded.

She winked Oliver's way as she flipped over and obeyed. "He's not done abusing my backside, is he?"

"Not even close," Callum admitted. He would never be done. It was his new hobby.

Rory shoved out of his slacks and hopped on the bed. "While he's prepping you, sweetheart, I think you should really take care of us. I seem to be in need of attention."

Oliver moved beside their brother. Callum approved of giving their girl something to do while he prepared her.

"Get them ready, love. It's time to get your men ready to fuck."

"Yes, I can see they need so much help," Tori replied.

That earned her another hard smack. "Your arse is going to be so grateful when that smart mouth of yours has something to do other than get you in trouble."

"You're probably right." She sucked the head of Rory's cock into her mouth.

Callum moved between her legs, placing the plug on the small of her back. "You take care of them but don't move too much. If this falls on the floor and I have to clean the plug again, we'll start all over."

"Dear god, Tori. Don't piss off the Dom. He'll keep us all in hell until he gets his way," Oliver moaned as she moved to his cock.

He would. Things should be done in the proper fashion. Rory and Oliver might run the business, and he would follow them in the real world, but here he was the leader. They would play things his way. Tori was very still even as she sucked Oliver with enthusiasm.

He parted her cheeks. The tiny streak of sadist in him flared to life at what he was about to do. "This is going to be a little cold, love."

She whimpered as he poured the lube on. The sweet sound went right to his dick. He massaged the lube in, letting his finger rim her over and over, warming her up. After her initial reaction she went back to her work, though he could feel her relax under his hand.

"You're going to be so tight." That tight hole would strangle his cock. He would have to be very careful or he might go off the moment he got inside her. He would have to replay a match in his head or try to remember the names of Henry VIII's wives, but he seriously doubted he would be able to think of anything but how hot Tori was, how right it felt to be inside her.

He allowed his finger to dip just past the ring protecting her. Yes. She clenched around him, proving his point about her tightness. Despite their work with the plug, she was still incredibly taut. It would still be difficult to coax her flesh to take all of him. He slid another finger inside, her heat nearly scorching him. He stretched her, forcing her to open wider.

When he'd played with her and stretched her opening to his satisfaction, he grabbed the plug with his free hand and settled it to her. With slow precision, he twisted and pressed. After a moment's resistance, she accepted the plug, the piece sliding in inch by inch.

"God, I think she likes it. I can feel her moaning around my cock." Rory fisted a hand in her hair.

Callum fucked her gently with the plug, certain now that she was as ready as she ever would be to take him. With a sigh, he pressed the plug home, seating it deep inside her. When he took it out again, it would be his warm flesh pushing inside her.

He kissed the small of her back and watched as she alternated attention between Rory and Oliver.

"Keep it up, love." His heart was full as he strode to the bathroom to clean up.

* * * *

Tori had never imagined she would enjoy this type of play. Of course she'd never thought to use the word play in the bedroom before she'd met these men, but now it seemed to be one of the sweetest words in the world. *Play*. It was something lovers did with trust and openness.

As Callum had worked the plug into her backside, she'd been overwhelmed with the sensation. It wasn't pain. There had been pressure, then an added sense of relief as she'd opened to him, and he guided the plug in and out. She'd felt a sense of satisfaction that she'd been able to do this. Pride, even. It wasn't merely for them. She wanted to own her sexuality, and for her, that meant trusting them and letting them guide her into this new, sensual world.

The plug in her backside stretched her wide, but she had

no doubt that Callum would fill her even more. She licked the cock in front of her, rolling her tongue over the warm skin of Oliver's dick. She loved the little bead of liquid that coated her tongue. It pulsed from the slit of his cock, salty and clean and wholly masculine. His hand found her hair and he thrust the head into her mouth. She softened around him, allowing him inside as she sucked.

They were playing with her, without any real intent to come. It was evident in the gentle way they were fucking her mouth. When Oliver wanted oral, he could be deeply aggressive. He would never hurt her, but he would take control, thrusting himself in and out while holding her head in his hands. She didn't have to work when he took over, merely follow his lead. Today, they were playing, allowing her to explore and revel in her power. Every groan she elicited made her more confident in her ability to please a man. Three men, to be precise.

She sucked softly on Oliver's cock, rubbing her tongue down the underside as she took him in slow pulls of her mouth.

Before she could really work her way down, Rory was gently tugging her head to the side. She couldn't forget him. No. She had to give them equal time, and she was sure in a moment that Callum would want his, too.

"Look at me," Rory demanded.

She raised her head, gazing at his beauty. Rory's sandy blond hair was mussed, and she loved how young and happy he looked. He was always impeccable in his three-piece suits, forever the very image of a captain of industry. Here, he was her lover, her eager Master. He smiled down at her.

"I love you," he said. "You should know that and I intend to tell you every single day."

Those words had frightened her so much once. But as she'd held Oliver the day before, she'd known that no matter what could have happened, she wouldn't have traded her time with him. If she ached, then it was because she'd loved. Even the ache would be better than the emptiness of her life before them, without them. She'd been a ghost walking through the world with no thought past protecting her wounded heart. Now she knew her purpose. It was to love and be loved by them.

To be their wife. Their friend. Their partner and their sweet sub.

"I love you, too. I love you all." Now that she'd made the decision, she couldn't imagine her life any other way. She would have been so lonely without them.

"Turn over slowly," Oliver commanded. "Whatever you do, don't lose that plug. Callum will start all over again, and I might die. I'm very delicate, as you know."

Yes, Oliver was so delicate. Actually he'd been a big baby about getting shot and hitting his head. He'd moaned and required excessive handholding. He'd insisted on keeping her close. Even his brothers had acquiesced to letting Tori stay by his bedside because he'd seemed so pathetically needy.

What Rory and Callum didn't know was that when they'd left to eat supper, Oliver's delicate self had pinned her to his hospital bed and had his way with her. He'd claimed he needed sex in order to heal. He'd taken full advantage of his time with her and one nurse had seen way too much of them.

Funny, she would have been horrified even a few weeks ago. Now all her fears and hang-ups seemed so silly. Everyone made a fool of themselves from time to time. The only real mistake was to take herself too seriously.

She had no doubt they would all make a habit out of getting alone time with her. However, she would always enjoy the times they were all together.

"But I wasn't done with you two." She'd wanted to bring them both to orgasm, to have them fill her mouth and drink them down. She'd been intending to up the ante and get her way. It wasn't like they couldn't go again after a brief rest. They could be insatiable.

"Not going to happen today." Oliver clasped her waist and helped her turn.

The plug seemed huge in her backside. She clenched around it, not wanting to begin again any more than the rest of them did. She had to think about every move she made. This was what Callum wanted, for her to be aware of parts of her body she'd never thought about before.

As she twisted, the cheeks of her ass ached. It was a nice reminder of the spanking they'd given her. She would likely feel it tomorrow and remember how breathless she'd been. How she'd held her ankles and anticipated that moment when they would strike. She moved gingerly so as not to disrupt the plug, but she felt every muscle. He wanted her thinking about how every pore and cell of her body belonged to them and that they would bring her pleasure. They would show her intimacy.

With gentle hands, Oliver lowered her down. She could feel the softness of the comforter at her back. Oliver stared down at her as Rory took his place at her left.

"Do you know how beautiful you are?" Oliver asked. He brushed his hands over her breasts, making her arch her back.

"I know how beautiful you make me feel." And they were the gorgeous ones. Oliver looked like an angel with his stark blue eyes and perfectly chiseled jaw.

"Then let us make you feel like the most beautiful woman in the world," he whispered as he lowered his lips to her breast.

Rory followed suit on his side. "Because that's what you are to us."

She gasped as she felt the heat of their mouths, one on each of her nipples. They sucked her into their mouths, pulling on her. The sensation went straight to her pussy, lighting her up and sending sparks through her whole body.

She needed this. She needed them all. She wasn't complete without them.

As though she'd conjured him through sheer want,

Callum appeared at the end of the bed, his athletic body on full display. She stared at him, boldly looking at his cock as it twitched her way. It was a thing of beauty. Long and impossibly thick, it stood out from his pelvis. She wanted to touch him, to stroke his thick flesh and know it was all hers.

He'd been through so much. All of them had. Now her place was surrounded by them, her right to love and comfort them, to find joy in their own unique happiness.

He sobered as he stared at her. "Do you know how hard it was to stand there yesterday and say those things?"

He was trying to get her to think when she should be feeling. Oliver and Rory were working her nipples, sucking and laving them with affection, but apparently Callum needed a different sort of affection. He needed reassurance.

It was time to tell them some truths.

"It should have been easy because I knew what you were doing. Not once did it cross my mind that you were telling Thea anything other than what she wanted to hear. You should have trusted me to know and then you wouldn't have believed that crap. I knew when I realized she was in the room that you would save me. That's what people in love do."

He fell to his knees, his head between her legs. "Is it? Well, I think we've done all the saving we need to do for a long while. Now we're going to settle down. We're going to be a perfectly boring family."

She doubted they would manage that. Especially since her heart raced every time one of them looked at her or called her name. There was nothing boring about the Thurston-Hughes boys. "Unless you have some other crazy stalkers."

Oliver chuckled against her skin. "No. I think the crazies in our lives are gone now. Mine is. Callum's is."

"I wasn't foolish enough to fall for a crazy." Rory winked down at her.

He wasn't off the hook. Rory wasn't some blushing innocent. "No, just three hundred supermodels."

He had the grace to blush. "None of whom could hold a candle to you."

Rory was smart. She sighed when his lips touched hers. "You always know what to say."

"Let us show you how we feel." Callum's mouth hovered above her pussy and she could feel anticipation pound through her system.

Rory moved back to her breast, his teeth finding the edge of her nipple, then biting down lightly.

He gave her the bare edge of pain, just enough to make her squirm and writhe.

That was when Callum chose to part her labia and run his tongue from below her clitoris to her channel. She stared up the length of her body as he laved her sensitive flesh. He teased her, running his tongue all around the edges of her pussy. He nosed her clitoris. The pressure made her gasp.

He took her to the edge and then brought her back. Sweet frustration welled. Between Callum at her pussy and Oliver and Rory at her breasts, she couldn't breathe. They held her down, Oliver and Rory pinning her arms to the mattress and Callum opening her thighs with strong hands. She was weighed down by them in a decadent splay, open and ready for their pleasure. Tori couldn't move. She was utterly helpless, and it was all right because she trusted these men.

She lay beneath them as they did their best to make her scream. Over and over, their tongues and hands stroked her. Callum suckled her clit before plunging his tongue deep. Rory moved from her breast to her mouth, kissing her with graceful ease. He played his tongue against her own, and kept her off balance while Oliver concentrated on her nipples. He bit down, then soothed the little ache with his kisses. He rolled the opposite nipple with his fingers as he did. On one, he poured love and affection. The other he gave a quick bite of pain that sent shivers through her system.

And all the while she couldn't forget the plug in her ass. She clenched. It filled her up. It was as if there wasn't any part of her body they weren't touching, stimulating, loving. Every cell and inch of her flesh was theirs, especially her heart. She was laid open and bare to their love.

Callum stroked his tongue through her folds, all the while pinching her clit as Oliver nipped her breast. The orgasm sneaked up on her, and Tori screamed as it rolled through her system, sending fire along her veins. Rory caught her strangled scream, kissing and calming her. Even Callum's hands were gentle as he grasped her ankles.

"It's time." Rory whispered along her skin. "I can't wait to get inside you."

She was still in the afterglow of the first orgasm, her body relaxed and her mind hazy. They were moving all around her, their hands caressing her body. This was where she wanted to be all the time, surrounded by them, filled by them.

Rory shifted with her, his mouth on hers even as they realigned their bodies, rolling her so he lay underneath. She could feel his erection already seeking its place. The broad head of his penis thrust against her labia, sliding easily through the slick arousal there.

Even as Rory moved into position under her, Oliver rose to his knees in front of her, his cock in his hand. It looked like she would get her way with one of them. She licked her lips as she stared at that gorgeous piece of masculine flesh. It jutted out from his perfectly muscled body, and below she could see the tautness of his balls as they moved while he stroked himself.

She shivered as Callum parted the cheeks of her ass and touched the plug. It sent a jagged sensation through her, jolting her from her languor. There was more pleasure to be had and she didn't want to miss an instant of it.

Callum pulled the plug out and she felt her muscles clenching, trying to keep it in. Rory's cock rooted at her core and finally his hips shifted and she felt him filling her.

"God, you're so tight. You feel so good." Rory clasped

his hands around her hips, pulling her down to impale her on his dick.

He was the one who felt good. He was so big inside her, reminding her how amazing it felt to be with them. When they made love, they combined to become something more than they were as individuals. Something profound and lovely.

"Rory, hold her still for me." Callum pushed against her virgin hole.

Oliver rested a hand on her head while Rory held her steady.

"Be still, darling. Don't fight him. Relax. The rest will be pure pleasure," Oliver cajoled.

She whimpered as she felt the pressure. Callum moved in short strokes, opening her up with little thrusts. She could feel him taking more and more with every thrust. Every pass brought them closer. And every time Callum moved, Rory had a countermove. While she felt the burn of being opened up, Rory ground up and hit her clit, sending a wild thrill through her.

"Almost there. You're doing beautifully." Oliver whispered words of praise.

Callum took his time. She could see the strain on Rory's face, but she loved them both for taking it easy with her. They were careful, making her feel their love and protection even as they inundated her with their desire.

Callum moaned behind her, his hands circling her waist as he thrust in. "Just a bit more. We're almost there."

She gasped when he finally breached her fully. The sensation was totally different from the plug. The plug was cold and sterile. This was Callum, all passion and fire. His heat flashed through her. They were connected on a base level. She was giving him something she'd never thought to give, and the sheer intimacy of it floored her.

Rory reached up and brushed away tears she hadn't known she was shedding. "We should stop. She's crying."

"No," she said as quickly as she could. "I'm not in pain. Don't you dare stop."

"She's happy we're finally together," Oliver said, his voice thick with emotion. "She's happy we're finally whole."

She nodded. Oliver was complete again and she loved the man he was becoming. Though they hadn't had the same issues, Rory and Callum needed this, too. And she'd come so far. She was only now realizing her potential, and it was all because of them. She let herself feel with her body and mind and heart. All three were finally aligned and she felt more powerful, more content than she'd ever been before.

And a little restless because she could feel them holding back. The time for that had passed.

She flexed her hips, feeling Callum's cock slide even further inside her body. And there, just as she'd hoped, he gave her a hard smack to her ass.

"Trying to take control again?" Callum hissed as he pulled back slightly. "Oliver, you should move because I don't think either one of us is going to last long."

She sent Oliver a smile as he aligned his cock with her lips.

"Suck me hard, darling. I'm ready to fill you up." Oliver's hand found her hair, his fingers tangling as he showed her that, this time, he meant business. There was no playing, just the hard thrust of his cock against her lips and the demand that she pleasure him. It was a demand she intended to meet since they'd already brought her more satisfaction than she could imagine.

She wrapped her lips around Oliver's cock and gave over to him. He fucked her mouth hard, gaining ground as Rory and Callum did the same. They worked themselves inside her until she couldn't remember where they ended and she began.

Her body relaxed as though it knew her Masters would take care of her. She let them control the flow of passion. She rode the wave between them. Rory stroked inside while Callum pulled out. When he did, a flurry of sensation startled her. She hummed out, the vibrations causing Oliver to tighten his hand and stroke in harder. It was as if a hundred new nerve endings came alive deep inside and they all flared with sizzling sensations.

They rode her body like the Masters they were, creating a rhythm she could only marvel at. Any way they pushed or pulled her brought another pleasure, another new intimacy.

Oliver hissed and lost his rhythm as he began to spill inside her mouth. "Take it all, love. Every bit. Take all of me."

She drank him down as he came on her tongue. She wanted everything he had, wanted to be filled with him, to know that she had his essence inside her as she moved through her days.

Rory thrust and ground against her, his cock as deep as it could go. Over and over, he slammed up, hitting just the right spot. She hadn't thought she could orgasm again so soon. She hadn't minded giving her body to them, had expected only the intimacy of surrendering to her men, but they'd brought her to the edge. She gasped, dragging air in, the taste of Oliver still on her tongue.

"Give it to us," Oliver insisted, staring into her eyes. "I want to watch you. Let me see you come for them. Come, Tori."

Callum flexed inside her, and she went careening over the edge. She could feel them losing control, their thrusts becoming fierce. They fucked her hard, and she was lost in them. Pure sensation became the air she breathed. She didn't need anything but their hands and mouths and cocks. She screamed as she came again, harder this time. They threw her into an ocean of sweet fire and she didn't want it to ever stop.

Rory shouted her name as she felt the hot wash of his pleasure. And then she was filled with Callum as he ground himself into her, holding her tight and giving up everything he had.

She fell in a heap of flesh, her men holding her tight.

She couldn't help but laugh. Her whole body felt light, but her heart was so full. Full of love for them, full of gratitude, full of hope for the first time in forever.

Callum smiled down at her. "Rest now, love."

She'd rested her whole life, holding herself back and allowing nothing to truly touch her. She was so done with that.

She growled a little and kissed him, dragging his bottom lip into her mouth. "You're not ready for the next round?"

Oliver chuckled, and Rory suddenly thumbed her nipples.

"We've created a monster," Rory said, and she could feel him stirring once more.

"As long as she's our monster." Oliver bent and kissed her with reverence.

She was theirs. Now and forever.

SCANDAL NEVER SLEEPS
The Perfect Gentlemen, Book 1
By Shayla Black and Lexi Blake
Now Available

They are the Perfect Gentlemen of Creighton Academy: privileged, wealthy, powerful friends with a wild side. But a deadly scandal is about to tear down their seemingly ideal lives...

Maddox Crawford's sudden death sends Gabriel Bond reeling. Not only is he burying his best friend, he's cleaning up Mad's messes, including his troubled company. Grieving and restless, Gabe escapes his worries in the arms of a beautiful stranger. But his mind-blowing one-night stand is about to come back to haunt him...

Mad groomed Everly Parker to be a rising star in the executive world. Now that he's gone, she's sure her job will be the next thing she mourns, especially after she ends up accidentally sleeping with her new boss. If only their night together hadn't been so incendiary—or Gabe like a fantasy come true...

As Gabe and Everly struggle to control the heated tension between them, they discover evidence that Mad's death was no accident. Now they must bank their smoldering passions to hunt down a murderer—because Mad had secrets that someone was willing to kill for, and Gabe or Everly could be the next target...

* * * *

"I want to see you."

Even in the low light, he noticed her breath hitch. "You want me to turn on the lights?"

"That's not what I meant." He never took his burning

336

gaze from her. "I want to see you naked. Take off your dress. Show me your breasts."

"I'll close the curtains." She started to turn to the windows.

He caught her elbow, gently restraining her. "Don't. We're high up. No one can see in. Take off your dress. Let me see you in the moonlight."

Her gaze tangled with his, and he could see a hint of her trepidation. A gentleman might have backed down. But he knew what he wanted. She must want him too or she wouldn't have agreed to spend the night with him. He wasn't giving Eve the easy way out.

Finally, she turned her back to him and lifted her arms, struggling to reach the metal tab. "There's a zipper down the back."

He moved closer. "Let me."

Gabe ran his hands up her spine before finding the zipper. She lifted her curls out of his way, exposing the graceful column of her neck. Her skin looked pale, almost incandescent in the low light. He couldn't help himself. He leaned over and kissed her nape, feeling her shiver under his touch.

Slowly, he eased the zipper down, his fingertips brushing her spine. Once he passed her neck, she let her hair fall free, the strawberry-blond mass tumbling well past her shoulders, gliding over her skin. Her tresses were soft, too. Not severely flat-ironed. Different, like the woman herself. Fuck, he could lose himself in Eve.

She shrugged, allowing the straps of her dress to fall past her shoulders and drop to her waist.

Her bra looked plain and white. He was used to delicate garments meant to entice a man, so he had no idea why the site of her utilitarian bra made his cock jerk. She hadn't been seeking a man this evening, much less intending to seduce a lover. When she'd dressed, it had been for comfort. But now, she was here with him, slowly peeling away her clothes.

With practiced ease, he unhooked her bra with a twist of his hand and slid his fingers under the straps to strip them off. He closed his eyes and allowed his hands to roam across the wealth of smooth skin he'd just exposed. He drew her back against his chest and grazed his way up her abdomen until he found her breasts. Full and real, he loved the weight of them in his palms. He drew his thumbs over the nubs of her nipples and Eve rewarded him with a long intake of breath.

"That feels so good." As she leaned back against him for support, she shuddered and thrust her breasts up like twin offerings.

He would absolutely take everything she had to give.

Gabe filled his hands with her flesh, cupping and rubbing and discovering every inch of her breasts before he grew impatient to have her totally bare and pushed the dress over the curve of her hips. It pooled on the floor at her feet.

Her underwear matched her bra. If she were his, he would buy her La Perla. He would dress her like a goddess in silk and lace and know that she wore the most come-hither lingerie for his eyes only. She could wear her ladylike dresses and cover herself with all appropriate modesty if she wanted—but only until they were alone.

As he stripped off her panties, a wild possessiveness blazed through his system. Gabe turned her to face him, well aware that he needed to slow down but utterly incapable of doing so. He took in the sight of her breasts. They looked every bit as perfect as they'd felt.

"You're beautiful."

"I don't feel that way." She tilted her face up to his, drinking him in with her stare. There was nothing coy about her expression. She looked at him with naked yearning. "Not most of the time. But you make me feel sexy."

"You are. I want to be very clear about how beautiful I think you are." He kissed her again, lifting her up and out of her dress, heading back to the bedroom while his mouth ate hungrily at hers.

She didn't fight him, didn't fidget to make him set her back on the ground. She simply wrapped her arms around his neck and let him carry her. Her fingers sank into his hair and she held tight while her tongue danced against his.

Luckily, he knew Plaza suites like the back of his hand. He maneuvered her toward the bed, his cock throbbing insistently.

He wouldn't last long. God, he couldn't believe he was even thinking that. Usually, he could go for hours, but Gabe knew the minute he got inside Eve, he was going to lose control. He needed to make it good for her now because he'd barely touched her and already he wanted to throw her against the wall and shove his way inside her.

As he approached the mattress, he stopped and eased her onto the luxurious comforter. She lay back on the elegant duvet, her hair fanned out and her legs spread. Wanton and yet so innocent. He pulled at his shirt, hearing a button or two pop off, but at the moment he didn't give a shit. The need to be skin to skin with her drove him to haste. He unbuckled his belt and shoved his pants down.

"Foreplay." Freaking hell. He was so ready to go, he'd forgotten about that. Women liked foreplay. It tended to be necessary for them.

She shook her head. "The kissing was foreplay. We're totally good."

Shit. He had to slow down. He wasn't exactly a small guy. She needed to be ready to take all of him.

Gabe took a deep breath. "Need you aroused. It's okay. Just give me a minute."

"Gabriel, I am as aroused as I have ever been in my life. I'm a little worried about what kind of stain I'm going to leave for the staff on this duvet. So really, can we get this train moving?"

He gripped her ankles and slid her down the bed, spreading her legs wider in the process. His cock twitched when he saw that she was right. Her pussy was wet. Juicy. He could see its slick gloss from above, even in the shadows. A little kissing, some groping, and she was ready to go. He'd never had a woman respond to him so readily. "Tell me again."

"I'm ready," she vowed. "I am *really* ready."

"No, tell me this isn't normal for you," he corrected. It was stupid. She was right there, able and willing to give him the pleasure he sought—but he craved more. He needed to know that tonight was special for her. "Tell me you want me and not just sex."

She gave him a sheepish smile. "This isn't at all normal. I guess I've gone a little crazy tonight, but I don't do one-night stands. I can count the men I've had sex with on one hand and I wouldn't need all my fingers. And I've never, never wanted anyone as much as I want you right now. Gabriel, I don't need foreplay, just you."

Want another alpha male who makes a headstrong beauty his? Meet Noah Weston.

I hooked up with my temporary roommate. Now I'll do anything to claim her for good.

Check out MORE THAN LOVE YOU, part of the steamy, emotional More Than Words Series.

MORE THAN LOVE YOU
by Shayla Black
(available in eBook, print, and audio)

I'm Noah Weston. For a decade, I've quarterbacked America's most iconic football team and plowed my way through women. Now I'm transitioning from star player to retired jock—with a cloud of allegation hanging over my head. So I'm escaping to the private ocean-front paradise I bought for peace and quiet. What I get instead is stubborn, snarky, wild, lights-my-blood-on-fire Harlow Reed. Since she just left a relationship in a hugely viral way, she should be the last woman I'm seen with.

On second thought, we can help each other...

I need a steady, supportive "girlfriend" for the court of public opinion, not entanglements. Harlow is merely looking for nonstop sweaty sex and screaming orgasms that wring pleasure from her oh-so-luscious body. Three months—that's how long it should take for us both to scratch this itch and leave our respective scandals behind. But the more I know this woman, the less I can picture my life without her. And when I'm forced to choose, I'll realize I don't merely want her in my bed or need her for a ruse. I more than love her enough to do whatever it takes to make her mine for good.

Discover Lexi Blake writing as Sophie Oak

Texas Sirens

Every girl dreams of her alpha cowboy, the one who sweeps her off her feet. In Texas Sirens, every girl gets two.

Set in both small Texas towns and cosmopolitan cities, Texas Sirens features beautifully broken heroes and heroines who discover that unconventional love is their best chance at happily ever after.

Small Town Siren
Siren in the City
Siren Enslaved
Siren Beloved
Siren in Waiting
Siren in Bloom
Siren Unleashed, Coming Spring 2019
More coming in 2019!

* * * *

Nights in Bliss

Bliss, Colorado, is home to nudists, squatchers, alien hunters, a bunch of ex-military men, and a surprising number of women on the run. Bliss is a place where cowboys hang out with vegan protestors, quirky is normal, and love is perfectly unconventional. So grab a chair and settle in. If you can forgive the oddly high per capita murder rate—and the occasional alien sighting—you'll find that life is better in Bliss.

Each Bliss story is a standalone, though found family is important so expect the characters to stick around, playing a part in each novel.

Three to Ride
Two to Love
One to Keep
Lost in Bliss
Found in Bliss
Pure Bliss, Coming March 5, 2019
More coming in 2019!

ABOUT SHAYLA BLACK

Shayla Black is the *New York Times* and *USA Today* bestselling author of more than sixty novels. For twenty years, she's written contemporary, erotic, paranormal, and historical romances via traditional, independent, foreign, and audio publishers. Her books have sold millions of copies and been published in a dozen languages.

Raised an only child, Shayla occupied herself with lots of daydreaming, much to the chagrin of her teachers. In college, she found her love for reading and realized that she could have a career publishing the stories spinning in her imagination. Though she graduated with a degree in Marketing/Advertising and embarked on a stint in corporate America to pay the bills, her heart has always been with her characters. She's thrilled that she's been living her dream as a full-time author for the past eight years.

Shayla currently lives in North Texas with her wonderfully supportive husband, her daughter, and two spoiled tabbies. In her "free" time, she enjoys reality TV, reading, and listening to an eclectic blend of music.

Connect with me online:
Website: http://shaylablack.com
VIP Reader Newsletter: http://shayla.link/nwsltr
Facebook Author Page:
    https://www.facebook.com/ShaylaBlackAuthor
Facebook Book Beauties Chat Group:
    http://shayla.link/FBChat
Instagram: https://instagram.com/ShaylaBlack/
Twitter: http://twitter.com/Shayla_Black
Amazon Author: http://shayla.link/AmazonFollow
BookBub: http://shayla.link/BookBub
Goodreads: http://shayla.link/goodreads
YouTube: http://shayla.link/youtube

If you enjoyed this book, please review it or recommend it to others.

Keep in touch by engaging with me through one of the links above. Subscribe to my VIP Readers newsletter for exclusive excerpts and hang out in my Facebook Book Beauties group for live weekly #WineWednesday video chats full of fun, community, book chatter, and prizes. I love talking to readers!

ABOUT LEXI BLAKE

Lexi Blake lives in North Texas with her husband, three kids, and the laziest rescue dog in the world. She began writing at a young age, concentrating on plays and journalism. It wasn't until she started writing romance that she found success. She likes to find humor in the strangest places. Lexi believes in happy endings no matter how odd the couple, threesome or foursome may seem. She also writes contemporary Western ménage as Sophie Oak.

Connect with Lexi online:

Facebook: Lexi Blake
Twitter: https://twitter.com/authorlexiblake
Website: www.LexiBlake.net

Sign up for Lexi's free newsletter at
http://lexiblake.net/contact.html#newsletter.

ALSO BY SHAYLA BLACK AND LEXI BLAKE

Their Virgin Captive
Their Virgin's Secret
Their Virgin Concubine
Their Virgin Princess
Their Virgin Hostage
Their Virgin Secretary
Their Virgin Mistress

SERIES BY SHAYLA BLACK

For more info about Shayla's books, visit ShaylaBlack.com!

MORE THAN WORDS
Contemporary romances that depict a love so complete, it can't be expressed with mere words.

DEVOTED LOVERS
Steamy, character-driven romantic suspenses about heroes who will do anything to love and protect the women bold enough to be theirs. Begins where Wicked Lovers ended.

WICKED LOVERS
Dark, dangerous, beyond-sexy romantic suspenses about high-octane men and the daring women they risk all for, even their hearts.

PERFECT GENTLEMEN
Suspenseful contemporary romances about the "Perfect Gentlemen" of Creighton Academy. Privileged, wealthy, and powerful friends—with a wild side.

MASTERS OF MÉNAGE
Very sexy romances about men of power and danger who share a kink—and a special woman. Though she's inexperienced, she isn't afraid to embrace all she desires.

SEXY CAPERS
Sassy, sinful contemporary romances with a pinch of suspense that show both the fun and angst of falling in love while snaring bad guys.

DOMS OF HER LIFE: RAINE FALLING
Super-sexy serialized contemporary romances about one tempestuous woman thoroughly in love with two friends and

their battle to see who will ultimately win her heart.

DOMS OF HER LIFE: HEAVENLY RISING
Super-sexy serialized contemporary romances about one innocent and the two frenemies desperate to her touch, protect, and claim her as their own.

MISADVENTURES
Fun, sexy, rompy standalone contemporary romances with a fun premise, fast pace, and high heat.

STANDALONES
Romances published independent of a series, some sexy, some sweet, all with a happy ending that's finished and complete.

HISTORICALS
Sexy stories about the bold rakes and audacious beauties of lush eras gone by.

PARANORMAL
Set in contemporary London, magic, myth, and emotions blend in the passionate, good-versus-evil Doomsday Brethren series.

OTHER BOOKS BY LEXI BLAKE

ROMANTIC SUSPENSE

Masters And Mercenaries
The Dom Who Loved Me
The Men With The Golden Cuffs
A Dom is Forever
On Her Master's Secret Service
Sanctum: A Masters and Mercenaries Novella
Love and Let Die
Unconditional: A Masters and Mercenaries Novella
Dungeon Royale
Dungeon Games: A Masters and Mercenaries Novella
A View to a Thrill
Cherished: A Masters and Mercenaries Novella
You Only Love Twice
Luscious: Masters and Mercenaries~Topped
Adored: A Masters and Mercenaries Novella
Master No
Just One Taste: Masters and Mercenaries~Topped 2
From Sanctum with Love
Devoted: A Masters and Mercenaries Novella
Dominance Never Dies
Submission is Not Enough
Master Bits and Mercenary Bites~The Secret Recipes of Topped
Perfectly Paired: Masters and Mercenaries~Topped 3
For His Eyes Only
Arranged: A Masters and Mercenaries Novella
Love Another Day
At Your Service: Masters and Mercenaries~Topped 4
Master Bits and Mercenary Bites~Girls Night
Nobody Does It Better
Close Cover
Protected: A Masters and Mercenaries Novella

Enchanted: A Masters and Mercenaries Novella

Masters and Mercenaries: The Forgotten
Lost Hearts (Memento Mori)
Lost and Found, Coming February 26, 2019

Lawless
Ruthless
Satisfaction
Revenge

Courting Justice
Order of Protection
Evidence of Desire, Coming January 8, 2019

Masters Of Ménage (by Shayla Black and Lexi Blake)
Their Virgin Captive
Their Virgin's Secret
Their Virgin Concubine
Their Virgin Princess
Their Virgin Hostage
Their Virgin Secretary
Their Virgin Mistress

The Perfect Gentlemen (by Shayla Black and Lexi Blake)
Scandal Never Sleeps
Seduction in Session
Big Easy Temptation
Smoke and Sin
At the Pleasure of the President, Coming 2019

URBAN FANTASY

Thieves
Steal the Light

Steal the Day
Steal the Moon
Steal the Sun
Steal the Night
Ripper
Addict
Sleeper
Outcast

LEXI BLAKE WRITING AS SOPHIE OAK

Small Town Siren
Siren in the City
Away From Me
Three to Ride
Siren Enslaved
Two to Love
Siren Beloved
One to Keep
Siren in Waiting
Lost in Bliss
Found in Bliss
Siren in Bloom
Pure Bliss, Coming March 5, 2019
Siren Unleashed, Coming Spring 2019

Made in the
USA
Monee, IL